4

A
PARTICULAR
Eye for
VILLAINY

By Ann Granger and available from Headline

Inspector Ben Ross crime novels

A Rare Interest in Corpses
A Mortal Curiosity
A Better Quality of Murder
A Particular Eye for Villainy

Fran Varady crime novels
Asking For Trouble
Keeping Bad Company
Running Scared
Risking It All
Watching Out
Mixing With Murder
Rattling The Bones

Mitchell and Markby crime novels
Say It With Poison
A Season For Murder
Cold In The Earth
Murder Among Us
Where Old Bones Lie
A Fine Place For Death
Flowers For His Funeral
Candle For A Corpse
A Touch Of Mortality
A Word After Dying
Call The Dead Again
Beneath These Stones
Shades Of Murder
A Restless Evil
That Way Murder Lies

Campbell and Carter crime novels
Mud, Muck and Dead Things
Rack, Ruin and Murder

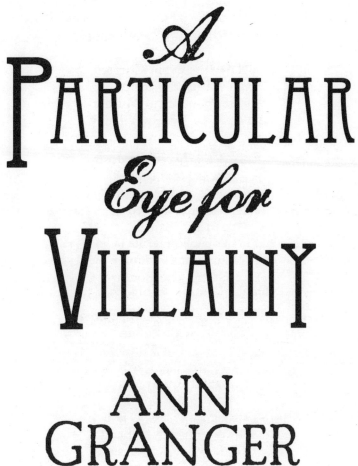

A PARTICULAR *Eye for* VILLAINY

ANN GRANGER

headline

First published in 2012 by
HEADLINE PUBLISHING GROUP

1

Cataloguing in Publication Data is available from the British Library

Hardback ISBN 978 0 7553 4912 8
Trade paperback ISBN 978 0 7553 4922 7

Typeset in Plantin by Avon DataSet Ltd,
Bidford-on-Avon, Warwickshire

Printed and bound in Great Britain by
Clays Ltd, St Ives plc

Headline's policy is to use papers that are natural, renewable and
recyclable products and made from wood grown in sustainable forests.
The logging and manufacturing processes are expected to conform to
the environmental regulations of the country of origin.

HEADLINE PUBLISHING GROUP
An Hachette UK Company
338 Euston Road
London NW1 3BH

www.headline.co.uk
www.hachette.co.uk

I would like to thank Radmila May, both for her friendship, and for her kindness in helping me research various points of the Victorian legal system, during the writing of this book.

Chapter One

Elizabeth Martin Ross

A FINE spring day in London isn't to be compared with spring in the countryside but the city does its best. Its dusty trees are green with new shoots. A pall of smoke still hangs above the roofs but it is thinner than the evil black blanket smothering the streets in midwinter. Pedestrians are no longer muffled to the eyebrows now the sleet and biting winds have vanished. They look happier as they hurry about their business. After being the prisoners of our own homes most of the past months, this was all too tempting. I put aside any tasks, told Bessie our maid to do the same, and the pair of us set out for a good long walk to feel the warmth of the sun on our faces.

The river really didn't smell too foul that day as we crossed it from the south side, where we lived, to the north. We have Mr Bazalgette and his new and improved sewer system to thank for not having to hold a handkerchief to our noses. My plan was to walk along the new embankment until Blackfriars and then, if not too tired, continue until we reached the looming fortress of the Tower. There we'd definitely turn back for home because we would have covered a fair distance. Beyond that point, in any case, lay St Katherine's dock on the upper pool of the port of London and the district of Wapping.

'Wapping', said Bessie firmly, 'ain't a place where a lady like you should go walking. Nor me, neither, come to that!'

She was right, of course. Wapping heaved with activity centred on the port and London docks. Seamen of all nations thronged its streets and taverns. Chandlers' shops jostled opium dives. Cheap lodging houses neighboured brothels. Dead bodies were regularly pulled from the river at Wapping Stairs and not all of them had met their deaths by drowning. I know all this because I am married to an inspector of police, although happily he is based at Scotland Yard.

'We might not get as far as the Tower,' I said to Bessie as we stepped off the bridge. 'But we'll do our best.'

At that point we were hailed by a voice behind us. We turned to see Mr Thomas Tapley scurrying past the tollbooth, waving his battered umbrella in salutation. It didn't look like rain, but Mr Tapley never left his umbrella behind when he sallied forth, every day, for what he liked to call his 'constitutional'. He was a short man; so spindly in build it looked as if a breath of wind would bowl him over and send him tumbling along like a carelessly discarded sheet of newspaper. Yet his pace was always brisk. He was wearing what I shall always think of as his uniform: checked trousers and a frock coat once black but now faded to a bottle green as iridescent as shot taffeta in the sunshine. A hat with a low crown and broad curling brim topped his outfit. The style of headwear had been fashionable some twenty years earlier. I remember my father donning a similar hat before setting out to make his house calls. It had cost him a pretty penny but my father had justified the expense. A doctor, he'd pointed out, should look prosperous or patients will think he's little in demand and there must be a good reason. Tapley's hat had suffered the passage of time and was spotted and scuffed, but it was tilted at a jaunty angle.

'Good afternoon, Mrs Ross! A fine day, is it not?' He answered his own question before I could. 'Yes, a beautiful day. It fairly makes one's heart sing! I trust you are well? Inspector Ross keeps well too?'

His wide smile crumpled his skin like a wash-leather; his eyes twinkled brightly and showed he had most of his teeth in reasonable condition considering his age. I supposed him in his sixties.

I assured him that Ben and I were both in good health and gave Bessie, walking beside me, a nudge to let her know she should stifle her giggles.

'You are taking the air!' observed Mr Tapley, bestowing another kindly smile on Bessie.

Ashamed, she made an awkward curtsy and mumbled, 'Yes, sir.'

'And you are right to take the opportunity,' continued Tapley to me. 'Exercise, dear madam, is of the greatest importance in the maintenance of good health. I never fail to take my constitutional, come rain or shine. But today one can only feel particularly fortunate!'

He made a theatrical sweep of the umbrella towards the river behind us, sparkling in the sunshine and dotted with shipping of all kinds, busily chugging up and down. There were lighters, coal barges, doughty little steam tugs, even a vessel marked as belonging to the River Police, while wherries bobbed back and forth between them all, often, it seemed, avoiding collision by a miracle.

'Our great city at work, on land and on river,' observed Tapley, using the umbrella as a schoolmaster uses a cane or rule to point out chalked details on a blackboard. Seamlessly, he continued: 'My regards to Inspector Ross. Tell him to continue his stalwart efforts to rid London of scoundrels.'

He tipped his hat, beamed, and walked on. We watched him skirt a small crowd that had gathered round a street entertainer, bounce across the road on his small neat feet and head north through the narrow streets leading up into The Strand.

'He's a funny old gent, ain't he?' observed Bessie disrespectfully but accurately.

'He's obviously fallen on hard times,' I told her. 'That's not his fault – or we don't know that it is.'

Bessie considered this. 'You can see he's a gent all right,' she conceded. 'He must have had money once. Perhaps he gambled or drank it away . . .' Her voice gained enthusiasm. 'P'raps he had a business partner who made off with the cash or perhaps he—'

'That's enough!' I said firmly.

Bessie came to join Ben and me when we married and set up home. She has the stunted but wiry build of one raised 'on charity' with the quick wits and sharp instincts of a child of the city poor. She is as ferocious in her loyalty as she is in her opinions.

As for Thomas Tapley, no one knew very much about him. Bessie was not the only one to have speculated on what might have brought him to reduced circumstances. He lodged at the far end of our street in a house that was not part of our recently built terrace but much older, here long before the railway came. When it was built there must have been fields around it. It was a four-square Georgian building with fine pediments, a little chipped and knocked about now, and an elegant door case. Perhaps it had once belonged to some prosperous merchant or even some country gentleman of independent means. It now belonged to a Mrs Jameson, the widow of a clipper ship captain.

The street had been surprised when she took in Thomas Tapley as a lodger six months or so earlier, because she was a lady with some claim to status. If she needed to let one of her rooms to supplement her income, she could have been expected to select a professional man for her tenant. But Mr Tapley was possessed of a certain charm and innocence of manner. For all his down-at-heel appearance, the street soon decided he was 'an eccentric' and approved his presence.

How odd it was that a chance meeting and a simple exchange of courtesies should draw both Bessie and me into a murder investigation. But no one could have guessed, that fine, bright spring morning, that we were among the last people to see Thomas Tapley alive, and to speak to him, before he met a violent death.

We did reach the Tower. The sun was so pleasant without being hot that we were surprised to find we'd come so far. We turned back conscious of a long walk home again. The river here was possibly even busier, with larger vessels. There were the colliers that had brought the coal on which London's fires and steam power depended. We saw a pleasure craft carrying some of the first day-trippers of the season and even, in the distance, the tall masts of a clipper ship that made me think of Tapley's landlady. But it was a fleeting thought and poor Tapley was immediately out of my mind again.

We were growing weary as we approached Waterloo Bridge once more. The embankment here was always a busy spot, with passengers making their ways to and from the great rail terminus of Waterloo on the farther side by cab and on foot. Inevitably, street entertainers, peddlers of small items 'useful for the journey' or out-and-out beggars had stationed themselves here. They didn't venture on to the great bridge itself because of the guardian of the tollbooth who wouldn't have permitted it. The police, if they caught them, also moved them on. The offenders always came back. Being occasionally arrested for causing an obstruction didn't deter them.

Bessie's sharp eyes had spotted something. She tugged at my arm and hissed, 'Missus! There's a clown there. Do you want us to turn back?'

But by now I'd seen him too. He had taken up a pitch about ten yards ahead of us where it would be impossible to step on to the bridge without passing close by him. I remembered the small crowd earlier, when we crossed on our outward path. Perhaps it had been watching this same fellow. If so, the watchers had obscured him from my view. I could hardly have missed him otherwise, or have come across a greater contrast to shabby little Thomas Tapley. The clown's brightly coloured form was unmistakable: a middle-aged man of portly frame clad in his 'working uniform' of a patched woman's gown, loosely cut, with a hemline a little below his knees revealing striped stockings and overlarge boots. A wide frill, a sort of tippet, was tied round his neck and reached his shoulders to either side. Over a garish orange wig with ringlets dangling about his ears, he had crammed a peculiar bonnet, very difficult to describe. It was rather like an upturned bucket, decorated with all manner of paper flowers and tattered ribbon bunches. The whole was secured with a wide ribbon tied in a bow beneath his double chin.

He was harmlessly engaged in juggling some balls, pretending to drop one and catching it at the last minute, while keeping up a shrill patter in a falsetto mimicking a woman's voice. His antics didn't bother me. It was his painted face: a dead white, eyes outlined with blacklead with long eyelashes drawn above, mouth coloured vivid scarlet with lips pursed as if about to bestow a kiss, and another large round scarlet spot on each of his puffy cheeks.

I've never liked clowns, though the word is inadequate to describe the real horror they inspire in me. I panic at the sight. My heart pounds and terror tightens my throat so I can barely swallow. I can hardly breathe. You'll think me foolish but nothing so real can be dismissed as nonsense.

The abiding fear dates from an incident in my childhood. I was six years old. My nursemaid, Molly Darby, persuaded my father that I'd enjoy a visit to a travelling circus that had set up camp on fields at the edge of our town. My father was doubtful. As a doctor he knew the dangers of being in unwashed crowds. But there were no fevers running around the town at that moment and Molly insisted. 'She'd love it, sir. Why, all the little ones do.'

She meant, of course, that she would love it.

My father, still hesitant, turned to me and asked if I'd like to go. Carried away by Molly's assurances of the wonders I'd see, I told him I would. So my father agreed with the proviso that Mary Newling, our housekeeper, should go along with us. I think now he didn't quite trust Molly's motives, out and about with only a six year old as chaperone. He probably suspected an assignation with an admirer. If so perhaps he was right, for Molly's face certainly fell when she heard that Mrs Newling was to be of our party. But she cheered up because we were at least going.

As for Mary Newling, it took an hour to persuade her. 'It's not a place any decent woman should be going. There will be thieves and vagabonds everywhere and folk doing things they shouldn't!' This last claim was accompanied by a meaningful glare at Molly.

She blushed but stood her ground. 'Dr Martin says it's all right.'

So, with Mary Newling still grumbling, off we set. I hopped along full of anticipation. If anything, Mary's warning of vagabonds had made the trip more exciting. I wasn't sure what a vagabond was, but it must be an interesting beast.

My enthusiasm flagged a little by the time we'd taken our places on a hard wooden bench in the huge tent. ('The big top!' Molly whispered to me. 'That's what it's called.') I had never been in such vast (to me) gathering. We had paid extra and it entitled us to sit at the very front. But from behind us came much argument and exchange of insult and profanity as the crowd heaved and pushed, fighting for the best vantage points. Mary Newling scowled and placed her large work-worn hands over my ears, clamping my head in a vice. It was very hot and the air smelled bad.

We faced a circular area floored with sawdust called, said Molly importantly, the ring. It was empty but any moment wonderful sights would fill it.

'We're packed like herrings,' groused Mary Newling, unimpressed, 'and a lot of the folk here are strangers to soap and water, it seems to me. If a body were to be taken faint there'd be nowhere to fall. They'd have to lay the poor soul on that . . .' She pointed to the sawdust floor.

Just then a band took up its place on a podium to one side. It was no more than a couple of fiddles and a trumpet-player, together with a man either banging on a drum or rattling an instrument of his own invention: a pole with various bits of metal attached. It made a wonderful racket when he beat the end of his staff on the ground. I was more than ready to believe Molly's assertion that it was a proper orchestra.

When the orchestra fell silent, into the ring strode a fine moustachioed gentleman in hunting pink and dazzling white breeches. He saluted us with his top hat, bid us welcome and to prepare to be amazed. He then turned and pointed with his long whip to a curtained spot behind him.

To my delight, the curtains were dragged aside by unseen hands and in cantered a line of beautiful white ponies with feathers nodding between their ears. They galloped around the gentleman in hunting pink as he cracked the whip. Then in came another horse, fantastically bedecked. There were gasps and whistles from the crowd because balanced on its broad back, *standing up*, was the most beautiful woman I'd ever seen. She was scantily glad in a fringed corset of emerald green satin and bright pink tights. As the horse circled the ring, the vision in green satin struck various poses with her arms and then, incredibly, bent to place both palms flat on the pad on the horse's back and up went her legs, straight as anything, and she stood on her hands as the horse still cantered round.

'Disgusting!' declared Mary Newling, 'showing all she's got!' But no one heard her for the wild applause, whistles and cheers.

When, her display over, the rider was on her way to the exit she did actually fall off, landing on her back with her pink legs kicking. But she was cheered again, most people believing it part of the show.

Next came the strong man in leopard-skin leotard and scarlet boots. He lifted terribly heavy-looking barbells with ease.

'Fake!' growled Mary Newling. 'Filled with air, more than like!'

But by now I was clapping and cheering with all the rest, having a wonderful time. Then the orchestra struck up again and in ran the clowns.

They were the stuff of my nightmares, misshapen, grotesquely garbed and painted. They tumbled and fell about, tripped one another up, threw buckets of shredded paper over one another and into the crowd and played all manner of tricks. I understood at once, in my childish way, that some cruel mischief had invaded the ring. It wasn't funny; it was threatening. Just then, one of the hideous creatures broke away and ran straight towards me with grinning scarlet mouth and outstretched arms . . .

I had to be taken out, of course, and that wasn't easy. The

crowd didn't want the show interrupted nor to give way and let Mary and Molly carry me out between them. They swore and catcalled; shouting out that Molly should 'stop the brat's howling!'

I bawled all the way home. Molly Darby cried, too, because she'd be blamed for the whole disaster. Mary Newling divided her time between consoling me, scolding Molly, and declaring triumphantly that she'd said from the first it would end in tears.

All these terrors returned now as I gazed at the clown, poor harmless fellow that he was, trying to earn a few pennies. Bessie gripped my arm and said loudly, 'Don't worry, missus. We'll walk on and cross further up over Westminster Bridge! It ain't so much out of our way.'

But I was footsore and knew Bessie must be tired, too. The thought of making an unnecessary detour just because of an irrational fear embarrassed me. I was ashamed to behave stupidly before a sixteen-year-old girl. I rallied and said firmly, 'No, Bessie, we'll walk past him and cross this bridge as we intended. It isn't his fault. Wait . . .' I thrust my hand into the drawstring purse on my wrist and took out some coins. 'Go and drop those in his bowl.'

Bessie took my offering and walked briskly up to the clown. 'Here you are!' she said loudly into his painted face. 'Though you're a sight fit to frighten folk, do you know that?' She let the coins clatter down into the wooden bowl at his feet.

The clown chuckled and looked past her, straight at me. He took the strange hat from his orange curls and bowed in my direction. All the time he kept his dark glittering eyes fixed on me. There was something so knowing and sharp in his gaze

11

that I quite froze for the moment, hearing nothing of the noise around me and unseeing of anything else. I wanted to look away from him but couldn't. He straightened up and replaced his hat but still kept his eyes on me.

'He'll know you again, won't he?' Bessie was back at my side. 'Staring like that. No manners, that's what, even if he is a clown. Even a clown ought not to go staring at decent ladies out walking!' She gestured angrily at him.

It broke the spell. He looked away and I awoke from my paralysis. 'Come along!' I said and marched past him on to the bridge, Bessie trotting alongside me.

Then, ahead of us, we spotted Thomas Tapley again, also walking home. Provided he had not stopped off somewhere in the meantime, he must have walked quite as far as Bessie and I had done, but his step was still brisk. We wouldn't overtake him. But, at that moment, someone else overtook us. To my horror, it was the clown.

He had left his post! Was he following us? My heart leaped painfully. But we were not of interest to him. He padded past us and I saw his garish attire moving ahead, slowing to a walk, and keeping several paces behind Tapley. If Tapley had turned, he still might not have spotted the fellow at once. The bridge was busy and it seemed to me the clown was careful to keep other walkers between him and the shabby bottle green frock coat. But Tapley did not turn. Like us, his mind was doubtless on soon being home and hearing the welcome whistle of the teakettle on the hob. Both were walking faster than we were and the crowd, which had parted before the clown, now closed behind him, blocking my view. They must have reached the far side well before we did so it wasn't surprising that when we got there, both of them were out of sight.

I was filled with misgiving. It must be my imagination playing more nonsensical tricks, I told myself. But to me it had appeared that the clown was following Thomas Tapley.

Chapter Two

I DIDN'T mention the clown to Ben that evening. I'd earlier warned Bessie to say nothing. When we'd reached home we'd concentrated on making the steak, ale and oyster pie for supper and didn't speak of the episode even to one another. I was ashamed of my cowardice, as I now saw it. But I was still a little worried about Tapley, despite telling myself that my concern for him was only an extension of my own fear.

I did tell Ben we'd met Mrs Jameson's lodger. I passed on Tapley's good wishes and hope that Ben would rid London of scoundrels.

'We do our best,' said Ben wryly. 'But it's a little like chopping a head off that Greek monster that grew seven heads in place of each lopped one.'

'The Hydra,' I said.

'That's it. London's underworld is like that. We arrest one villain and deliver him to the court. The judge sends him off to prison. But before the process is even complete, another couple of rogues has taken up where the original one left off.' He paused to eat a mouthful of pie. 'That's the only person you met, then?'

'The only person we knew,' I said, satisfying honesty and discretion at the same time.

Nothing further happened until the following evening. It had been a busy day. We were sitting by our parlour fire after supper and chatting. The evenings were still cool enough to require some extra warmth of an evening. It was a dark room that didn't get the sun and was often chilly. From the kitchen we could hear Bessie washing the dishes in her usual noisy fashion with much clanging of pots. Suddenly there was an even more tremendous clatter and the sound of Bessie's voice, crying out in distress.

'Bother that girl!' grumbled Ben. 'Has she broken another plate?'

But I was already on my feet because Bessie's shrill cry of alarm suggested more than a broken dish. Sure enough, the parlour door was flung open and she appeared, still wearing her damp apron and with her cotton mob cap askew.

'Oh, sir, oh, missus!' she gasped. 'Something 'orrible has happened!'

Ben, accustomed to dealing with horrors on a near daily basis, merely shrugged and picked up his newspaper, leaving it to me to deal with whatever domestic emergency it was.

'What is it, Bessie?' I asked, hurrying towards her. As I did I caught the sound of another female, sobbing in the kitchen.

'There's been a dreadful murder, missus! Oh, sir, you've got to come straight away!'

Ben put down his newspaper with admirable calm and asked, 'Just where has this murder taken place, Bessie? Outside in the street? We heard nothing.'

'No, sir. It's Mrs Jameson's housemaid!'

'Murdered?' Ben's tone sharpened and he rose to his feet.

'She's in our kitchen?' I asked, guessing the origin of the sobbing noises. I didn't wait but hurried past Bessie and arrived in the kitchen with Ben on my heels, to find a girl of similar age to Bessie. She'd collapsed on to the stone-flagged floor and was sitting there weeping. When we arrived she gave way to a dreadful roaring and began to roll about.

'She's having a fit!' Ben exclaimed. 'Get a wooden spoon and put it between her teeth. She'll bite her tongue!'

'No, no, she's only terrified,' I snapped. I ran to seize the girl by her shoulders and force her to keep still, though she still crouched at my feet like some sort of animal unable to stand on two legs only. 'What's your name?'

The girl stared up at me, her mouth working silently.

'She's called Jenny,' Bessie informed us. 'Here, Jenny, stop acting stupid and get up on your feet. Don't you know no better?' She accompanied her words with action, striding across to the hapless housemaid and physically hauling her up on her feet, though the wretched visitor looked as if she might collapse again at any second.

Ben took over, hastily pushing a kitchen chair forward. Jenny sank down on that, still looking up at us with tears rolling down her cheeks. Bending over her, Ben asked gently but firmly, 'Now, Jenny, what's it all about?'

'You've to come at once, sir, if you please,' she whispered. 'My mistress said to run and find you. It would be quicker than finding the bobby on his beat.'

'Is Mrs Jameson harmed?' he demanded.

'No, sir, it's Mr Tapley, her lodger. He's dead, sir, all horribly battered about and covered in blood! He's lying on . . .' But here Jenny could manage no more and began to sob noisily again.

Ben straightened up. 'I'll go and see what's amiss. This girl had better stay here. Bessie, make her some strong hot tea. I won't be long, with luck, Lizzie, but if things should—'

'But I'm coming with you!' I interrupted him. 'Whatever's happened, poor Mrs Jameson is alone in the house now. She must be in a terrible state of distress and even in danger. At the least, she'll need someone to support her. While you investigate what's happened to Mr Tapley, I'll look after Mrs Jameson.'

'Yes, yes, all right then!' He was already on his way out without pausing to take even his hat.

I ran after him and together we arrived quickly at Mrs Jameson's house. The front door stood open and the gas mantles downstairs were all burning brightly. It was now almost dark enough to warrant artificial light, but I guessed Mrs Jameson had lit them to ward off any intruder who might still be lurking. I peered into the shadows around us, but there was no one to be seen, nor could I hear footsteps.

Ben called out the widow's name as we climbed the few steps. She must have seen or heard us, for she was already in the hall, waiting. She was pale and shaking, on the verge of losing her composure, but greeted us civilly.

'Thank you for coming, Inspector, and Mrs Ross, too. I am so sorry to have troubled you but poor Mr Tapley . . .' Her voice faltered.

Ben said quietly, 'Where is the body?'

'Upstairs, Inspector. In his little sitting room. He occupies the two rooms on the first floor overlooking the street.'

Ben bounded up the stairs. I took Mrs Jameson by her arm and led her into her parlour.

'I'll make you some tea,' I said, when she was seated.

She half rose until I pushed her gently down again. 'Oh, no, Mrs Ross, you mustn't take so much trouble, Jenny can . . .'

She broke off, apparently remembering she'd sent Jenny on her errand to fetch Ben.

'Jenny is sitting in our kitchen with our maid, Bessie,' I said. 'She'll be back as soon as Bessie has calmed her down enough. Perhaps something a little stronger than tea would help. Have you any wine, sherry or Madeira, perhaps?'

At that she rallied and said firmly, 'Oh no, no strong drink of any sort ever comes into this house, Mrs Ross.'

'I didn't mean to suggest . . .' I apologised.

She closed her eyes briefly. When she opened them, she appeared to have collected her thoughts. 'No tea either, thank you, Mrs Ross, but I admit I am glad to have your company.'

From above our heads came the sound of a door closing and then Ben came clattering down the stairs.

'I'm going directly to the Yard.' He hesitated. 'It's not a good idea to leave you two women here unprotected. Perhaps you'd better both go to our house.'

So Thomas Tapley *was* dead, I thought. It wasn't some dreadful mistake or even an injury leaving him unconscious. I looked up at the ceiling and wondered if it was in the room above this parlour that he sprawled lifeless.

'I shall stay here,' said Mrs Jameson suddenly with unexpected firmness. 'Dreadful as it is to know poor Mr Tapley is lying dead upstairs, to leave the house quite empty apart from his corpse seems altogether wrong. It would be as if everyone had abandoned him. It would not be decent. I am not afraid of a dead man, Mr Ross.'

I thought it was probably the living that Ben was more worried about. But a look of obstinacy on the landlady's face told us both her mind was made up. She had decided it was right to remain, observing a kind of death-watch. When someone like Mrs Jameson had made up her own mind as to what was right, there would be no shifting her.

'I am prepared to wait here with Mrs Jameson, if that is what she wants,' I said.

I could see Ben wasn't happy with this, but he was anxious to get to the Yard, and nodded. 'Officers will come as soon as I can bring them. If I see the local man on the beat I'll send him round before that. But in the meantime, no one, no one at all, can enter that room. Is that clear? Lizzie, make sure, won't you, that no one goes upstairs?'

I promised and followed him to the front door to secure it behind him.

'And lock that parlour door, too. I wish you'd both go to our house,' he repeated.

'It will be all right,' I told him optimistically.

With a promise to return with all possible speed, he left and I went back to the widow. I turned the key in the parlour door, as Ben had requested, conscious of Mrs Jameson watching me.

'All this is a terrible shock,' she whispered as I took a seat opposite to her. 'A barbarous business, how else can I describe it? And the victim Mr Tapley! He is, he was such a good tenant.' She folded her hands in her lap and looked at me helplessly. 'Who could be so wicked as to do such a dreadful thing? And in my house!'

I thought she must be about sixty, perhaps a year or two younger than her late tenant. Her grey hair was still thick and parted centrally, smoothed back on either side in two wings and twisted at the nape of her neck in a bun. She wore a maroon gown with lace collar and cuffs and looked the very picture of respectability. My eye fell on her hands and her wedding ring. She wore no other jewellery. My thoughts, you see, were running along the lines of a violent burglar, disturbed perhaps by Tapley. But the parlour, around which I quickly glanced, was like a thousand others up and down the land. All in all, it wasn't a poorly furnished room but neither did it indicate wealth. I saw a set of comfortable chairs; a faded Turkey carpet; a couple of low tables, on one of them an opened Bible. The only other items of any interest were a portrait of the late Captain Jameson, surmounted by a black silk bow; a pair of Chinese vases on the mantelshelf, perhaps brought back by him from some voyage, and between them a solid ebony-cased clock ticking monotonously. On the wall hung an alphabet sampler worked by a childish hand.

It was all so normal in every way. The only oddity, if you could call it that, was more unexpected than strange. It was a child's rocking horse standing in one corner. The amiable animal was painted white with scuffed black patches and had a long black mane and tail of real horsehair. Its red velvet saddle had faded and looked well worn. Her late husband had left Mrs Jameson fairly comfortably off, I decided, but she had still felt obliged to let her first-floor front rooms to a lodger. Was it only financial need or, perhaps, loneliness? Was it the

21

security of knowing another person, a man, lived there? To have someone under the same roof other than herself, getting on in years, and a very young maidservant would be encouraging, especially during the hours of darkness. Not that poor Thomas Tapley would have been much use defending the two women. He had not, it seemed, been able to defend himself.

She had noticed my interest in the rocking horse. 'It belonged to our little daughter, Dorcas,' she said. 'She died at the age of ten. It was the diphtheria. Several children in the neighbourhood caught it and all of them died. We are not so far from the river here and fevers used to be very common, as indeed they still are. Dorcas loved Dobbin even when she'd grown too big to sit on him. So Dobbin stays there in his corner, keeping me company now that both Ernest and Dorcas have gone before me to a better place.'

'I am so sorry,' I said. 'So sorry that as well as your losses you have now to deal with this.'

I hesitated. I didn't want to press the poor woman when she clearly had the greatest difficulty in maintaining her calm manner. But my curiosity overcame me. 'You heard nothing? There was no sign of any intruder?'

She shook her head. 'Not a thing. To be sure, the walls are solid in this house but I do believe I would have heard Mr Tapley cry out. And he must have cried out, mustn't he?' She looked bewildered. 'If he looked up and saw an assassin advancing on him with – with some implement in his hand? Oh, Mrs Ross, I had never thought to see such a sight. So much blood and the carpet quite soaked.' She broke off, distracted by this domestic detail.

'He might not have cried out if he didn't look up,' I pointed out. 'If the assailant crept up . . .' I stopped quickly because the image wasn't one to introduce now.

She leaned forward earnestly. 'He must have stolen into the house and up the stairs as quiet as a mouse. Neither Jenny nor I saw or heard the wretch. I can't believe it. It seems incredible that a complete stranger, a murderer, came into my own home! How?'

That is what the police would want to know, I thought. 'Had you seen Mr Tapley earlier today?'

'No, but that was by no means unusual. Mr Tapley rose rather late and went out to a coffee house for his breakfast. I would have been happy to have him eat his breakfast here; but he said it was his habit to go to a coffee house and read the newspapers. I don't know what he did the rest of the day. He was accustomed to join me at supper. It's – it was the only meal he took here. He had his own key to the street door, you see.'

She saw my surprise and hurried on. 'At first I hadn't intended to give any tenant his own key. But Mr Tapley asked if he might have one and promised not to lose it. I agreed. There are only Jenny and myself here and if by chance we were both out, he would not have been able to get back in until we returned. It seemed sensible that he should be able to let himself in. At any rate, he was usually back here in good time for supper. But tonight he didn't come down. I thought perhaps he had fallen asleep and sent Jenny up to knock on his door. I am talking of his sitting-room door. He didn't reply and she opened it to see if he was there – and she saw him . . .'

Her fingers tightened their grip on one another in her lap. 'She came screaming downstairs declaring Mr Tapley murdered. Of course, I told her not to be foolish because how could such a thing be? Who would want to kill such an inoffensive sort of person and *here*? I ran up there myself to take a look and found it was as she said. It was an awful sight.' She shuddered. 'Nothing will persuade me to go and look at his corpse again, not even if the police demand it of me.'

'I shouldn't think they would,' I said, 'not if you can tell them you are sure the body is that of Tapley.'

'Oh, but it is!' she insisted. 'His features, you understand, are not so much – damaged. It is the back of his head . . .'

She put a hand to her face.

'Try not to dwell too much on the detail of it now,' I urged. 'Just tell me what happened next.'

'Oh, well, I knew I must act at once!' Her tone became brisker. 'There was little point in sending for a medical man, so I sent Jenny to find your husband. I thought he would be at home by now. I am very glad that he was, and came so quickly.'

I thought all this over. Establishing the time of death would be important. The doctor brought by the police might have an opinion on that. But Tapley had been a quiet tenant, slipping in and out of the house almost unnoticed. Had he even gone out, as usual, for his constitutional? His landlady had seen nothing of him in the normal course of the day until evening. Bessie and I had met him the previous day. But had anyone met him today? Where did he go between rising to go out and take his breakfast at a coffee house and appearing at Mrs Jameson's supper table, I wondered. Did he spend the daylight hours walking about London? Or did he pass them in various coffee- or chophouses, reading rooms, the capital's museums or just sitting in public parks? Or, having taken his exercise, did he slip back into the house and spend the rest of the day quietly in his rooms?'

Then the most terrible possibility of all struck me. Thomas Tapley had a front-door key. Had he met his killer somewhere in town and invited him back to the house? Using his own key, had the victim – unaware of the threat – let them both in?

Tentatively I began, 'Can you tell me – I mean to say, the police will want to know everything you can tell them about Mr Tapley. How he came to lodge here, for example. Had you placed an advertisement? Did he bring references?'

'Everything?' Mrs Jameson looked alarmed. 'But I know virtually nothing about him. Oh dear, that sounds so odd, because I allowed him into my house and if I knew nothing . . . But he was such a nice, quiet, happy sort of gentleman. I felt I could trust him, even with the key. Of course, I'll give the police all the information I can.'

At that moment the mantelpiece clock chimed, making us both jump.

She drew a deep breath. I think talking helped her because it was as if some impediment had suddenly been removed and the words fairly poured out.

Chapter Three

Patience Jameson

'MY HUSBAND'S name was Ernest, as I mentioned, and he was master of the clipper ship, the *Josie*. Seafarers are obliged to be away from home a great deal and I used to tease him, declaring that the *Josie* was more of a wife to him than I was, since he spent so much more time with her than he did with me.

'On his last voyage he sailed to the West Indies. During the voyage back to London, he fell sick with fever and died. Ernest and I both came from Quaker families and neither of us touched a drop of alcohol in any form, nor did Ernest allow the crew to drink spirits. But on that last voyage the cargo included some casks of Jamaica rum. The bos'un, who took over command when Ernest died, had the idea that Ernest's body could be preserved in that and brought home to me for burial. Otherwise they could have buried him at sea but Mr Brand – the bos'un – thought I should wish to lay Ernest to rest in England. It was a kindly thought of Mr Brand's. So they broached a cask and tipped the rum into some other receptacle. Then they got Ernest's body, folded in some fashion, into the cask and topped it up with rum again and replaced the bung. I don't know what they did with the rum left over. I fear they probably drank it. But the procedure was very successful and Ernest was returned to me, preserved in alcohol. I saw him buried in his home town of Norwich; and it was a comfort.

'It was a very odd thing, you know, but when the undertaker was engaged in preparing Ernest's body he asked me if I would wish him to shave the deceased and cut his hair, before I saw my dear husband in his coffin. I told him I was sure that wouldn't be necessary. But then he explained to me that Ernest's hair, beard and moustache had continued to grow after death in the barrel during the weeks it took to reach port. He now looked like a brigand or some sort of hermit. So I agreed that the undertaker should trim hair, beard and moustache so that Ernest would look like a Christian again.

'I was used to spending long periods alone here while my husband was at sea, and to making all the necessary decisions and arrangements, meaning I was better placed than many widows. Ernest had taken out a life insurance so that I should not be left without means. Of course, the house became mine too. But as I have had to watch my daily expenditure very carefully, I decided to take in a lodger. I thought I should like to let the rooms to an older gentleman, if possible. Young men are unreliable. An older man would give less trouble. Young professional gentlemen, on the other hand, are capable of giving quite a lot of trouble, Mrs Ross, and rolling home inebriated is only one of the scrapes they get into! I first made enquiry among the Quaker community, but no one was in need of lodgings at the time. I then put an advertisement in one of the local papers, wording it very carefully and stressing that this was a teetotal household. The very next day Mr Tapley called.

'He was a little down-at-heel in appearance but clearly a gentleman by family and education. There was a kind of – a kind of goodness in him, in his face and voice and manner. I can't describe it otherwise. You might say a sort of innocence.

'Normally I'd have hesitated to take in a gentleman completely unknown to me, without any real recommendation. He did bring one letter of reference but it was only from the landlady of his previous lodgings in Southampton. It said he had been an excellent tenant, always paying his rent on time and causing no disturbance. The landlady was sorry to see him leave. I asked him why he left and he told me he had a fancy to return to London where he'd lived as a younger man.

'It sounds very unsatisfactory, but Mr Tapley proved an excellent tenant during the six months he was here. He did always pay his rent promptly. He never took a drop of drink that I ever saw any sign of. He was very quiet. He went out nearly every day for his "constitutional" as he called it. If it was rainy I think he spent some time in public libraries and museums. He often brought home books that he'd bought from street stalls. He once showed me a very fine leather-bound volume that he'd acquired for only sixpence, he said, from a man selling from a barrow in Whitechapel. He was a great reader.

'And that is all I can say. There was never any sign of anything being wrong. It seems beyond belief that this could happen. I don't think I shall ever be able to take in another lodger.'

Elisabeth Martin Ross

Mrs Jameson had only just stopped speaking, and was mopping away the tears that had begun to roll down her cheeks, when we were both alarmed by a loud rat-a-tat at the front door. She jumped up, staring at me in terror. I told her to stay seated in the parlour and I would find out who it was. It was probably, I told her, Ben returned with the help from Scotland Yard. She sank back on her chair, only partly reassured. I wasn't so sure myself, as Ben had hardly had the time to reach the Yard, much less return. So I went to the window and, peering out, saw a burly caped figure wearing a police helmet.

More confident, I opened the street door. I found the officer standing on the doorstep and pretty well filling the space between the doorposts. His cape was rain spotted. I was distracted enough to peer past him and see a veil of fine drizzle that had begun to patter down on the cobbles.

'This will be the household where there's been an incident?' enquired the newcomer, stepping forward as he spoke.

I had no intention of being bundled out of the way and asked briskly, 'Who told you? What's your name?'

He gave me a scathing look. 'I am Constable Butcher, madam, and this here . . .' He gestured at the street behind him. 'This here is part of my regular beat. I was patrolling it as usual, just got to the far end of it, when I met an inspector from the Yard who told me to come immediate. There had been an incident that would need investigating. So here I am and I'd be obliged, madam, if you'd allow me in. You are at present obstructing me. Will you be the owner of the house?'

'No, I am Mrs Ross, the wife of the inspector you met and

who sent you here. The owner is Mrs Jameson and she's in the parlour . . . and the *incident*, as you refer to it, is a murdered man in a room on the first floor.'

I couldn't help but sound exasperated, but I did step aside as I spoke to allow him in. Mrs Jameson appeared in the parlour doorway behind me.

He plodded past us, divested himself of his cape, hesitated and then folded it carefully and hung it over his arm where it began to drip on the hall carpet. Mrs Jameson made a little mew of protest.

'As to whether it is a murder, madam, that is to be established. Until the matter is sat on by the coroner, it is an incident. Where is the deceased? Upstairs, you say?' He began to make his way to the staircase.

'My hus— Inspector Ross asked me to ensure no one went upstairs before he returned!' I said loudly.

Constable Butcher paused and looked round, his boot already planted on the first tread of the stair. ''E didn't mean *the law*, madam!' Now both his look and his tone were scathing.

I was obliged to stand there while he laboriously climbed the stairs. I could hear him moving about up there and then I heard him exclaim, '*Strewth!*' Subsequently I heard doors opened and shut as he searched, I supposed, for the culprit. He then reappeared on the landing and began to descend again.

'I will guard the house, madam, until the arrival of the Yard,' he announced. 'You'd best go and sit in the parlour with the other lady.'

At that moment there was distant clatter towards the rear of the house and the sound of voices.

'Intruders!' exclaimed Constable Butcher, grasping his truncheon and preparing to tackle them.

I caught his sleeve as he started forward and told him, 'It will only be the maidservant who ran to tell us what had happened. She'll have returned with our maid.'

'We'll see about that, madam!' said Constable Butcher. 'Until I have investigated, it is possible there are intruders. You have a body upstairs, all bloodied and awful to look upon, and the miscreant what done it might still be on the premises. At any rate, there are desperate criminals about!'

I thought, and devoutly hoped, the murderer had long left the house. But at least Butcher had promoted Tapley's death from an 'incident' to an act of violence, even without the assistance of the coroner.

He strode forward and I hurried along behind him. He threw open a door and sure enough, there were Jenny and Bessie, sitting at the kitchen table. They jumped up in alarm as Butcher burst in. Jenny screamed and looked as though she might start sobbing again.

I pushed past him into the kitchen and told him, 'It's as I said. That young woman is employed here and the other one is my maidservant.'

'If you say so, madam,' he agreed reluctantly. Then, fixing the two girls with a glare, he demanded, 'How did you get in?'

'Through the back door,' snapped Bessie. 'How do you think? We don't come in and out the front door. We're servants.'

Butcher surveyed the back door, perplexed. I guessed he was working out how he could guard both front and back doors at the same time. At last he plodded across to it and dropped the bar across that secured it against entry from outside. He then moved to the kitchen window and rattled the catch.

Only then he turned back to the three of us and announced. 'That bar stays there until an officer of the law removes it. You go back to the parlour, Mrs Ross, that's your best course of action. And you two girls . . .' Butcher stared mistrustfully at them. 'You stay here and don't touch that bar across the door, not if the Angel Gabriel himself was to come knocking to be allowed in. I shall now go and make a thorough inspection of all the other downstairs windows and guard the front door. If anyone calls, I shall answer and deal with the situation as I see fit.'

To our great relief, he stalked past us en route to carry out these duties.

'Who's that great lump?' asked Bessie, exasperated.

'It's the constable whose beat this is.'

'He ain't going to be the one investigating, is he?'

'I most sincerely trust not,' I said. 'But don't worry. Inspector Ross will take care of it. How are you feeling now, Jenny?'

'Something awful, all shook up inside, missus,' said the wretched girl.

'Make her some more tea, Bessie. Jenny, the police will want to speak to you when they come from the Yard, so pull yourself together.'

'I can't drink no more tea,' protested Jenny, 'I'm all awash with it.'

'Then just sit quietly. Bessie, make up the fire in that range and stay here with her.'

I went back to the parlour and assured Mrs Jameson all was well and under control. At that point we heard the clatter of hooves and the grinding roll of wheels. I ran to the window yet again. Outside a closed four-wheel cab, of the sort called a growler, had just drawn up. The rain had painted it with a coat of gleaming lacquer and made the heavy caped coat of its driver glitter as if with spangles. To my relief, Ben jumped down from the cab, followed by two other men. One of them, the younger, I recognised as Constable Biddle. The other was a stranger to me, an older man with a grey moustache, but he carried a familiar bag. It was the doctor, brought both to certify death and give an opinion as to how long poor Tapley had been dead.

They hastened towards the front door and I heard Butcher greeting them, then their voices in the hall.

'It's all right,' I soothed Mrs Jameson, who was looking at me with frightened eyes. 'It's the Yard.'

Chapter Four

Inspector Benjamin Ross

I HAD left the house with great reluctance. I thought Lizzie would have enough sense not to go upstairs. As for Mrs Jameson, having seen the body once, she would have no wish to see it again. All in all, I could be confident they'd stay in the parlour with the door locked. But they were alone and that wasn't desirable with a murderer on the prowl. I set off in the direction of Waterloo Station where I could find a cab to take me to the Yard. It had begun to rain, a light persistent drizzle that found its way down the back of my neck. I had left home without my hat, too, but had no time to go back for it. I turned up my coat collar and hurried through the now empty streets, glimmering in the gaslight.

Then I had a bit of luck. I turned a corner and saw, proceeding towards me in a stately fashion, the unmistakable form of a police constable on his beat. He was better protected against the weather than I was, wearing his cape. I hailed him and he responded by turning on his bull's-eye lamp and playing its beam over me.

'It'll be Mr Ross, if I'm not mistaken, sir!' he said in a surprised voice.

'You're not mistaken and for goodness' sake, turn that beam away from me. You're dazzling me!'

He obliged, turning the lamp off altogether. I peered at him and thought I recognised a man who regularly patrolled this beat. 'It's Butcher, isn't it?'

'Yessir.' He was pleased I knew his name. 'All in order here, sir.'

'I am not checking on you, Constable. I leave that to your sergeant. I'm on my way to find a cab to take me to the Yard. I'm afraid all is not in order!' Quickly I explained the situation and asked him to go at once to the house and mount guard on it.

'There has been some bad business done here tonight and two women waiting unprotected in a house with a murdered man lying upstairs. And one of the ladies is my wife, as it happens.'

Butcher drew himself up. 'If it's been done on my beat, sir, I shall of course proceed there immediate. You may rely on me!'

He set off at a cumbersome jogtrot.

The wheels of the law sometimes turn slowly but they turn efficiently. No one would get past Butcher once he took up guard at the house. I could be relieved on that account.

I found a cab quickly enough at the railway station but it was still late when I got to the Yard. Sergeant Morris had gone off duty and was at home in Camberwell. It was, as it happened, a busy evening and I had to make do with Constable Biddle. I had told the cab that had brought me to wait, and so pushed Biddle into it and gave the driver the address of the nearest police surgeon. By the time we'd picked up this gentleman and set off back across the river time was ticking by and I was growing increasingly impatient, but we could not have returned to the house faster. The surgeon, Dr Harper, did not look best pleased at being dragged out – he had been halfway through his dinner – but Biddle was clearly elated. He is young and enthusiastic, good qualities both, but I would have preferred to have Morris there. I wondered what the total of my cab fare was going to be and hoped the expense wouldn't be queried.

When we got back to the Jameson house, I was relieved to see the door opened by Constable Butcher.

'All quiet, here, sir,' said Butcher as soon as he saw me. 'The ladies is in the parlour. There's also a pair of servant girls, a-sitting in the kitchen. One of 'em works here and the other works for you, Mr Ross. They're drinking tea and talking the hind leg off a donkey. One keeps blubbing. They wasn't here when I got here but turned up just after. I have secured the back door – that leads out of the kitchen, too. But it occurs to me that the villain made good his escape that way and very possible his entry, too! I've examined all the windows on the ground floor, sir, and none of them's been forced.'

'How he got in will be the first mystery to solve,' I murmured to Harper as we climbed the stairs. 'But if there is only the one servant employed here, and if she left the kitchen door unlocked, it wouldn't be difficult.'

We had reached the room on the first floor where poor Tapley lay. Although I'd seen him earlier and braced myself for seeing him again, it was still a sickening sight.

I have dealt with murder more often than I could have wished. Usually, in my experience, it takes place at the rougher end of society. Men kill one another in tavern brawls. They kill their wretched women in fits of drunken jealousy. Motives often seem petty and out of all proportion to the horror of the crime. Recently I had dealt with the case of a pawnbroker, killed in his shop by a customer who couldn't raise the money to redeem his mother's wedding ring so decided to retrieve it the direct way. I've known murder done for a penny-a-week life insurance. Life is hard for those on the street and little better for the labouring poor. Temptation is always at hand.

The middle classes are on the whole subtler in dealing with a problem or an obstacle. They can afford to pay a lawyer his fee to argue their cause in the courts. They are conscious of their reputations. Of course there is violence in such homes, too. I've seen the signs of that also. But it seldom comes into court because they cling to a 'good name' with the zeal of a fanatic. The beaten wife swears she walked into a bedpost. The abused servant girl is silenced with a mix of money and threats. But murder cannot be hidden so easily. Murder is a stain that cannot be washed clean. The police cannot be turned away from an investigation into murder with a firm 'not today, thank you!'. It is the rarity, therefore, of such an event in such a setting that makes it particularly shocking. And this time in a peace-loving Quaker home, too! There was a horrid irony in that.

Thomas Tapley, the scholarly recluse, had been down-at-heel but, in the opinion of all it would seem, 'a gentleman'. He would not have expected to leave life in such a way as this. Nor would I have expected to find someone like him beaten to death. I gave myself a mental shake and told myself to stop philosophising and get on with the practical details.

The poor fellow was as I had left him earlier before hurrying out to Scotland Yard. He sprawled on one side with his face turned towards the hearth. But if he had glanced in that direction before he died, he'd have seen no dancing flames. No fire burned in the grate nor was there any sign that one had been lit that day. The iron grille at the base of the grate was free of ash or cinders. In fact, the room was so cold I guessed no heat had warmed it in many weeks. I felt it even through my jacket. I wondered at anyone wanting to sit and read in such a chilly room, and why the lodger had not asked for a fire. Had he been required to pay extra for it?

Tapley's eyes and mouth were open and the features still seemed to show his incredulity at the event. The back of his skull was a bloody pulped mess. Head wounds bleed copiously and this had caused a pool of blood and brain matter to seep out and into the carpet beneath. The victim was a small man and in death looked even more shrunken, a tiny helpless figure. To overcome him would not have been difficult. But there was no sign of a struggle. I guessed that he had been reading the book that lay, open, spine uppermost and clearly blood spotted, nearby. His assailant had opened the door quietly, approached the absorbed reader across the carpet and raised his weapon . . .

Fire irons are always the first thing to check in such a situation, but the stand usually called a companion set, in the neatly swept pristine hearth, appeared to have a full complement of these – poker, shovel, tongs – and none was bloodstained. The murderer had evidently brought some weapon with him and taken it away again. This was not a disturbed sneak thief, I thought. The intruder was someone who had come with no other purpose than to kill. But why on earth should anyone harbour murderous intentions towards such a harmless little fellow as Tapley?

Biddle had given a little gasp when he saw the body and turned pale but assured me, when I gave him an enquiring look, that he was all right.

'Go down to the kitchen and interview the housemaid, Jenny,' I told him. 'Ask particularly if there were any visitors to the house today and that includes visitors to the kitchen.'

Would-be thieves sweet-talking housemaids in order to gain entry was a common enough occurrence; and it would be a necessary line of enquiry. Jenny might not want to admit to a 'follower'. But she might speak more freely to Biddle who was nearer her age.

Dr Harper had gone to the body and was kneeling over it. 'A bad business,' he observed.

I took a more careful look round the room while he examined the dead man. This had been Tapley's parlour, so his landlady had told us. It was a small sitting room but large enough for a single man to take his ease in. Again I wondered at the lack of a fire. Probably there was an understanding that he could join his landlady in the heated parlour after their supper taken together.

The most significant piece of furniture was a bookcase stuffed with volumes. I took down a few at random. Most were well thumbed and their condition suggested they were second-hand. Some were novels or poetry, but others dealt with a wealth of practical subjects: health, the law, history, travel . . . There were quite few notes made in the margins, all in the same small, spidery hand. I would ask Mrs Jameson if she recognised the writing as being that of her lodger, as I suspected it was. Tapley's interests had been scholarly and eclectic. Had he brought some of these books with him when he moved in? I wondered. Or had he bought them all in the past six months?

I left Harper to his examination and went into the next-door room. Mrs Jameson had said Tapley occupied the front two rooms, so this should be his bedroom. It was. A marble-topped washstand was furnished with bowl and ewer, together with a shaving mug painted with forget-me-nots. The bed was neatly made. Another book lay on a small table beside it, together with a candlestick and an empty china pin tray. I opened a wardrobe and saw his coat hanging inside it as sole occupant, apart from an empty, battered travelling grip standing on the floor. Opening the drawers of a dresser I found only some handkerchiefs, a spare shirt, a set of woollen 'long johns' and some knitted stockings. Mr Tapley had travelled light. I returned to the book on the bedside table and examined it to see if it was one of devotions. But it was a translation from the German of Goethe's travels in Italy. It occurred to me that I had seen no religious texts of any sort among the books. The lodger had not been drawn to a Quaker house because he was a man of deep personal faith.

I was beginning to be intrigued by the character of Mr Tapley. His meagre belongings suggested a man of few means, but he had found the money to buy books and pay his rent. Was he, perhaps, in receipt of some small pension? Did he enjoy the income from a small sum wisely invested?

I left the room and investigated the rest of the passageway. Mrs Jameson's bedroom was a large room at the back. The view over the yard was uninteresting but the room offered more privacy than one overlooking the street and would also, I conjectured, let in the morning sunshine. A marble-topped washstand here was twin to the one in Tapley's room.

By what route did Jenny bring up the morning's hot water? I completed my exploration to the far shadowy end of the passage and found a narrow iron spiral staircase that must lead down to the kitchen. If Tapley's murderer had come in via the kitchen, then he would have used this spiral stair to access the upper floor and to make his escape.

I went back to the victim's sitting room, where Harper still knelt above the victim, He was slowly working around the upper body. As I watched, he cupped the victim's jaw and moved the head a fraction. The doctor then sat back, balanced on his heels, his hands hanging loose above his knees, staring thoughtfully at poor Tapley. I took my notebook from my pocket. I drew a careful diagram showing the position of all the furniture in the room and the body. I also made one of the first floor with its two points of access from below. I was putting the finishing touches to this when Harper sighed and stood up.

'Well, Inspector, your man was killed by at least two heavy blows to the back of the skull by the usual blunt instrument, something like a jemmy, for example.' His tone was matter-of-fact.

'A *jemmy*!' I exclaimed. Were we, after all, looking for a burglar? This short, solid iron bar was the standard tool of the housebreaking fraternity, prising open windows, doors, locked boxes, anything needing to be forced. It went without saying it doubled as a useful weapon if the villain was cornered. But housebreakers are cautious coves nowadays, since burglary alone no longer leads to an appointment with the hangman. Tapley had been a frail man and a good shove would have pushed him over without further violence. I frowned. No, a housebreaker would not go out of his way to creep up on an unsuspecting old gentleman, sitting in a chair reading. All the fatal blows were to the back of the cranium. If Tapley had heard the intruder, had jumped up and confronted him, he would have been struck on the front or side of the head. The assailant would then have fled. If, on the other hand, Tapley had not heard him open the door, if the intruder had spotted Tapley engrossed in his book and oblivious, the burglar would have closed it quietly again and made good his escape.

Constable Butcher had examined the ground-floor windows, something I'd failed to do before I left for the Yard, and I believed him when he said none was forced. Butcher was a man of experience who would have been called to numerous break-ins. He wouldn't make a mistake over a thing like that. It all confirmed the theory that the intruder had slipped through an unsecured window or door, probably in the kitchen.

'I only use "jemmy" as an example,' explained Harper. 'Something weighty enough to do a lot of damage at a single blow. I would say considerable force was used, more than required.'

'Can you give me a time of death?' I asked.

Harper allowed himself a small, professional smile. 'My dear Inspector Ross, you know as well as I do that such a thing is very difficult to judge. But in this case we are, if the expression doesn't seem unfortunate, in luck. Despite faint early signs of it, rigor is barely setting in. Even the jaw and neck muscles can still be manipulated to some degree and they, as you know, are among the first to set.'

'So he has not been dead long,' I said.

'No, Inspector. It will be some hours before rigor has advanced enough to render all the muscles completely stiff. I would venture to say the unfortunate man had not long died when you paid your first visit to his house and saw him. What time was that?'

'A little after seven thirty.' My mind was racing with possibilities, all of them unwelcome, and I knew my voice sounded dull.

Harper took out his pocket watch and consulted it. 'Well, it is now nearly half past nine. So, some time between five and when you found him, shall we say? Or rather, when the maidservant found him at about a quarter past seven.'

I hoped Biddle was making a thorough job of the interview with the maid. Someone had entered this house during that recent period of time, killed Tapley, and slipped out without being seen. He might still, I realised with dismay, have been hidden in the house when I entered this room. He'd escaped while I was here – in this room viewing his handiwork! Mrs Jameson and Lizzie had been downstairs in the parlour. Jenny had still been at our house with Bessie. The murderer could have left without any hindrance, certainly not from me. I should have searched the place! I might have been too late already; but I might have confronted him and, even if he'd knocked me down, and then fled, I'd have laid my eyes on the wretch and known what he looked like.

Harper was watching me quizzically. I dare say he knew exactly what was in my mind.

'You'll want to be on your way, Doctor,' I said to him. 'Thank you for your promptness in coming tonight.'

He nodded. 'I will arrange for the mortuary van to come and take the body.'

We went downstairs together. I shook hands with Dr Harper and he left. In the parlour I found Lizzie and Mrs Jameson engaged in conversation. The moment would come when the house owner realised that the murderer might still have been on the premises when she sent Jenny running to fetch me. But it could wait. I asked her if there had been any visitors at all that day and particularly during the afternoon. She shook her head and insisted it had been a quiet day and no one had called. The kitchen, then, was increasingly looking like the murderer's way in. But I had to make sure.

'Your lodger lived in the two front rooms upstairs,' I said. 'If he had been watching from one of his windows and had seen a potential visitor to himself approach, could he have gone downstairs and opened the front door to that person? Taken him upstairs, without your knowledge or the knowledge of your maid?'

She admitted it was possible. Her day was a busy one. The devil made work for idle hands. She did her sewing, mending and letter-writing in the small back sitting room. Jenny lit the parlour fire at five o'clock in the winter months and of a cool evening, such as today.

I couldn't help but mention the lack of a fire in the lodger's rooms.

She was anxious to explain. The upstairs parlour for his use had had no fire lit in it for the past three weeks now, since the onset of milder weather. But, she assured me, it had been Tapley's own request to discontinue the fire in the grate.

'I several times asked him not to suffer cold unnecessarily,' she told me. 'I had the impression, you see, that he was used to making economies of that sort, and that was why he didn't ask for one to be lit now the winter is past. I assured him he was welcome to enjoy this parlour fire from five onwards. But the cooler evenings didn't seem to trouble him and, as Jenny has more than enough to do, I admit I didn't press him. Jenny has this hearth to tend and the supper to help me cook. Then she must serve the supper to both Mr Tapley and me, clear the table and wash the dishes. After that she must make the dining room ready for my breakfast. She's a willing girl, but it would be unfair to expect her to run up and down the stairs tending a second fire in the evening, and clearing a second grate of its ashes in the morning, if the lodger didn't want it. It was a different matter in the middle of winter, of course. He didn't refuse a fire then. I should have insisted, even if he had.'

Her voice trailed away and she looked distressed.

Lizzie caught my eye and said, with an apologetic glance at Mrs Jameson, 'Mr Tapley had a key to the house, a street-door key.'

This was important. I hurried back upstairs. Tapley's frock coat hung in the wardrobe and I searched its pockets first. I then knelt by the body and slipped my fingers into the pockets of the clothes he wore. My search turned up a gold half-hunter watch, which was interesting, and not only because a robber wouldn't have missed it. Tapley had not been reduced to selling or pawning it. At some time in the past he'd been well off enough to buy it in the first place. I opened the case hoping for an inscription but there was none. I closed the case again and contemplated it. The watch was dented and a little rubbed, suggesting it had resided in his pocket for years, but it was an expensive item.

However, there was nothing like a street-door key. A further search in all drawers and any other likely spot failed to turn up any key whatsoever.

I went back downstairs. 'Mrs Jameson,' I told her, 'I strongly advise you to send for a locksmith in the morning. Have him change the lock on the front door. Tapley's key may be upstairs but I haven't found it. So we have a possibility that his killer took it and if there is something in Tapley's rooms that the killer wants, but may not yet have found, he could return.'

'Mrs Jameson and Jenny must both come to us tonight!' Lizzie said at once. She turned to the landlady. 'They will soon take Mr Tapley away. There will be things to be done here by the police. You won't want to be here at that time. The missing key – it may have been taken by the intruder. Please come to us.'

Mrs Jameson looked up at me. 'Will it be in order for me to go up and pack a small bag, Inspector?'

I admit I hesitated. We had not yet conducted a thorough search of the house. We had no idea if the murder weapon was still here. Normally I'd intervene to prevent any article leaving the house, especially if possibly concealed in a bag. Suspicion, unfortunately, must fall on this respectable widow lady and her maid, as it falls on all unlucky enough to find themselves involved in a murder inquiry. But, I told myself, if Mrs Jameson had wanted time to hide some small object (in this case the fatal 'blunt instrument'), then she'd already had the opportunity to do so after sending Jenny to fetch me. She'd had at least fifteen minutes alone in the house to wash blood off and dispose of it. She wouldn't have waited until I arrived.

In the same way she could have taken Tapley's key in an attempt to muddy the water of the investigation. She had but to return it to her own ring of keys.

Jenny, likewise, could have disposed of incriminating material before falling through our back door into Bessie's arms, bawling her eyes out. The girl had appeared demented with terror when she arrived at our house, but she might also be a clever little actress.

I thought guiltily that there'd already been enough time for the villain to get halfway across the country, let alone slip out of the house, and toss the murder weapon into the Thames, only a step away.

'Of course,' I told Mrs Jameson. 'Pack whatever you'll need for a few nights, but only that, if you please.'

When she'd left us, I asked Lizzie what else she had learned from the lady and was given a precise account of the conversation.

'Lizzie,' I asked, 'would you say Mrs Jameson was a foolish, naive or gullible woman?'

My wife shook her head decidedly. 'No, I'd say she was a practical one, very capable and intelligent.'

'Then our Mr Tapley,' I replied, 'was also a very clever fellow, it seems to me. He talked his way into this house and into renting the two rooms upstairs, without a single written reference of any significance. I don't count the letter from his previous landlady who probably knew as little about him as this one does. He persuaded Mrs Jameson to let him have a key to the house, and gave no information about himself or his history while he was here, nor where he went during the day. He received no visitors that we know of before today.'

'You think he let his murderer in?' Lizzie asked quietly.

'We have to consider it. However, it does appear he was attacked while reading. He wasn't sitting and talking to someone. I'm inclined to believe the killer slipped in through the kitchen.

'But it's possible Tapley may have sneaked in a visitor or two on prior occasions. He has been in contact with someone outside of this house, Lizzie, and I'll have to find out who that person is! Otherwise, supposing this not the work of a thief so incompetent he overlooked a gold watch, we are looking for a total stranger. A man who, for no obvious reason, walked into an unknown house and there killed a man he'd never seen before.' I shook my head. 'I find that difficult to accept.'

There was another rumble and clatter of wheels and hooves on the cobbles outside. I got up and glanced from the window. A sombre, windowless van had drawn up. Two men were unloading a plain deal coffin.

'Lizzie, would you go up to Mrs Jameson and ask her to stay in her room for the next half an hour? Keep her company and the door shut. The van is here to take the victim to the mortuary and it's not a sight either of you would wish to see.'

Lizzie hurried away up the stairs while I opened the door to the mortuary workers. So much activity so late at night had occasioned a lot of interest up and down the street. Curtains were twitching at bedroom windows. Faces showed as pale ovals against the panes, caught by the gaslight in the street lamps. By morning few would be in ignorance of what had happened here. I showed the men up to the room where Tapley lay and watched them lift his battered body into the coffin. Their faces were expressionless and their movements brisk and capable. They did not speak, even to each other. To them it was merely another death. They had done the job before.

Tapley was carried downstairs and loaded up. The van clattered away. Curtains at upper windows fell back into place.

I went back and climbed the stairs to the first floor. I had forgotten Jenny, but she was seated on the topmost step of the spiral stairway down to her kitchen, a bundle in her arms. Biddle stood over her. It looked as if he had supervised her packing, if rolling her nightgown and hairbrush into a shawl could be called that. His attitude looked custodial. It was not that which bothered Jenny.

'I suppose I'll have to scrub that carpet,' she said resentfully.

'But not tomorrow,' I told her. 'There will be police officers in the room tomorrow.' I could hear the voices of the two women in Mrs Jameson's room and rapped on the door panels. 'You can come down now.'

Lizzie opened the door. Behind her I could see Mrs Jameson, a small portmanteau held in one hand and her Bible gripped in the other.

'We are ready to leave.'

I asked Mrs Jameson if she wouldn't mind first accompanying me around the house to find out if anything was obviously missing or disturbed other than in Tapley's room. The police would search the premises later, I explained. But if there were any sign of theft, we would have our motive.

'You want me to come, too, ma'am?' asked Jenny.

'Let her come too,' I said. 'She may notice something.'

So Biddle found himself carrying both the portmanteau and Jenny's bundle downstairs. Lizzie followed him.

Both women declined to enter the murder room itself but we looked everywhere else. They assured me nothing appeared to be missing or to have been moved. The sad signs of an evening so dramatically interrupted were seen in the dining room, where the table was set for the meal never taken. The kitchen smelled of the roast pork congealing in its pan; but it had mysteriously disappeared from sight.

'I put the joint in the meat safe in your larder, missus,' announced Bessie to Mrs Jameson. 'If you was to leave it here on the table overnight, rats would get it.'

'If I might have the house key, ma'am,' I asked. 'So that we can secure the premises when we've finished. You shall have it back in the morning.'

'Of course,' she murmured.

When all four women had left the house, Biddle and I conducted a quick second search but turned up nothing helpful. In particular, we didn't find the missing house key. It looked as if the killer had taken it. If so, it could only mean he intended to return. Why? Had he, too, been disturbed and had no time to search for something? Not the gold half-hunter. Although a prize, it would not be worth risking his neck to return for that alone. We couldn't yet rule out a burglar – Harper's use of the word 'jemmy' worried me – but I felt strongly that this was premeditated murder. We'd have to work hard to discover what motive lay behind it.

'Right, Constable!' I said to him. 'What about that girl, Jenny? What did she have to say? Did you ask her if anyone at all called here during this past week? Any hawkers, peddlers, tradesmen or delivery boys? Beggars?'

'The baker's roundsman came yesterday,' Biddle said, taking out his notebook and consulting it ostentatiously. 'That's his regular call, sir. The same man has been doing the round as long as Jenny's worked here. That's nearly two years, sir,' added Biddle. 'That's how long Jenny has had a place here, I mean. She's not London-born. She comes from Chatham where her pa and brothers work in the dockyard. But she's got an auntie in service with a Quaker family in Clapham and that's how she comes to be working for Mrs Jameson. Her auntie found her the place. She isn't a Quaker herself, Jenny, but she likes working in a Quaker house because it's a good recommendation if she wanted to seek another place later. No drinking nor gambling nor bad language and so on . . . and everything kept as clean as a new pin.'

I begged Biddle to cut short Jenny's personal history and future prospects and get on with the events leading up to the fatal day. It came down to no one calling at the house except the bread roundsman at the kitchen door that day, and a pair of Quaker ladies who'd come to take tea with Mrs Jameson the previous afternoon. The milkman's cart came down the street both days. Jenny had gone out with a jug to fetch milk from him. He did not come round to the back of the house. Mr Tapley had received no visitor that Jenny saw, but she agreed he might have let someone in himself and taken that person upstairs unbeknown either to her or her mistress. Had she ever suspected he'd done that? No, not that Jenny had ever discovered. But she didn't think Mr Tapley was the sort of man with anything to act furtive about. He didn't know anyone to come calling; that was her opinion. She had not seen him on the day of the murder. She supposed he'd gone to a coffee house in the morning as usual, because he'd left his rooms when she went up to make the bed and dust. Everything had looked normal.

'Just his books everywhere,' Jenny had said. 'All them words, thousands of them. Wonderful, really.'

Biddle had been inclined to agree.

Jenny could read and write and had once looked into some of Tapley's books. But the print had been too small, the words too long and unfamiliar, and the subject matter dull.

'He was a quaint old gentleman,' Biddle had written verbatim in his notes, 'and very old fashioned in his clothes and ways. He always spoke of taking a "dish" of tea. But he was always very polite.'

The mystery – why anyone should deliberately set out to murder such a man – deepened. My policeman's suspicious mind had already decided there must have been more to Thomas Tapley than had met the eye. But would we be able to find out what it was?

Biddle had established one last point and it was an important one. The back door, in the kitchen, was not secured during the day because Jenny was 'in and out' all the time. The woodpile to keep the kitchen range going, the coalhouse from which to feed the parlour fire, and the pump supplying the household's water needs, were all in the yard. Mrs Jameson also kept a few chickens in a shed in the back yard. Jenny fed them and collected their eggs.

At this news I asked if the chickens were let out to roam free during the day. Biddle said there was a moveable wire cage where the birds spent the daylight hours before being locked inside again at night. Jenny had taken Biddle outside to show him.

'It means Jenny can move the chickens around from spot to spot and they clear out all the beetles and such on the ground. But they were all back in their shed by five. I asked her to take me outside and show me,' added Biddle, 'because the other one, your maid Bessie, kept interrupting and I wanted to get Jenny on her own.'

I could imagine the scene and thought Biddle shrewd to have got Jenny away.

'It's pity it didn't rain earlier today,' I grumbled. 'We might have had some good footprints in the yard.' I thought about the chickens. 'Might they have squawked if disturbed by a stranger coming through the yard?' I wondered aloud.

But Biddle thought otherwise. 'They wouldn't raise the alarm, sir, begging your pardon. It's geese what cackle when strangers come near them. Not chickens, silly things they are. Geese are as good as a watchdog. My grandpa keeps them. He's got a pig, too, in his backyard and it'll eat all your rubbish. A pig's very useful.'

I deferred to Biddle's superior knowledge of animal husbandry, and praised the lad for having done a good job interviewing the servant girl and checking the yard. I told him to write it all out nicely so that it would go on record. Biddle blushed red to the tips of his rather prominent ears and began to thank me fulsomely until I ordered him to stop.

Oh, and Jenny didn't have a follower, Biddle threw this fact into the pot. Mrs Jameson wouldn't allow it. 'Though she's quite pretty, that Jenny,' opined Biddle.

I told him to go home now and to concentrate on the report he was to write in the morning; and not start getting unprofessional thoughts about witnesses.

Biddle now turned even redder and I feared his head would burst into flames in the only case I'd ever seen or was likely to see of spontaneous combustion.

Chapter Five

DAWN WAS breaking before I made my own way home. I like this time of day and even tired as I was, and worried about this new case, I breathed in deeply of the morning air that was still relatively fresh and unpolluted. The first workers were on their way to their places of labour, picking their way round the puddles that dotted the cobbled street and had gathered in the gutters. Chimneys puffed out the first smoke of the day as housewives or sleepy servant girls got the range lit. I could easily guess the topic of conversation over the breakfast would be all about the comings and goings at the Jameson house the previous night.

No one was yet rattling about in our kitchen and the parlour fire had long gone out. But the room was still warm and I settled down in the chair before the ashes and fell asleep.

I was awoken later by movement and voices and opened my eyes to see Lizzie standing over me with a cup of tea in her hand. I glanced up at our clock and saw I'd been sleeping for about an hour and a half. From the kitchen came the sounds of breakfast being prepared by Bessie with Jenny's help.

'Mrs Jameson will be down shortly,' Lizzie informed me. 'I hope the poor woman was able to get some sleep. I slept like a log,' she added frankly. 'I'll tell one of the girls to take a jug of hot water upstairs so you can shave.'

Later when I came down, shaved and wearing a clean shirt, Mrs Jameson and Lizzie were at the breakfast table. I asked our guest how she'd slept.

'Not well, Inspector, though the bed was most comfortable and I'm very grateful to you and Mrs Ross for your kindness. But I won't impose on you for a second night. I keep worrying about the locksmith. I do know of one. I think he will come at once. I must get back to my house immediately. I don't like it to stand empty. Only think, if someone has the key he may have returned and left with everything of value he could find.'

'Constable Butcher was keeping an eye on the house,' I assured her, but she looked unconvinced.

Before she and Jenny left us, I sat them down in our parlour and interviewed them again. I began with Jenny, as I hadn't spoken to her at length myself and she had found the body. I was worried she might start rolling about and roaring again but under her mistress's eye she behaved quite sensibly. Biddle had thought her pretty; I was inclined to agree. She had a pink and white complexion of the sort traditionally associated with milkmaids, round blue eyes and copper-coloured hair. I wondered again about followers. Surely such a pretty girl must have a sweetheart? Perhaps he lived back in her hometown of Chatham. Or perhaps he had crept up the back stairs and struck down Thomas Tapley, dead on the carpet.

'Your mistress sent you to see what kept Mr Tapley from coming down to supper. Tell me exactly what you did, anything you noticed or heard.'

'I only knocked on the door, sir, and called his name.

I didn't see nor hear nothing strange before that. Honest, sir, I never let no one into the house that day. Someone might've come in through the kitchen when I wasn't in it, and gone out that way, but he took an awful risk, sir, because either me or Mrs Jameson could've walked in at any time. He was pretty clever at getting in and out of folk's houses, if he did.' Her round blue gaze stared at me guilelessly.

I have met such a gaze more than once and from a hardened criminal, so that, in itself, didn't impress me. But, to be fair, she seemed a girl who wore her emotions on her sleeve and not a natural deceiver. Nor did I wish to frighten her. Honest or guilty, if they think you believe them, they relax and are less guarded in their speech.

'Yes, yes, Jenny. Go on from when you knocked on the lodger's door.'

'He didn't answer, sir, so I thought perhaps he'd dozed off in his chair, him being an elderly gent. He'd done that once or twice before. So I opened the door and looked in, thinking I'd wake him. Ohmigawd . . .' Jenny broke off and gave her employer a furtive look. 'Sorry, madam, it sort of slipped out. I meant to say, oh *my goodness* . . .'

Even Mrs Jameson looked a little amused at this hasty correction.

Jenny carried on, 'He was lying on the carpet all bashed about and bleeding. I never saw such a sight in my life. Not never. My pa works in the docks at Chatham and they have accidents there sometimes and men gets mangled but I bet they don't see sights worse than that one I saw. I hopes never to see such a horrible thing again, no, not for the rest of my days!'

When I'd been a young boy, working down in the mines of my native Derbyshire, I'd seen mangled bodies, too. It had still shocked me to see one in a private house and Jenny's terrified display the previous day was to be excused.

Jenny then returned to insisting no one had visited or called at the door during the day. The kitchen door had not been locked because her duties took her into the yard at frequent intervals; but she couldn't understand that anyone had slipped in past her.

'He was a wicked sneak thief, sir, that's what he was. Poor Mr Tapley disturbed him and the horrid creature beat the poor old gent's brains out.'

Jenny might be right, at that, but I still didn't think so. The way Tapley lay sprawled suggested to me the murderer had disturbed him, and not the other way round. But I left it there for the moment and told her she could go back to Bessie in our kitchen while I spoke with her mistress.

Jenny got up, still protesting vigorously that it wasn't her fault if anyone had got in. Her day was a busy one. She couldn't be expected to have eyes in the back of her head. I set aside my theory – never a strongly held one – that some admirer of Jenny's had been responsible for the savage deed. The girl might be possessed of a vivid imagination and she might be inclined to panic – I would not easily forget her roaring on our kitchen floor – but she was shrewd enough for all that.

When Jenny had left us, I turned to Mrs Jameson. She gave me much the same account as she'd given Lizzie the previous evening. I was again struck by how easily Tapley had talked his way into her small household. She was aware of it and regretted it now.

'Indeed, I can't blame Jenny if someone slipped in through the kitchen, when I took in Mr Tapley with no proper references. I wish I could explain to you how it came about, but he was such a pleasant, harmless sort of person.'

Of a type I'd certainly met before, I thought grimly. 'Mrs Jameson, please be frank, did Mr Tapley at any time seek to borrow money from you?'

'Oh, no, Inspector!' She looked shocked. 'Certainly not. He always paid his rent regularly and never sought extra time to find the money.'

She then surprised me by adding, 'I do not think he was a confidence trickster, as I believe such people are called.'

Lizzie was right. Mrs Jameson was a very sensible woman and by no means naive. She'd been unwise to let her rooms to the man, but at the time perhaps there had been no reason why she shouldn't. Were all my suspicions about Tapley unfounded?

I accompanied her back to her house, Jenny trailing dolefully behind us. I wondered how soon she would be using her Quaker references to seek a new place. Before I left them, I warned them that neither must go into either of the rooms rented by Tapley. Nothing must be disturbed until the police gave permission.

'I shall probably be back again later today myself, with another officer,' I told them. 'Because we'll need to search those two rooms thoroughly by daylight.'

Search his rooms again was all we could do for the moment. Apart from that I would make sure news of the murder reached the later editions and the evening papers. With luck someone would come forward with information or at least to confirm the identity of our man. We would need as much luck as we could get.

When I reached the Yard that morning, Sergeant Morris was waiting for me. He'd been told of the case by Superintendent Dunn and ordered to assist me. Thank goodness for that, I thought. I also found Biddle's report on my desk, neatly written out.

'Well, well,' I said to Morris, 'that boy will make a detective yet! Have you read this, Morris?'

'I have, Mr Ross,' Morris replied lugubriously. 'And it seems a very nasty affair to me, very *untoward* as you might say.'

'You might, indeed, Sergeant. There are a number of mysteries around the deceased. Not the least of them is how he acquired his skill at talking his way into the homes of respectable women, renting rooms from them, even persuading this one to let him have a street-door key giving free access to the house, with no other reference than one from his previous landlady. His appearance was down at heel. He was well spoken and educated but appeared out of thin air in response, Mrs Jameson says, to an advertisement she'd placed in the local press. That might suggest he was already living locally – or it might not.'

'He'd kissed the Blarney stone, by the sound of it,' observed Morris.

'We've no reason to suppose him Irish, or Welsh or Scottish or, come to that, English. He told this respectable Quaker widow he had a wish to return to live in London where he'd lived many years earlier and that was all he told her. She took him on trust. But that does not mean *we* have to take anything about him on trust. That includes his apparent straitened means. He never tried to borrow money from her or to delay payment of his rent. He spent a fair amount on books, even if most of them do appear second-hand. He went to a coffee house every morning to make his breakfast, though his landlady would certainly have been willing to have him eat it in her house at no extra cost. He told her it was because he liked to read the newspapers. He dined with her in the evenings.'

'What did they talk about, while they were having their supper?' asked Morris.

People who don't know him sometimes underestimate Morris. That is their mistake and many wrongdoers have made it.

'I don't know,' I said. 'But you are quite right. If he didn't talk about himself, what did he talk about? Not religion, I shouldn't think. The lady is a Quaker but there's no Bible in Tapley's rooms, nor any other devotional book. We shall have to ask her, Morris.'

'A Quaker lady, you say?' Morris said thoughtfully. 'They're inclined to see the best in people, are Quakers.'

'The lady is not naive, Morris. I've spoken with her. She's sharp enough. It makes it all the more remarkable that she let the two rooms to him.'

'What I meant to say, sir,' Morris explained, 'was that they're good people themselves – though I dare say they have their occasional black sheep – and they look for good in others. They reckon the world a sinful place and no police officer will argue with that! But they pride themselves – although they don't go in for pride, it being sin – on seeing the good in others. Perhaps this Quaker widow lady trusted Tapley because she saw something in him that others might not.'

'Hm, well, I'll bear that theory in mind, Morris. Now I'd better go along and see Superintendent Dunn and get his view of the matter.'

Dunn's view was predictable. I didn't need to hear it from his lips to know it. The superintendent believed in taking the direct line between two points. It was sometimes difficult to dissuade him from any conclusion so reached.

'Well, it's a dreadful business, of course, when a respectable gentleman is murdered in a decent household, with the roast ready to come to the table and a scripture-reading lady downstairs in the parlour. But from the police point of view, Ross, it is a simple matter. A thief broke in, Tapley disturbed him – or he was alarmed to come upon Tapley reading – so the miscreant struck out in a panic, having in hand some implement of his criminal trade, and killed the poor old fellow.' Dunn looked satisfied at having arrived at this. But, because he knew me as I knew him, he waited for my objections.

'There was no sign of any break-in,' I ventured. 'No forced window.'

Dunn waved this away. 'He slipped in through the kitchen, then, while the maid had her back turned, he went up this servant's stair . . .' Dunn tapped my plan of the upper floor. 'He used this spiral stair to reach the first floor. He left the same way after committing his heinous assault. We have to seek among London's criminal fraternity, Ross! First port of call, known housebreakers.'

'But why should he attack Tapley, if Tapley was reading quietly and hadn't noticed that the door had opened behind him, sir? Why creep in and strike the victim down? It was unnecessary and, frankly, madness. It is one thing to be charged with housebreaking, and another to be charged with murder. We don't hang a man for theft any longer in this country but we do hang him for a murder.'

'Housebreakers are not reasoning beings, Ross. They plan their break-in and nothing more. Anything more is due to their low, violent instincts.' Dunn nodded in agreement with his own words.

I was not ready to give up my argument. 'Habitual housebreakers operate by night or at dawn, when the household is asleep, sir. An opportunist sneak thief, on the other hand, doesn't go upstairs, where he may be trapped. He seizes a purse left lying on a table, a small ornament of value, something of that nature, and clears out as fast as he can.'

Dunn began showing signs of irritation. 'So, are you saying the culprit entered the house with the express purpose of killing this blameless man, in his sixties, who spent his days in coffee houses and his evenings reading? Who was apparently in receipt of some small income, enough to prevent him pawning or selling his gold watch, but not enough to buy a new set of clothes or make him worth robbing?'

'It does sound very odd, sir,' I had to agree. 'But we have to consider it. The victim, Thomas Tapley, is something of a mystery figure. We know nothing about him, nor did his landlady.'

Dunn sighed and yielded with bad grace. 'You will investigate, of course, to see if it is indeed a deliberate murder. It's a rum business, I admit. But don't waste time or manpower looking for complications where there are none, Ross. We are short of both those commodities here at the Yard.'

'I am aware of that, sir.'

'This female, Mrs Jameson, ought not to have let her rooms to him,' the superintendent went on crossly, rubbing his hands through his wiry hair. 'It was very unwise of her. Bound to be trouble sooner or later, perhaps not murder, but some problem. She knew absolutely nothing about the fellow! What on earth made her take him in?'

'Sergeant Morris thinks perhaps she identified some good qualities in him,' I ventured.

Dunn snorted. 'I wish I had a guinea for each time some deceived woman has told me that! They usually offer it as an excuse after the man has spent all their money, or run off with the nursemaid, or turned out to be a bigamist. Your Mrs Jameson wasn't the first woman he'd charmed in that way, apparently,' Dunn rumbled on, 'because he showed her a letter from his previous landlady in – where?'

'Southampton, sir.'

'A port . . .' observed Dunn thoughtfully. 'There is a regular packet service to and from France sailing from Southampton, is there not?'

'I have wondered if that means anything, sir. He certainly might only recently have arrived in this country after spending some years abroad. That would account for his not being able to produce any other references.'

'He might have been abroad, or in gaol or in the madhouse. Do we have this letter of reference?' Dunn looked fiercely at me.

'So far we have nothing, sir. That includes his house key – and it looks increasingly as if the murderer took that with him. If he did, it will be of no use to him now. Mrs Jameson is fetching in a locksmith this morning. But it indicates he intended to return and that suggests something he wants is there. We have to find it. But without knowing what it is, identifying it in the first place will be a problem.'

'Tapley will have kept that letter of reference from his former landlady,' mused Dunn. He got up from his chair and walked to the window where he stood with his back to the room, his hands clasped at the small of his spine and balancing on the balls of his feet. His shiny, uncreased boots looked brand new. Distracted, I wondered if he found them tight.

The superintendent spun round and fixed me with his small but piercing grey eyes. 'Find that letter, Ross! It was the only bona fide piece of recommendation the fellow had. If he'd ever intended to move to new lodgings he'd have need of it again. He'd have kept it, mark my word. We must trace his former landlady in Hampshire. She may be our only lead.'

'I'll be taking Morris with me to the house shortly, sir, to search Tapley's two rooms again,' I said. 'Before we leave I'll arrange for the report of the murder to appear in this evening's newspapers. I will tell the pressmen that we are anxious to confirm the identity of the corpse; and that there is a possibility the victim lived briefly in Southampton. That may spark some interest. If we can find the coffee house he was in the habit of frequenting, he may have chatted more freely to someone there. I'll get Biddle on to that when he reports back on duty again. The youngster did very well last night, sir.'

Dunn squinted at me, the grey iris of his eyes almost invisible. 'Experience tells me, Ross, that this nice old gentleman, who wouldn't hurt a fly and collected books, was on the run from something or someone!'

It wasn't the first occasion when Dunn had abandoned a fixed point of view and taken up another. The speed with which he'd changed his mind this time was still disconcerting. So, from seeking known housebreakers, I was now to chase down Tapley's history and seek a reason for murder. The next step would be for Dunn to decide this had been his idea from the first.

'Yes, sir,' I said.

I sent a man out to go round the newspaper offices and make sure the murder made the late editions. Morris and I then returned to the Jameson house where we found the locksmith busy at his trade, and Mrs Jameson standing over him. She looked unhappy, as well she might, because removing the old lock had made a sorry mess of the front door, leaving an unsightly gap around the newly fitted replacement. The next person to be called to the house would be a carpenter, I guessed.

I explained to the lady that, as soon as the work was finished, it would help us if she would go and stay with my wife – or perhaps with some other acquaintance – for a few hours so that we could search the house.

'It's better you are not here, ma'am,' I told her. 'It gives us a free hand and we'll be moving about a great deal in the two rooms rented by Tapley. That might upset you. But I am glad of a chance of a word with you. When Tapley dined with you, did he speak much of himself?'

Mrs Jameson took her eyes reluctantly from the locksmith. 'Oh, well, no, he didn't, Inspector. Now that you come to mention it, he hardly told me a thing. I didn't *pry*, naturally.'

'Naturally. So, if I may ask, what did you talk about?'

She looked vaguely up and down the street as if something there might jolt her memory. 'He read the newspapers, every day without fail. He must have read them in coffee houses or public libraries because he never brought one into the house. I should have noticed, or Jenny would have done. I don't allow a newspaper into the house, you see, Inspector. The papers are full of all kinds of unsuitable reports of people misbehaving in every way. I wouldn't wish a young person like Jenny to find one and read of it. Having a young person in the house is a great responsibility, Inspector, as I expect you find with your maid.'

She didn't know Bessie, I thought. Banning newspapers from the house wouldn't have kept Bessie from hearing the gossip and any shocking news in particular. Maidservants operate a sort of telegraph system of their own by which anything like that runs round like wildfire. No doubt Jenny, too, would gather this sort of intelligence. Morris was right. There was a kind of innocence of the world about Mrs Jameson. Jenny would be much more alert to its pitfalls.

'So,' Mrs Jameson was saying, 'of an evening, if he came down and dined with me, he told me of any current events he thought might interest me. I think I shouldn't have known what was going on in the wide world if poor Mr Tapley hadn't told me. I don't mean he told me details of lurid murders—'

She broke off and looked at me in distress. 'Oh, dear . . . and now the press will be reporting his murder.'

'But he spoke to you of, perhaps, international affairs? What the government intended to do at home?' I tried to sound reassuring. 'Of course he didn't report scandal.'

'Yes, yes, that's it! In fact, he made me realise how lamentably ignorant I have become since poor Ernest died.' She turned her attention back to the locksmith. 'I shall miss Mr Tapley. Have you finished?'

I thought she meant, had I concluded my questions, but I realised she had addressed the question to the locksmith.

'Yes, ma'am,' he said. He sounded relieved.

'Then you may be on your way and I will call and settle the bill with your employer.'

The locksmith, a sturdy fellow with close-clipped hair, prepared to set off, gathering up his tools and a small canvas sack that appeared to be heavy.

'Wait!' I called to him. I pointed at the sack. 'Is that the old lock?'

'Yessir . . . the lady don't want it. Mr Pickles might have a use for it.'

'He works for Mr Pickles,' Mrs Jameson explained. 'Mr Pickles is a member of our society.'

'Society?' I asked.

'The Society of Friends, Inspector. He is a fellow Quaker.'

I nodded understanding. 'But, if you don't mind, I'll take charge of the lock for the time being. I'll write you a receipt for it.'

Both of them looked surprised. 'What do you want with it?' demanded the locksmith.

'I don't know,' I told him. 'But this house was the scene of a murder last night and that lock was part of the house at the time. We are not sure yet how the murderer entered. We may have to examine it.'

'He didn't pick this lock,' said the locksmith, holding up the sack. 'The only way he'd open this lock is with a key. This is a Bramah, this one is. That's the best you can buy, you ask anyone in the trade.'

'Really?' I asked.

'Yus, really,' said the locksmith. 'There was a feller picked one a few years ago, or reckoned he did, but it took him hours and hours and he done it with no one watching him. It was a special lock the company had put on show in their window. They were offering two hundred pounds if anyone could pick it. That just shows you what a good'un the company thought it had made. So this feller, he had a go and got it open after weeks fiddling with it. But no one saw him actually do the opening of it, did they? So they don't know how he done it. He might've picked it and there again, he might not. I, myself,' added the locksmith, 'know a bit about locks and I couldn't pick a lock like that one I just took out of the lady's front door.'

'Just leave it there,' ordered Mrs Jameson, cutting short this flow of information that I was actually finding quite interesting.

The locksmith shrugged, set the bag with the old lock down on the ground, and trudged away. I scribbled out a receipt for the lock and handed it to Mrs Jameson, who murmured, 'I am sure there is no need . . .'

'Regulations require, ma'am, that if I take possession of something at the scene, I give you a receipt for it.'

Mrs Jameson was impressed by regulations. She said she

would go to another Quaker lady's house for the day. In exchange for the receipt for the old lock, she handed me her friend's address on a scrap of paper. I thanked her for her help and forbearance. Mrs Jameson departed, taking Jenny with her.

As she passed by me, Jenny whispered, 'I'm glad we're going out for the day, sir. I don't like it in this house no more. It fair gives me the creeps. Every little sound makes me jump and I don't see how I'm going to sleep here. I won't even be able to get my work done, not with looking over my shoulder every two minutes.'

As I'd already guessed, Jenny would soon be seeking a new place, Quaker references in hand.

'If you leave here during the next few weeks, you must leave us the address of your new place of employment,' I told her. 'In case we need you.'

'Whaffor?' asked Jenny indignantly.

'It's procedure,' I assured her.

'If I get a new place, the lady there won't want the police coming round the minute I start working there!' Jenny declared truthfully, if impolitely.

'Then I advise you to stay here for the meantime, until we've finished our enquiries.'

Jenny rolled her eyes at me. At that moment her mistress called her and she hurried away without further argument.

'She'll stay, at least for the next few weeks,' said Morris, who'd been listening. 'She won't have any choice. Everyone will know she's been working in a house where the police are making enquiries. It'll cast a shadow over her, as it were. She won't get offered a new place soon. She'll have to wait for it all to quieten down.'

Now we had the house to ourselves and went upstairs to search Tapley's rooms thoroughly.

'The letter, Morris, from the landlady in Southampton, that must be somewhere. The superintendent is right in believing Tapley would have kept it. We are also looking for the missing house key. The murderer, if he has it, can't now use it. But if he took it, I want to know.'

We looked under the carpets. We pulled out drawers and checked to see if anything was taped to the back of one. In the end we found the letter in the place where Tapley would most obviously have hidden it: in the bookcase. We had to take out every single book and open each at every page, but we found the former landlady's letter tucked neatly into a volume of Cowper's poetry. The volume was bound in green cloth and I made a mental note to wash my hands carefully before I ate. Arsenic is less used now to produce the colour green, since the danger of absorbing the poison through the skin is known. But it is still to be found in older books.

The earlier landlady's name was Mrs Holland and she lived in St Michael's Alley, Southampton. Mr Thomas Tapley had lodged with her from February in the previous year until the end of July. He had then moved out. He had been an excellent lodger, caused no disturbance of any kind, paid on time and had been unfailingly courteous and helpful. She was sorry to see him leave.

'Well,' I said to Morris, 'this is what we expected. It tallies with what Mrs Jameson remembers of it. It tells us nothing new about the man. But I'll telegraph my opposite number in Southampton. I'll ask him to speak to Mrs Holland and find out if she knows where Tapley lived before he arrived on her doorstep with that air of trustworthiness that so impressed both landladies. Mrs Jameson says he never tried to borrow money from her; but Mrs Holland's experience may have been otherwise.'

'Doesn't sound like it from that letter,' observed Morris, staring gloomily at the sheet of paper in my hand.

'I agree, it doesn't. But I need her to confirm it. For one thing, if she does, it confirms he had a regular source of income. I want to know what that was.'

We didn't, however, find the missing house key despite our thoroughness. The murderer, if he had it, would find it useless now; but it did suggest he'd meant to come back. What had he been seeking, and why had we found no private papers of any kind?

We returned to Scotland Yard. I sent a telegraphed message to Southampton, requesting any information about Thomas Tapley who had resided briefly the previous year in St Michael's Alley – and asking that someone go and interview the landlady.

Biddle returned in the late afternoon, footsore and perspiring, having trudged round every coffee house south of the river in the vicinity of Waterloo Bridge rail station. He had also crossed the bridge and asked questions in the many coffee houses and cigar divans of The Strand and the immediate streets around it, on the north side. Two days earlier, Lizzie had met Tapley near Waterloo Bridge heading for the busy area beyond. Returning, quite some time later, she'd seen him again, ahead of her on the bridge this time, making for the south bank and home. I wanted to know where he'd been in the meantime.

But Biddle's search had been curiously unproductive. Several waiters thought they remembered a small gent in a shabby coat who came in occasionally, but he had not been a regular. Of that all the waiters were certain. They knew their regulars. Moreover, their establishments saw a fair number of small shabby men who drifted through, spending little cash and making the most of a warm room and a free newspaper. They could not be sure the man Biddle was asking about was any one of them.

Those who thought they remembered Tapley at all, as an individual, agreed he had not been talkative. 'Not a chatty gentleman,' said one of them, 'other than to remark on the weather, like most of 'em do, especially if it's raining. They always come in from the rain talking about it – as if it never rained in London.' Tapley? He had read the newspapers, drunk his coffee – or smoked his cigar as the case might be – and left. They didn't recall him greeting or being greeted by anyone else as an acquaintance. But then, they couldn't swear that the customer had been Tapley at all.

Emerging from this collective vagueness of memory, the only thing they were certain of was that, whoever he was, he'd not been one to leave the small change for the waiter. They remembered generous tippers.

'Kept moving lodgings and kept changing coffee houses,' I said sourly to Superintendent Dunn when I went to report on my lack of progress at the end of the day. 'He'd not wanted to attract attention or invite questions, if you ask me.'

Dunn leaned back in his chair and rubbed the palm of his hand over his stubble of grey hair. 'Why?' he asked simply.

'Well,' I told him, 'either Thomas Tapley did not want to

give an account of himself to anyone or . . . or he was anxious not to leave a trail that could be followed.'

'Hiding from someone?' Dunn mused. 'Yes, yes, just as I said earlier, on the run.'

'It's possible, sir. However you look at it,' I declared, 'that man had a secret.'

'Then find out what it was, Ross,' said Dunn with the serene confidence of the man who doesn't have to do the job himself.

Chapter Six

Elizabeth Martin Ross

I HAD waited up for Ben to return the previous night for as long as I could. At last, as I kept nodding off in my chair, I went to bed. I found my husband sleeping in the same chair, before a cold fire, in the early morning. After such a disturbed night, it wasn't surprising Bessie and I lacked enthusiasm for our usual morning tasks. I watched Ben leave, escorting Mrs Jameson and Jenny home. I wondered how he would manage the opening of what might prove to be a difficult investigation when he'd spent most of the night awake.

Bessie, yawning, was despatched to the butcher to ask if there were any mutton chops to be had. I warned her not to linger gossiping about the events of the previous night, and to come straight home again. I set off myself to visit a lacemaker to view the progress of a commission I'd given her, to make collar and cuffs that I hoped would brighten a plain gown. My route took me by the great rail terminus of Waterloo. Here it was always crowded and I knew to watch out for my purse. It was because I was keeping this sharp lookout that, on my return from the lacemaker, I noticed Coalhouse Joey.

It was purest chance. Joey did not want to attract attention. Attention, as far as he was concerned, generally meant trouble. Vagrancy was an offence. But my eye caught the flicker of movement and there he was, scurrying along the street, keeping to the walls, just as any of the rats or stray cats might have done. His small, skinny frame stooped almost double to avoid being spotted by shopkeepers and any forces of the law that might be about. On impulse, I called out his name. I thought he might bolt into the nearest alley and vanish into the maze of courts and lanes beyond, but he hesitated, eyeing me warily.

'It's Mrs Ross. You know me, Joey!' I called again, and beckoned to him.

Bessie would not have approved. 'You want to keep away from that boy, missus,' she had told me on numerous occasions. 'You'll very likely catch something if you go anywhere near him. He's got lice and nits and ringworm, and he smells something awful.'

She was right, at least about the smell. I caught a strong whiff of it as Joey sidled towards me. I doubt he'd even been bathed as a baby or troubled to wash himself since; and the resulting layer of grey-brown served as a varnish on his skin. It was hard to imagine how he had survived infancy, or what wretched girl had given him birth. He was a child in both years and in stature; and an old man in experience. His scrawny body was wrapped in a motley collection of filthy rags. His teeth were pointed like an animal's and a few had been lost. When I'd first become aware that he lived in our neighbourhood, I'd asked Ben if something couldn't be done for him.

'Like what?' asked Ben.

'Perhaps he could be apprenticed to a trade.'

'No tradesman would take him on,' said Ben. 'Though he's the right build for going up a chimney.'

At that I held forth at length on the wrongs done to climbing boys. Ben had responded by reminding me he had begun his working life as a trapper in the Derbyshire mines. 'Crouching for hours in the dark and cold, terrified of rats and of being forgotten at the end of a shift, left down there for ever. But for your father's generosity, I'd still be down there, digging out the coal.'

'Then you should be sympathetic to Joey,' I'd argued.

'I am sympathetic,' said Ben. 'I've twice caught him creeping out of our coalhouse and not run him in for breaking and entering. London is full of child vagrants, Lizzie. You can't adopt them all.'

That is how Joey had acquired his nickname of 'coalhouse'. It was his habit on cold wet nights to crawl into people's outhouses, or even into their cellars, his small frame squeezing through narrow gaps or tiny windows. It was a wonder house thieves had not sought to exploit this talent of his. Joey would leave at daybreak and the only sign of his presence might be the smudged print of a child's hand or of a small foot in the coal dust. He didn't steal from the properties he visited clandestinely; householders and servant girls would shrug and say, 'It's only Coalhouse Joey.' Perhaps, in time, he would become a figure of folklore, like Will o' the Wisp, or gain a more sinister reputation as he grew older, like Springheeled Jack. (Ben has told me that from time to time the police still receive reports of a claimed sighting of that strange being!)

79

I had bought some apples my way back. I took one from my basket and held it out to him. Joey sidled up, with a gleam in his eyes. But, like a feral animal, he wouldn't take it from my hand. So I set it down on the pavement. Joey darted forward to seize it, then retreated, gripping it tightly. He stared at me from beneath the matted fringe of hair that grew right down to his large dark eyes and muttered his thanks.

'I haven't seen you for some days, Joey,' I said.

'Old Butcher is after me.' I was quite surprised to hear him speak up clearly.

'Constable Butcher?'

'Yus, but he don't catch me. He can't run. He's too fat.'

'Well, he might catch you one day, Joey. Why don't you present yourself at the workhouse? They'll take you in.'

'I ain't going in no work'us.'

'You'd be fed.'

'I gets food.' He held up the apple. 'Like this. People give me bits of bread sometimes. I goes round the kitchen door of the chophouses and some of the cooks know me. They give me the stuff what comes back from the dining room on the plates, what's not eaten, you know.' Joey's brow creased in wonderment. 'Folk do send it back, not eaten. A whole potato sometimes, fat off the meat, with the gravy on it . . .' Joey looked wistful at the memory of these treats. 'Anyway,' he added, 'I don't need no work'us.'

He squinted at me. 'There's been a murder done in your street,' he said suddenly.

'Oh, you've heard about that, have you, then?' I asked, surprised.

'O'course I have. I know everything what goes on around

here. It was the little old fellow what got croaked, as I heard it.' He looked at me expectantly.

I realised that some sort of trade was in progress. I'd given him an apple. He wanted to show his gratitude – or ensure future small gifts of food – by offering me something in return.

'That's right. His name is, or was, Mr Tapley. Thomas Tapley.'

'Didn't know his name,' said Joey. 'Only that he went out walking every day, even when it rained. He'd got an old umbrella. He didn't half look funny with it.'

'Sadly you won't see Mr Tapley again, Joey.'

'Suppose not,' said Joey carelessly. He tilted his head on one side. 'I saw his visitor, though.'

I was startled and tried not to show it. But I fancy Joey knew he'd surprised me because he gave a little grin of satisfaction. He had hoped to offer me some information I didn't already have, in return for the apple, and he'd been successful.

'When was this, Joey?'

He frowned. 'I don't know different days. They're all the same to me, excepting Sundays when the bells all ring. It was about three or four days, maybe a week, before he got croaked.'

'Did this visitor come to the house?'

Joey nodded. 'But it was on the quiet. The lady what owns the house, she'd gone out.' He paused to reflect on what he knew of the address. 'It's no good asking her maid for anything to eat. Some of the maids will give me a bit of bread when the missus is out of the way. But not yours, mind you!' Joey fixed me with a resentful eye. 'She's a real bad-tempered one, your maid. The maid in the murder house, that one with the red hair, she's the same, wouldn't give me nothing, so I don't bother to go round to the kitchen and ask. When I saw the lady leave, I stayed where I was, sitting just inside the side alley across the road.'

'And?' I prompted him impatiently.

'Then I saw a young fellow come along the street. Not very big, he wasn't. He had a black coat, with one of them high collars, and a hat pulled down over his ears, so you couldn't see his face much. But I reckoned he was really young by the style of him and the way he walked, not plodding along like ole Butcher but light as a fevver.'

'Fevver? Oh, *feather* . . .'

'That's wot I said.' Joey was annoyed by my interruption. 'You want to know or not? He crossed over to my side – I mean to where my alley was. So I squeezed m'self back in a bit more, into the shadow, and didn't make no noise. 'Cos I reckoned he was up to something, see? He'd stopped, standing right there just a bit in front of me. I could've reached out and touched him. He didn't know I was there. He just stood looking up at the front of the house. Then ole Mr Tapley, as you call him, he came to the window upstairs and looked out. He saw the young fellow, looking up at him, so he opens the window and leans out. He didn't call out nothing. He just pointed down at the street door, and put his finger to his lips, like this.' Joey put a grimy forefinger to his mouth in the traditional sign for silence. 'So the young fellow crosses back over and stands by the street door. Then it opens and I can see old Tapley himself has opened it – not that red-haired maid. The visitor nips inside and Tapley closes the door real quick and quiet. He was sneaking him in, that's what. On the quiet, you know? He didn't want anyone knowing about him.'

It certainly appeared so. Ben would want to hear about this.

'How long did the visitor stay there, Joey?'

'Not long. Well, perhaps half an hour. Then Tapley lets him out again and the young chap sets off down the street, real quick.' Joey gave me a fleeting grin. 'And I followed him, 'cos I wanted to know where he was going.'

'And where did he go?'

Now there was no disguising the look of triumph on Joey's face. 'That's the best bit. He marches off, round the corner and down the road towards the river. Then I see a carriage, a closed one and a real smart affair, with a beautiful pair of horses. I like horses,' added Joey. 'These was the tops, a matched pair, golden chestnuts with pale yellow manes and tails. Cor, they must have cost a fortune, them horses.'

'So we're talking of a private carriage,' I said.

He nodded. 'No cabbie ever drove a matched pair like that, nor any old carriage for hire. This carriage was painted all shiny and polished up. The coachmen had a smart coat and a top hat, and all. The young fellow, the one that had visited old Tapley, he jumps up into the carriage and off they go down the street, heading towards the bridge.'

This was a curious and secretive affair, indeed. 'The visitor never came back, Joey?'

He shook his head. 'Not as I saw him ever. I never saw that carriage again, neither. I looked out for it because I wanted to see them yellow horses again.'

'Joey,' I said earnestly, 'my husband will want to know about this. It's a murder investigation and information is very important. Will you come to my house tonight and tell Inspector Ross what you've told me?'

But this was asking more than the apple was worth. 'I don't speak to no peelers,' said Joey firmly. 'Not even the plain-clothes sort like your old man.'

And in a blur of rags, he was gone, slipping away among the crowds like an eel among rocks, and out of sight.

I hurried back to our street and to Mrs Jameson's house. The locksmith had been and completed his task, as I could see from the scored wood of the door around a new lock. But although I beat the brass knocker loudly several times, I couldn't summon either Ben or Morris; yet Ben had told me he had intended to take Morris there to help him search poor Tapley's rooms. I even went down the passage leading into the back yard but the only living things there were Mrs Jameson's hens, pecking away in their coop. The kitchen door was fastened and peering through the windows rewarded me with nothing more than a view of the kitchen range. Probably the two men had just left, and I'd missed them by minutes.

I looked around the yard. It wouldn't be difficult for someone to slip into it, as I had done, wait until Jenny had left her kitchen and enter the house on his way to murder. But Tapley's earlier visitor had not come that way. He'd clearly made an arrangement with Tapley to come as soon as Mrs Jameson had left the house. He'd waited across the street, Tapley had looked out of his window for him and let him in by the front door. Why had this visitor taken the bold way in and not the surreptitious way from the rear of the house, as the murderer appeared to have done? Because, I reasoned, the mystery visitor had arrived in the vicinity by private carriage. This was someone who would no more dream of entering a house by the servants' and tradesmen's route than he would take a public cab to get there. Tapley's youthful visitor had been a young gentleman of means.

I put aside my speculations, remembering that Ben would want to hear Joey's story before he came home that night. There was nothing for it but to take a cab and go to Scotland Yard myself.

It seemed sensible to run to the rank at the nearby railway station, so I hurried there. I was looking for a growler, being alone and knowing that only women of dubious virtue rode around unescorted in a hansom cab. Sure enough, there was one free and waiting for hire. As I approached it the driver, who had been chatting with others of his trade nearby, spotted the approaching fare, detached himself from the group and came towards me. We recognised one another at the same moment.

'Why, Mr Slater!' I exclaimed. There was no mistaking his battered ex-prizefighter's features.

'Hullo!' returned the cabbie. His mouth formed a wide grin revealing his broken teeth. 'It's Miss Martin, as I stand here. What are you doing running around railway stations? Not looking out for dead bodies, I hope?' This was, to him, a joke recalling our original meeting at the time of my first arrival in London. He chuckled hoarsely.

'Well, yes, as it happens, Mr Slater. There has been another murder and I'm anxious to get to Scotland Yard. Oh, and I'm Mrs Ross now and my husband is an inspector in the plain-clothes division of the Yard.'

He bent a stern eye on me. 'Is he, now? Well, I congratulates you on your marriage, and hopes you'll be as content as Mrs

Slater and yours truly. Though married to a plain-clothes jack out of the Yard, eh?' He shook his head sorrowfully. 'Not that I'm surprised to learn it, mind you. You always had a funny sort of interest in corpses. Ladies do have hobbies, I know that. Only generally it's painting flowers or bothering the poor with their good works. But your pa was a sawbones, I recollect you telling me. So I suppose it runs in the fam'ly. You certainly have a particular eye for a murder.'

'Yes, yes, Mr Slater, if you want to put it like that. But will you take me to Scotland Yard, as quickly as possible, please?' There was no persuading him I wasn't of a particularly ghoulish turn of mind.

'Course I will,' he said. 'Jump up in the cab. I washed it out yesterday inside, all clean. I must've known you would come along.'

We did make good speed. Before we parted, he wished me good luck with my investigations and hoped he'd see me again. 'Like as not whenever a body turns up!'

I hurried inside the building.

'Hullo, Mrs Ross,' said the young constable who greeted me. 'The inspector's with Superintendent Dunn. You sit down there and wait and I'll go up and tell him you're here, the minute he's back in his office.'

'Lizzie?' said Ben, a few minutes later, his face registering his surprise. His voice sharpened. 'What's happened now?'

I told him about Joey and the mysterious visitor to Tapley.

'I shall have to find that boy,' he said. Then he made an impatient 'tsk' noise. 'Morris and I were certainly at the house this morning to search Tapley's room and I wish I'd still been there when you came. We could have gone at once to the area where you saw Joey, and searched for him, all three of us. I shall ask that Constable Butcher or any other officer who patrols that beat keep an eye open for the boy.'

'They won't catch Joey,' I told him. 'He keeps both eyes well open to spot a policeman in uniform. But I'll ask Bessie to ask among the other maids in the street to tell her if Joey comes to their kitchen door begging food scraps. He doesn't come to ours, unfortunately, because Bessie chases him away if I'm not there. Mrs Jameson's Jenny shoos him away, too. If I am at home and see him about, I usually give him something to eat. I really wish we could do something for him. He is very fond of horses, Ben. He could make a stable boy.'

'He could hang around the mews and hope the ostlers would give him a penny or two to help out, but as to any one actually letting him take care of a valuable beast, I doubt that.' Ben's black brows furrowed in thought. 'But the "yellow" horses, as you say he called them. They should be easily spotted if we knew which part of London to look in, certainly a wealthy part. I'll send word out round the districts, to tell their men to watch out for a matched carriage pair like that, and send word to the Yard immediately.'

Ben stretched his arms above his head and sighed. He looked tired and still had the rest of a long day ahead of him. 'Let's hope I hear from Southampton tomorrow or that news of the murder in the evening papers may stir up some interest. Our Quaker widow's lodger is an intriguing case, Lizzie, but we'll ferret out his secret yet!'

At that moment a heavy footstep sounded in the doorway and Superintendent Dunn's burly form appeared.

'Well, well, Mrs Ross!' he exclaimed. 'A pleasure to see you, ma'am.'

And what are you doing here? was the unspoken query, signalled by his bushy eyebrows rising up to his hairline.

Ben hastily explained about my encounter with Coalhouse Joey.

'What should we do without you, Mrs Ross?' rumbled Dunn. 'Yet again you bring us valuable information. It is a great pity we cannot employ ladies to be detectives. They seem most adept at turning up clues and witnesses.'

How much I preferred Wally Slater's honest opinion that I was a strange sort of female with odd interests; but that it was to be accepted. Anything rather than Dunn's patronising smile.

'Yes!' I said briskly. 'It is a great pity you do not employ women here at the Yard. But I sincerely hope the day will come when you do.'

I don't know which of the two men looked the more horrified. I beamed at them and left them to contemplate the Awful Female Future. Good. And if Superintendent Dunn wanted further proof that Scotland Yard would benefit from employing women, then I'd do my very best to see that he got it.

Chapter Seven

Inspector Benjamin Ross

IT WAS frustrating to think that Lizzie had just missed me at the Jameson house. I certainly wanted to talk to that boy, Joey. If we could find him, I could still quiz him. But in the short term I didn't have much hope of it. Joey would realise that I'd be looking for him, and he'd be keeping out of the way. Even so, he couldn't hide for ever. The area around Waterloo Bridge Station was his hunting ground. By his own admission it was here he foraged around the kitchen doors of households and chophouses. Here they knew him and he knew where those well disposed towards him were to be found. Joey wouldn't starve where there was a regular handout of scraps to be had. He would lie low for a while, but he would come back. Hunger would speak louder than caution.

After Lizzie's meeting with Dunn, she'd bounced out, skirts a-quiver, in a way that led me to fancy she had taken offence at something Dunn had said. That was a pity, because I knew Dunn admired her sharp wits. But women, or so I've been given to understand, are sometimes touchy in the oddest sort of ways. A simple remark on the pork chops being a little dry is immediately interpreted as the whole meal being spoiled, it all the fault of the cook. An intended compliment on always having liked to see the lady in a particular gown draws a cross remark about always having to wear the same thing. Compliment too much and that's suspicious. Say nothing at all and you risk accusations of being unobservant or uncaring. Of course I don't refer to Lizzie. She is too sensible and intelligent and I hope we understand one another too well for silly squabbles of that sort. I am talking generally, based on the lamentations of my married colleagues. Mrs Morris is particularly sensitive, I gather, on the subject of her culinary skills.

In the meantime my best hope, the following morning, was the report of the murder in the previous day's evening newspapers. There were missing people a-plenty in London and those anxious to find them. With luck, the latter would soon be beating a path to Scotland Yard.

By early afternoon I had had three eager visitors, all in response to the press report of the murder, all convinced that the dead man was the missing person they'd been seeking. Unfortunately, in none of these cases did the details of their missing man remotely correspond with those of our corpse.

The callers were unwilling to be told this. They all insisted the dead man must be their absconded husband, defaulting tenant, or the man who had persuaded them to invest in a certain scheme to make money on the stock exchange. In two of these cases there was no cause for optimism at all. I did send the man whose tenant had done a moonlight flit down to the mortuary, with Biddle as escort. But it was always an outside chance. Biddle came back to say that the gentleman had not recognised the corpse and departed in high dudgeon, declaring that Scotland Yard had wasted his valuable time.

It was just gone two in the afternoon, and, not having lunched, I was beginning to be distracted by the pangs of hunger. I was wondering whether to send Biddle out for a veal pie, when the lad himself appeared. He announced breathlessly that a Mr Jonathan Tapley presented his compliments, and his card, and wished to speak to me. He held out the visiting card, his hand trembling with excitement.

Tapley! My heart leaped. 'Send him in!' I ordered Biddle, and got up to greet the visitor. I should have taken a second to read the little white card Biddle held out. I'd have been forewarned. But, anxious to see anyone by the name of Tapley, I didn't. I deposited it carelessly on my desk and waited with excitement equal (though hopefully better concealed) to Biddle's.

I suppose, having seen Thomas Tapley occasionally in the neighbourhood (and his dead body rather closer to hand), I expected to meet someone very like him in appearance, perhaps even a double. At any rate, I was ready for someone rather short and perhaps shabby. So I was taken aback when into my office strode a very tall, lean and stately gentleman, radiating authority. He wore a frock coat that was a miracle of tailoring and carried an ivory-headed malacca cane. He sat down, uninvited, and placed his spotless silk hat on my desk. His black curling hair was silvering at the temples. He was a handsome man, no denying.

'You are Inspector Ross?' he enquired. His voice didn't exactly boom, but it resonated impressively, filling the little cubbyhole the Yard has allotted me. His manner suggested I had inconveniently called on him.

This was all the wrong way round. I was supposed to be in charge here. I hastened to correct the situation.

'I'm Inspector Ross,' I agreed, 'and you . . .' I glanced ostentatiously at his card and, to my dismay, now read there, 'J. G. Tapley Q.C. Barrister at Law'.

Of course I had heard of him and of the highly respected and long-established law chambers of which he was a member. But he specialised in arguing or defending the legal causes of the wealthy. He had not made his reputation in the criminal courts. It followed I'd never seen him face to face in action in any trial in which I'd had an interest. I certainly hadn't expected, when Biddle announced him, that my visitor would be *that* Jonathan Tapley. Whatever had brought a famous barrister to the Yard, in person, the mystery of how Thomas Tapley had come to be Mrs Jameson's first-floor front lodger could only deepen. Supposing, of course, that the two men were connected. It would seem that my visitor, at least, had reason to suppose they were. Yet, our poor battered corpse and this distinguished gentleman sitting in my modest office? It was enough to make any head spin.

Caught off-balance, I did my best. 'You are well known to me by name, Mr Tapley. I am honoured to make your acquaintance, sir. In what may I be of assistance?' So far, so good. But then I couldn't help blurting, 'You have some information for us, perhaps?'

Tapley parried this effortlessly. 'You have some information for *me*, I hope, Inspector.'

He folded his kid-gloved hands over the ivory pommel of the cane and sat there, looking at me expectantly. There was something of my old headmaster about the direct stare of his dark eyes. To my further discomfiture I felt myself regress to twelve years of age, standing accused once again of fighting with my schoolfellows. I sat down hastily. 'Perhaps you'd care to tell me what brings you, Mr Tapley.'

Wrong, Ross, wretched boy! Remember that an act of charity brought you here. If you are not to disgrace the good name of this ancient and respected school, and grieve your generous benefactor, at least keep your wits about you.

My visitor didn't say it but his look expressed similar sentiments.

'You cannot be unaware, Inspector, of the reports in yesterday evening's press of the discovery of a murdered man in lodgings near to Waterloo Bridge Station. You are possibly even the origin of that news item.'

'Well, yes,' I confessed. 'The body was discovered the day before yesterday, in the evening. I made sure the news was in the press the next day. We cannot be sure of the deceased's identity. His landlady knew very little about him. He did not speak to her of any family. We therefore have no knowledge of next of kin, and no one close to him has yet come forward and identified him. The landlady herself had only known him for about six months and he told her almost nothing of his circumstances. He may have given her a false name. Without confirmation of identity, we're hampered in our investigations.'

Jonathan Tapley raised a kid-gloved hand to interrupt me. 'I should like to see the body. There is no problem about that?'

'No, sir, none. But may I ask what interest—'

He cut me short again. 'The report did not say how he died. But since it was reported as murder, it was obviously not due to natural causes.'

'He was battered about the head, Mr Tapley.'

'Is the face damaged?' The fellow sounded dashed cool if our corpse was a relative of some sort.

'No, Mr Tapley. The back of the head took the force of the blows.'

'Then,' said my visitor, rising to his feet and taking up his silk hat, 'perhaps you'd be so good as to conduct me to the place where the corpse is presently to be found.'

I was more than eager to do so. Perhaps, on the way there, he'd deign to reveal what his interest was. But he was playing his cards close to his chest, as they say. If the body was nothing to him, he could depart having told me nothing. But some well-concealed secret fear had brought him to me. I wondered if, when he saw the body, his composure would be shaken. But it wasn't, at least not outwardly.

'Yes,' he said briefly, his eyes fixed on the waxen face.

'Sir?' I prompted.

'What?' He looked at me, momentarily startled, as if his mind had wandered from the sad sight that lay before him. He rallied at once with a brisk, 'Yes, I can identify him. The late gentleman is my cousin, Thomas Tapley.'

He looked back at the corpse. 'Is that the name he had been using? His own is the name he gave his landlady?'

'Yes, now that you have confirmed it is indeed his.'

Jonathan Tapley paused for a last look at his cousin's body. Then he turned away. 'Curious,' he remarked.

Outside the mortuary, he set his hat squarely on his head. 'I have now to carry the sad news to the rest of the family, Inspector. You will understand that is my primary duty. Perhaps you'd care to call on me later, in my chambers in the

Gray's Inn Road. Shall we say five o'clock?'

'Well,' I objected, 'if you could spare time for even a brief talk now, it might give us a lead . . .'

'I doubt I can give you a lead, as you call it, Inspector. I hadn't seen my cousin or been in direct contact with him for some time. I didn't know he was in London. But I am as anxious as you are to know what has happened here. You'll appreciate that, I hope?'

'Yes, sir, of course.' The questions were leaping to my lips but piled up there unasked. There was no use pressing him. He would speak when ready and I had to accept it. The problem for me was that he – and other family members – would have had time to correlate their statements.

He raised his cane, grasped by the neck, straight up in a farewell salute. I noticed that the ivory pommel was carved in the form of a skull. It looked a solid bit of work.

Jonathan Tapley was experienced at reading a witness's reactions. His lips curled slightly in a mirthless grimace. 'Yes, Inspector, it is a fine piece of carving. The cane is Malay craftsmanship. I always carry it. But I did not use it to beat my cousin's head in. Good day, Inspector. Until five o'clock.'

He strode off and I saw him raise the cane again, this time to hail a cab.

I made good use of the just over two hours I had before I kept my appointment with Jonathan Tapley. I tried to find out as much as I could about both him and other Tapley family members. I sent Sergeant Morris to Somerset House and took myself to the nearest reference library. We combined what we'd found out shortly before I set out for Tapley's chambers.

The barrister was easy enough to track down in books of reference. He was the son of a colonel of the Foot Guards. He had been born in 1816, so was at present, in this spring of 1868, fifty-two years of age. I speculated, digressing, that his soldier father had returned from playing his part in scotching the ambitions of Napoleon Bonaparte at Waterloo to set his own ambition at establishing himself in peacetime as a married man with family.

Jonathan had studied at Oxford and made steady progress through his chosen profession of the law. He had married a Miss Maria Harte in 1846. There was no recorded issue of this marriage. I was interested to learn that he had a London address in Bryanston Square. He also had a country property in Buckinghamshire. Mr Jonathan Tapley Q.C. was a very successful man, and also a very wealthy one. Had he inherited his fortune, made it all through his distinguished career at the bar, or had he, in the popular phrase, married money?

His cousin, Thomas Tapley, was a different kettle of fish when it came to looking him up. I couldn't find any trace of him at all. His birth would be recorded in the register of baptisms of the parish where he was born. But I had no knowledge of where that might be, as it would have taken place well before the requirement that all births be officially registered with a government office. He was not entered in any of the published directories of professional gentlemen, law, medicine or the Church, nor did he appear in the army or the navy lists. It would seem, therefore, that he'd been in possession of sufficient private income all his life to avoid having to work for a living. But even so he had finished up in Mrs Jameson's first-floor front rooms with only a change of underlinen and a collection of second-hand volumes to his name.

Morris had possibly done rather better. He hadn't found a birth, but the records of Somerset House had contained details of a marriage in January 1848 between a Thomas Tapley, gentleman, with an address in Harrogate, and Eulalia Sanders, daughter of Alexander Sanders, gentleman. The marriage had taken place in Harrogate. Was this our Thomas or another of the same name? Jonathan would be able to tell me. Morris, in a regular tour de force of research, had also discovered a record, still in Harrogate, of a female infant, named Flora Jane, born to Thomas Tapley, gentleman, and his wife Eulalia in October 1848. He found no information about any more births to the couple.

'The plot thickens, Morris!' I exclaimed. 'We may be in danger of haring off down the wrong track, but if this Thomas Tapley is our lately deceased Tapley, then where now are the wife and daughter?'

'Very likely he done a bunk, left 'em in the lurch,' said Morris, whose view of human nature has been sadly soured by his experiences as a police officer.

'We'll see . . .' I said, taking up my hat and setting out.

The senior clerk in Tapley's chambers was a dry-looking fellow whose complexion suggested he rarely saw the sun. He wore a pince-nez and removed it, holding it aloft in his hand, as he conducted me to Tapley's lair.

'Inspector Ross, Mr Tapley,' he announced in a voice as dry as the rest of him.

Tapley's study was comfortable and well furnished. I

compared the room mentally with my office, back at the Yard, a product of Metropolitan Police thrift. Here a fire crackled in the hearth. Two leather-covered armchairs stood either side of it and a sherry decanter graced a small table conveniently at hand. There was a handsome mahogany desk. The walls were lined with leather-bound tomes. A glance told me all dealt with aspects of the law. If Tapley was unsure of a point, he had but to stretch out his hand to look it up.

My scrutiny of the surroundings had not gone unnoticed.

'It is a comfortable room but rather small for the purpose,' Tapley remarked. 'I share it with a colleague. He is out of Town at the moment and won't interrupt us.'

He indicated with a graceful sweep of his hand that I should be seated. I sank down into one of the leather chairs. He, however, remained standing. This put me at something of a disadvantage, as he towered over me. Tapley the barrister, I thought sourly, knew all the courtroom tricks.

'Sherry, Inspector?'

'Thank you, sir, but we are not permitted,' I said. And you know that, don't you? I nearly snarled.

'Of course.' He walked to the window and stood, with his hands clasped behind his back, looking out.

'You were able to carry the sad news to your family?' I prompted him, determined he should not manipulate me like a marionette on strings.

He turned to walk back towards me. 'Indeed, yes, that is to say, I told my wife. She was very upset, naturally. I have left it to her to inform Flora, my niece.' He took a seat at last in the armchair facing me.

Flora? I thought. It began to look as if the Thomas Tapley

in Harrogate unearthed by Morris might be the unfortunate Thomas, late lodger of the Quaker widow.

'I would be glad,' I said politely, 'of any and all details concerning your late cousin that you can give me.'

He inclined his head. 'I shall do so, even though it will cost me some pain and embarrassment.' He drew a deep breath. 'We are both of us toilers in the cause of upholding the law, Inspector. We both know that the most respected citizens, and the most respectable of families, may harbour secrets they would not wished revealed to public knowledge. We both know that when murder occurs, thorough enquiries follow. They will, one hopes, lead to someone being charged with the crime. They will also bring secrets to the surface, wished or unwished. The thorough preparation needed to prosecute or defend such a charge in a court of law also makes of some wretch's life an open book.'

He'd had ample time to prepare this pretty speech. I read his implication as easily as he meant me to do. I replied, as I knew he hoped:

'Secrets must, indeed, be revealed to the investigating officers. But they are of interest only when they have a bearing on the particular crime. What's necessary must be made public. What is not of public interest, has no bearing on the crime, well, that needn't become known to all and sundry.'

I fancied he looked relieved. 'Quite,' he said. 'Thank you, Inspector.'

I was sorry to damage his confidence. 'But I should remind you that the gentlemen of the press have quite another agenda. One can't keep everything from them, at least not easily. What they do with the knowledge is beyond my powers to control.'

'I am aware of that,' he replied bitterly. 'However, I don't expect you to control the press, Ross. It'll be up to me to try to do that. I realise I might not be successful.'

'The press can also be very helpful to us in this kind of affair,' I warned him. 'Had I not been able to put the report of the finding of a body in the evening papers here in London, you would not have seen it, and we wouldn't be having this conversation now. Further references to the case may jog the memory of someone, somewhere, who may come forward with valuable information. On the other hand, we don't want the worst kind of sensational journalism or we'll get inundated with wild stories and claims. We will try to keep anything personal and embarrassing to the family out of it. But if we want the press's help, we have to offer something in return. It's a matter of treading a fine line, Mr Tapley.'

He nodded, took a deep breath, and placed the tips of his long, slender fingers together. 'You appear to me – you won't take offence at what I say, I hope – to have a more subtle nature than most police officers. I have, in my time, had to deal with some deeply unimaginative ones – and some out-and-out blockheads. You are obviously not in that category. I know you will treat anything I tell you with sensitivity.' He paused. 'Are you going to write any of this down?' He raised one dark eyebrow a little quizzically.

I felt myself flush. 'With your permission, I will make a few notes, Mr Tapley. It will save me having to return to you again unnecessarily.'

I fished out my notebook and pencil and sat ready.

'Well, now,' he began. 'My father was the younger of two brothers. He made his way as a soldier. His elder brother managed things rather differently. He married an heiress. In 1806 my cousin Thomas was born. You may have already discovered that I was born in 1816 . . .'

I felt myself flush once more and hoped it wasn't visible or that he'd put it down to being seated near the fire. I reflected again that Tapley had a barrister's nimble mental footwork and I'd have to be ever alert to keep ahead of him. So far, he seemed to be keeping marginally ahead of me.

'And that, therefore, Tom was a full ten years older than I. For that reason we were not close as boys. I was a squalling infant when he already fancied himself quite a fellow. By the time I was ten years old, Tom was out in the wide world. But Tom's childhood was greatly affected by the death of my uncle, his father, when Tom was seven. After that he was brought up by his devoted mother. He was educated at home, because she had decided he was too delicate to go away to school . . .'

Jonathan Tapley paused before adding, with what might have been either dry humour or resentment: 'Nobody thought I was too delicate to be sent away from home at a young age to cope as best I could with the rigours of a public school education!'

'At ten years of age,' I said with some asperity, 'I was working down a coal mine.'

I had, at last, wrong-footed my companion. He looked startled. 'Were you, indeed?' He stared at me long and hard. 'My cousin Tom had a far easier life than either of us, then. How, may I ask, did you escape the coal mine for the police force?'

'A generous benefactor, a local doctor, was responsible for

taking me and another boy out of the mine and paying for us both to be educated,' I told him.

'Then your benefactor has been well repaid.'

Dr Martin had sadly not lived long enough to see his prodigy become a police inspector, or to see me marry his daughter. Perhaps the last was just as well.

Tapley was continuing his story. 'Tom stayed at home, cosseted by his mamma and a bevy of aunts and other assorted spinster ladies. There is a portrait showing him to be an attractive child. He found it easy to please all the womenfolk who surrounded him. He had an excellent brain and would, if encouraged, have made a first-class scholar. As it was, he turned out a dilettante, dabbling in literature, the arts, the natural sciences: any subject that took his fancy at the moment and for the moment.'

'In his lodgings, where he died,' I told him, 'he had quite a library.'

'Poor Tom,' said his cousin. 'He did love books even if he skimped the tasks set him by his long-suffering tutor. But he did learn one skill from his upbringing, Ross, and learned it well. He discovered how to play on the soft natures of older women. He adopted the attitude that there would always be a female presence to look after him. Of course, as he grew older, the ladies he'd known in childhood either died or dropped out of his life. His mother passed away when he was in his late twenties. But he always seemed to find another to take her place.'

As he had found Mrs Jameson and, before her, the landlady in Southampton who had written so warmly recommending him.

Jonathan Tapley had begun, for the first time since I'd

made his acquaintance, to look ill at ease. 'He was sent up to Oxford but only stayed there briefly. He left, as they say, under a cloud. There was an incident . . .' Now Tapley was clearly unhappy. 'He was discovered with another student in what the law declares to be an unnatural act and a crime. In those days, all this happened in 1824, it was a hanging matter. That awful sentence, thank heaven, has at last been abolished for the offence. But as you'll know it remains punishable by imprisonment with hard labour. As a result, a culture of secrecy has grown up around the matter. Still, you're a police officer and I don't need to tell you that.' He made a dismissive gesture.

'At the time, it was dealt with quickly, efficiently and privately. It was in the interest of both families and of the college, to say nothing of the wretched youngsters themselves. Tom was barely eighteen at the time and terrified out of his wits at the danger he found himself in. But it didn't frighten him into lifelong celibacy. Other later encounters had to be hushed up. It was obvious that, while Tom saw women as providers of home comforts, those did not include that of the shared bedchamber. His personal preference, in that respect, was for his own sex.'

There was a silence. I quickly reviewed the tale Coalhouse Joey had told Lizzie, of the young fellow who had so secretively visited Tapley when the landlady had been away from the house. This could be the explanation, an assignation of a sexual nature. But would Tapley take such a risk in the house where he lodged? Actually bring a young male lover there? There were other places where he might go and meet such a person without danger of being caught. Yet people do behave foolishly when a physical urge overrules commonsense. There was no need to repeat Joey's story now. I hadn't interviewed the boy himself. The story came second-hand from Lizzie. Besides, any man who sat down to play with Jonathan Tapley should, I'd realised, keep a poker face and cards out of sight.

'I see,' I said aloud. 'But yet your cousin married?'

'Yes. His experience at Oxford had, at least, taught Tom the importance of discretion. Our society displays a remarkable degree of hypocrisy, Ross. You can't be unaware of that! What is known of, but never spoken of, is largely left undisturbed. But public knowledge, scandal, is greatly to be feared. It brings swift retribution. I don't know what your private view of the subject is, Inspector. I do however know that you, as I am, are required to uphold the law. I personally feel the law is too harsh. Tom could no more help his nature than any other man. But, like others of his persuasion, he was obliged to live a double life with an ever-present fear of one day finding himself breaking rocks on Dartmoor.

'As he grew older the temptation to acquire the protection of marriage, as plenty of other fellows like him have done, grew. Also, only through marriage, quite apart from keeping scandal at bay, would he ensure that a doting female of the respectable sort would run his home, preside over his dinner table and take the place of all those devoted female relatives of his childhood. The lady of his choice, of course, would know nothing of his sexual preference and, naturally, no one would explain it to her. Women of good family are generally ignorant on that subject and there is a consensus of opinion in our society that they should remain so. Tom took the marriage route in 1848. He was already in his early forties. His continued single status – bear in mind he was a well-to-do man who could afford to marry – was causing some comment. He chose carefully. His wife wasn't a young woman. She was in her late thirties. Her family was alarmed at the thought of her, the spinster of the family, sitting in a corner in some relative's house until she died. She probably didn't relish the prospect either. She was delighted to become mistress of her own household. My father, who had a soldier's robust sense of humour, remarked that forty-eight was indeed the Year of Revolutions, since Tom Tapley had walked up the aisle.'

Jonathan Tapley actually smiled. 'To the astonishment of us all, this union proved very happy and even, most unexpectedly, bore fruit. A daughter was born later in the year, almost nine months to the day. Her name is Flora and she's now nineteen years of age. Tom, once he got over the surprise, was quite the proudest father I ever saw.

'Sadly, his wife died when Flora was only three. Doctors had told my wife and me we must resign ourselves to never having a child of our own. We offered to take Flora into our household and bring her up. Tom was grateful. My wife and I were overjoyed. It is not too strong a word. To us, it was a gift from above. Flora's presence has transformed our lives, Inspector. No natural daughter born to us could be more dear.'

He fell silent and I could find nothing to say. To hear and see this self-assured, rather pompous stuffed shirt of a man reveal his humanity and his vulnerability was deeply moving.

'So,' I said, 'the "niece" of whom you spoke earlier is, in fact, what? A young cousin once removed?'

Jonathan Tapley made a visible effort to pull himself together. 'Yes. In view of her young age, it was more convenient for us to refer to her as a niece and for her to call us Uncle and Aunt.'

It also blurred her relationship to her father, your cousin Thomas, and any stories that might be circulating, I thought. Introduced to the world as your 'niece', no one would automatically think of Tom and the whispers about him.

'So, you see, it was all neatly arranged . . .' Tapley was saying, 'except in one respect. As Flora grew older and showed signs of growing into a very pretty and charming young lady, we had to give some thought to her future. She was ten when my wife and I decided something must be done to ensure no unpleasantness cast a shadow over it. Ten is still a child. But the years fly by, and all too soon she'd be going out into the world. We hoped she would meet a very suitable young man and marry happily.' He fell silent again and seemed to be waiting for me to identify the problem aloud, although it was obvious enough.

'If there should be a scandal concerning her father, or if his name should become known as a frequenter of certain circles, and if it came out that she was his daughter, her prospects would be blighted,' I said. 'Good families cherish their reputations. They flee public notoriety. Passing her off as your niece might be interpreted by some as an attempt to mislead. There would be no good marriage for Miss Flora.'

Your own good name, I thought, might also have a shadow over it.

'Quite,' Tapley said briefly, 'although I object strongly to your use of the expression "passing off". We never attempted to mislead anyone. That was not our purpose. For her to call me "Uncle" seemed obvious at the time. She was an infant when she came to us.

'I knew my cousin was anxious about his child's welfare, although he'd had little personally to do with Flora since she lost her mamma and came to us. He visited occasionally, bearing some expensive gift. I fancy he found the visits difficult, however. But he would want only her happiness. I took him aside and put a proposition to him. It was that he should put his affairs in order, drawing up a will naming Flora as his heir, and me as her guardian. Tom would then go abroad and stay there. He might live wherever and in whatever manner he chose. But he would remain outside of this country.'

'A remittance man . . .' I murmured. So, that was it.

'Strictly speaking, he was not that because he wasn't paid by me to stay away,' Tapley corrected me. 'Tom was a wealthy man. He would draw upon income from his investments and rents through an arrangement with a bank wherever he was, for his own support. He agreed it would be in Flora's best interest. Besides, for him life might be easier. In Europe, Inspector, the laws are generally less vindictive than they are here regarding Tom's situation. In France, for example, the act which had nearly sent Tom to the gallows when a student ceased to be a crime late in the last century.

'My cousin agreed willingly. It was all settled and he left. I heard from him from time to time, not very often. For a while he lived in Italy, then in the south of France. Then came a period of silence. I was wondering whether to make enquiries when the matter became urgent. Flora turned nineteen last autumn. A most eligible young man, the younger son of a peer of the realm, presented himself as suitor. Flora fell in love.

The young man's family approved. Of course she is still very young, but my wife and I are sure the attachment is genuine. Naturally, the young fellow first came to me to ask permission to offer for her hand—'

'And you had to tell him that Flora's natural father was still alive and as she's not yet one and twenty, permission had to be sought from him,' I interrupted.

He nodded. 'Yes. That's when things became very difficult. I wrote to Thomas at the last known address in France because I believed him to be in that country. I explained what had happened and assured him the young man was no fortune hunter. I asked that Tom write, giving his consent to the marriage, and with the letter properly attested by a notary public. There would be no need for him to come home.

'I sent the letter to his last known residence. It was returned to me, apparently unopened. I wrote others, but received no reply. In desperation, I wrote to our embassy in Paris. I eventually received intelligence from them that Tom was last heard of living on the outskirts of the French capital. But he was no longer registered as living there; and where he was the embassy could not say. They had not been informed of the death in France of any British subject of that name. We assumed, therefore, he was still alive. But the Continent is full of travelling Englishmen. He could have returned to Italy, decided to see the Swiss Alps, been taken with an impulse to explore the Austrian or the Turkish empires, gone, in fact, anywhere.'

Tapley took out a fine lawn handkerchief and mopped his brow. 'I told the young couple that they must, in any case, wait until Flora was twenty-one before any marriage could take place. That gave me a little time. First of all I established, through enquiry in this country, that Tom was still drawing an income from his investments here, so was still alive. But, and here's the distressing thing, it had all along been a very modest income. He could barely have been living in comfort all those years. He wanted, I am sure, to leave as much as possible of his fortune for Flora. The poor fellow stinted himself in every way.'

'He certainly presented a down-at-heel appearance,' I told him. 'His clothing was shabby. The clothes press in his lodgings contains only a change of linen. He had only one coat. If he spent any money, it was on second-hand books.'

Jonathan Tapley closed his eyes. 'Poor Tom,' he murmured again. 'He was the kindest, most good-natured fellow, and his own country persecuted him.'

This was not the time to discuss the law regarding homosexual acts. Jonathan Tapley had been right in saying both he and I were bound to uphold the law as it stood.

Jonathan Tapley sat back as if bracing himself. 'I then received a severe shock. Failing to get a reply from France, I contacted the firm of Harrogate solicitors who handled, still handle, all of Tom's business in this country. I learned that Tom had visited them early last year, January, *in person*. He had returned to Britain! You can imagine my reaction – my stupefaction, you might say. He told the solicitors he had not yet established a permanent address here and would let them know as soon as he had one. They were still awaiting his notification. They had assumed I would know where he lived. Between us, you might say, we had lost him.'

The curious disappearance of Thomas Tapley was throwing

up all manner of possibilities. Why had he chosen to behave in this way? Because he feared his cousin Jonathan's disapproval when it was discovered he'd come back to England, breaking the arrangement made nine years earlier? He did not know, of course, that Jonathan was looking for him or that his daughter, Flora, wished to become engaged. But even when he had quitted the rooms rented from Mrs Holland in Southampton and had established himself more permanently with Mrs Jameson in London, Thomas still hadn't informed his solicitor of his address – or his cousin, who lived across town in the more fashionable area of Bryanston Square. Tom Tapley had also misled Mrs Jameson when he had told her he'd wished to return to London because he had previously lived there. But it seemed he'd lived in the North before leaving for the Continent. His wish to return to London was because here he had a daughter. Had he intended to contact her and then lacked the courage?

'Mr Tapley,' I said briskly, 'I take it you were in correspondence with your cousin while he was abroad.'

Jonathan looked discomfited for a moment. 'Not regularly, I confess. Perhaps only once a year, to let him know Flora was well and there were no changes in our situation. He seldom replied.'

'That is regular enough. There are people living in this country who don't correspond with their relations more frequently than that. Did you, at any time, travel to Europe and visit him there? When was the last confirmed sighting of him in France, Italy or any other country before he returned here? This is very important. It would help us narrow down the most likely date of his return. Was it just before he visited his solicitor in Harrogate last January, or earlier? There is a second question. Did he take abroad with him all his personal documents, those relating to his investments, for example, or a copy of his will? Nothing was found at his lodgings.'

'That one I can answer easily. He must have had some personal documents with him; but most items of that nature are lodged with the firm of Newman and Thorpe of Harrogate, the solicitors in question. They have represented my cousin's interests for many years and it would be a wise move for a man living a wandering life, staying in lodgings and hotels. I suggest you contact Newman and Thorpe. I shall shortly be writing to them myself. I understand I am an executor of his will. I can answer your question about the last sighting of him in Europe, but only to raise another mystery.'

He got to his feet and began to walk up and down the room, hands clasped behind his back again.

'The year before last, I happened to run into an old acquaintance, a fellow I'd been at school with. We chatted about this and that, catching up on our news as one does, when suddenly he floored me with a remark I really hadn't expected.

' "By the way," ' he said, "I ran into Tom Tapley recently. Isn't he a cousin of yours?" I was staggered – and alarmed. Had Tom broken his promise to stay out of England? Where? I asked at once. "Walking on the beach at Deauville," he told me.

'It seemed Parker, the chap's name, had been walking along the seafront at Deauville. Coming towards him he'd seen a gentleman with a female companion on his arm. Nearing them, he recognised Tom whom he'd met a few times in London some years before. He'd hailed him asking if he wasn't Tom Tapley? Tom had acknowledged it and asked what brought Parker to Deauville. Parker explained he'd come for the horse racing. Tom had replied that he was resident now in France, and was in Deauville to recuperate following a period of poor health. They agreed the air on the Normandy coast was invigorating. Parker wished Tom a speedy return to good health and they parted. It was Parker's impression Tom didn't wish to stay and talk more. He thought Tom not best pleased at the encounter. Both parties experienced some embarrassment.'

'And the lady?'

'Oh, that, in Parker's view, was the oddest thing. All the time they spoke, the female was clinging to Tom, while at the same time simpering and giving him, Parker, the glad eye. I am quoting Parker. But Tom didn't introduce her, which was very odd. She was French, in Parker's opinion, well turned out, and of what the French call "a certain age". Let's say, over forty. But her bold attitude and worldly air made him uneasy. Frankly, in his opinion, she was of the *demi-monde*. He was very surprised because he knew Tom wasn't interested in women, not in *that* way. He was the last fellow you'd expect to see with a courtesan.'

'What did you make of it?' I asked.

'I supposed Tom had found another older woman to take care of him. But I shared Parker's unease. Other older ladies who'd taken him under their wing had always been of irreproachable reputation. Well, now, perfectly respectable people do visit Deauville! I believe the Empress Eugénie has been seen there. But it is also known, although perhaps less than its sister-resort of Trouville, as the sort of place fellows take their mistresses. Seaside towns tend to have a racy reputation, in this country also. That was what flummoxed Parker.'

'Did you write to your cousin about it?'

'I set pen to paper, but I tore up the draft of my letter. It was not my business. My cousin was a free man. Besides, what if Tom wrote back saying the woman was the wife of a friend, whom he was escorting as a favour? I'd sound a perfect fool if I wrote suggesting otherwise. One thing Tom certainly never had was a mistress.'

'Just one last question, Mr Tapley,' I said, preparing to scramble out of the depths of the armchair. 'You came to see me as soon as you read of the discovery of a body. What made you think it might be that of your cousin?'

Jonathan Tapley raised his black eyebrows. 'My dear Inspector, my cousin had disappeared! He had failed to contact his solicitors with his new address, as he had promised. He had made no attempt to contact us, my wife and me. Though apparently in this country after an absence of almost nine years, he had shown no interest in visiting his daughter. The press report said the dead man was believed to have lived briefly in Southampton. It is a Channel port. It had already entered my mind that some misfortune could have befallen Tom. I can tell you that I was on the verge of consulting the police and reporting him missing.' He hesitated.

'At the risk of distressing you more,' I said, 'I must point out that if you had reported him missing, you and I would not be here now. Thomas Tapley lodged with a neighbour of ours, of my wife's and mine, on the south side of the river, not far from the railway station. I should have recognised the name and put you in touch.'

Jonathan Tapley frowned. 'That certainly doesn't make me feel any better. But I was not to know that! Yes, I agree, I should have contacted the police earlier. But, don't forget, there was also the possibility that he had not remained in England. He could have returned to France. That could have been the reason he sent no new address here to Newman and Thorpe.'

I thought that Mr Jonathan Tapley Q.C. was constructing a plausible explanation, others would call it an excuse, for his dilatoriness in contacting the police. I wondered if the truth were as simple as that.

'Well,' said Dunn thoughtfully when I reported all this to him. 'So Thomas Tapley had something of a history. Perhaps instead of sending Constable Biddle round the coffee houses, you should have sent him round the bathhouses, Ross.' He sat back and scowled at me.

I knew this didn't mean I'd displeased him particularly. It meant he was thinking it all over and was about to pick on some aspect that worried him. He was choosing his words.

'We must not offend Jonathan Tapley, Ross,' the superintendent began slowly. 'We must not appear to bungle any aspect of this investigation. He is an eminent barrister and if we make mistakes we should call down on our heads the wrath of him and all his brethren of the wig and gown. Besides, he has friends in high places. He has argued the interests of noblemen, members of parliament, fashionable society of all sorts. There must be no such errors. There must be no unnecessary scandal. No lurid tales in the popular press. All enquiries from now on must be handled with the utmost tact. Keep Biddle out of it, unless it's interviewing housemaids. Morris can be trusted for most things, but not to deal with Queen's Counsel. You'll have to do the sensitive work yourself.'

'We cannot rule out Jonathan Tapley as a suspect, sir,' I said as firmly as I could without sounding argumentative, 'unless, of course, he has an alibi for the time the fatal attack took place. We know approximately when that was. The doctor was certain Thomas Tapley had not been long dead when found. The courts would have risen for the day by then. But if Jonathan Tapley were at his chambers, others should have seen him. If he were at home his household should be able to vouch for him. But someone has to find out where he was and I suppose it must be me?'

'Of course, it's you, Ross!' said Dunn crossly. 'Weren't you listening? You must do the sensitive interviews yourself. Go back and see the distinguished counsel again. If you can manage to interview him at his house, so much the better. The man isn't a fool. He will be expecting you to ask him where he was at the time.'

'And will have arranged to have an alibi, well before he came to see me at the Yard. As you say, sir, he isn't a fool.'

Dunn squinted at me. 'Do you seriously think he's likely to have dashed his cousin's brains out?'

'It could be argued he has a motive. He and his wife look upon the young woman, Miss Flora Tapley, as their own. She is on the brink of a very advantageous marriage . . . to the younger son of a peer, no less. It represents the summit of their ambitions for her.'

Dunn harrumphed but I ignored him to continue.

'He wanted his cousin to send written approval for the marriage. He didn't want him to turn up here, claiming his rightful privilege, as father of the bride, to lead her down the aisle.'

Dunn muttered furiously under his breath again and jabbed a stubby finger at me.

'We need to find our villain quickly. The longer this drags on, the more likely it is the press will get hold of the background. Only think of the players in this drama! Beautiful and pure young woman – I suppose Flora Tapley to be both – on the brink of marriage. Son of a peer. Eminent barrister. Mysterious Frenchwoman of dubious background seen with the victim on the beach at a Continental watering hole. Good grief, Ross, this business has all the ingredients of a shilling shocker!'

Chapter Eight

Elizabeth Martin Ross

'IT'S MY opinion,' I told Ben that evening, when he had summarised his talk with Jonathan Tapley for my benefit, 'that he and his wife have been very selfish, even cruel. He practically forced his cousin Thomas into exile so that he might continue guardianship of little Flora. How dare he later write to his cousin requesting a letter, certified by a notary public no less, giving Thomas's consent to the marriage . . . but forbidding the poor man to come to England, give his consent in person and even see his daughter married?'

Indignation at the thought of the injustice done to poor Thomas filled me and I went on energetically, 'It would not, surely have caused any scandal now if Thomas had turned up? No one was going to remember an event that took place at Oxford forty years ago, or any rumours about his behaviour between then and leaving the country. He had been gone almost ten years!'

'Jonathan and Maria Tapley weren't so confident about that,' Ben said mildly.

I was having none of it. 'I'm not surprised Thomas slipped

back quietly, without informing his cousin. He wanted to see his daughter; it's only natural. I know if it had been my father—'

'But he wasn't Dr Martin,' Ben interrupted me brusquely. 'When your papa found himself a widower with a young child, he undertook to bring you up himself. Thomas handed his daughter over to his cousin like a shot. But he's to be excused. Don't overlook the difficulty of his position. Dr Martin's daughter may be well informed and broad minded about sex but most nice young women are brought up lamentably ignorant. Suppose Thomas had been caught up in another scandal. Who would have explained it all to young Flora? Thomas understood the wisdom of going abroad. And don't assume that you know his motives in returning home. If he wanted so badly to see his child, why did he linger first in Southampton with Mrs Holland, then at Mrs Jameson's house as a lodger, without contacting Jonathan or trying to contact Flora?'

'His nerve failed him,' I suggested. 'Poor man, the girl doesn't even know what he looks – looked – like, or I suppose not. Or perhaps Thomas wanted to delay giving his consent?'

Ben gave me a triumphant look. 'You're overlooking an important fact, Lizzie. Thomas *didn't know* Flora was engaged and wanted to marry, because the letter Jonathan sent to his last address in Nice, with that news, was returned and further attempts to contact him failed. Thomas's solicitors saw him in January of last year. He promised them his new address, as soon as he should have one, but he never sent it. You set too much store by Thomas Tapley's complete innocence. Perhaps, instead of thinking of him as a scholarly old gent who resides with a Quaker landlady, you should try picturing him as a man who strolls on the beach at Deauville with a lady of dubious background on his arm!'

He concluded his objections with this bull's-eye and waited for me to fire off mine at him.

I was ready. 'He didn't inform Jonathan because he knew what the reaction would be. The first letter was returned. Jonathan sent other letters afterwards, didn't he? To anywhere he remembered Thomas ever having lived? Were *all* those letters returned to him? Who is to say one of them didn't reach Thomas?'

'Because Thomas appears to have already returned to England,' was Ben's prompt answer. 'We now know that, after visiting the solicitors in Harrogate and fobbing them off with an unfulfilled promise to keep in touch, he returned to Southampton at the other end of the country. Why the hasty departure from Harrogate? Did he fear running into an old acquaintance or two who might remember him? From February to July, he lodged in Southampton. Was he thinking of returning to France? If so, it seems he abandoned the idea, because he came to London, but not with the intention of seeking out his cousin. From July until his death this spring, he lodged quietly with Mrs Jameson. Thomas, in the popular phrase, was lying low.

'Jonathan started bombarding the Continent with letters around October of last year, after Flora's nineteenth birthday, when the suitor appeared asking for her hand. But he was wasting his time and letter paper. Tom Tapley was *already here*. No wonder none of the post reached him. He'd flown the coop, returned to England . . . and it wasn't because he wanted to get in touch with his cousin or his child.'

119

There was a silence during which Ben took the poker and stirred up the fire. I sat mutinous, having been forced temporarily to concede the upper ground. But I was not completely out of ammunition. I considered that this might be the time to tell Ben about the clown. I should have told him the night Thomas Tapley died, but somehow the incident had slipped my mind while I'd been sitting in Mrs Jameson's parlour.

'I do believe this is a more complicated affair than getting permission for a marriage,' I began. 'I haven't told you about the clown.'

'Clown?' Ben returned the poker to the companion set and sat back.

'Yes, the clown Bessie and I saw on the new embankment, entertaining passers-by. That is, he was entertaining them until he stopped to follow Tapley across the bridge.'

Ben groaned and buried his thick mop of black hair in his hands. Looking up, he said hollowly. 'Dunn called this a shilling shocker. Now you are going to throw in a clown and make it a regular fairground? What is this all about, for pity's sake?'

I related my story and when I'd finished, Ben was silent for a few minutes before beginning in what I call his 'reasonable' voice. 'I'm sorry you and Bessie met this fellow on the embankment. I know how you feel about clowns. But I really do believe you're letting your personal experience influence your feelings in this whole business of Thomas Tapley's murder. It influences your view of Jonathan Tapley and his wife and their actions. It influences your view of Thomas's motives in returning to England. A fear born of a child's visit to a circus influences this episode of the clown.'

'No!' I protested. 'I saw—'

'You *saw* a man, dressed in a garish outfit, with a painted face, juggling on the embankment. The sight frightened you.' He leaned forward to take my hand. 'Later you see the same fear-inspiring figure crossing the bridge ahead of you. By your own admission, he pays no attention to you. The interest is directed all from you towards him. As it happens, Thomas has begun to cross the bridge moments earlier, and so is ahead of the clown. To you, in your panic, it seems the clown must be following Thomas . . .'

I opened my mouth in protest but he signalled me to wait until he'd finished.

'To you, you must understand, the clown is a sinister figure and must have a correspondingly sinister purpose. He cannot, to you, just be a street entertainer with no plan other than to gather enough pennies from generous-minded passers-by to take home to, probably, his wife and children. They have to be fed and the rent for their room paid. He has no other trade. I would suggest, Lizzie dear, that you are ashamed of your irrational fear. Therefore, you seek to justify it. The clown is a villain, he must be. But no, my darling, he isn't.'

It's true this tied in very much with my own thoughts as I'd rolled pastry for the pie the evening of the day I'd seen the clown. I'd told myself then that my fear for Thomas Tapley was an extension of my own fear. But I did not like to hear Ben say it with such confidence, not in view of what had happened since. I withdrew my hand from his. 'Very well,' I said stiffly. 'I won't mention the clown again. But I am entitled to my opinion. Moreover, I was there and you weren't.'

'I can't argue with that. I don't want us to argue at all. But at the risk of offending you further, Lizzie, I must tell you I shall not be home until late tomorrow evening. I'll get myself something to eat in a chophouse. Don't cook for me.'

'Where are you going?' I asked curiously.

'As it happens, I'm going to try to catch Jonathan Tapley at home. I want to interview him on his own ground. I want to meet Mrs Tapley and, especially, I want to meet Miss Flora Tapley. I should like to present my condolences to both. He has a house, by the way, in Bryanston Square, not so very far from your Aunt Parry's in Marylebone.'

'They are in mourning,' I warned. 'They won't like you calling, particularly unexpectedly.'

Ben gave a grim smile. 'Nobody likes the police calling and it is our bad habit to turn up when unexpected. I agree, Jonathan won't like it at all, but neither will he be surprised. I am a miner's son and missed out on all the social niceties. I have no scruples about disturbing a gentleman enjoying his after-dinner port and cigar. So far that man has manipulated me very skilfully. Well, it's time our master of courtroom tricks found himself on the defence.'

'You don't like him,' I said, with a certain triumph creeping into my voice. 'Any more than I do.'

'You haven't met him,' he reproved me.

'I don't need to meet him. I disapprove his actions. Anyway, *you* don't like him and I am to respect *your* opinion before forming any judgement, it seems. *You* are right about the clown so *you* must be right about Jonathan Tapley.'

There was another silence. 'I haven't heard the last of this, have I?' Ben said with resignation.

'No, Inspector Ross, you haven't. But don't worry. I shan't

raise the matter again unless I have some new information for you. If you're interested in any information I may acquire, that is.'

'Lizzie . . .' he warned. 'Be careful.'

'Oh, I won't upset Superintendent Dunn!' I promised.

'Since you will not be home to dine this evening,' I said to Ben at breakfast, 'I think I'll go and call on my Aunt Parry. It's some time since I saw her. She always complains of being neglected. I'll go this afternoon. Bessie can come with me and visit her friends below stairs.'

Before coming to work for us, Bessie had been kitchen maid in my aunt's household.

'How will you get there?' he asked, drinking his coffee too fast and getting to his feet.

'We'll walk up to the railway station and take a cab at the rank there.'

'Good, good, give your aunt my warm regards.' Ben was struggling into his coat as he spoke. 'I'll see you later on this evening.' He grabbed a piece of toast and hurried out of the door.

Bessie was delighted with the prospect of another day out. Accordingly, we set off in the early afternoon. As we walked to the railway station I looked out for Joey, but there was no sign of him. Bessie had been asking up and down the street if he'd appeared at kitchen doors, but no one had seen him. We would have to wait until he returned, as Ben was sure he eventually would.

I had also hoped to see Wally Slater waiting at the cab rank. But he was not there. Several trains must have come at much the same time because only one growler waited for hire and we had to take it. The driver was a surly man whose nose suggested close acquaintance with the bottle and whose horse looked ill fed and neglected. I told him so (about the horse, that is) when we reached our destination. He replied that I knew nothing about horseflesh and his animal was as fit as a fiddle. I retaliated remarking that the animal's harness was dirty and ill fitting. He replied that if I didn't like his cab, I was free to have taken another. Moreover, he was a working man with a living to earn and he couldn't wait about here, listening to wealthy women tell him his business.

I could have replied I wasn't wealthy but, since he had delivered me to a house in a very expensive area and the butler had just opened the door to admit me, he'd only have laughed.

My Aunt Parry never appeared before noon. Her mornings were spent in bed, eating a light breakfast and attending to her correspondence. By one o'clock, however, she was dressed and ready to sit down to a substantial luncheon. When we arrived, at three, she was in her upstairs parlour about to drink tea with her companion.

I had originally come to London to fill that same post. It had led to my meeting Ben again, for the first time since our childhood, so all had turned out well for me. On the other hand, the arrangement had not altogether suited Aunt Parry. I had put her in the annoying position of having to find another companion. She had not been sorry to see me leave. I was too outspoken and my behaviour was considered by her to be outlandish. Despite this, she still insisted I had abandoned her selfishly in order to marry – and marry a policeman at that.

Since my departure, three companions in quick succession

had passed through the household. She was now 'trying out' the fourth unfortunate. I found them sitting either side of the fire, my aunt in purple satin and the companion, Laetitia Bunn by name, in dark green glazed cotton. Both were short and stubby in build. The impression given was of a ripe plum that had fallen from a small rounded tree.

'Oh, Elizabeth my dear,' cried Aunt Parry. 'At last! I had begun to think you had left London and gone back to, where was it? Some place in Derbyshire. Not a word from you. How are you and how is Inspector Ross?' Before I could answer, she indicated me for the benefit of Miss Bunn and added, 'This is Mrs Ross, my niece, Laetitia. I have spoken to you of her.'

To be accurate, I wasn't her niece. She was the widow of my godfather. But we'd settled on 'aunt' as a mode of address.

I don't know what Aunt Parry had told Miss Bunn about me but the poor girl stared at me as if I'd escaped from a menagerie.

'I am very pleased to meet you, Miss Bunn,' I said to her. 'I hope you are settling in well here?'

'Oh, yes,' whispered Miss Bunn, 'oh, very much so. Mrs Parry is so kind.'

She seemed a mousy female, anxious to please, in dread of being dismissed, and generally in the wretched situation of most companions. I felt sorry for her but there was an army of Miss Bunns out there up and down the country, of respectable family but of no fortune and with no relative left able to take them in. I am critical of Aunt Parry, but I had been in the situation of Miss Bunn when Aunt Parry had invited me to London. At the time I'd been grateful and I told myself now not to forget it.

'It is very draughty in here,' announced Aunt Parry. 'Just ring the bell, Laetitia, so that Simms can bring more tea. And run and fetch my shawl – the light blue cashmere one. Thank you, my dear.'

Miss Bunn jumped to her feet; pulled the bell rope so hard that it was a wonder it didn't come off, and scurried out to fetch the shawl.

'Oh, my dear Lizzie,' confided Aunt Parry as soon as the companion had left. 'She is driving me quite out of my mind. She plays a wretched game of whist, can't count, you see, poor child. Muddles her hand all up. She has no conversation. Uneducated, lamentably uneducated. When she reads to me she has to stop before any really long word and think it out. She stammers and puts the stress on the wrong syllables and, well, really it's painful having to listen. How I miss you, dear Elizabeth, and how I wish you were still here. But, there, you would run off and marry that policeman.'

Fortunately I hadn't to reply to this speech as Simms, the butler, arrived at that moment and was despatched to bring fresh tea and another cup for me. 'And perhaps a few scones!' added Aunt Parry brightly, ignoring the fact that she'd not long eaten luncheon.

'Are you well, Aunt Parry?' I asked. 'Are there any other changes in the household? Is Nugent still with you?'

Nugent was the much-put-upon lady's maid.

Aunt Parry gave a squeal of dismay at the prospect of being Nugent-less. 'If I hadn't Nugent I should really be in a dreadful state. And no, I am not well. I suffer dreadfully with indigestion and the powders don't help a bit.'

Eating less might help, I thought.

'Mrs Simms misses that kitchen maid you took with you,' Aunt Parry continued her litany of complaints. 'Of course I took on another girl to replace, what-was-her-name, Bessie, yes, Bessie. Another charity girl, but Mrs Simms says she is a very slow learner. But there, you would take Bessie with you when you left. You know, Elizabeth, fond of you as I am, I have to tell you that you played havoc with my household when you went off to get married. You might have given me some consideration. Oh, there you are, Laetitia, whatever kept you so long?'

The next few minutes were spent arranging the blue shawl around Aunt Parry's plump shoulders and then Simms appeared with the fresh pot of tea and the scones, so it was a little while before conversation resumed. We spoke first about Frank Carterton, Aunt Parry's genuine nephew, who had entered the Foreign Office and was at present, to her great distress, in Peking with Her Majesty's newly established Legation there. For years the Chinese had steadfastly refused to allow the British barbarians to have an official representative in Peking. The emperor had eventually been forced to concede to our wishes; although the Chinese still made it clear that the newcomers' red faces were unwelcome in their capital. For once Aunt Parry had some reason for concern. Typically, however, her first worry was that Frank wouldn't be eating properly.

'Living on rice, poor boy,' she said, dabbing butter from her chin. 'I am sure it's so. He writes me that a very varied diet is available to him, although all of it prepared in the Chinese manner, as that is the only way the cooks know how to do it. But I think he is only trying to calm my nerves. I do worry about dear Frank. I worried about him when he was in Russia, because of the Cossacks; and now I worry because the Chinese emperor is so very devious.'

'I'm sure he's safe, Aunt Parry. Frank is very resourceful.'

'Well, he could have stayed home here with me. First you left me and then Frank went. I don't know what you both imagined I should do here all on my own. But I dare say neither of you gave me a thought. It is the way of young people. I have Laetitia now, of course.' Aunt Parry gazed gloomily at the companion who rattled her cup in the saucer, opened her mouth, closed it again and remained speechless and apprehensive.

'Is there anything happening in the neighbourhood?' I asked. I was seeking a way to introduce the topic of the Tapley family who, according to Ben, lived not far away. They might all attend the same parish church; or at least be on nodding acquaintance.

As it turned out, all I had to do was ask that simple question.

'My dear Elizabeth,' Aunt Parry leaned forward and gripped the shawl at her bosom in dramatic fashion, 'such a business. The Tapleys, a very well-respected family, you may not have heard of them, Elizabeth. Mr Jonathan Tapley is a very famous barrister. Well, can you believe it? Mr Tapley's cousin was found murdered here in London, when he was supposed to be living in France, or was it Italy? One of the two. And his daughter, I mean the murdered man's daughter, has lived all her life with Mr Jonathan Tapley and his wife and they quite regard her as *their* daughter. Indeed, I was under the impression she was their own child until all this happened. Poor little Flora Tapley . . . there is a very suitable young man,

I believe, wanting to marry her, although with murders taking place in the family, perhaps he won't want to now. One never knows who might be next.'

Laetitia Bunn, showing herself to be far more astute than Aunt Parry gave her credit for, asked, 'Is your husband, the police inspector, involved in any way, Mrs Ross?'

Both women stared at me.

'I believe he may know something about it,' I said. 'Since he works at Scotland Yard, he is bound to have heard something. Are the Tapleys, then, neighbours, Aunt Parry?'

'Just a short walk away in Bryanston Square,' said Aunt Parry. 'It's altogether too much excitement. This is a very quiet part of town. That is, until you came, Elizabeth, and Madeleine Hexham got herself murdered.'

'I do believe, Aunt Parry, that Madeleine Hexham was murdered before I arrived,' I protested. 'It was to replace her that I came to you.'

Miss Bunn asked quickly, 'Miss Hexham was companion here, in this house? To you, Mrs Parry?' She turned her slightly protruding pale blue gaze on her employer.

Aunt Parry looked momentarily discomfited. 'Yes, but her death had nothing at all to do with this house. She was a very silly sort of girl, the kind who always gets into trouble. I don't recollect the details.'

Miss Bunn looked thoughtful.

As Simms showed me out of the front door, Bessie came running up the steps from the basement where she'd been visiting her old friends.

'I expect Mrs Simms and the maids were pleased to see

you,' I said to her as we set off. 'Let's walk in the general direction of Oxford Street. We shall easily find a cab along the way to take us home.'

'We had a good chat,' said Bessie with satisfaction. 'Of course, all the talk round here just now is about the horrible murder of Mr Jonathan Tapley's cousin. Staff, including Mr and Mrs Simms, were all really interested to hear I'd seen the poor gentleman not long before.' Bessie smiled at the memory of her moment of glory when imparting this news. She went on, 'Wilkins, the housemaid here, is walking out with the Tapleys' footman. He told her that their household is in a terrible fret; no one knowing what's going to happen from one minute to the next. Of course, it's very sad for Mr Thomas Tapley although none of the staff knew him because he'd lived in France. But they are all sorry for Miss Flora, that's the thing that's causing the most upset.'

'She's lost her papa, her real papa,' I said. 'It's to be expected she's distressed.'

'I don't think she hardly knew him,' said Bessie bluntly. 'I think she was still in the nursery when he went to live in foreign parts and left her with her uncle and aunt. But she's being courted by a very fine gentleman. He's the younger son of a lord. If anything happened to his elder brother, then Miss Flora's gentleman would become the heir to a title. So they can't be doing with any scandal in the family. Mrs Tapley's in a rare old state about it; and Mr Jonathan Tapley is in such a temper none of the staff dare speak to him.'

Jonathan Tapley may be angry now, I thought ruefully, but he'll be furious when Ben arrives on his doorstep this evening.

We had arrived in Bryanston Square, an elegant and

spacious area with many smart carriages rattling up and down it. Fashionably dressed people sauntered along its pavements.

'I can't see a cab,' said Bessie, putting a hand to her eyes to shield her gaze from the sun. 'We'd do best to go on down to Oxford Street.'

'I wish I knew,' I said, scrutinising the rows of black-painted doors, 'which house belongs to the Tapleys.'

At that moment a boy, not Joey but a street urchin of similar type, ran past us, brushing up against me. I gripped my reticule, fearing he meant to snatch it. But instead, to my surprise, I felt some sharp-cornered object pressed into my hand. I opened my fist to find nestling on my palm what appeared to be a small, oblong card similar to a visiting card. The boy had already disappeared in the crowd.

'It will be advertising something,' said Bessie knowledgeably.

I read the legend on the little card aloud. 'Horatio Jenkins. Private Enquiry Agent. Discretion Assured.' It was followed by an address in Camden High Street.

'Yes, it is advertising something,' I said slowly to Bessie. I turned it over. Printed on the reverse in pencil were the three words, WOULD BE OBLIGED.

'But I am not quite sure what,' I added and put the card in my pocket.

Inspector Benjamin Ross

I had mixed feelings when I set out that evening to call on Jonathan Tapley and his family at home, unannounced. I didn't underestimate the man's intelligence. He would probably be expecting something of the sort. But a clever fellow like him would have made his preparations for the event, should it happen. He would have his answers to any questions ready and so would Mrs Tapley and Miss Flora. The older couple would not have neglected to prime her. She, too, had a real vested interest in not upsetting the applecart. Her future marriage was at stake. If, indeed, the murder had not already resulted in the marriage being indefinitely delayed; and perhaps never now taking place.

I timed my ring on the doorbell very carefully. Dinner should be over. The butler, who opened to me, gave me a look that clearly told me I should have presented myself at a tradesman's entrance. He took my card as if contact with it would contaminate him. After a glance at it, he whisked me indoors and closed the front door smartly behind us before anyone passing by saw me, and disappeared to tell his master that I was even now sullying the parquet with my boots.

He returned quickly and led me to a small back parlour when I was shut in and again left alone. After a few minutes, however, footsteps approached and the door flew open to reveal Jonathan Tapley, choleric with anger.

'This is unacceptable, Inspector Ross!' He marched into the room and the door clattered shut behind him. 'We are a family in mourning. You and I have twice spoken already, once in your office and once in mine. There is no reason whatsoever for you to come here, at this time of the evening, and disturb our family meal.'

'You are still eating?' I asked. 'I am so sorry. I left it late enough to avoid disturbing you before you'd finished, or so I thought.'

He snorted at me and, had he been a bull, would have

pawed the ground. 'Did you, indeed? Well, you are here. Sit down and tell me what you want. Be quick about it, if you please.'

'I have a couple of points to clear up. And I would like to meet the ladies, sir, if that is convenient.'

'No, it is not convenient, damn it!' he shouted at me.

Above our heads the glass drops in the chandelier tinkled in the disturbed air. Perhaps that sobered him.

'It can hardly be convenient,' he said more moderately. 'The ladies are in deep shock after hearing of my cousin's death.'

I nodded sympathetically. 'But one of them, Miss Flora Tapley, is the deceased's next of kin, his daughter, no less. I understand the shock she and your wife must both be feeling. But you will understand, Mr Tapley, that I have to talk to her. It cannot be avoided. I am the officer in charge of the investigation. I do not, naturally, expect the young lady to come to Scotland Yard. I thought you'd appreciate it if I came here.'

'Did you, indeed?' he returned sarcastically, knowing he was being outmanoeuvred.

I suddenly became tired of the whole silly game. Perhaps it was the sarcastic tone that did it. 'Come, now, Mr Tapley,' I said briskly. 'You can't be so very surprised to see me. We have both of us spoken the lines this piece of theatre has called upon us to speak. You have expressed indignation. I have been apologetic. Now I need to ask questions. It is what, as a detective, I do. My first question – I am sure easily dealt with – concerns your own whereabouts at the time Mr Thomas Tapley died. You will understand that this is necessary to exclude you from enquiries. No doubt you can tell me and give me the names of witnesses. Then we can move on.'

I thought, as I ceased speaking, that he might throw me out, or have a couple of footmen do it. But to my surprise he merely gave a very mild snort. He assessed me again through narrowed eyelids and said, 'I begin to feel you may be in the wrong branch of the law, Inspector Ross. You would have made a very good courtroom lawyer. You stick to the point and know when to drive it home.'

I made no reply. He sat down at last and said, 'Thomas died the day before news appeared in the evening newspapers, you have told me. Have you been able to establish what time of day the fatal attack took place?'

'The victim died between five and seven of the evening, according to the medical man who attended to certify death.'

He nodded. 'I was in court all the day in question and I set out for my chambers in the Gray's Inn Road around four. I arrived there about half past four. I had lunched lightly and was unsure if I should be late home that evening or not, so I sent out the page for half a roast fowl. The boy will confirm the time. I ate hastily in the room where you and I had our conversation. I had arranged a case conference and expected the interested parties at any moment. They arrived and our discussion started at around a quarter past five and continued until well gone six. I will write down their names. It must have been half past six when I left my chambers and hailed a cab. Again, the clerk will confirm that. It was a little after seven when I arrived home here. My wife and the servants can confirm that! The traffic was heavy that evening. A cart had overturned in High Holborn, shedding its load and causing mayhem not only there but also in all the surrounding streets.

I was told the horse had dropped dead in the shafts, poor beast. You may check all this easily. The police attended the scene. Dinner was about to be served, so I washed hurriedly and sat down to dine with my wife and Flora. Afterwards I went to my study here and continued to work on the papers I had brought home with me. It was then nine o'clock or thereabouts. My wife, Flora and my staff here can vouch for my presence. Harris, the butler, brought me some coffee a little later, about ten. I told him no one need wait up for me. But by that time, as I understand you, my cousin had been dead some hours.'

'That seems to take care of it,' I said. I had taken out my notebook and written all this down. 'Now, if it's convenient, I should like to talk to the ladies, in particular Miss Flora.'

He stood up and reached for the bell rope. But then his hand fell by his side. 'I will go and fetch them,' he said.

He wants to be sure they have all the right answers in their heads before I see them, I thought.

I had expected him to return with the women, but when the door opened only the two ladies entered with a rustle of skirts. The older led the way. She was a stately woman in black taffeta embroidered with jet beads and with a ruffle of black lace on her head. She looked me directly in the eye as I rose to my feet but not a muscle of her face moved. I was put in mind of some Greek statue.

The younger woman had cast her eyes down. She wore black silk, but no jet beads. The only decoration on her dress was a bunch of ribbons at each shoulder. Around her neck was a simple gold chain and cross.

They sat down, side by side, on a gilded bench in the

135

style of the previous century. The older one folded her lace-mittened hands and the younger one simply placed one hand on top of the other on her lap. Her hands were small, plump and childlike but I had noticed on entering that she was nearly as tall as her aunt. Perhaps her late mother had been tall, because Thomas Tapley had been a short man.

I bowed politely and, as I did, the door of the room closed quietly behind the ladies. I didn't know if Jonathan stood behind it in the hall, or Harris, the butler.

'I am sorry to have disturbed your evening,' I said by way of opening the conversation. It seemed I would have to start. Neither woman showed signs of speaking. I had not been invited to sit down so I took it upon myself to do so.

Maria Tapley answered, her voice as expressionless as her face. 'I dare say it cannot be helped, Inspector.'

She might just as well have said, 'I dare say you know no better,' because that was what she meant.

I turned to the younger lady. Because her head was tipped forward, my eyes looked at the centre parting in her light brown hair. It fell in straight shiny wings either side of her face before it was twisted into a small knot at the back of her head. A black ribbon had been tied round the knot and the ends dangled to rest on the nape of her neck. A disturbing image came into my head: one of Henry VIII's wives, Anne Boleyn I believe, putting her head on the block and telling the executioner that her neck was very small.

'I am very sorry for your loss, Miss Tapley. Your father was briefly a neighbour of ours, of my wife's and mine.'

At that Mrs Tapley narrowed her eyes and the young woman looked up, surprised.

'But I can't say I knew him at all, really,' I confessed. 'I only saw him a few times in the street. I believe my wife exchanged a few words with him from time to time.'

She smiled uncertainly. She had a rounded chin and wide-spaced brown eyes beneath straight dark brows. When she was older she would be called handsome. Now she was striking, rather than beautiful, and had I been an artist, I would have wished to sketch her.

'Thank you for your sympathy, Inspector Ross,' she said.

There was little point in talking to Maria Tapley. She was there in the role of duenna and her husband's spy. I concentrated on Flora. I sensed she was now well disposed towards me. There was none of the hostility that flowed from her aunt. I might just as well think of the Tapleys as uncle and aunt to Flora, since the girl herself did. After all, Lizzie called Mrs Parry 'Aunt' though the lady was no blood relative. It was a convenient term. I ought not to have suggested to Jonathan Tapley that he and his wife had sought to blur the relationship with the young girl they'd taken in.

'I am sorry if what I have to ask you causes you any pain,' I said. 'But it is the way of police investigations that questions must be asked and answered. You didn't know your father very well, I understand?'

'I was only just ten when he left England,' she said. 'He called here on my tenth birthday to wish me happiness and good fortune and give me a present.' She touched the gold cross and chain at her neck. 'It was this. He also brought a little ivory-inlaid box. He said it was made in India and was for my "jewellery", as he called it. At the time I had only the necklace he'd just given me, and a little silver bangle from my christening. Being a child, I burst out, "But I don't have jewels!" He laughed and said, "One day, dear Flora, you will have diamonds, just see if you don't!"'

She gave a sad little smile and fell silent. I thought about these words of Thomas's. Had he meant that one day, when he was dead, she would be rich? He had only drawn a small amount in living expenses all those years. Jonathan had suggested it was because he had wanted to leave Flora a decent inheritance. Had he wanted to leave her seriously wealthy? I must contact those solicitors in Harrogate, I thought. Just how much was Thomas Tapley worth? Money is one of the oldest motives for murder.

'Did he give any hint that he might be going away? Do you recall anything?' I asked as gently as I could.

'I remember everything he said,' she returned simply.

I heard a rustle of taffeta as Maria Tapley shifted a little beside her on the bench.

'He said he would be going away soon. He hoped I would be a good girl and mind my kind relatives who had taken me into their home. Also that I'd say my prayers before I went to bed and remember him in them.'

I saw the glitter of a tear in her eyes. She looked down again, blinking.

'Is this quite necessary?' Maria Tapley said harshly. 'The events of a child's tenth birthday? What relevance can they have to the dreadful thing that has happened now?'

'I never know what might be relevant, Mrs Tapley, so I have to ask about everything,' I returned. But I didn't look at her as I spoke. I was watching Flora. She had produced a lace-trimmed scrap and dabbed at her eyes. Then she put the inadequate handkerchief away and looked fully at me. The tears had gone.

Her 'uncle and aunt' have trained her well, I thought. She has been taught it is bad form to show emotion. Poor child. Perhaps Lizzie is right. Thomas should have stayed here, tried to avoid being caught up in scandal, and brought up his child himself with the help of a governess. Perhaps Jonathan and Maria had persuaded him too easily that he was doing best by his daughter in abandoning her. Thomas had been newly bereaved and vulnerable. I couldn't help but remember that they, a childless couple, had also served their own interest in getting him to surrender Flora.

'Did your father ever write to you after he left for the Continent?'

'No,' she said.

She had control of herself now and if the fact was hurtful, she didn't show it or let it echo in her voice. But I did wish I could discuss it with her more.

Why had he not written? I wondered. Why had he not visited more often before that sad tenth birthday parting? Jonathan had declared to me that Thomas had found the visits 'difficult'. How did he know? Had they been rare because Jonathan had persuaded him that 'a clean break' would be best? That the little girl would settle more easily with her new parents if the original one made no contact? Of course, this was supposition on my part. It had been a tragic and difficult situation for Thomas and for the child. All the adults concerned had probably believed they had acted for the best. Perhaps they had? Who was I to criticise?

I reminded myself that it had not been such a clean break,

after all. Flora had been three when given into the care of Jonathan and his wife. But it was not until Flora had reached the age of ten that Thomas had been persuaded to leave England for the Continent, never to return. Between the ages of three and ten, her father had had some contact. How had Thomas really felt on leaving his only child behind for ever as he boarded the packet for France?

And what of Flora's feelings in all this? Had the child looked forward to his rare visits? From the few words she had spoken I had the distinct impression she had loved her absent papa, or at least loved the idea that she did have a real flesh and blood father somewhere.

I had no wish to distress the poor girl any longer. I got to my feet. For the first time some emotion showed on Maria Tapley's marble features. She looked relieved.

'Thank you both, ladies, for your forbearance,' I said.

Maria jerked at the bell pull before Flora could answer.

'Harris will see you out,' she said crisply. 'Come, Flora.'

In a swirl of black taffeta and glitter of jet she swept from the room. Flora gave me an apologetic look and hurried after her.

I was left alone in the room but not for many minutes. Harris arrived to show me out. He first held out a silver tray on which lay a white envelope inscribed with my name.

I opened it. It was the list of names promised me by Jonathan, individuals who'd seen him on the day of the murder. It was a very long roll call. I returned the sheet to the envelope and put it in my pocket.

'This way, sir,' invited Harris.

I followed his rigid back to the front door and was ejected with as much courtesy as was absolutely necessary and no more.

However, I had not gone many steps when I was conscious that the door, behind me, had been opened again. A female voice called my name.

I turned as light footsteps pattered towards me and beheld, to my amazement, Miss Flora Tapley, holding up her black silk skirts and running in a way her Aunt Maria would not approve.

'Inspector!' she gasped as she reached me.

'Take time to catch your breath, Miss Tapley,' I urged her. 'I can wait.'

She took a deep breath and scrutinised my face. I tried to look encouraging but obviously failed.

'I only wanted to say, before you go, that you must find the man who killed my father,' she blurted.

'That's my intention,' I returned mildly. 'That's why I called tonight.'

'You will not find the killer in our house!' she retorted fiercely. Her cheeks glowed a deep pink, the smooth wings of hair had become a little dishevelled and she looked younger than her nineteen years. 'I don't know where you will find him, but you *must*! You must promise it!'

I didn't reply at once but stared at her thoughtfully, which seemed to disconcert her.

'Why won't you?' she demanded. She put up a hand and began nervously to tuck the straying strands of hair back into place.

'Why not promise? Because I'd be a fool to do anything so rash. Detection isn't a straight, smooth path. There are wrong turnings I may take. There will be many stumbling blocks and I might fall flat over any one of them. Some individuals may

141

seek to mislead me. I am a man lost and feeling his way in a fog. But if I ask the right questions, get the right answers from the right people, the fog will lift and I'll see my way. There is a desperate villain out there, Miss Tapley. His own life is at stake. He's not going to make anything easy for me. But I'll do my very best, Scotland Yard will do its best, I promise that.'

'Thank you,' she said quietly. 'I understand. I am sorry if our family appears unhelpful to you. We – we are very distressed.'

'That's natural.'

'Natural . . .' she repeated the word as if seeking out some inner meaning to it. 'Inspector, I would not wish you to think my father had abandoned me, in going to France to live as he did.'

'Of course not. He left you in a comfortable home, with relatives who cared for you and clearly still care for you deeply.'

'I particularly don't want you to think badly of him,' she urged, staring at me intently.

'Nor do I. I wonder, Miss Tapley, if there is something else you would like to say to me. Something, perhaps, you felt you could not say in front of your Aunt Maria?' Again I tried to sound encouraging.

'No!' she snapped. Then, glancing behind her, 'I must go back. I'll be missed.'

A swirl of silk and she was running back to the front door that opened at her approach. Harris had been waiting. I wondered if he would tell his master about this little escapade. But the staff here would have seen Flora grow up. It was likely they'd protect her now as they probably shielded her from censure when she'd been naughty as a child.

I also wondered just what she had intended to tell me when she came running after me as she had done; and why she had changed her mind at the last minute.

'Well,' I said to Lizzie when I reached home at last to find my wife seated comfortably before the glowing embers of our parlour fire. A dish of cold cuts had been awaiting me in the kitchen. I'd carried it through and sat down opposite her setting my tray on an occasional table. 'I bearded Jonathan Tapley in his den, or in the bosom of his family, and I've survived.'

'I dare say,' returned Lizzie with a grin, 'he wasn't dining on cold cuts when you found him.'

'He was at dinner, or just finishing, so not best pleased – as you foresaw. On the other hand he wasn't entirely surprised. Neither, I fancy, were the two women. I told you they wouldn't be. They are a family at bay, Lizzie, and constantly on the alert.'

'What is Flora like?' Lizzie asked immediately.

'She's not a beauty, but nevertheless a very attractive young lady. Her face shows character, suggests depth. She would stand out in a group of girls of only conventional prettiness. I think she's probably intelligent and resourceful. But she's a young woman with something on her mind.' I related how Flora had run after me in the street.

Lizzie looked thoughtful. 'How much do you think she really knows about her papa?'

'About his scandalous past, you mean? Perhaps a little more than her uncle and aunt, as she calls them, imagine. Her Aunt Maria, Mrs Jonathan Tapley, is somewhat fierce or would be, if roused.'

'And she would be roused if anything or anyone appeared to threaten Flora or Flora's marriage prospects?' Lizzie asked shrewdly.

'Oh, yes,' I replied, probably a little indistinctly as I was chewing. 'She would, indeed, and she wouldn't be a woman to flinch at taking any steps she thought necessary.'

'So, she is a suspect as well as her husband?' Lizzie asked eagerly.

'I don't know that I have any suspects,' I told her. 'But some interesting possibilities are beginning to emerge. Lizzie, I need to go to Harrogate and speak to someone at the solicitors' firm, Newman and Thorpe, there. They handled all Thomas Tapley's affairs – and since they presumably have his will – still do. Flora is supposed by everyone to be his sole heir. But is she? No one has mentioned that. In any case, Thomas lived in Harrogate before leaving for the Continent. He married there and Flora was born there. If I travel up tomorrow on the first available train I should be able to arrange a meeting at the offices of Newman and Thorpe. They may, in turn, be able to suggest some other persons I could profitably speak to. I fancy I'll have to stay overnight if I'm to complete all my enquiries. I'll have to persuade Superintendent Dunn that the expense is necessary.'

And that might be the most difficult part of the whole exercise.

'How did you find your Aunt Parry?' I remembered to ask.

'Oh, very well. She has a new companion, Miss Laetitia Bunn.'

'Think she'll last?'

'Not long,' Lizzie admitted. 'Not now she knows that one

of the previous companions was murdered. She'll be writing letters already seeking a new place.'

'Like Mrs Jameson's Jenny,' I observed.

'Aunt Parry knows all about the Tapley family and Thomas Tapley's death. It's the talk of the neighbourhood. Bessie learned that one of Aunt Parry's housemaids is walking out with the Tapley footman. She has it from the housemaid, via the footman, that Mr Jonathan Tapley is in a bad temper and the household very upset.'

'I dare say it's even more upset now I've called there,' I told her. 'Anything else of interest?'

It seemed to me my wife hesitated but then she said, 'No, not really.'

I left it at that. If Lizzie didn't want to tell me yet, it was useless to ask further.

Chapter Nine

Elizabeth Martin Ross

BEN SPENT a good part of the evening consulting Bradshaw's railway timetable and departed early the next morning for Harrogate. He might return late that evening, but feared he would be away for at least one night. If he found out anything of interest that required following up, then possibly he might stay for two nights. A telegraphed message had been sent to the Yorkshire police to let them know he was on his way. They had replied that an Inspector Barnes would meet him off the train at Harrogate.

'So, Bessie,' I told her, when Ben had left for King's Cross Station, 'you and I are free to dispose of our time as we wish. I suggest we begin by calling on Mr Horatio Jenkins, the private enquiry agent, as he terms himself.'

'I don't know about that, missus,' said Bessie doubtfully. 'Sounds a funny way to earn a living to me. Still,' she cheered up, 'no harm in taking a look at him, is there?'

To take a hackney carriage all the way to Camden would be expensive so we made our way there by omnibus. It is a slow, crowded and uncomfortable way to travel. Frequency of stops to pick up or deposit passengers, together with the press of other traffic, meant the horses seldom went faster than a steady plod, occasionally breaking into a cumbersome trot for brief stretches. Passengers were crammed together unpleasantly, and we were obliged to keep a sharp eye open for those thieves who specialised in preying on omnibus travellers and could operate almost with impunity in the crush. But at last we reached our destination without mishap, and stood on the pavement in Camden High Street, across from the address printed on the card. Bessie was examining her outer clothing gloomily.

'I wouldn't surprise me, missus, if you and I ain't picked up a flea or two on that *ommybus*.'

'Then we shall find out later. Never mind now. That is the place, do you think?'

We were looking at a greengrocer's shop. Above the door was printed A. WEISZ PROP. To either side of the entry stood wooden tables displaying produce. It was all neatly set out, fruit on one side, vegetables on the other. A slim man of medium height, in a houndstooth check suit of knickerbockers and jacket and with his face shadowed by a soft felt hat, was inspecting the fruit. He was picking up one piece at a time and examining it on all sides, before putting it down again and trying the next piece.

A middle-aged man with waxed moustaches, wearing a green baize apron, presumably A. Weisz himself, stood with folded arms in the doorway and watched this prospective customer closely.

'It's a shop,' said Bessie simply. 'You sure we're at the right address, missus?'

I took out the card and checked the street number. 'This is definitely the one, Bessie. Let's go and ask.'

We crossed the road and I asked the shopkeeper if he knew of Horatio Jenkins, enquiry agent.

Without unfolding his arms or taking his eyes from the fussy customer, Mr Weisz replied briefly, 'Upstairs.'

He had not moved out of the way and still blocked the entry so I asked, 'Are we to go through the shop?'

Mr Weisz now unfolded his arms, but still without taking his eyes from the fellow in the check suit, pointed to his left. 'Door.'

There was, I saw, a narrow door, badly in need of a coat of paint, tucked into a shadowy recess next to the shop window. When we went to inspect it, we were able to read painted on it a little inexpertly, *H. Jenkins, Private Enquiry Agent, 1st Floor*. Also on the first floor we'd find *S. Baggins, taxidermist*. On the second floor we would find *Miss R. Poole, milliner*.

I gave the door an experimental push and it opened on to a dark flight of uncarpeted stairs.

'Come on, Bessie,' I encouraged, and we started up.

Sure enough, on the first-floor landing we found ourselves in a dusty, dark corridor with two doors leading off it to the right and a third door facing us at the end of the corridor. The first door to our right bore the legend H. JENKINS DETECTION AGENCY boldly printed in large capitals on it. There was no bell so I knocked loudly and after a moment we heard movement on the other side and the door opened.

The man who stood there was middle aged with greying curls, a coarse complexion, and small dark eyes. His coat was shiny with wear and his linen didn't look too clean. A dusting of crumbs covered his shirtfront.

I was about to ask if he were Mr Jenkins, when he spoke.

'Mrs Ross, ain't it?' he said. His lips curved in a wide smile that didn't reach his eyes. 'Nice of you to take up my invitation, Mrs Ross. Why don't you come on into my office?'

Even my corset didn't disguise Bessie's warning prod in my spine. I ignored it and her and strode boldly inside, my boots clumping on the bare boards. Bessie followed with a gusty sigh.

Just inside the doorway, rather like a footman waiting to announce us, loomed one of those coat and hat hangers constructed to look like a tree with inward curling branches. Nothing hung from its leafless arms but a battered rusty black umbrella and bowler hat to match. The rest of the 'office' was no more imposing. A large ink-stained desk had long ago seen better days. Behind it stood a chair facing the entry. In front of it were two more chairs for visitors, positioned with their backs to the door. On the desk lay implements for writing and a stack of cheap notepaper, but no sign of any work being done. The folded copy of what looked like a sporting newspaper suggested how Mr Jenkins had been passing his morning. In one corner of the room stood a large wicker laundry basket. Another corner had been curtained off and I suspected that was where Jenkins slept. It struck me that the private enquiry business did not appear to be prospering. There was a faint aroma of cigarette smoke and stale beer.

'Sit down, ladies, make yourselves at home,' invited Mr Jenkins, indicating the visitors' chairs with a broad, hairy hand.

I sat down and so, after some hesitation, did Bessie. She

continued to take stock of our surroundings and the downward droop of her mouth expressed her opinion. I elected to stare Jenkins in the eye.

'Would you like to take tea? Ruby Poole makes it.' Jenkins pointed to the ceiling. 'Up there where she makes her hats. If I've got a client I give a rap on the ceiling with that brolly there,' he redirected his finger to point at the hat stand, 'and I give as many raps as cups of tea required.'

'Thank you,' I said. 'We will not trouble Miss Poole. I'm sure she is busy.'

'She makes a very good mourning bonnet,' Mr Jenkins informed me, 'should you ever find yourself in need of such a thing, which of course I hope you won't. She trims it up with feathers and little satin rosettes, all black, veil if you want.'

'Mr Jenkins!' I interrupted him. 'I don't want tea nor do I need a mourning or any other bonnet. What do you mean by having that boy put your card into my hand in Bryanston Square? How do you know who I am? Were you in Bryanston Square yourself? You must have been. What were you doing there?'

He gave me another of his slow, wide, mirthless smiles. 'Doing much what you were doing, Mrs Ross. I was keeping an eye on the residence of Mr Jonathan Tapley.'

'Why?' I demanded crisply.

'Well, Mrs Ross, again I have to say that it was probably for much the same reason as you were giving it a good look-over.'

I did not like his familiar manner bordering on the insolent. Nor did I like the idea that, while I had been watching Tapley's house, this man had been watching me. A sardonic twinkle gleamed in his small dark eyes and, at that, I recognised him.

'You are the clown,' I gasped.

Bessie unexpectedly leaped up and marched across to the wicker basket in the corner.

'Here!' shouted Mr Jenkins, starting to get up from his chair. 'You keep your nose out of that! That's private property.'

'Here, yourself!' retorted Bessie, flinging open the lid. 'You're right, missus. It's all in here. Look!' She delved into the basket and held up the clown's wig. 'Lots of other stuff too, all for dressing up.'

'Disguises, if you don't mind!' snapped Jenkins. 'Not dressing up.'

'I'll call it what I want,' Bessie told him. 'It's a very strange way of going on, if you ask me, not normal.'

Jenkins sank back into his chair and appealed to me. 'Can't you put her on a leash or something?'

'I believe Bessie and I have every right to know what you keep in that basket,' I replied. 'I think you must explain yourself, Mr Jenkins.'

He placed his large hairy hands flat on the desk and leaned over it towards me. 'I am an enquiry agent, that's how I earn my living. I am sometimes called upon to adopt disguises.'

'I couldn't care less why you dress up – adopt disguises – but I do care when you do so to spy on Thomas Tapley.'

He sighed and sat back. 'I knew you'd spotted me,' he said. 'I knew from the way you looked at me on the Embankment that you'd guessed what I was about.'

Strictly speaking, I hadn't. I had merely been unreasonably terrified out of my wits at the clown's garb. But now I felt a little better about my fear. I pressed home my advantage.

'Yes, I did think you were up to something suspicious. I told my husband about you.'

'Ah,' he said with another sigh. 'I was afraid you might have done that.'

'My husband is an inspector, plain clothes, at Scotland Yard.'

'I know who your old man is, Mrs Ross.' He leaned back. 'Let me explain myself. Are you sure you won't let me rap on the ceiling for tea?'

'Just get on with it!' I told him sharply.

Bessie, who had been rummaging in the basket, closed the lid at last and returned to her seat.

'Seen enough, have you?' Jenkins asked her sourly.

'Yes,' said Bessie. 'I'll remember all the stuff you've got in there and if I see you anywhere wearing any of it, I'll recognise you straight off!'

'I'll be watching out for you, too,' retorted Jenkins. He turned back to me. 'Best I start at the beginning, so you know who I am and how I come to be in this business. When I was a young chap I decided to go travelling. I went to America, landed in New York. Now, that's a city you want to try and see. I did a variety of jobs but I didn't settle and decided to move on. I'd heard you could make your fortune in the Californian goldfields. So I set out West but, by a series of misadventures I needn't trouble you with, I found myself in Chicago. That's not the West, more in the middle. I needed to earn some money before I moved on again, still planning on reaching California. I asked around if any one knew of any company hiring. I met a fellow who said he worked for Pinkerton's. I had no idea what Pinkerton's was and so he explained it was a private detective agency. He suggested I come along with him to their offices and perhaps they might take me on.

'Along I went. I met the fellow who'd founded it, Allan Pinkerton. He wasn't an American by birth. He was a Scotsman who'd got an itch to wander, like me, and decided he could do better if he crossed the Atlantic. He engaged me as one of his agents. The work suited me very well. You might say I turned out to be a natural at it. It was at Pinkerton's I learned about disguises, and how to adopt a false identity to infiltrate criminal gangs and other plotters. People, Mrs Ross, judge very much by first appearances. What they see is, they reckon, what they're getting. They're not all as sharp as you! Most folk see a clown and think, ho! That's a clown. But you can't trust your own eyes, that's the truth.

'Anyway, I was doing well. But then the recent Civil War over there started and that wasn't good news. Two things were pretty obvious to me. First, the war was likely to last years, rather than months. Second, the nature of the work we'd undertake would be different. Pinkerton saw his opportunity in the Union cause. He got close to President Lincoln, you know, after he found out about a plot to assassinate him. But I'm not a political man, certainly not one for getting caught up in politics in a foreign country. Also, I saw no need to get involved in a war. I'd have joined the army if I wanted to do that.

'I no longer had the urge to get to California, either. I'd met a few men coming the other way, all of whom had either failed to make their fortunes, or who had been robbed of what they had found by fellows with quicker wits than theirs.

In the end I decided it was time for me to sail home to Britain.

'I had the idea that, with my experience working for Pinkerton, I could set up something similar here, a private detective agency. So I did. I haven't done as well as I'd hoped, I admit. Not as well as Allan Pinkerton has done over there. But there again, we do things differently here. But I've made a living. You can't say fairer than that, can you?'

He paused on this appeal and looked at me, waiting for my answer.

'Please go on, Mr Jenkins,' was all I said.

When telling me of his American adventures he'd been at ease. Now he began to look and sound cautious. 'I was recently approached by a client. There hasn't been much work about and I was very pleased to think I could earn some money. Perhaps I should have been more cautious but beggars can't be choosers. It was a job of work, there!

'The client wanted me to find a man called Thomas Tapley. Tapley had been living in France but the client believed he'd returned to England. He had a relative, name of Jonathan Tapley, living in London in Bryanston Square. But when the client made enquiries and found out what manner of man Jonathan Tapley was, it didn't seem such a good idea to approach him directly and start asking questions. So the client came to me. I was given a photograph of Thomas, a studio portrait taken in France, and a very good description of the subject as well.'

I interrupted him. 'Do you still have this photograph?'

'I do, madam. But let me finish my tale. I managed to find out that Thomas Tapley had indeed returned to England. I tracked him from Southampton to London. But where he was in London, ah, that was a different matter. The quarry seemed to have vanished. If you want to get lost, London is the place to choose, that's the truth.

'So I tried a new tack. I kept watch on the Bryanston Square house. I established very quick that Mr Jonathan kept a carriage and a very showy pair to pull it. I'd seen horses like that in America. Palominos, they call them, almost gold in colour, with pale manes and tails. Sort of thing would please the ladies, you know, and there were a pair of ladies living in the house. One afternoon, as I was making my way towards the Square, I saw that carriage trotting along the road, going in the direction of the river. There's not another carriage pair like that around, I thought! I set off after it. There was a lot of traffic that day, so it wasn't so difficult to keep it in sight until it got to Waterloo Bridge. It started across the bridge and I meant to do the same, but I had bad luck. A couple of cabbies got themselves into an argument over who had the right of way and a crowd built up. I got through it at last, and across the Bridge, but no sign of the carriage now. I'd lost 'em.

'My first thought was that probably it had been making for the railway station and someone was hoping to catch a train. I therefore made for the station, too, but I didn't see the carriage around there. So, I thought to myself, where else might it be have been going? Could it be that Thomas Tapley was living south of the river, and whoever was inside the carriage was visiting him? If that were so then Thomas, so I reckoned, would sooner or later cross the bridge. For there ain't nothing but the railway station on the south side. I adopted my clown disguise and took up my post on the Embankment. On the third day I stood there, juggling and making little jokes and earning quite a few pence, when I saw him coming towards me. I waited for him to come back and I followed him and established where he was living. That was my good luck. The bad luck was you spotting me.'

'Your client', I said, 'didn't want to ask Jonathan Tapley if he knew where Thomas might be found, because your mysterious client had found out Jonathan practises at the bar. Your client, I suspect, is avoiding the law, Mr Jenkins. That is why he came to you.'

'I dare say you're right, Mrs Ross,' agreed Jenkins. 'But not everyone wants to go to the police or lawyers, do they? That's why they come to me, see? That's how I make my living. Anyhow, I reported to my client that I'd tracked the quarry down. I was paid my fee, on the spot. I had previously arranged that I should be paid as soon as I found my man.

'I felt pretty pleased with myself. A good bit of detection and a good bit of business. But I stopped feeling good about it very quickly, I can tell you. A few days later I read in the evening papers that a man had been found murdered in that very street. He'd been lodging there after previously lodging in Southampton. I didn't like the sound of it. I felt sure the corpse would turn out to be Thomas Tapley and I'd been tracking him. In no time at all the police might be tracking me! Even worse, the day after the evening press carried the story, my client turned up again here. This time I was asked to approach Jonathan Tapley. But I smelled danger so first off, I refused.'

'How did your client seem?' I asked. 'Anxious? Surprised? Not at all put out?'

'Oh, very anxious indeed. As I was, eh? Talk about a couple

of cats on hot bricks! We neither of us wanted to find ourselves accused of being involved in any murder. The pair of us stood in a very bad light. But my client didn't want your Thomas Tapley dead, Mrs Ross. My client very much wanted him alive. I didn't want to make an enemy of the client who might put the police on to me. But I didn't want to be involved any further, either. Real pickle I found myself in. So I said to the client, give me some time and I'll cast about to see what's happening. I carried on watching the house in Bryanston Square, too, because that's at the centre of it, in my opinion. I'm a man, remember, of some experience in detection. That's when I saw you again and thought to meself, ha! The lady's playing at detective too!'

'Nevertheless,' I said firmly, 'you must go to the police now. To continue as you have been, snooping about on your own, risks making things look even worse for you. Persuade you client to go with you to Scotland Yard. My husband is out of London at the moment. He will not return until tomorrow evening, or possibly even the day after. But ask for Sergeant Morris, or even for Superintendent Dunn himself.'

Jenkins was shaking his head vigorously. 'No, no, that won't do. My client wouldn't hear of it. In this first place, you see, my client isn't "he". My client is "she".'

'A lady?' I asked in surprise.

'Yes, Mrs Ross, and a foreign one at that, a French one. I did mention going to Scotland Yard, but the very idea terrifies her. I established that Inspector Ross is in charge of the inquiry and my client would agree to meet the inspector here, at this office. She speaks some English but would probably need some help. As it happens I know a little French and could help out in any interview. Will you tell your husband so?'

It was on the tip of my tongue to tell him that I spoke good French, and could interpret if needed. But I stopped myself. The less information Jenkins had about me, the better. He was quite capable of finding out enough for himself.

'Then I should tell the Yard myself,' I said. 'This is a murder inquiry and all information should be given to the police at once. I should pass on immediately all you've told me.'

Jenkins began to be agitated. 'No, no! If you do that, I'll have rozzers all over this office. What good is that to a private enquiry agent, discretion assured? I'd never get another client, once word got round. Besides, my client would get wind of it and she wouldn't turn up. She will meet Inspector Ross here, on his own, or no one.'

'What is the lady's name?' I asked.

He gave me one of his slow, unsettling smiles. 'I'm like a lawyer myself, Mrs Ross, that or a priest. I keep my clients' secrets until they tell me I may speak. It's all a matter of trust, see? Clients tell me all manner of things because they believe I'll keep a confidence.'

'I'll think about it,' I said, standing up.

'I'd rather have your word,' Jenkins said.

That put me on the spot. 'My husband may return late tonight, or not. I will wait until tomorrow. If he doesn't come then – if he has to remain away any longer – I shall go myself to the Yard. My suggestion to you is that you contact this lady. You have all the rest of today to do it. Persuade her to confide in the authorities, if possible before the day is out. If she has nothing to hide, she need have no fears.'

★ ★ ★

'I don't know as if you've agreed to the right thing there, missus,' said Bessie as we reached the street and set off homeward.

'No more do I know it,' I confessed. 'But if I run straight away to Superintendent Dunn and he sends Morris or someone over here, then it is possible this elusive lady client of Jenkins's will disappear and we'll not find her again. We don't know her name, only that she is French and, if frightened, will run straight away back to France.'

'What did she want our Mr Thomas Tapley for?' asked Bessie. 'And why does she now want to get in touch with Mr Jonathan Tapley? She didn't want to get in touch with him before; not once she found out he was a lawyer. If you ask me, she has got something to hide. That's why she's keeping out of sight.'

'We won't know that until she chooses to tell us – tell the police. That depends on Jenkins producing her. I shall do as I promised Jenkins and wait. If the inspector does not return tonight from Harrogate, then I shall go directly to Superintendent Dunn tomorrow morning. We shall have to risk losing the lady.'

As I spoke, we passed by a man standing on the corner and munching an apple. I thought I recognised his knickerbockers and felt hat.

'After picking over every piece of fruit on show,' Bessie, who'd recognised him too, muttered, 'he only bought a single apple from that poor man's shop. You would think he could have done that without so much fuss!'

Her remark made me turn my head towards the man and I met his eyes, fixed on me. They were very large, dark eyes, with a sort of mocking twinkle in them. They stared at me so frankly, assessing me in a way that seemed so personal, that I was embarrassed. I'm not usually confused by being stared at. Not, I hasten to add, that I attract too many glances of the openly admiring variety. I don't think I'm bad looking but I was never a great beauty of the sort to turn all heads. Nor was the fellow himself, strictly speaking, really handsome. But there was a sort of rakish, man-of-the-world confidence about him. He had thick curling black side-whiskers and his skin was of that pale olive shade that wasn't quite English. Perhaps that was why he wore a tweed suit. He fancied it made him look less foreign.

He'd noted my confusion and it amused him. He grinned, showing strong white teeth, and then bit into the apple again with an audible crunch.

I hurried by him prey to a feeling I couldn't quite explain and didn't care to dwell on too much.

Chapter Ten

Inspector Benjamin Ross

I HAD been told to look out for Inspector Barnes, my opposite number at Harrogate, at the town's railway station. During my journey I wondered how I'd know him. As it turned out I could hardly have missed him, as he was bigger than anyone else there. He had spotted and identified me almost before I had both feet on the platform, and bore down on me.

'You'll be the chap from London!' he boomed, gripping my hand. 'Ross, isn't it?'

'Yes,' I gasped, easing my fingers free. 'You're Inspector Barnes?'

'That's me, all right. Now, before anything else, what do you think of our station?' He waved a massive paw at our surroundings. 'We're very proud of it, y'know. It's not been open long, only six year. Before that, trains fetched up at the old Brunswick Station and that weren't much more than a garden shed compared to this. You've got the one bag, have you?'

He was shepherding me briskly through the crowd as we spoke. I managed to say the place seemed very busy.

'A lot of folk come here to Harrogate,' he informed me.

'That's why we needed a new station. It's on account of the mineral springs. There's folk swear by a pint of Harrogate waters. The Pump Room is never short of visitors. They even come here from abroad, our waters are that famous. It's the high concentration of minerals, you know, cures just about everything. If you've got time afore you leave, you ought to get yourself down to the Pump Room and try it.'

'What's it like?' I asked with caution.

Barnes gave that a moment's thought. 'It's what you might call an acquired taste. But it'll do you a power of good and my old mother always said that no good medicine ever tasted nice.'

I resolved that urgent need to return to London would not allow me time to down a pint of the famous waters.

'Now, it's all arranged,' Barnes went on. For an awful moment I thought he meant a pint of the dread fluid was already lined up for me. Luckily, he continued, 'I've booked you a room for tonight at the Commercial Hotel. You'll be comfortable enough sleeping there. But Mrs Barnes is looking forward to seeing you at our table tonight. She's got a wonderful light hand with pastry, my wife.'

That sounded much better. Barnes was assuming that my business here wouldn't allow me to set off home tonight; but I'd warned Lizzie that might be the case. I would, however, need to telegraph the Yard and let them know my plans. Perhaps I could get a message to my wife at the same time. Aloud, I said I was looking forward to meeting Mrs Barnes.

'From the way you talk, you'll not be a southerner?' enquired Barnes.

'I'm originally from Derbyshire.'

'Mrs Barnes will like that,' he told me approvingly. 'She's what you might call a bit suspicious of southerners.'

'I am myself, and I live among them,' I told him. At that he roared with laughter and clapped my shoulders so heartily I almost fell flat on my face.

Fortunately he'd hailed a cab and I found myself bundled into it. Barnes shouted out an address to the cabbie and climbed in beside me. The cab rocked and seemed to settle lower on its springs. I am a solidly built fellow myself and I felt sorry for the horse that had to pull the pair of us.

'We are going to the hotel?' I asked doubtfully, since Barnes hadn't given the driver the name of the Commercial.

'I thought it best I take you straight to Newman and Thorpe's offices,' he told me. 'I've set up a meeting with Fred Thorpe. Young Mr Thorpe, that is.'

'How young?' I asked immediately. I wanted, if possible, to speak to people who'd dealt with Thomas Tapley before he departed for the Continent and knew something about him as a person.

'Fred's around my age,' Barnes said. 'And I'm forty-one. They call him Young Mr Thorpe to distinguish him from his father, Old Mr Thorpe, also called Frederick.'

'Old Mr Thorpe is retired?'

'He does a little, just to keep his hand in. Folk are traditional around here and some of his older clients don't want to deal with anyone else. So I wouldn't say Old Mr Thorpe is retired. Now, Mr Thorpe Senior, he *is* retired. He's in his eighties.'

At least three male Thorpes living. I made a quick calculation.

'The *senior* gentleman would be Fred's – Young Mr Thorpe's – grandfather?'

'You've got it. Old Mr Thorpe's pa and young Fred's – as we tend to call him – grandpapa. A very old-established firm is Newman and Thorpe.'

'What about Newman?' I asked, wondering how old he was.

'Dead,' said Barnes. 'But they haven't got round to taking his name off the doorplate.'

'I see. When did he die?'

'Twenty year ago. Now,' continued Barnes, 'I'll introduce you and then, if you like, I'll take your bag along to the Commercial and drop it off. Then you can make your own way to the hotel at your leisure. Ah, here we are.'

I was briskly decanted from the cab and the driver ordered to wait. I was propelled into the outer office of Newman and Thorpe, where an aged clerk rose creakingly to greet us. He looked to me as if he might have started work there as a youngster in Mr Thorpe Senior's day.

'Here he is, Walter,' announced Inspector Barnes. 'This is Inspector Ross from Scotland Yard, down in London. We get the top people coming to us in Harrogate!' He gave me another mighty clap on the shoulder. 'See you later, lad,' he said and, to my relief, departed.

Walter looked me up and down suspiciously in silence. I wondered if he quite understood why I was there.

'I understand,' I prompted, 'that Mr Thorpe – Young Mr Thorpe – is expecting me.'

'I didn't hear the fire cart's bell,' replied Walter. 'All in good time. London folk are always rushing about, as I'm told. I'll take you to him.'

He shuffled ahead of me to a door, opened it and managed to slip through it quite nimbly, pushing it smartly to behind him, so that I was left staring at the oak panels.

'It's yon fellow from London,' I heard him say through the crack.

There was a scrape of a chair, a brisk footfall, and the door was opened wide.

'Come in!' cried a jolly looking, red-faced and curly-haired man. 'Sit down. Yes, yes, Walter, that's fine.' He shut the door, excluding my escort. 'Don't mind Walter,' he added. 'He's a very cautious old boy, you know, doesn't care for strangers.'

'You deal mostly with established clients, then?'

'Mostly,' agreed Thorpe. 'Glass of sherry?'

'Yes, please,' I said. 'I know I'm on duty here, but it was a long journey.'

Thorpe leaned forward. 'If you'd prefer, I'll send over the road for a jug of ale.'

'Even better,' I told him. 'But how long will it take Walter to fetch it?'

Fred Thorpe chuckled. 'He won't go himself. He'll send Charlie, the office boy.'

I didn't ask how old Charlie was. The way things were at Newman and Thorpe, he was very likely at least sixty.

Fred settled back in his chair. 'You've come about poor old Tom Tapley, then?'

'I have. You have heard he's dead, obviously. May I ask, did Barnes tell you – or did you read it in the press?'

'We don't see the London evening papers here, but this morning, the murder victim was named in *The Times*.' He tapped a folded newspaper on his desk.

'I haven't seen it,' I said regretfully. I had read the *Morning Chronicle* during my train journey. The paper had devoted much of today's edition to its zeal for reform. Poor Tapley's death suggested no copy for an interesting leader on social conditions. He had not died of cholera in a squalid slum but in a respectable Quaker house. Perhaps, having reported the original discovery of a body, the *Chronicle* was now waiting for an arrest. It would then send a man to cover the trial and fill its columns with sensational details. I hoped the press wouldn't have to wait much longer. That was why I was here in Harrogate: to find a lead. I had a childish impulse to cross my fingers.

'But, as it happens,' the solicitor was continuing, 'I had already heard the sad news from Sam Barnes. He came round here last night to tell me and arrange for me to be here today when you were expected. I'm glad to see you, Ross. I should have been getting in touch with you myself, otherwise.' He paused. 'I'll have to contact Jonathan Tapley, too, though I dare say I'll be hearing from him, probably by tomorrow's post.'

'I think you may,' I agreed. 'Mr Jonathan Tapley believes he is the executor, or one of them, of his cousin's will. Is that right? You have the will here?'

'Oh, yes, we have it, and his other papers. You are correct. Jonathan Tapley is one executor. My father is the other.'

'I confess,' I told him, 'that I had rather hoped to speak to someone who had known Tapley personally.'

'You can speak to my father tonight, when he gets back.'

'I am pledged to dine with Inspector Barnes, and don't want to disappoint Mrs Barnes.'

'Oh, that's all right,' said Thorpe cheerily. 'People around here dine early. You can eat your dinner and then come over to our house to meet my father afterwards, take a glass of port with us. Bring Sam Barnes with you. You can meet my grandfather, too. Might as well see us all in one lot. Father and grandfather both knew the Tapley family.'

'Thank you,' I told him. It sounded as if the Thorpes all lived together.

'But I knew Tapley, too, you know,' said Young Fred with a mischievous look in his eye.

'You did?'

He knew he'd surprised me and chuckled away to himself. I was beginning to find his irrepressible good humour as wearing as Barnes's boisterousness. But anyone who had to deal daily with Walter would need a robust sense of humour.

As if on cue, the ale arrived, carried in by Walter. Charlie was probably not allowed into this inner sanctum.

'Your good health!' Thorpe toasted me when he'd poured our ale. I raised my glass in return salutation. There was a pause while we savoured our ale. I remarked it was a very good brew.

'It's our water,' said my host.

'Not the stuff down at the Pump Rooms?'

'Good Lord, no. I never touch that. Mind you, Grandfather swears by it.' He returned to business. 'Fact is, Tom Tapley came here at the very beginning of last year.'

Of course he had, Jonathan Tapley had told me. But somehow I had imagined Thomas would have seen the older partner, young Fred's father, not the younger man.

'It was right at the end of January with snow on the ground, a difficult time to travel.' Fred took another drink of the ale. 'He was wearing a shabby old frock coat, as I recall, and a plaid shawl draped over it. It put Walter in quite a state when he walked into the outer office. Walter knew him years ago and was very upset to see him so down at heel and half frozen as well. It gave me a start when I learned who he was. Charlie was sent over the road to fetch a hot toddy for him. Tapley had asked to see my father. But the old man was out visiting a local landowner on a matter of business, just as he is today. I explained to Tapley he had to make do with me or return later. He said he would deal with me. I was, after all, a Thorpe.

'He told me he'd just returned from France where he'd been living for some years. He'd brought me some documents to add to those we already held for him. He explained that he was temporarily lodged and when he had found somewhere permanent he would let me have that address. But he never did, so I presume he hadn't found anywhere?' Thorpe paused and raised his eyebrows and his mug of ale to his lips at the same time.

'He stayed with a lady in Southampton and then in London with a Quaker lady. It is at her house he died. If he stayed anywhere else we don't know of it.'

Thorpe set down his mug. 'He was very nervous, poor old boy. I marked it at once.'

Ah. The jollity deceived. Thorpe was shrewd as a third-generation solicitor would be.

'How did he show it?'

'In almost every way he could. I liked him, by the way. He seemed a nice old gentleman, about my father's age, two and sixty. I told him my father would be most sorry to miss him, and certainly wish to see him again, but he said he couldn't wait until the evening, much less come back next day. He must start back south. I don't know what the hurry was. He didn't tell me.

'I did ask him what had brought him back from the Continent and if he intended to stay in England? He said he was planning to settle here now. He confided that he'd had "a bad experience" in France, not long before. It was one reason he was anxious to deposit a box containing all his private papers with us the moment he'd returned. "Lest anyone get their hands on them," he said. "Has that happened?" I asked him. But he became more agitated, said he didn't know, couldn't be sure. He had been ill for some time, in France, he said, about six or seven months earlier. He had lain delirious for two whole weeks and at death's door for almost a month. Consequently there was a gap in his memory. So, working back through the calendar, I reckon whatever it was, it happened at some point the year before last, during this illness.'

The year before last, I thought. Later that year he was seen, by a Mr Parker, on the beach at Deauville with a mysterious woman on his arm. He had told Parker that he'd been ill and was at the coast to recuperate.

'Mr Thorpe,' I said, 'what manner of documents did Tapley bring to deposit with you?'

'There is a passport issued by the Foreign Office with which he'd had the foresight to equip himself before leaving England. It is in a well-worn and generally sorry state, rather like poor Tapley. As a private gentleman travelling with no diplomatic position and not wishing to engage in any trade, he did not, of course, strictly speaking need such a document. But he anticipated that officials sometimes like to see these things, especially at border crossing. He also deposited the various letters of introduction which he'd carried around with him on his travels. Some are so out of date now that I can't imagine anyone to whom he might have shown them would have been much impressed. There was also a mixed bag of correspondence: some from us, of which we had our copies, of course. However he wanted us to keep his originals, too. There was correspondence from his bank, but no private letters. He said he had been obliged to destroy those. He didn't give a reason, just that he had had to do it. It was one of the things that underlined how nervous he was. I wish now, of course, that I had pressed him for details. But even if I had, I doubt he'd have given any. I should tell you that, from time to time over the years, he had sent bundles of correspondence to us to keep here. Otherwise he wouldn't have needed just a box, he'd have needed a trunk to store them all.'

'He corresponded with this office frequently?'

'Fairly regularly during all his stay in France. That is why I didn't doubt he'd send us his new address in England when he had one. He managed most of his affairs through us and his bank. We also acted as his land agent. That was, perhaps, a little unusual. But it's how he wanted it.'

'Land agent?' I gasped. 'Did he own extensive property?'

Thorpe shook his head, raising a hand in protest. 'I wouldn't call it *extensive*, but certainly not to be sniffed at. There is one fair-sized property, consisting of a large house and grounds, and a farm, originally part of the same property but now leased out separately. The house is – and has been for a number of years – leased to a tenant. He is a retired military gentleman, Major Griffiths. The farm has a different tenant, a local family.'

So what on earth, I wondered, was Tom Tapley doing, living in rented rooms? The income from this estate alone must be respectable.

'As a matter of fact,' Fred Thorpe was saying, 'I have arranged to take you out to the house this afternoon, if that's all right with you. I thought you might like to take a look at the property yourself and meet Major Griffiths. The major would rather like to meet you. I sent a message there to inform him that the owner of the property had died, as soon as I had the news from Barnes.'

I had to hand it to Barnes, Thorpe, Griffiths and all the rest of them I'd not yet had the honour to meet, they were nothing if not efficient. They had my timetable planned down to the last half-hour of my stay in Harrogate.

'This property', I began, 'now forms part of the late Mr Tapley's estate? It is disposed of in his will?'

'Yes,' agreed Thorpe.

A thought struck me. 'Among the papers he brought you last year, he didn't bring a new will, did he?'

Thorpe shook his head. 'No, but I raised the matter. I asked if, since it was many years now since the will had been drawn up, there were any changes he wished to make to it. At that, the poor old fellow looked so upset I thought he would faint clean away. He was most insistent he wanted no changes to his will.'

'May I ask,' I began, 'who is the principal beneficiary?'

'His daughter, Miss Flora Tapley,' Thorpe replied. 'There is no reason why I shouldn't tell you. She resides in London with Mr Jonathan Tapley and his wife,'

'I have met the young lady,' I said. 'The property at present leased to Major Griffiths, does that also form a part of the bequest to Miss Flora?'

'It does.'

'Major Griffiths was probably concerned to hear of Tapley's death. But the lease would still have some time to run? His position as tenant is not immediately threatened?'

'The present lease runs for another couple of years, unless the new owner wishes to terminate the agreement before then. There is a clause in the tenancy agreement. I imagine, with so little time to run until the end of the lease, the new owner may simply wait. It would be almost as quick as waiting for the law to grind its course. But Major Griffiths is nevertheless anxious to see you, Inspector. May I suggest we go there now? I have arranged a pony and trap to take us.'

By now I would have expected no less. 'Let us go there, then,' I said, taking up my hat. It was all proving quite an adventure. What surprises would Major Griffiths spring?

Our journey to see Major Griffiths took us across open moor and along country roads that made the trap rattle and bounce and precluded much conversation. Thorpe did his best.

'You do meet these eccentrics!' he shouted at me, holding on to his hat in the stiff wind.

'Tapley does seem to have been quaint in his ways!' I bawled back, holding on to mine.

'All Tapleys a bit odd!' contributed our driver over his

shoulder. 'Well known for it! Not all touched, mind you! Just a bit different!'

'William is a local man!' explained Thorpe, indicating the driver. 'It's true, the Tapleys were all considered, well, different, in the days when they lived around here. People didn't mind, though, did they, William?'

'Folk used to it,' retorted William simply. 'Haven't seen any of 'em around for years. Mr Thomas dead, you say?'

'Murdered!' shouted Thorpe. 'In London!'

'Ah!' replied the driver. 'It'll have been in London. He'd not have got himself murdered around here.'

For some minutes we'd been following a stone wall on our right-hand side. Now we drew up before a pair of closed wrought-iron gates. Our driver climbed down and tugged at a bell affixed to the wall. It jangled loudly, its discordant notes echoing around us and breaking the silence as harshly as a gunshot would have done. In reply, the door of a small lodge opened and a sturdy fellow in gaiters and moleskin waistcoat, who looked like a gamekeeper, came out. He dragged open the gates and we clattered through.

The gate/gamekeeper raised a hand in salute and stared at me in an unfriendly manner, or so it seemed. His living and his home, as with all those employed by Major Griffiths, had suddenly become uncertain with the death of the owner of the estate and the lease only having two years to run. The tenant farmer and his family must also be apprehensive. I must expect to be viewed as the harbinger of doom.

The house was soon reached. The solid Jacobean building of regular proportions and with rows of identical windows had been so long here that it had settled into the landscape like a natural feature, and its tall slender chimneys appeared to spring from its mossy roof as long-necked birds stretching their heads skyward.

'This is The Old Hall,' said Thorpe, as we scrambled down from the trap. 'So called because the family who originally owned it decided to build a New Hall, a more fashionable seat, elsewhere around 1790. The old house came into the Tapley family through marriage. Thomas Tapley's mother brought it as her dowry.'

'A fine dowry,' I observed, remembering that Jonathan had told me his uncle, Thomas's father, had 'married money'. In this house young Thomas had grown up, cosseted by his mamma and all those doting female relatives. I entered it with a lively interest.

Major Griffiths turned out to be as solidly built as the house. He was a man of some seventy years but with an upright soldier's bearing still, and a fine mane of silvering hair.

'I am pleased to meet you, Inspector,' he said. 'I appreciate you have made time to come out here. Has Mr Thorpe told you why I was so anxious to talk to you?'

'Er, no . . .' I replied, glancing at Thorpe.

'Thought it best you explain, Major,' said the solicitor. 'Because the inspector will have questions and I couldn't answer them.'

'Quite so, quite so. Do make yourselves comfortable, gentlemen. I can have them bring tea, or a glass of Madeira might suit you more.'

After our bone-shaking journey, we gratefully accepted the Madeira. Accompanied by plain cake, it arrived carried in by an elderly butler.

'I'll explain it all as quickly as I can,' began Griffiths. 'I dare say you have other matters to attend to before you go back to London, Inspector. When Mr Thorpe sent a message to me yesterday, telling me you were expected, I sent a reply back by the same carrier, making clear my urgent need to talk to you. At least, it seems urgent to me. I am – or was – Thomas Tapley's tenant, as you'll know. I am still the tenant for the next two years, unless the new owner wants to turn me out. I hope we'll be able to come to some arrangement about that, Thorpe! I should like to see the lease out here. In two years' time I shall be ready to move out of my own accord and retire to a mild climate. I have a fancy for the South-West, Sidmouth, to end my days by the sea. I know the late Duke of Kent, our gracious Queen's father, took the chill there that carried the poor fellow off, but I like the place. Where was I? Ah, yes, Ross.'

To my relief, he turned his attention back to me. If this were telling it as quickly as he could, I would hate to be subjected to what Griffiths would consider a lengthy explanation.

'I don't get many visitors here, you know, and those who do come, come by my invitation. It is an out-of-the-way spot. But at the beginning of November last, a hired carriage drew up here and out got a couple I'd never set eyes on, who requested to view the house. They were, they said, on a tour of Yorkshire. I thought they had left it rather late in the year. The weather was cold. They were foreign, French. The man introduced himself as Monsieur Hector Guillaume and he presented the lady as his sister.'

Major Griffiths gave a snort. 'I am an old soldier. I've been around. She was no more his sister than she was mine! What's

177

more, she was a type who, if younger, I'd have described as a camp-follower. She was a handsome female, I'll give you that. She had fine eyes but the look in them was wary and her mouth was hard. These things always give away a woman of questionable background. She carried herself well. I suspected the dark red colour of her hair was helped with henna. There was a great deal of it, the hair, all piled up in a complicated way. She would have passed for forty-something in a kindly light, but was probably nearly fifty-one or -two. I am not an expert at judging ladies' years. Paint and powder disguise the passage of time and this lady had applied plenty of both.

'The man was, I would say, a good deal younger. He was not unprepossessing, but dressed in the manner I fancy he thought someone visiting the English countryside should dress. He wore tweed knickerbockers and matching jacket of a rather loud check. He had some kind of scented oil on his hair, which no country gentleman of my acquaintance would affect. I don't know what they do in Town these days. Never trust a fellow who perfumes himself is my motto. I also found his manner . . .' Griffiths paused to seek the word.

'There was something not quite right about him!' he concluded. 'I can't say he was rude. I'd have shown them the door at once if he had been. On the contrary, he was very polite, *too* polite. Both were all smiles. I wouldn't have trusted either of them. However, a number of foreigners come to Harrogate for the waters. They are not a strange sight. When visiting, they do often take the opportunity to tour Yorkshire and they do turn up at country houses. The Old Hall clearly has considerable age and would catch the eye. These travellers made their request courteously. If they overdid it a bit, perhaps they were just nervous. It put me in something of a quandary. I didn't wish to appear inhospitable or unfair. One can't expect a foreigner to act like a straightforward Englishman. I'd no wish to appear prejudiced. So I said I would show them around the ground-floor rooms, but not upstairs. I regretted I was not able to offer them any other hospitality.

'They assured me they only wished to look round the main reception rooms. I saw no objection to that. But they asked questions, oh my, they did. They first wanted to know, reasonably enough, about the age of the house and its history. They then asked if it had been long in my family? So far, so good. But when I replied I was only the tenant, they expressed some surprise. Thereafter, their questioning became more specific and, to my mind, bordered on the impertinent. What of the owner? His name? Tapley? They were surprised he did not wish to live here himself, in such a charming house. Were there no other Tapley family members who might want to live here? What had caused him to leave? Where did he live now?'

Major Griffiths gave a kind of growl. 'To the last I replied I had no idea where he lived and was not myself in correspondence with him. I was now most anxious to be rid of them and deeply regretted giving way to their request. I recommended them to consult Newman and Thorpe in Harrogate if they wished to know more about Mr Tapley, and I hurried them out. To be frank, once they realised I didn't know where Tapley could be found, they showed no inclination to linger, or so it seemed to me. They took themselves off. I instructed Hartwell, my gamekeeper who lives at the lodge and whom you probably saw when you arrived, that if they returned, they were not to be admitted. I also sent a letter to Thorpe here, telling him about it. I warned him they might turn up at his office.'

'But they didn't,' said Fred Thorpe, who had been nodding agreement. 'We discussed it, my father and I, and wondered if we ought to get in touch with Jonathan Tapley about it. You see, we didn't know where Thomas Tapley was. As I explained, he hadn't sent me his present address as he'd promised. But his cousin might know. In the end, I confess we didn't contact Mr Jonathan Tapley because, after all, there was nothing specific to tell. The couple had left the area. I made sure of that by enquiry. They were certainly not in Harrogate. They may well have been genuine visitors, as they claimed, and if their manner seemed odd, well, they were foreign. We get everyone in Harrogate, as the major said, and our countryside is well worth visiting. All sorts come, artists, poets . . . and tourists.'

Now the major was nodding. 'Quite so. During the week before those two turned up, Hartwell had reported he'd met a fellow tramping over the moor with a folded easel over his shoulder and a satchel of art materials in hand, disturbing the birds. He told him to be off. If the Guillaumes had arrived on foot, he'd have sent them packing. But they arrived in a carriage and that flummoxed the poor fellow. He assumed they must be gentry.'

'I see,' I said. 'I am very glad you've told me of this, Major.'

'Thought you should know,' said Griffiths. 'Glad to have it off my mind.'

'I'll be honest with you, Ross,' said Fred Thorpe when we were alone outside the house, waiting for our trap to come round. 'I wish now I'd written to Jonathan Tapley about the Guillaumes. I may have slipped up there.'

'It would have made no difference,' I consoled him. 'Jonathan Tapley didn't know where his cousin Thomas was living either. He'd been trying to find him.'

'Eventually it was Jonathan Tapley who wrote to us, asking if we had an address for his cousin. We replied in the negative. Apparently, he had been trying to contact Thomas at his French address without luck. Mr Jonathan Tapley told us he had not known his cousin was back in England. I'm afraid we appear remiss.' The solicitor shook his head ruefully.

'In my experience as a police officer,' I told him, 'if a person wishes to disappear, he can show remarkable ingenuity. Thomas Tapley gave you the slip, as we'd say.'

'We should have realised it earlier. You think this pair of foreigners were trying to find him, too?' He squinted at me in the stiff breeze.

'Yes, I do.'

'Then, is it possible that he didn't give anyone his address because he was hiding from them?' the solicitor asked bluntly.

'Yes, Mr Thorpe, I think it entirely possible.'

The trap rattled round the corner and drew up, waiting for us.

'I don't like it,' said Fred Thorpe fiercely. 'Given what happened to poor Tapley, I don't like it at all! Well, at least they didn't get an address for him from Griffiths.'

No, I thought but didn't say aloud, but they did get a good look at the property. That alone would have told them Thomas Tapley was a wealthy man.

He had also been a frightened one.

Chapter Eleven

ON MY return from The Old Hall and after parting from Fred Thorpe, I managed to find the telegraph office. I sent my message to the Yard. It was then time to make my way to Barnes's home where I was royally received by Mrs Barnes and dined splendidly on a beef pudding and fruit tart.

By now, having had a long and eventful day, I was ready to retire to the Commercial Hotel and my bed. But instead I had another appointment to keep. I'd promised Fred to call later that evening and meet his father and grandfather. So, together with Sam Barnes, I set out for the Thorpe residence.

This turned out to be a substantial house where we found all the Thorpe family gathered, including the ladies. They were Fred's wife and mother and a Thorpe maiden aunt. Young Fred, I learned, had children, but they were very young and fast asleep in the nursery. The house was fairly crammed with Thorpes. After the usual formalities of introduction and small talk, the womenfolk retired. Sam and I found ourselves comfortably seated before a crackling hearth, in company with the three Thorpe men. The port was passed round.

It did occur to me that I had drunk more alcohol that day than at any time since Christmas. I sipped cautiously at the port and resolved to keep a clear head. It was not easy, what with fatigue and so much new information running round my brain after my meetings that day.

Fred's father was very much a mature version of young Fred, his curly hair now grey but still abundant. To think that this robust man was of an age with the late Thomas Tapley only served to underline how unfairly Fate had treated the latter. To designate Fred's father as 'Old Mr Thorpe' seemed equally unjust, but he seemed happy to be called so. Mr Thorpe Senior, the grandfather, however, was a fierce-looking ancient, brandishing an ear trumpet and swathed head to toe in tartan shawls. I foresaw certain difficulties of communication.

'We were all of us very sorry to learn what happened to Tom Tapley,' began Fred's father.

'What's that?' demanded Thorpe Senior shrilly, holding the trumpet to his ear and leaning forward in the winged Queen Anne-style chair; where he strongly resembled a tartan parcel that had been deposited there and forgotten.

'Tom Tapley, Grandpapa!' bawled Young Thorpe.

'Let the side down!' squawked Thorpe Senior. 'When he was a lad.'

'You do him an injustice, Father!' objected Old Mr Thorpe vigorously. 'And you forget you speak of an old and much respected client.'

'No, I don't!' snapped his parent. 'He did let the side down. There was a big fuss when he was up at Oxford and he had to leave very suddenly. His mother took it badly, not because she knew what he'd been up to, but because she didn't. He was caught with another fellow in what they like to call a compromising situation. No one would tell her and she thought he'd been in some boyish scrape like seducing a serving girl. It was easy enough to let her think that was the case and that the girl had been paid off. She was a woman who always accepted what she was told. But it wasn't girls he fancied, it was fellows!'

Well, I thought, Thorpe Senior might be hard of hearing, but there was certainly nothing wrong with his memory.

Old Mr Thorpe turned to me and spoke in a low voice. 'What my father says about the reason for Tapley being sent down is true. But although the news that he'd been disgraced couldn't be disguised, very few people here in Harrogate knew the real cause of the scandal, or if they did, they didn't speak of it. His mother never knew until her dying day.'

'But your father seems to have known all about it.'

'What's that?' yelled Thorpe Senior, brandishing the ear trumpet.

'Inspector Ross says that you knew the true facts, Grand-papa!' shouted Fred Thorpe.

'Had to know them! His uncle came to see me, warned me it might come to court, if the truth got out, and we'd need to seek counsel. Serious offence! Hanging matter back then. But it didn't come to that. All hushed up. Well, all for the best. He wasn't the first and he won't be the last.'

'Tom later married,' Fred's father said to me before turning to his own father and repeating the words *fortissimo*. '*He later married!*'

'Yes, wisest thing he could have done. I advised it myself. Landowner in his early forties, sound in wind and limb, no sign of wanting an heir, tongues got wagging again. "Get him a wife!" I said. So he married one of Alexander Sanders' daughters, the plain one!' declared Thorpe Senior with relish. 'She had a squint.'

'Tom and his wife then also had a daughter, Grandpapa!' from young Fred.

'Surprised he managed it. Has she got a squint?' asked the old fellow with interest.

'No, Mr Thorpe!' I took it upon myself to shout at him. 'I have met the young lady, Miss Flora, and she is very handsome.'

Thorpe Senior grunted and slumped down among his shawls.

'Mrs Thomas Tapley died, sir, and Miss Flora has been brought up by Mr Jonathan Tapley and his wife.' I found I was now shouting everything.

'Shrewd fellow, young Jonathan,' muttered the ancient. 'Got his wits about him. Tom never had any wits. Took after his mother, probably.'

'He went to live in France, Grandpapa!'

'Best place for him, I dare say,' mumbled Thorpe Senior.

Disconcertingly, he then fell asleep.

'This is a late hour for my grandfather,' young Fred apologised to me.

After my busy day it was a late night for me, too. I took the opportunity to thank them all for their hospitality and help, and expressed my pleasure at meeting them. I shook hands with Fred Thorpe and his father. Grandfather Thorpe was snoring gently among his tartan shawls so I asked Fred to say my goodbye for me later.

'Very likely by tomorrow he'll have forgotten you were here tonight,' said Fred ruefully.

'I thought his memory wonderfully clear.'

Fred smiled and shook his head. 'Anything that happened years ago is as yesterday to him. But real yesterday itself, that's another matter.'

'Well?' asked Sam Barnes as he walked with me back to the Commercial Hotel. 'Any ideas?'

'To tell you the truth,' I confessed, 'I have learned quite a lot today, but whether it's led to anything definite? Not yet. I must return to London tomorrow on the early train.'

'I'll call by and walk with you to the station, see you off,' Barnes promised. 'Hope you've enjoyed your visit.'

Elizabeth Martin Ross

'It's a pity we've got to go home,' said Bessie as we climbed aboard the omnibus for our return journey.

Her tone was wistful. I reflected that she seldom made an expedition to anywhere new and today was a treat for her. But we did not have to go home, not straight away. Ben would not be back before evening, if he returned today at all. He might not do so until tomorrow. Besides, perhaps Horatio Jenkins had judged me right. I was as much bitten by the detection bug as he was. He had hung about Bryanston Square in the hope of making some progress – and had been rewarded with the sight of me. I would do the same and hope for similar good luck.

'We'll go first to Bryanston Square, where Mr Jonathan Tapley and his family live,' I said firmly.

Bessie's eyes opened wide. 'You're never going to knock on his door, missus!' she gasped.

'No,' I told her with regret, 'I can't do that. I am sure Maria Tapley would not allow me to see Flora. But we'll go there and walk around the area and, well, who knows?'

'I'd like to see his house,' said Bessie.

Bryanston Square was quiet and, in the spring sunshine, invited strollers to linger. There was a pretty shady park in the middle of it protected by railings. Today the gates stood open and a pair of nursemaids pushed their charges, in wicker bassinets, up and down the paths. Bessie and I went in and sat down.

'I liked living in Dorset Square when I worked at Mrs Parry's,' observed Bessie, adding hastily, 'but I like working for you and the inspector an awful lot more. What I meant was, Dorset Square is like this, with a bit of green in the middle.'

'There's certainly no greenery around Waterloo Station,' I admitted. Mention of Aunt Parry led me to wonder if, since we were so close, I ought to go and call on her again, should nothing of interest happen here. As I'd been so recently at Aunt Parry's, I wasn't keen on visiting again so soon. She might interpret that as wishful thinking on my part. I certainly didn't regret leaving her house.

'Missus!' hissed Bessie, gripping my arm.

Daydreaming as I'd been, I hadn't noticed that the front door of the house had opened. Two female forms emerged. Both were young, so neither could be Maria Tapley. One was well dressed, but in mourning. The other, plainly dressed in grey, wore the discontented expression of a ladies' maid. They were crossing the road towards the park where we sat.

'They're coming 'ere!' gasped Bessie. 'Do you reckon that one in black is poor old Mr Tapley's daughter?'

'I do indeed,' I told her. 'I'm certainly going to find out!'

The two girls had entered the park and begun to make a

leisurely tour of it. They were not talking. Flora, if it were Flora, walked a little ahead of her companion, her head slightly bowed so that I couldn't see beneath the brim of her bonnet. The maid followed behind, demure but still sullen, carrying a shawl over her arm in case her mistress suddenly felt cool. I was on tenterhooks watching them until they had almost completed their circle and had neared Bessie and me. At this point I stood up.

'Forgive me,' I said to the young woman in black. 'But are you by chance Miss Flora Tapley?'

She looked up in surprise. 'Yes,' she said simply. Then she frowned. 'But I am afraid I don't know . . .'

'I'm Elizabeth Ross, the husband of Inspector Ross who is investigating your father's death. I would like to say how sorry I am about the dreadful thing that happened. I was slightly acquainted with your father. He lodged not far from us. I used to see him walking about and we would exchange the time of day.'

Her face lit up with pleasure. 'You knew my papa?' She glanced at the maid. 'Wait here, Biddy, I'm just going to take a turn about with Mrs Ross.'

We walked on, leaving the two maids standing together watching us. Bessie looked excited. The other girl, Biddy, was openly scowling. She has had instructions from Maria Tapley, I thought, never to leave Miss Flora alone. What did Maria fear?

'What's brought you here to Bryanston Square, Mrs Ross?' Flora asked.

'I – I have a relative who lives in Dorset Square. Her name is Parry and you may have come across her. I was thinking of visiting her.'

That was not untrue. I had considered visiting Aunt Parry again – and had decided against it. But I had no need to tell Flora that.

'It looked so pretty and peaceful in the park here, I decided to sit for a while,' I added.

'It is nice here,' agreed Flora in a sad voice. 'And it's about the only place I am allowed to go without Aunt Maria to watch me. Even now she sends Biddy along to make sure I don't get into any mischief.'

Mischief? That was an odd word to use. Again, I wondered what mischief Mrs Tapley imagined her well-brought-up niece would be tempted to undertake.

'You are to be married, I understand,' I fished. 'She is guarding you zealously.'

'Oh, I don't know about my marriage,' returned Flora in an offhand way. 'It may not take place. A problem has arisen because of the manner of my father's death. George's parents don't like that at all. They have grown distinctly cool towards the whole idea and me. My uncle and aunt – although they are not really related in that way – are in quite a state about it. They were so pleased when George asked to marry me. But if George doesn't care for me enough to marry me despite what's happened, well, I don't know that I want to marry him, after all. He should defy his parents if they object. Don't you agree?'

'Well,' I said cautiously. 'I don't know the gentleman or his family . . .'

'George is very kind and never wants to upset anyone.' Flora made an impatient movement of her hands. 'I mean, naturally he doesn't want to upset *me*, but he wouldn't wish to upset his parents, either. His parents are nice, but fearfully

stiff and proper. Then there is the question of the title, you
see, which is so important. Of course, George isn't the heir.
His elder brother Edwin is that. But if any accident befell
Edwin . . .' She paused and then added, 'Not that it's likely
to. Edwin is very dull and doesn't go climbing mountains or
anything. He studies moths, if you please. He sits outside in
the garden in the evenings with a lantern and a net to catch
them. But suppose Edwin were to fall mortally ill, let us say
develop pneumonia, sitting outside half the night. If he died,
then George would become the heir. George has had that
drummed into him since the nursery. So there must not be
any scandal concerning his future wife, that is to say, me.'

Flora gave a little 'tsk!' of annoyance. 'It's not as if Edwin
shows any sign of getting married himself and having a son of
his own. That would free George to stand up for what he
wants. But without that I am afraid George will never fight for
anything if it means going against his parents. If we were to
marry, it would still be the same. I have come to realise that.
I have always had to do what Uncle Jonathan and Aunt Maria
want me to do. And if I were George's wife, I'd have to do
what his family wants. I find that very tiresome. Why do you
think, Mrs Ross, no one ever asks me what *I* want?'

Poor George, I thought, brought up to understand that his
role was to be understudy to his brother. No one ever asked
him what he wanted, either. I wondered why Edwin, the heir,
had not married or even become engaged before his younger
brother. Was Edwin, too, relying on George to free him from
the burden of ensuring the title? One thing, however, did
seem clear. Her future marriage might now be in jeopardy,
but Flora was hardly heartbroken. I might have said she

seemed relieved at the possibility that the engagement was now 'off'.

We had almost made a complete circuit of the little park and were nearing the bench where the two maids had been sitting and chatting. Both had stood up at our approach. Flora signalled them to be seated again and we started out on our second tour. Biddy hesitated, but Bessie started talking at once and forced her to turn her attention away from us. I knew I could depend on Bessie to keep Biddy anchored there on the bench for as long as possible.

'Inspector Ross seemed very certain he would catch the scoundrel who murdered my papa,' said Flora now. 'Do you think he will?'

'He'll do his very best,' I assured her.

'That's what he said to me. But I am afraid that he won't. Poor Papa. I wish I could have spent more time with him.'

A tingle ran along my spine.

'When you were a child, you mean?' I prompted cautiously.

'Oh, yes, then, of course. But I was thinking of recently, after he returned to London. But there was so little time.' She gave a muffled sob and sniffed into a handkerchief. 'Is Biddy looking? I hope not. She reports everything to Aunt Maria.'

I had been so startled at her words that I'd stopped in my tracks I gasped, 'You knew he'd returned to England?'

Flora blushed a deep red and looked far younger than her nineteen years. 'You won't tell, will you?'

I had to be truthful. 'It may be necessary to tell Ben – to tell the inspector. But he's very discreet, Miss Tapley. How did you find out that your father was in London – and when?'

'Oh, only very recently, just a couple of weeks before –

before someone killed him. I knew that Uncle Jonathan had been writing to Papa in France to get his consent to my marriage to George. But the letters were unanswered. Uncle Jonathan then wrote to some solicitors in Harrogate who manage Papa's affairs. They told him he had returned to this country, but they had no address. It threw both Uncle Jonathan and Aunt Maria into a regular panic. But, as Papa had not contacted us, they decided he had probably returned to France.

'But I kept hoping that one day he'd come to see me. Then it happened. I had gone to the circulating library. It is about the only place Aunt Maria let me go alone and now she won't even let me go there. Well, on that day I was in the library when a gentleman came up to me and spoke my name. Just like that, "Flora?" in a questioning way. He wasn't young and he sounded nervous. He looked a little down-at-heel; but one does see a number of elderly gentlemen like that in the library, particularly on cold days. But he knew my name so I turned round and saw it was my father. I knew him at once even though it was such a long time since he left.'

Flora fell silent. 'I was very moved and so was he. He had tears in his eyes and it was all I could do not to throw my arms round his neck. We went outside the library lest anyone notice. He explained he had returned to England because his circumstances in France had altered.'

'In what way?' I asked.

Flora frowned. 'He didn't explain and there was so much we wanted to say to one another, and so little time, that I didn't ask. He said he was so very pleased to see me and so grown. I asked him why he had not come to our house and where he was living. He said he had no wish to meet Uncle

Jonathan just yet. He begged that I would not tell either his cousin or his cousin's wife that he was still here in England. There was something that had to be settled first. I asked if he'd received any of the letters sent to France but he said not. I told him I was to be married. It came as a great shock to him. He asked who the young man was and begged me not to be hasty. We couldn't linger talking longer. We were both afraid of being observed by some busybody who would tell Aunt Maria.'

Flora glanced over her shoulder. 'Is Biddy watching?'

I looked towards the bench. Bessie was talking earnestly and Biddy seemed rapt. What on earth was Bessie telling her? Something lurid about police work, I suspected. At any rate, it was having the desired effect. Biddy had forgotten she was supposed to be keeping an eye on Miss Tapley.

There was another bench nearby, unoccupied, so Flora and I sat down on that.

'That's when I had my brilliant idea,' said Flora with satisfaction. 'Papa didn't want to come to our house. To meet him in public elsewhere would be risky. So I would go to him where he was living.'

'But how could you?' I protested. 'You would be seen!'

'Oh no,' said Flora complacently. 'I thought of a way round that. I have a friend, Emily Waterton. Her brother is away at Eton. He is fifteen, much my height, and slender in build. While he's away at school, some of his clothes remain in a closet in their house. So I went to Emily and told her I was planning a practical joke. I would dress as a young man, persuade Joliffe the coachman to drive me across the river to near where my father told me he lived, and get him to wait for me with the carriage round the corner. Of course, Emily would have to come too; it depended on that. Joliffe probably wouldn't have driven me there if I were alone. But if Emily came along and waited in the coach while I went to see Papa, Joliffe might agree, thinking it some prank. Emily is such a good sport and when we were at school she was always into mischief.

'The next meeting I had with Papa I explained my plan. We met not far from here, near St Mary's church. We didn't risk the library again. He was alarmed at first but I persuaded him it was really very simple. He told me there would be an afternoon that week when his landlady went to one of her meetings. She was a Quaker lady. If I would come and wait in the street, he would look out for me. I was not to ring at the door because the housemaid there was "a sharp little baggage", that's how he described her. She might know, if she looked at me closely, that I wasn't a boy.

'So that is what I did. I didn't stay long. Just long enough to see the rooms where Papa was living. We spoke briefly about my marriage. He said, if I were really certain in my own mind about it, he would write a letter of consent – or go and see Uncle Jonathan and sign any necessary document. But he wanted me to think it over very carefully. "Once you are married, my dear," he said, "I can do nothing for you. Nor can Jonathan. You will be quite in the power of your husband and his family. You say they are a titled family, with a position in society. You will live very comfortably no doubt, moving in a fashionable world with many entertainments and every material thing you could wish. But these alone cannot guarantee you happiness. I would wish, above all, to know you happy. So, please, be very sure in your mind about your love for the young man." What he said impressed me very much. I said I would think carefully and let him know.'

Flora fell silent. 'But I never saw him again. Before I could arrange it, Uncle Jonathan brought us the dreadful news.' She looked towards the bench where the two maids waited. Biddy was now looking our way. The girl got to her feet.

'She's coming to tell me it's time we went home,' said Flora. 'I must go.'

'Miss Tapley,' I said quickly, 'did either your uncle or your aunt discover anything of this escapade? Did they learn your father was living in London?'

'Oh no! Uncle Jonathan knows nothing of my dressing up and having Joliffe drive me in the carriage, with Emily, across the river. But Aunt Maria found out. Joliffe told her, in the end. He was frightened that if it came out, and he'd said nothing, he'd be turned away and with no references to get a new position. Aunt Maria ordered him to keep quiet about it and not tell Uncle Jonathan. She quizzed me dreadfully. I swore it was just a prank played by Emily and me on a girl we'd been at school with. She didn't believe me. She accused me of forming another attachment, not to George, but to someone altogether unsuitable. She insisted on knowing where I had met this person, so I told her, quite truthfully, at the library.'

Flora pulled a face. 'I thought she would faint away with horror. She demanded to know if I were quite out of my wits. She said, "To behave scandalously! When my husband and I have taken such pains to put you in the way of a very suitable match. The young fellow you ran off to see in secret, on the other hand, will have the worst of motives. These bounders hang about in museums, art galleries, public exhibitions, even libraries I don't doubt, on the lookout for unaccompanied young females!"

'She lectured me for nearly an hour. I felt like a damp rag at the end of it all, but I didn't confess the truth. She still doesn't know it was Papa I visited. I kept that and his presence here in London a secret. If Aunt Maria wants to believe I am such a noodle I'd let myself be bamboozled by some rake, met by chance and bent on seduction, well, then let her. It is often much easier to let people think what they want, you know. She warned me Uncle Jonathan must never find out; and I must never risk my reputation so foolishly again, or no truly eligible young man would ever think of marrying me.'

Flora sighed. 'Since then, she has kept me so close to her I might as well be shackled like a convict.'

'Miss Flora?' Biddy was standing before us, giving me mistrustful looks.

'Yes, Biddy,' said Flora briskly, rising to her feet. 'We must get back or Mrs Tapley will be worried. My dear Mrs Ross,' she held out her hand, 'it has been a real pleasure to meet you. Thank you for the kind words and sympathy about my father. To think that you knew him a little and to learn that he was living comfortably in such respectable lodgings is a great comfort. My regards to Inspector Ross.'

She set off with Biddy trotting along behind.

'What do you think, missus?' asked Bessie hoarsely.

'I think,' I told her, 'that Miss Flora Tapley is altogether a remarkable young woman.'

I also hoped she didn't allow herself to be badgered into marrying the spineless George. For this spirited and enter-prising girl it would not be a happy situation. Thomas Tapley had been able to spend little time with his daughter, but he had rendered her great service in making her see that.

I don't know what made me look back as we left the little park. Perhaps I only wantcd to see if Flora had gone into the house. But there, unnoticed by me while I'd been in the park, was a man standing beneath a tree. He was quite still and his check tweed suit blended well into the dappled shade thrown by the branches above his head. I dare say I wouldn't have noticed him if I had not seen him only a little earlier. He wasn't eating an apple this time or doing anything but stand there, watching. As before, he caught my gaze on him and he put a hand to the brim of his felt hat and touched it politely in salutation, inclining a little as he did.

I felt an unwelcome tide of red creep up my neck to my cheeks and turned quickly back. Good heavens, Mrs Ross; I said to myself, trying to laugh away my unease. At this stage of your life, respectably married and turned thirty, you have literally attracted a follower!

But I wasn't amused, not one bit.

We had not long arrived home, Bessie and I, when a loud rat-tat was heard at our front door. For one awful, foolish moment, I thought the wretch in the tweed suit had followed me even to my own home. I listened apprehensively as Bessie went to answer it.

A small commotion resulted during which Bessie could be heard declaring, 'Well, you're not walking over my clean floor tiles in them boots! Take them off and leave 'em there. You ought not to have come to the front door, anyway. You ought to have gone round the back to the kitchen.'

A young man's voice, aggrieved and faintly familiar, retorted, 'I didn't go to the kitchen door because I didn't come to see you, did I? I came to see Mrs Ross. Is she here? 'Cos if she is, why don't you go and tell her.'

'Don't you give me orders!' snapped back Bessie. 'That uniform don't give you the right to come barging into a respectable house with them muddy boots on.'

'Who is it, Bessie?' I called.

More rustling and grumbling from the hall and then the door opened. Bessie appeared first, flushed with determination. Behind her loomed a uniformed figure.

'It's that Constable Biddle,' said Bessie. 'Wanting to see you.'

'Do come in, Constable,' I said, getting up to welcome him. 'Have you brought me a message from my husband?'

Biddle shouldered his way determinedly past Bessie and stood before me in his stockinged feet with his helmet under his arm. 'Yes, ma'am. Inspector Ross has sent a message by the telegraph to the superintendent. He's coming back to London tomorrow morning. He asked if someone could let you know, ma'am. So Mr Dunn said as I should come here and tell you.'

'Thank you,' I said. 'I appreciate your coming so far out of your way. I'm sure Bessie will give you a cup of tea, won't you, Bessie?'

Behind him, Bessie rolled her eyes at me. However, she led him away and a few minutes later the murmur of voices from the kitchen, interspersed with the occasional unexpected giggle from Bessie, led me to understand peace and harmony had been restored.

So Ben wouldn't be home tonight. It was a pity, as I'd so

much to tell him. I could tell Biddle all about it now, and ask him to pass it on. But it was a lot to explain to a young constable like Biddle. I didn't know how garbled the account would be by the time it reached Superintendent Dunn. Besides, the news that I'd been investigating ('interfering' as Dunn would no doubt call it) would much better come from Ben. Dunn already thought I took too much interest in police matters. I could imagine his initial reaction, although he wouldn't be able to deny I'd learned several facts material to the investigation.

Ben would be home tomorrow and I'd be able tell him then. I wouldn't tell him about the fellow in the tweed suit, of course. He would only lecture me on the folly of walking around the streets with no specific purpose and only a sixteen-year-old housemaid as escort. Besides, I wanted to put the man right out of my mind. Nevertheless he was lodged there, a disconcerting image with his dark eyes gleaming and his white teeth biting into the shiny green apple.

More laughter from the kitchen, Biddle joining in with Bessie's squawks of merriment. I hoped I hadn't started something there. It did occur to me with a pang of alarm that she might be telling Biddle of all our adventures that day. But no, Bessie would be discreet. She had her head screwed on the right way.

A further peal of female laughter came from the kitchen. Well, I hoped she had.

Chapter Twelve

Inspector Benjamin Ross

I TOOK the earliest train from Harrogate, was obliged to make only a single change en route, and arrived mid-morning back in London. I should perhaps have gone directly to Scotland Yard to make my report. But I decided to go home first, leave my bag there, and check that all was in order. As things turned out, it was as well that I did. I could not have anticipated all that Lizzie would have to tell me.

'It's a good job you come home, sir,' said Bessie ominously, on opening the door to me.

'Why, what's happened?' I asked in alarm.

'You wouldn't guess at it, that's for sure,' she continued, grabbing my coat. 'Oh, we're all safe and well, don't fear. But we've had such adventures, the missus and me!'

The first sense of relief on hearing all was well was immediately dispersed by the word 'adventures', and replaced with deep alarm.

'Missus!' called Bessie. 'Here's the inspector come home!'

I wondered if Bessie would ever develop into the sort of well-trained maid who led new arrivals to the parlour and announced them with a respectful curtsy. But then Lizzie was running to greet me and I forgot about that.

'Now then,' I said, when I was seated with a cup of tea before my own hearth. 'What is all this about adventures?'

'I told Bessie not to say anything to you before I saw you,' said Lizzie crossly. 'But I suppose she couldn't help it. Tell me first how you got along in Harrogate.'

'I got along very well, thank you. Everyone was very hospitable and I learned one or two interesting things. I need to go as soon as possible to the Yard and report it all, so please, Lizzie, just tell me what you've been doing, Whatever it is or was, if it's got any bearing on this case, I need to know before I see Dunn. I have a horrible feeling that it does have something to do with the case.'

Lizzie folded her hands in her lap, took a deep breath and began. I suppose she expected me to interrupt frequently. But such was my dismay that I listened bereft of speech. This worried her rather more than my jumping up and shouting. I noted a distinct lessening of her confidence as she went on. But Lizzie being Lizzie, she stuck to her guns and reached the end of her account of her visit to Jenkins, and subsequent talk with Flora Tapley. I was aware that at some point Bessie had come into the room and was standing behind Lizzie in a protective attitude, watching me apprehensively.

Silence fell, only broken by the ticking of the mantelpiece clock. It sounded unnaturally loud. Perhaps I was just stunned. I heard myself speak – or croak.

'You had better come with me to the Yard, my dear. You can tell it all again to Superintendent Dunn yourself. He will have questions to put to you and you will have to write out a statement.'

'Oh, I've done that already,' said my wife, cheering up. 'I wrote it all down last night.' She got up and fetched a small wad of densely written papers which she handed to me. When I took her account and glanced through it in silence, she asked, 'Is it official enough?'

'If it's complete and accurate and you've signed and dated it, as I see you have, it is official enough. You do realise, don't you, that this –' I brandished the wad of paper – 'that your actions might spell the end of my career?'

'I realise Mr Dunn will be angry with me,' returned my wife. 'But he's an intelligent man and he won't be able to dismiss the importance of what I found out, will he?'

I rubbed a hand over my face and rose in silence. Truth to tell I was afraid to begin any speech for fear of not being able to stop. I went back to the hall and retrieved my coat from the hook where Bessie had left it. Behind me, I heard Bessie say, 'He took it very well, didn't he, missus?'

I cannot, unfortunately, relate that Superintendent Dunn took it very well at all. His short spiky hair bristled more than usual. His complexion turned puce. Beads of sweat formed on his brow. He seemed to experience some difficulty in breathing. I was wondering whether to summon help or, at the very least, a glass of water, when he found speech.

'I am dismayed, Mrs Ross. I fully understand you have a way of . . .' He struggled to express himself politely. 'You have a way of taking a lively interest in criminal cases and making comments. Some of your comments have, in the past, been very apt. I don't deny it. But this . . .' Dunn's quivering forefinger tapped Lizzie's statement. 'This goes far beyond any reasonable action. When you first came into the possession of the visiting card belonging to this so-called private enquiry agent . . .' Here Dunn's already florid complexion darkened to a dangerous hue of deep red. 'Whatever such a person may be, you should have reported it and given the card to an appropriate official. That is to your husband or, in his absence, to someone here at the Yard. To me.'

'But I didn't know who Jenkins was,' Lizzie explained. 'I didn't know then he was the clown.'

Dunn hunched his shoulders and leaned forward. 'Yes, this business of the clown . . .'

Here I thought I should interrupt in Lizzie's defence. 'My wife did report to me the presence of the clown by the bridge, sir.'

'And she told you the clown appeared to be following Tapley?' he snapped, transferring his attention to me.

'Yes, sir, but at the time, I thought that was unlikely. I am sorry to report I dismissed her suspicions.'

'It was because he knew I have a fear of clowns. I always find them sinister,' confessed Lizzie, despite my warning glance.

'Just as a matter of interest,' said Dunn to her with dangerous calm, 'is there anything else you have not thought fit to tell us? Any little thing at all, mm?'

'No, I don't think so, I think you know all of it,' said Lizzie, but I fancied she hesitated, just fractionally.

Dunn sighed. 'We shall have to discuss your behaviour later, Mrs Ross, in greater detail. You have interfered with an official investigation and that, as I am sure you realise, is a serious matter. Whether you have actively hindered the police, or not, is yet to be established. If it turns out that you have done so, you will find yourself in a great deal of trouble. However . . .' He raised his hand to forestall protest from either of us. 'The investigation itself has primary importance and someone must interview this fellow Jenkins at once. You had better get over to Camden and do it, Ross.'

'Yes, sir.'

'And I had better go along, too,' said Lizzie disastrously.

Dunn's hand crashed down on his desk with such force that all the papers on it jumped and a pen rolled off it on to the floor. 'No, Mrs Ross! You had *not*!'

'Because of the speaking French,' explained Lizzie, undeterred. 'Ben doesn't. You don't, do you, Ben?'

'Speak French? No,' I admitted.

'This fellow Jenkins is French?' Dunn demanded incredulously.

Lizzie shook her head. 'No, Mr Dunn. But he said his client was a French lady and he offered his own services as interpreter if needed. But you couldn't trust any translation done by Jenkins, could you?' Lizzie paused for comment but Dunn only stared at her, eyes bulging. 'What I am thinking,' my wife carried on hurriedly, 'is that if Jenkins has his client close at hand somewhere, and were to produce her when we – when Ben goes to see him, then it would be best if Ben – the police have the services of a *reliable* interpreter.'

'Speak *good* French, do you?' Dunn asked her brusquely.

'Yes, quite good,' was Lizzie's confident reply. 'I had a French governess when I was a child.'

This reply served to impress the superintendent. His confidence, I was pleased to see, was visibly shaken. Of course, he didn't know what I knew, because Lizzie had told me, that the French governess in question had been a woman of rather questionable background who had eventually been dismissed for drinking herself insensible on Dr Martin's brandy.

'Then go with your husband. Ross!' Dunn's bloodshot gaze turned to me. 'I want a full account. If Jenkins does produce his client and she makes any sort of statement, in French or in English, make sure she signs it. If you can bring her here, it would perhaps be even better.'

'Yes, sir. We'll go to Camden immediately. We'll take a cab.'

'It will come out of your expenses allowance,' said Dunn sourly. When Lizzie had left his office and I was about to follow her, he added: 'You have not heard the last of this, Ross. I have spoken to you before about controlling your wife.'

'I am afraid I don't – can't – control my wife, sir, not in the way you mean. But I shall make sure she understands the foolhardiness of her actions.'

'Will you, indeed?' said Dunn unpleasantly.

I thought Lizzie and I had come out of that encounter rather well, all things considered. It would not have surprised me if I'd found myself suspended. If our visit to Horatio Jenkins produced some important new evidence, it would be even better. Dunn would still grumble about her actions during my absence, but his sting would have been drawn. I felt quite optimistic as we made our way to Camden.

A fine rain drizzled down by the time we arrived. We stood for shelter under the awning of a dress shop across the road from the greengrocer's above which Jenkins had his so-called detective agency.

'It doesn't look very impressive,' I said, studying the uncurtained first-floor windows.

'It isn't,' said Lizzie. 'Nor is Mr Jenkins himself very impressive to look at. But you have to admit he does seem to know his business. He found Thomas Tapley for his client.'

'I'll give him credit for that. But I can't say I like the idea of this fellow running round investigating his fellow citizens' private affairs because someone has paid him to do so. Especially as the person who hired him is so shy about speaking to anyone in authority.'

We remained there for a further three or four minutes and during that time no one approached the street door to the staircase, or left by it. There was no sign of movement at the windows of Jenkins's office, nor was any gas lit inside although the afternoon light was now poor on account of the rain. The first-floor room looked quite deserted. The floor above that, where the milliner had her workroom, did show a lighted lamp at one window. Her work involved fine stitching. Inside the greengrocer's shop a glow announced gaslight.

'This was once a private house,' I mused aloud. 'The shop and its entrance have been carved out of the ground-floor rooms. I dare say the proprietor and his family live at the back. That street door once gave access to the whole house. Now, if what you told me is correct, it only lets visitors on to the staircase and the rooms for letting, above. They have been sealed off from the shop and proprietor's dwelling by some more recent brickwork and plaster.'

Lizzie understood that I was not just speculating idly. 'You wonder if Jenkins has another way out, other than on to the street. So he could escape if he saw us coming and decided he didn't want to meet us. I don't think he does. He could perhaps run up to Miss Poole's workroom and hide there. They sound to be on very good terms.' She frowned. 'He might be able to get into an attic or out on to the roof, from the top floor.'

'At the moment he shows no sign of being at home. But I agree that he will have thought out some strategy for emergency use. I doubt he's cultivated the goodwill of Miss Poole just for cups of tea. Come on, Lizzie, let's knock on this private detective's door.'

I set off briskly across the street with Lizzie darting past me in her eagerness and reaching the door first.

'One moment, Lizzie.' I put a hand on her arm. 'Just wait here while I ask something of the shopkeeper.'

Mr Weisz was selling onions to a customer and I waited until the woman had made her purchase and left the shop. Weisz then turned to me and looked me over carefully, head to toe. I took out my warrant card but before I could show it, he was ahead of me.

'You will be from the police?' His accent was faint but noticeable all the same.

I reflected that even those who had not been all their lives in this country knew an officer of the law in plain clothes as soon as he hove into view. There must be something about us.

'I have no trouble with the police,' Weisz was continuing. 'I am a respectable citizen. I work hard. My wife works hard. My younger children help. My eldest son is a clerk in a counting house. My daughter sews on buttons, piecework. We don't want any trouble.'

'I am not here seeking to make any trouble for you,' I

assured him. 'I only want to ask about the tenant on the first floor, Mr Horatio Jenkins.'

A look of derision passed over the greengrocer's face. He leaned forward slightly and hissed, 'He is a spy!'

'A spy?' I asked, startled.

'Yes, yes, a spy, an informer. He runs to the authorities with gossip. In the country where I was born and spent my boyhood, such people were everywhere and everyone knew them.'

'Mr Jenkins claims to be a private detective,' I pointed out.

'Hah!' exclaimed Weisz. 'What is that but a spy?'

'Have you seen him today?' I asked, cutting short the discussion of the nature of Jenkins's activities.

'No. There is a separate entrance. I don't see him come or go, only if I am standing outside.'

'And you haven't been standing outside today?'

'It is raining,' said Weisz simply. 'Also today we sort the potatoes. We buy at market in big sacks and we put them in smaller ones, or put them loose in that tray. They must be inspected, each one. One bad potato will make bad every other potato it touches. If you go into the backyard, you will see my wife and children bagging potatoes, also carrots.'

'In the rain?'

'They can take the work into a shed.'

I persevered with one last question. 'Perhaps, recently, while you have been standing outside in better weather, you may have seen a lady arrive to visit Mr Jenkins.'

He shook his head. 'No. I am busy man. Also there are many thieves. If I stand outside, it is to watch my fruit and vegetables. Small boys will steal an apple. Old ladies, too. You will not believe what old ladies steal. They conceal it in their shawls.'

He treated me to an aggrieved scowl. 'Where are police then?'

'We have other matters than apples to worry about, Mr Weisz, but if you speak to the regular constable on this beat, he will keep a lookout. Thank you for your time.'

I rejoined Lizzie who was waiting for me impatiently. 'How did you get on?' she asked.

'Not at all. Mr Weisz neither sees nor hears anything that is not his business. I fancy he hails from a country where it is unwise to behave otherwise. Let's go up and find Jenkins.'

We proceeded up the unswept stairs and arrived before Jenkins's door. It was not quite shut fast. A prickle of apprehension ran up my spine.

'Lizzie,' I said. 'Perhaps you had better wait downstairs. Weisz will let you shelter in his shop out of the rain.'

But Lizzie had already noticed the door. She leaned past me and gave it a push. It swung open.

I was, in my mind, already half prepared for what we'd see. Lizzie was not. She gasped and when I turned to her, she had a hand clasped to her mouth.

'Go downstairs!' I said sharply. This was not the moment to deal with a distressed female.

I should have known my wife better. She took the hand from her mouth and snapped, 'Certainly not!'

'Oh, well, stay then, but here!' I pointed at the floor. 'Don't come further inside.'

Jenkins had had earlier visitors. The small room was in complete disarray. The wicker hamper in one corner had been tipped over and fantastical garb of all kinds – Jenkins's disguises – lay strewn across the floor. The stained velvet curtain that had been drawn across the opposite corner had been wrenched from its hooks and also lay on the ground. The couch it had shielded had been dragged out, stripped of its bedding and slashed open. Shiny black horsehair filling spilled out. Even the pillow had been slashed in the same way and a dusting of feathers, like snow, lay over everything. Every drawer in the desk had been pulled out, the contents thrown around.

The body of the private detective lay behind the desk, huddled on the bare boards. I stooped over him. His face and, as far as I could tell, his skull were unmarked. He had not been bludgeoned, as had Tapley. A large damp patch on his waistcoat, staining my fingers crimson when I touched it, told me he'd been stabbed. He had been in confrontation with his visitor, I reasoned, and the assailant had been close enough to make one deadly thrust up between the ribs. This was a knifeman who knew his business. The victim had not been dead very long.

I didn't doubt we were looking for the same killer as had slain Tapley. But he'd changed his method. Why? Because he'd needed to talk to Jenkins and he wouldn't have had much conversation with a bludgeoned man. He had wanted something from Jenkins. Not information, something tangible. Jenkins hadn't given it to him and so the killer had ransacked the room, looking for it. Something small, therefore, something easily concealed. Had he found it?

Lizzie, predictably, had ignored my last instruction and stood a few feet away.

'As you're here,' I said to her, 'can you confirm for me that this is the man who introduced himself to you as Horatio Jenkins?'

'Yes, poor man,' she said, looking down at the sprawled form. 'I didn't like him but he looks so pathetic lying there.'

'Listen to me, Lizzie,' I said. 'And please, don't argue. This is now an investigation into a murder. Take a cab if you can find one and go to Scotland Yard and report what has happened here. Oh, before you do that, please ask Weisz to send one of his children to find the local constable on his beat, and bring him here. I must stay here, make sure nothing here is disturbed—'

A shrill shriek made my eardrums ring. We both spun round to see a woman standing in the doorway. She was a dowdy little soul, wearing spectacles and a pinafore with a large pocket. She backed away from us into the stairwell, and screamed, 'Murder! Horrible murder! What have you done? You've gone and killed poor Mr Jenkins! Oh, help, help! Police!'

I started towards her but she had turned and, with the speed of terror, had darted down the stairs and out into the street where she was already screeching, 'Murder!'

Weisz burst out of his shop and, seeing me emerge from the door into the street, demanded, 'What's amiss?'

'Jenkins is dead,' I told him, since this was obvious. 'Please send one of your children for the local constable and take this lady into your shop and give her some tea or something. Do you know her?'

'I know her. It is Ruby Poole. She makes hats. I send Jacob for the constable. He is an intelligent boy, and quick. Come, come, Miss Poole . . .'

She had begun to sob uncontrollably and allowed Weisz to take her elbow and lead her into the shop.

I went back upstairs. 'You need only go directly to the Yard, Lizzie. Weisz is sending a child for the constable.'

Lizzie nodded. 'I'll be back soon.'

I opened my mouth to say she had no need to return with the officers from the Yard, but she would do so, anyway. Besides, she was, after all, a witness. I returned upstairs and closed the door to the detective agency. I remembered that a taxidermist also had his workshop on this floor. Accordingly, I moved along to the next door and rapped on it. No one answered. I tried the handle and the door opened easily. I stepped inside.

At once I found myself in an extraordinary place beyond my imagination. The first thing to strike me was the smell. The air had a strange musty quality, with a hint of chemicals, and a lingering odour of meat. Death itself was everywhere, but in the form of a curious limbo in which creatures which had ceased to live and breathe still existed, in a halfway house between this life and total extinction. The room was inhabited by a menagerie of dead animals. They hung from the ceiling; they peered at me through the glass walls of boxes within which they had been tastefully mounted in naturalistic settings. They poked their snouts out from under the table and chairs, shelves, open cupboards. A window in this room gave on to the rear of the premises, and before it was a large porcelain sink and draining board. I made a cautious way towards it, conscious of so many glass eyes watching my progress, and looked down. A small dead dog of the miniature sort ladies like to carry round concealed in a muff lay in it, still entire but presumably a candidate for taxidermy.

Looking through the window I had a view of the back garden, if that was the word for it. I saw a patch of trampled mud, a washing line from which flapped the Weisz family linen; a brick-built privy and a shed. There was also a door in the back wall so an alley must run behind. Directly below, as I looked down, I could see a rough deal table, a couple of benches, some sacks of vegetables and signs of the work that had now been abandoned by Mrs Weisz and her children when the rain began.

There was a faint scuffling sound. I felt a moment's unreasoning panic that one of the glassy eyed creatures behind me might have returned to life and was reaching out its stiff paws or had spread its wings and was about to swoop down. I spun round and just glimpsed, from the corner of my eye, a movement behind a display cabinet.

'Come out!' I ordered.

With a moan a small man, wearing an apron and a skullcap crammed over straggling grey hair, emerged and sidled a few inches towards me. He looked as terrified as Miss Poole had done.

'Don't be afraid,' I reassured him. 'I am a police officer. Are you Mr Baggins?' I produced my warrant card.

'Yes,' he whispered, 'I'm Baggins, Sebastian Baggins, sir . . .'

'There has been an incident concerning your neighbour, Mr Jenkins.'

'I heard Ruby Poole screeching,' he confessed. 'She shouted it was murder. Is it murder? I hid.' He blinked at me pathetically. 'When you knocked at my door, I thought you were the murderer, come to find another victim.'

A polite murderer who knocked at doors, I thought. 'No, Mr Baggins, you are quite safe. The assailant has fled.'

He straightened up and heaved a deep sigh of relief. Then, with a twitch of fear, asked, 'He ain't coming back?'

'No, I doubt that very much, Mr Baggins.'

The murderer had either found what he sought in Jenkins's room, or he hadn't. Either way he wouldn't return. 'How thick are the walls here?' I gestured at the room.

'Reasonable,' said Baggins cautiously. 'You don't hear no conversation. That suits me just fine. You've got to concentrate on taxidermy. You can't go being distracted. The animal has to look lifelike. You can't have one cross eyed or with a hump in its back. I take pride in my creations. Why, that owl over there, you'd swear it was about to swoop down on you. When I'm working, I generally don't hear anything, not if you was in this room and spoke to me.'

I had been trying to ignore the owl in question. It had a decidedly unpleasant gaze fixed on me. I could see where this was leading. Mr Baggins, like Mr Weisz, would have seen and heard nothing. But I persevered.

'Did you know Jenkins had a visitor or visitors this morning?'

He hesitated fractionally. 'No, I would have to be out on the stairs to see that. I've been in here.'

'Did you hear anything?' I repeated. 'Don't deny it if you did, Mr Baggins. That would be withholding important information.'

His face crumpled in misery. 'Someone came, about two hours ago. I can't be exact. I didn't see him. But Mr Jenkins must have opened the door to him and I heard him – Mr

Jenkins – say, "What do you want?" I didn't hear any reply. They must have gone into the room. I didn't hear anything more.'

'You didn't hear voices raised in argument?'

'No,' said Mr Baggins firmly.

'You didn't hear furniture being moved? You didn't hear, say, a crash?'

'There was a bit of a bump at one point,' he admitted, 'but nothing to make me worry. It was about there.' He pointed at the wall between his room and the next one. He had indicated the spot where, on the other side, the wicker basket of disguises had stood. That would have been when the killer upended it in his search, I thought.

'Nothing more?'

'Nothing, sir. I didn't hear anyone leave. The first I heard was Ruby Poole screaming fit to bust.'

'Who is in the remaining room on this floor?'

He looked puzzled then said, 'Oh, you mean the little room next to this. That's my living room, sir, and my bedroom, too.'

'I should like to see it.'

Baggins pattered ahead of me to the remaining door on the landing, unlocking it after searching through a collection of keys on a ring. There were keys large and small, from sturdy house keys to modest cabinet ones, even tiny ones such as might have opened a tea caddy. I wondered why he needed so many, when he only had two rooms. He would need one for the street door, but that totalled no more than three. I asked him.

'Keys is handy,' he said vaguely. 'I never throw away a key.'

He opened the door. The room was much smaller, what is sometimes called a boxroom. Somehow, leaving hardly any space to move between them, a narrow bedstead, a table and a single chair had been crammed in. A kettle stood on a trivet before an unlit hearth. The view from the window was of the same patch of rear garden. I asked if he knew what was in the shed.

'Vegetables,' he said, confirming what Weisz had told me. 'A store for the greengrocery, downstairs.'

Prompted by the sight of the brick privy, I asked how he managed for necessary sanitation. Tenants all shared the privy in the garden below, I was told. Those upstairs such as himself and Jenkins and the milliner all had to go down to the street, round the corner and into the yard from a back alley through the door I'd observed.

'And above here?' I pointed upwards. 'Apart from Miss Poole the milliner, who else lives up there?'

'No one,' he shook his head. 'The back two rooms are unlet at the moment.'

'Who owns the building?'

'He does.' Baggins pointed downwards.

'Weisz, the greengrocer?' I was surprised.

'That's him. He's got a business head, he has. He wouldn't give you a bruised apple for free.'

I thanked him and warned him not to gossip, and that a constable would come eventually to take down his statement.

'I've got nothing to state!' he protested.

'You repeat what you told me, that you heard someone admitted to Jenkins's agency about two hours ago. You heard Jenkins ask the visitor what he wanted. You later heard a muffled noise, a bump, and you indicate the spot you showed me. You see? You know more than you think you do.'

This did not appear to cheer Mr Baggins at all. He trailed gloomily back to his glassy eyed companions.

A clump of footsteps on the stairs heralded the constable brought by the child. After a brief conversation I left him guarding the scene of the crime and went back to the shop.

Someone had put up a 'closed' sign, but when I tapped on the glass, Weisz emerged from the back room and led me there. The family was gathered around Miss Poole who was still sniffing noisily into a handkerchief. Mrs Weisz ushered her brood, all with eyes shining with curiosity and excitement, into a little room next door. She then went to stand by her husband facing me. Both looked despondent and wary. I felt sorry for them. They had worked hard in their adopted country, even becoming owners of property. Now they were involved with the police in a serious inquiry. Their experience was that, however innocent, it was not a good situation to be in.

'I'm sorry for the inconvenience this is causing you,' I said to Mrs Weisz, hoping to reassure her.

She murmured, 'Thank you, sir.'

I turned to Miss Poole. 'If you feel able, Miss Poole, perhaps you would return upstairs with me.'

'I can't go into his room!' wailed Miss Poole.

'No, no, you don't need to do that. But I'd like to talk to you in private.'

I also needed to take a look into her room. She got up and I followed her out of the shop into the street and up the staircase. We squeezed past the constable on guard, Miss Poole giving him a fearful look, and arrived on the top floor. Before going into her room I glanced up at the ceiling of the top landing. It had a small hatch in it. There was an attic, but the hatch showed no sign of having been disturbed, nor was there any way a person could reach it without a ladder.

The milliner's room was more comfortable than Jenkins's, but gave an impression of hard-working poverty. There was a threadbare carpet on the floor. The tools of her trade, in the form of a motley collection of scraps of fabric, ribbons, false flowers, cotton reels and so on, lay spread across a worktable. The oil lamp also burned there, giving the glow we had noticed from the street. On a low cupboard, in pride of place, stood a silver-plated container with a tap, fixed above a spirit stove. Having seen similar things before in immigrant homes, I recognised it as a samovar. I wondered from where Miss Poole had it. Perhaps she had bought it from a street stall or taken it in payment of a debt. A teapot stood beside it and, on a shelf above, a collection of cups.

As in Jenkins's room, a corner was curtained for privacy. Miss Poole slept up here.

I invited her to sit down and she did so, folding her hands in her lap. She answered my questions in a docile manner, giving no sign of concealing anything. From time to time she removed her spectacles to mop at her eyes.

She had known Mr Jenkins since he had moved in below this room. That was nearly a year ago. Yes, there was an arrangement that he would rap on his ceiling – her floor – when he wanted tea for a client. Otherwise she had no way of knowing who called on him. She might notice someone come to the street door, from her window, but she had to concentrate on her work. She didn't have time to sit staring down into the street. She had not seen anyone that day. Jenkins had been a good neighbour, very kind and helpful. How helpful? Well, he had put up a shelf for her, that one over there with the cups on it. He had carried up water in a bucket, from the pump in the yard. She could get water from Mr Baggins, who had a sink and a tap, but she didn't like to disturb Mr Baggins too much. Truth to tell, his room full of dead creatures gave her the creeps. The taxidermist himself also made her uneasy. What can you make of a man who spent his entire life messing around the dead things, skinning them, curing the skins and mounting them on frames? He sold the skinned carcasses to the dog meat trade, or so he said. It was her opinion that cat carcasses were trimmed and secretly sold to unscrupulous butchers, who in turn sold them as rabbit to unsuspecting purchasers. It was all horrid, in Miss Poole's view. She, personally, did not work with fur for her millinery, although Mr Baggins had once offered to cure a skin for her. But she left that to the professional furriers. It had been nice to have Mr Jenkins live below because he had been a professional gentleman. His had been clean work.

Some might have questioned that.

I asked her what had brought her downstairs when Lizzie and I were there. With much blushing and hesitation she whispered that she had been on to her way to the privy in the backyard. She then began to weep again.

My ear caught movement below; the officers from the Yard had arrived. I thanked her and left the poor soul to her grief.

Chapter Thirteen

Elizabeth Martin Ross

ON ARRIVING at the Yard with my news and message from Ben, I had been subjected to a brief but pithy lecture from Superintendent Dunn.

'You see, Mrs Ross? This could well be the result of your keeping information to yourself; information you should have brought immediately here. Someone would have been sent to interview Jenkins yesterday. If he'd had anything to tell, we'd have learned it. He might have led us to his client. He might be alive now. I am not blaming you for the actions of a murderer. But it might all have been different!'

'If' is a wonderful word, my father used to say. I did not repeat this to Dunn. I managed to listen in silence to his homily and nod.

'And now,' he announced, 'you will stay away from further investigation into this matter. Leave it to the professionals.'

Considering the professionals would not have known about Jenkins, his clown disguise, his being hired by a French lady to find Tapley and all the rest of it I was tempted to point out that my contribution had been very valuable. But this would not have been well received. I had to admit to myself, if not to him, the superintendent did have a point. Delay might have cost poor Jenkins his life.

'But I have to return to Camden,' I said, 'with Sergeant Morris.'

Dunn's eyes bulged.

'There is a lady witness, a Miss Poole,' I went on hurriedly. 'She is very distressed, on the verge of fainting away. Of course the police will take a statement from her. But if I sat with her she would be reassured by a woman's presence . . . and she might talk more freely to me.'

I thought Dunn would burst out angrily, denying me permission to approach a witness. But I was underestimating him. After surveying me thoughtfully for a moment, he folded his hands on his desk and leaned towards me.

'You are a shrewd woman, Mrs Ross. I do not approve of your interference in police matters or condone it in any way. I have been quite clear about this; and I don't want you to imagine I can be ignored. However, I confess I sometimes wish some of my officers had half your quick mind. I will agree to your return to Camden with Morris, and to your sitting with Miss Poole and comforting her. You will not talk to any other witness. You will not quiz her. You will not put any leading questions to her. You will not put ideas into her head. But should she, of her own free will and unprompted, confide in you about anything at all, no matter how trivial, you will tell either your husband or another officer *at once*.'

'Of course, Superintendent!' I promised.

★ ★ ★

Ben was surprised to see me back again and not pleased. 'There is nothing you can do here, Lizzie! I have spoken to Miss Poole. She has nothing of interest to say.'

'Superintendent Dunn thinks it a good idea.'

This silenced Ben completely for a full thirty seconds. 'I don't know,' he said eventually, 'how you managed to twist Dunn round your finger. But whatever trick Dunn has up his sleeve, or whatever permission he has given you, this remains my investigation. He has put me in charge of running it and in that capacity I – not Dunn – agree to your speaking to Miss Poole. Go ahead and comfort her. But I want a complete report back to me detailing every time she mops her eyes or blows her nose.'

'You shall have it,' I promised.

Miss Poole seemed unsurprised to see me and raised no objection to my making tea for us both. She watched me inspect the samovar and light its little spirit stove.

'It was a gift . . .' she said almost inaudibly.

'The samovar? It's very pretty.'

'It came from my former employer, with whom I trained in millinery. She was obliged to retire when her sight failed. I started up on my own here. She wished me well and gave me the tea urn. Yes, she called it a samovar. She had brought it with her when she left her original home, in Russia, I think.' Miss Poole's voice has gained in volume and confidence as she spoke of this domestic object. 'She always put a lump of sugar in the teapot with the tea leaves and poured the hot water over it. She never drank milk with her tea in the English fashion. She sometimes took a slice of lemon. I'm afraid I have neither . . .' Her voice faltered and she began to sound distressed. 'I was not expecting to entertain . . .'

I brought the teacup to her. 'Dear Miss Poole, don't worry about that. I seldom take milk with my tea. I prefer it without.'

She took off her spectacles and blinked at me myopically. I thought sympathetically that so much close work, often in poor light, had affected her eyesight as it had affected her former employer's. If Miss Poole were obliged to retire, what would she do? Had she managed to save a little money? How long would it last, if she had? Had she family to whom she could turn? I put her age at about forty-five or -six.

I couldn't but think, as I looked around me, how easily I might be living in a room like this, above a shop, doing whatever I could to earn a living. Aunt Parry, with all her faults, had rescued me from that.

'My husband tells me that Mr Jenkins would carry water up here for you.'

'Oh, yes, he was always so helpful. That is why I was always happy to make tea for his visitors.'

'Did you carry the tea down to his office?'

'Yes, but I never went in. I just knocked at his door and he would come and take the tray from me. I didn't meet his visitors. He explained to me that his work was very private. Often his clients, as he called them, were very shy.'

They probably often had good reason, I thought. 'You didn't see the French lady who called to see him?'

She hesitated. 'He seldom had lady visitors. I cannot imagine a lady wanting to consult a private detective! There was an occasion when a lady and a gentleman came together to see him. It was a few weeks ago. I only saw them from the doorway, you understand, when I took the tray down. So I didn't see their faces. They appeared well dressed.' Miss Poole's voice gained a professional enthusiasm. 'The lady's hat took my eye. Her hair was a deep chestnut red and quite elaborately dressed. Atop it sat a small round hat, with a lace edging at the brim and lavender silk rosebuds applied all round it. The top was decorated with dark green silk ruffles. A pair of lavender satin ribbons kept it in place, passing behind her ears and tied in a bow at the nape of her neck in a most becoming way. I should like to have seen the hat from the front, but she didn't turn her head. I thought it a very fashionable item and very much a spring design, just as you might see in a ladies' magazine. It would not have done in winter. Rain would have ruined it.'

'Silk rosebuds and ruffles? Yes, bad weather would have destroyed it. You didn't hear either the man or the woman speak?'

Miss Poole had not. 'I thought I might copy the hat, for example as a wedding item if a customer wanted such a thing. Not with lavender rosebuds, of course, unless the wearer were in half-mourning. Pink, perhaps.'

She fell silent and I guessed, from the way the animation drained from her features, that the memory of the hat had been replaced by a sadder memory. 'His room was in such disorder earlier, when I came upon you and your husband there. Did you do that?'

'Turn it all out? No, his killer almost certainly did.'

'But why?' She turned her gaze back to me, blinking back fresh tears. 'Wasn't it enough to kill him? Why do such an awful deed, anyway?'

I picked my words carefully, mindful of Superintendent Dunn's warning that I should not put ideas into her head. 'The two things were probably connected.'

'He disturbed a burglar, you mean?'

'Not an ordinary burglar, perhaps. Rather someone who was looking for something particular, something the murderer believed Jenkins had hidden.'

'Oh . . .' said Miss Poole thoughtfully.

I should never get anywhere if I followed Dunn's instructions to the letter. 'Miss Poole . . .' I put my hand on her arm. 'Did Mr Jenkins ever ask you to keep some small item of his up here in your room? To hide it for him, I mean. He knew you were a friend.'

I knew at once I had hit the mark. She turned a furious shade of red. 'Well, I . . . I suppose now that he is dead, I should give it to the police.'

'Indeed you should,' I urged her, 'anything at all. I could accompany you downstairs now and you could hand over the item to my husband.'

'Yes, yes, what a good thing you are here, Mrs Ross. I should be so nervous of going downstairs to the police alone. I'll fetch it.'

She rose and went behind the curtain hung across her sleeping area. After a moment she returned holding an envelope. 'This is it. It's nothing much. He asked if I wouldn't mind just keeping it for a little, lest he lose it.'

I longed to rip open the envelope and see what it contained, but I must let Ben do that. I hurried Miss Poole back downstairs where she handed over the envelope to Ben, with trembling hand.

Ben opened it at once and took out a piece of card. I could see that it was a photograph, but annoyingly I couldn't make out the subject.

'Thank you, Miss Poole,' said Ben to her. He pushed the photograph back in the envelope and put it in his pocket.

I could have screamed in frustration. Miss Poole was looking mournfully round the room, avoiding the spot where the body lay, concealed from view now by the velvet curtain that had been torn down from the sleeping alcove.

'I shall not easily come to terms with this,' she said. 'The memory of it will haunt me. I – I shall miss his friendship. Sometimes, when he had nothing else to do, he would come up to my workshop and just sit, drinking tea and chatting to me. He told me of his adventures in America. I always liked to hear about those. It seemed so cosy, sitting there with him. I did allow myself to wonder if . . .'

She did not go on. The tragedy was complete. Miss Poole had had hopes of Mr Jenkins.

Inspector Benjamin Ross

Lizzie conducted Miss Poole back to her workroom but, as I expected, she was down again almost at once.

'What is it?' she demanded eagerly as I opened the envelope again.

'It is a photograph,' I replied.

'Yes, yes, I can see that! But of whom?' She answered her own question at once. 'It is the photograph the French lady gave Jenkins, so that he would recognise Mr Tapley.'

'It might be . . . all right! Yes, it is. But don't speak of that to anyone.' I pocketed the photograph.

Lizzie was looking around the ransacked room. 'Clearly she wanted it back. Why did she not take it back when she paid Jenkins? That would have been the obvious time. She gave him his money. He should have returned the photograph.'

'But he didn't,' I said. 'Jenkins was a cautious person. He knew the sitter in this picture,' I tapped my pocket. 'The sitter was a man he had himself tracked down, a man who had just been murdered. This photograph was the equivalent of Jenkins's penny insurance. It is proof she had been in touch with him about Tapley. I don't know what excuse he gave her for not returning it. Perhaps he just said he had lost it. She would have been angry, but there would not have been much she could do.'

'You think this a woman's crime?' Lizzie was horrified.

'Oh, no, she had help. I don't believe a woman crept into Mrs Jameson's house and bludgeoned Tapley. Such a brutal attack is the work of a man. Nor do I see a woman knifing Jenkins. Whoever killed Jenkins had used a knife before. We are looking for someone you might call a professional.'

'She hired a killer?' Lizzie goggled at me.

'I'm not saying that. Rather that she had a male accomplice.' I could see Morris giving me an old-fashioned look. He thought I should not be chatting so easily to my wife about the case. But Lizzie, too, was looking unhappy.

She glanced at Morris who took the hint and removed himself to the staircase out of earshot.

'Ben,' said my wife, 'I have been stupidly vain, really, quite intolerably so.'

'I find this hard to imagine,' I said encouragingly. There *was* something else, and she had not told me. From vanity? Surely Lizzie would not have been swayed by such a silly thing. But she had turned a furious pink.

'There was a man . . .' She recounted her observation of the man in a tweed suit of knickerbockers (I had heard about such an outfit all too recently, too). 'He was watching this building when I arrived, wasn't he? Picking over the fruit and spinning out the time. He wanted to see if Jenkins had a visitor and when Bessie and I came, he was rewarded. He probably crept upstairs to make sure we had called on Jenkins, or perhaps he saw us through the window. At any rate, he followed us afterwards. I should have realised.'

That is our man, I thought with a mix of triumph and frustration. That was Hector Guillaume, for want of any other name. Where the devil is he now?

'Did Miss Poole have anything else of interest to say?' I asked.

Lizzie stopped looking disconsolate and gave me a rapid account of her conversation in the workroom, like the precise witness she normally was.

'Thank you,' I told her. 'That's very helpful. You really must go home now. Take a cab. Ask the local constable downstairs to go with you to make sure you find one.'

'To make sure I go home, you mean!' said my wife crossly. 'Don't worry, I shall do that. What will you do with that photograph?'

'It will form part of the evidence.' I sounded very policeman-like. My wife gave me a look that spoke volumes, but she did march out, head high.

'Sergeant,' I called out to Morris. 'I shall leave you in charge here now. I am going straight away back to the Yard to see Superintendent Dunn.'

'Very well, sir,' said Morris stolidly. 'The police surgeon will likely be here shortly. Not that he'll be able to tell us much more than we can see for ourselves.'

I looked for Lizzie in the street outside but there was no sign of her. However, the constable I'd ordered to go with her was plodding towards me.

'I put Mrs Ross in a cab, sir,' he announced. 'It was a growler not a hansom, all decent. I did hesitate to put your wife in it at first on account of the look of the cabbie. He was a big old fellow with a squashed nose, touch of the prizefighter about him. But he seemed to know Mrs Ross and she him, so I thought it all right. She hopped up into the cab quite happy.'

That could only mean her old acquaintance, Wally Slater. It was a bit of luck. He would make sure Lizzie got home. That is, if she didn't persuade him to drive her off somewhere on another detecting foray.

'Thank you,' I told the constable. 'I'm glad you found a growler. I think I know the cabbie.'

I next hastened to make my own way back to the Yard. As I entered, the sergeant on the desk hailed me at once. 'Mr Dunn is asking for you, sir. He said for you to go straight up to his office when you got here.'

Was this about Lizzie? I braced myself for another lecture and hurried up to Dunn's office. I tapped on his door and opened it, to be stopped in my tracks frozen in the doorway, very likely with my mouth open.

Dunn was not alone. A woman was sitting in a chair by his desk. She turned her head to look at me. She was a fine-looking female, not young perhaps, but with remnants of former beauty still in her face. She was smartly dressed. I have learned, since being married, that women expect a fellow to notice what they are wearing in some detail, as if a man didn't have enough on his mind. So I noted now that the visitor wore a pale grey skirt and a jacket that, to my mind, looked rather military. It had rows of frogging and brass buttons. She had a pile of black hair, intricately coiled, and I did wonder if it were all her own. Atop it was perched, tilted forward . . .

Ah, there was something in this taking note of a woman's dress, after all. I fancied I already knew the lady's hat, having had it described to me just under an hour before by Lizzie, courtesy of Miss Poole. The little hat was round with lavender flower buds on it and a lot of crunched-up green ribbons on the top. It was held in place by a couple of ribbons tied in place at the nape of her neck.

Dunn's face had been inscrutable as he watched me study the visitor. 'I am pleased to see you return so soon, Ross,' he said now in a voice just as devoid of expression. 'I wanted you to meet this lady and asked her if she wouldn't mind waiting a little. May I introduce Mrs Thomas Tapley?'

Chapter Fourteen

Elizabeth Martin Ross

WALLY SLATER drove me at a sedate pace across London and set me down at my own front door. He clambered down from his perch and accepted his fare with a sigh.

'I'm pleased to see you, ma'am, but not too pleased to know you're meddling in murders again. There's been another one, ain't there? Near to where I picked you up? That bluebottle as was sent out to find a cab for you, told me of it.'

'The constable should not have gossiped,' I said crossly.

'I asked him, didn't I? The minute I saw him bringing you along. What does your old man think of you poking your nose in like you do?'

'My husband,' I said with dignity, 'has learned to live with it.'

Wally chuckled. 'Well, I dare say he knew what he was getting when he married you.'

'You are going to tell me it's not respectable,' I interrupted.

'No, I'm telling you it's a dangerous business,' he retorted. 'But you'll do what you want, anyways, I dare say. Mrs Slater is of much the same turn of mind, only she ain't as yet taken up investigating corpses.'

'She keeps well, I hope?' I asked politely.

'Oh, the old girl keeps well enough, excepting her knees which gives her trouble. Well, neither of us is getting any younger. Nor is Nelson here.' He patted his horse's rump.

'He looks fit.'

'He is fit, 'cos he's well looked after. I spent an hour this morning early, grooming him and getting him ready to take out. That and cleaning all the harness and keeping the cab itself spick and span, it's a job in itself, without driving it round the town all day.'

'You could do with some help, perhaps?' I asked thoughtfully.

He nodded, grimacing. 'I'd have to pay and it would have to be someone I could trust. Nelson and I, we've worked together a few years now. I rely on him and he relies on me.'

Nelson swung his head round and blew gustily through his nostrils at us.

'He's asking', explained Wally, 'what I'm doing hanging around here talking to you when I could be out looking for a fare.' He turned to climb back on to his perch.

'Mr Slater!' I called up to him impetuously. 'If I could find a boy, who wouldn't cost you much and really likes horses, to help you out, would you be interested?'

He stared down at me. 'I might. I don't say yes and I don't say no. Depends.'

'I do have someone in mind. He's quite a small boy, I mean in size. I don't know how old he is, but I suppose him to be about ten or eleven. He's very observant and bright.'

'I respect your opinion,' said Wally. 'If you says he's bright, then he is. But he's got to be able to reach up to groom Nelson, so if he's a real little'un, that might be a problem.'

'Oh, I think he could do that, or stand on a box. He's the sort of boy who, if he set himself to do something, would find a way to do it.'

'Would he now?' asked Wally drily. 'Seems to me, meaning no disrespect to your good self, that you and this boy are much of a kind. Bring him along.'

'Leave it with me,' I said confidently. 'Only it might take me a little time. I don't know where he is at the moment. I shall have to find him.'

'I hopes', said Wally grimly, 'as I have not let meself in for something. And he'd have to pass muster with Mrs Slater, you know! Mrs Slater is very particular. She wouldn't have anyone hanging round the place she thought would look bad as far as the neighbours is concerned! If you get hold of him, take him to Mrs Slater. Then she'll decide on it and let me know what I think.' He chuckled.

'Rely on me, Mr Slater.'

He only gave me a look, touched the brim of his hat and called to Nelson to 'Walk on!' The growler rumbled away.

Inspector Benjamin Ross

Dunn's words had completely taken away my gift of speech for the moment. The woman in the hussar jacket seemed unperturbed. She nodded graciously at me in acknowledgement of the introduction and said, in English,

'I am very pleased to meet you, Inspector Ross. I understand you have been searching for the villain who murdered my poor husband.'

Two things occurred to me at once. One was that the lady spoke good English, with an attractive accent, in a low husky voice. Had Jenkins been lying when he'd told Lizzie that his lady client spoke little English? Had it just been a ploy to require his presence as interpreter at any future interview? Or had he really not known that she had good command of the language? I didn't doubt this *was* his elusive female client (even without a description of her hat to go by, and in spite of the colour of her hair now being black).

The second thing to strike me was how self-possessed the lady appeared. At any rate she was not pretending excess grief. She showed little at all. Perhaps she was someone with extraordinary command over her emotions. Perhaps she was just too shrewd to fake what she didn't feel. But could she really be the widow of Thomas Tapley, so recently deceased and whose mortal remains still lay unburied? Thomas's corpse had been removed, at Jonathan Tapley's insistence, to an undertaker's establishment. It rested there, encased in an expensive coffin, awaiting instructions.

Perhaps she could read minds or, at least, read *mine*. Not a muscle of her face twitched, but comprehension gleamed in her dark eyes as she watched me.

She said, 'Superintendent Dunn has seen my marriage certificate. Thomas and I were married in Montmartre, over three years ago. Montmartre is a small community, a village on the outskirts of Paris. It is a very popular place for Parisians to visit, to be out of the city and just to enjoy themselves. We have many restaurants, music-halls, ballrooms and open-air dancing in the summer. The atmosphere is bohemian. There are also a number of small hotels. In Montmartre no one asks questions . . .'

Her self-control slipped there for a second and she smiled coquettishly. At once she seemed to realise it was inappropriate in the circumstances. In the firm, contained way in which she'd begun, she continued, 'I have kept a lodging house of respectable name there for some years. Thomas came to live with me there nearly four years ago, first as a paying guest and then as my husband.'

For my benefit Dunn silently held up an official-looking document that had been lying on his desk. He barely met my eye.

'I have told Superintendent Dunn that I have no objection at all to his keeping my marriage certificate for a little, long enough to verify that the marriage is properly registered. But you will keep it safe, Superintendent?' she turned to Dunn. 'I must have it returned.'

'Of course, madame,' said Dunn gruffly. He dropped the certificate back on his desk.

It occurred to me that he was as much at sea here as I was.

'You speak very good English, madame,' I said, adopting the form of address Dunn had used to her.

Again that graceful inclination of her head. 'Thank you.'

But no indication of where she'd acquired the skill! This was a very clever lady. She placed her cards on the table one at a time, with great care. Information would have to be finessed from her. I began with the obvious.

'May I ask whether you have been able to pay your respects to your late husband? If not, it can be arranged.'

'I have just come from the undertaker's, Inspector. I needed to satisfy myself that it is indeed my poor Thomas, before I came here to see you.'

She had just viewed the body? And yet not even a tear?

'Mrs Tapley,' said Dunn woodenly, 'has signed a declaration that the body is that of her husband.'

'Mr Thomas Tapley,' I began tentatively to take my questioning further, 'returned to this country *alone* early last year. It seems it is quite some time since you last saw him – and he was then alive. I am indeed sorry for your distress.' (Not that she was showing any. If she thought my words ironic, then so be it.) 'But I must ask you about the circumstances under which you parted. Was there an estrangement? Had you agreed—'

'No!' she was quick to interrupt. 'It did not come about like that at all. It is true he disappeared early last year. I have been seeking him anxiously all the time since, Inspector. Unfortunately, I was looking in France.'

Dunn's features twitched but he said nothing, content to let me flounder.

'In France? You didn't think to find him in this country? Being an Englishman . . .'

'But one who lived and had lived for many years in France. Who had married me in France. Who lived with me in our home there. Who never spoke of leaving or had any reason to do so.'

Again she'd been quick to interrupt but perhaps I didn't look impressed. She broke off and sighed.

'It must seem strange to you,' she began again. 'Let me explain how it came about. You should know that Thomas was very ill the year before last. I nursed him back to health. Sadly, after he recovered he was a changed man. Before his illness he had been of a placid, cheerful disposition. We had been so content, he and I. But now, after his illness, he had become quite another person, irritable, suspicious . . . His mind wandered sometimes. I spoke to the doctor about it. The doctor told me that severe and prolonged episodes of fever sometimes had such a result, especially when the sufferer was older. Memory can be lost. It can play tricks; invent episodes. Thus my husband began to – to imagine things. This, too, the doctor declared was not unusual. I tried hard to return him to his former good state of health in mind as in body. I even managed to persuade him to visit the seaside, hoping a change of air would help. We went to Deauville. But after our return to Paris, I fear his condition grew worse.

'Then, one day, he disappeared without any warning at all. I returned to the house to find he had gone and taken his travelling chest with him. I traced a carter who had taken him from Montmartre into central Paris. The man had been delivering fresh vegetables to the market area of Les Halles. He had deposited Thomas, and his box, at a cab rank nearby. I hurried to this place but . . .'

She gave an elegant shrug. 'You have not perhaps visited the area of Les Halles. They call it the belly of Paris. There are so many people, so much produce of all kinds coming from all over France, so much business being done, such a noise, such a running to and fro. There is a hill of empty crates and boxes waiting to be taken away, and another of full ones being delivered by all manner of carts. The cab rank nearby is also busy. A cab arrives with a fare only to depart almost at once with another. The poor horses are ready to drop with fatigue. My question about a man with a travelling chest earned me only laughter. They see dozens of such every day. No one remembered Thomas. No one had time to talk to me. No one cared. I returned to Montmartre in despair.'

'You did not think he might have returned to England?' I insisted.

'At first, no.' She shook her head, drawing my eye again to the hat with the lavender rosebuds. 'Why should I think that? Thomas had always told me he had left England for good. He called it shaking the dust from his feet. Is that not the expression?'

'Yes,' Dunn and I chimed in unison. Then we exchanged furtive glances.

'I was afraid,' our visitor was saying, 'that Thomas, in a confused state of mind, was wandering somewhere in France. He might have forgotten his very name. Now I learn that he had not done that. But clearly he had forgotten our home in Montmartre. I am sorry to say that the French police were of no help. I put notices requesting information in provincial newspapers, to no avail. Eventually, in my desperation, I began to wonder if he had returned to England after all; and I must come to this country to seek for him, but . . .' she spread her hands in a particularly foreign gesture. 'To follow him here and search for him would cost me much money. I did not then have it. I had to save for a long time and only towards the end of last year, late October, did I have enough to allow me to make the journey and stay here to search for him. But now it is only to learn that I am a widow.' She cast down her eyes disconsolately.

'My condolences once more,' I said. 'May I ask from whom you learned of his death?'

She raised her dark eyes and stared fully at me. 'Thomas had spoken to me of a cousin, Jonathan, who lived in London. At first I did not want to approach him because I understood there to have been some disagreement between the two of them. But yesterday I sent him a note, explaining who I was. I had become quite desperate, you see, because I had found no trace of Thomas. This morning I received a note in return, asking that I call at an address in Gray's Inn Road. It is a legal chambers, as I believe they are called here. Jonathan Tapley is a lawyer – an *avocat* – and has his office in that building. So I went there earlier today, and he told me the tragic news. Poor Thomas is dead and worse, he has been murdered!'

Now she took out a handkerchief and dabbed her eyes. 'I cannot speak more of it now, *messieurs*. I am too shocked.'

'Indeed, you must be,' I sympathised. 'Are you all alone in London, madame?'

'Yes, quite alone,' she told me mournfully. She rose to her feet. 'I beg you will excuse me, gentlemen. You have my address, Superintendent. It is a small hotel, not expensive, you understand. But I shall stay there and you can easily find me – or send a message, and I will come here.'

Before either of us quite knew what was happening, she had risen and was on her way to the door. There was nothing to do but open it for her, and call to a constable in the room beyond to escort the lady downstairs to the street.

'Well, Ross?' Dunn asked when we were alone. 'What do you make of all that?'

241

'She'll return,' I said, 'because we have her marriage certificate and I don't doubt for a minute that, if we ask the French police to check it, we'll find the marriage properly registered. The certificate is genuine and she'll want it back.'

'But is *she* genuine?' Dunn squinted at me.

'Who knows? I fancy we are dealing with a clever woman, sir,' I said bluntly.

'Ah, yes, that, of course, and a fine-looking one.' Dunn turned his shrewd little eyes on me. 'But is she also, do you think, a murderess?'

I could only grin wryly. 'It wouldn't surprise me if she had it in her. She's as cool as an iceberg. But, if she killed anyone, I can imagine poison might be her method. Will you contact the French police, sir?'

'Yes, yes . . . you keep after this woman and question her again. See if she admits hiring a detective, this Jenkins. Oh, you had better look at this . . .' Dunn handed me the marriage certificate.

'My, my,' I said, casting my eyes over it. 'So before her marriage to Thomas Tapley, the lady was Mademoiselle Victorine Guillaume.' I returned the certificate to Dunn. 'Let's not forget the couple by the name of Guillaume who visited Major Griffiths at The Old Hall and showed such interest in The Hall's absent owners. They were supposedly brother and sister. Surely the surname being the same cannot just be coincidental? So, let us suppose Victorine was the woman. Who played the role of her brother? Where is this "brother" now?'

'We should expect another visit from Mr Jonathan Tapley, I suppose,' said Dunn. 'Now that he finds the young cousin he has brought up as a daughter has, in fact, a stepmamma.'

'Confound it!' I muttered. 'Did Madame Victorine Tapley know that her husband had a daughter here?'

'You had better ask her,' said Dunn. 'Well, Ross, get on with it. Don't stand here speculating. Get me some facts!'

'Goodness,' said Lizzie, when I had told her all this that evening at home. 'What an extraordinary thing.'

'That seems to me, if you don't mind my saying so, the very mildest description of it,' I replied.

'Cor . . .' murmured Bessie, who had been listening from the doorway. 'Who'd have thought it?'

It was pointless to tell her to return to her kitchen, she'd only have listened through the door panels.

'Would you say,' Lizzie began slowly, 'that as Victorine Guillaume or Tapley has come forward like this, it is a sign of her innocence? But where is the man Miss Poole saw with her in Jenkins's office?'

'I am working to find that out. I have to proceed very cautiously. I don't want our French visitor to fly away back to Montmartre and the respectable lodging house she keeps there! Also,' I felt I should remind my wife, 'Miss Poole only saw the back view of both visitors, and that for an instant. Were it not for her description of the hat with the lavender rosebuds or whatever they are, I would have no reason to believe the woman of the pair was Mrs Thomas Tapley. But even so, there must be other hats around with lavender flowers on them? It would be a risky thing to accept Miss Poole's description of a hat, briefly glimpsed, as solid evidence. Solid evidence is what I have to have to satisfy Dunn. What's more he seems to expect it to be found, by me, almost at once!'

'What about Jonathan Tapley?' asked Lizzie suddenly. 'What will he do now?'

'That, Lizzie, I think we shall also find out almost at once,' I told her.

'It's exciting, ain't it?' said Bessie.

Chapter Fifteen

I WAS right about Jonathan Tapley's imminent appearance at Scotland Yard. He was there first thing in the morning.

'I am required later today in court, Inspector. I therefore have little time to discuss the situation now, but it is imperative that you understand what a disaster this is! So I have made time to come and ask what you mean to do about it.' He struck the floor with the metal ferrule of his cane. I had half thought he was going to raise it and point it straight at me.

The thump of the ferrule on the floorboards caused Biddle's alarmed face to appear round the door. I signalled him away.

'We are investigating the lady's claim, Mr Tapley. We are asking the French police to confirm that a marriage between the two parties was properly conducted and registered at the place and on the date given on the certificate. I think Superintendent Dunn also intends to ask someone at the French Embassy to take a look at the marriage certificate today, and give an opinion as to its genuine appearance. I have to tell you, Mr Dunn and I are both pretty sure that it will turn out to be in order. Its authenticity is so easily checked that Mrs Victorine Tapley would be very foolish to come here and produce it otherwise.'

Tapley's appearance grew alarmingly choleric. '*Mrs Victorine Tapley*... It is out of the question that the woman can be genuine!' The ferrule struck the floorboards again, but Biddle didn't appear this time.

'No, sir, it is not,' I repeated mildly. 'You told me yourself that your cousin had made a practice of finding good-hearted ladies to take care of him.'

'I would not,' snarled Jonathan Tapley, 'describe that woman as "good hearted"! In the past the women who took it upon themselves to care for his wellbeing were all utterly respectable! His wife – his *first* wife, if we are to accept this second marriage – was of very good family. I doubt that is true of the female who appeared yesterday at my chambers.'

'I'm inclined to agree with you, sir. But you also explained to me that your cousin's first marriage was the result of necessity, to disguise his true inclinations. I suggest to you that this second marriage was also made from necessity. Not because the law in France disapproves of the activity of which your cousin stood accused, as our law does here; but because your cousin had grown older, his health was no longer so robust, and he needed a settled home and a woman to take care of his day-to-day comforts; nurse him when sick as this lady did. A younger, more dashing fellow might have got that without offering marriage. Your cousin could not. The lady would have insisted on it.'

'Tom was a fool,' Jonathan Tapley said bitterly. 'He was a fool to get into the situation. He was doubly a fool not to make a new will when it was suggested to him by Fred Thorpe that his existing one might need updating. It needed more than that! It needed an entire new will. By his second marriage his first will is revoked. As a result, he died intestate. Do you realise what that means? Victorine Guillaume – I refuse to accept her as a Tapley – is making considerable claims upon the estate! We shall contest that on behalf of Flora. Morally, in my view, Guillaume shouldn't get a penny. The pair no longer lived together. He was here; she in France. Clearly Tom considered the marriage over . . .' He snorted. 'If there was ever such a valid contract, despite what you have said about it!'

'The certificate produced by the lady appears to be in order,' I ventured to remind him. 'Although we have not yet heard from the French police—'

He interrupted me curtly. 'The document, in itself, may be genuine, as a piece of paper. But was the ceremony a valid one? Were both parties free to make such a contract? Tom, we can assume, was free to take a wife, but was he somehow coerced? As for Victorine Guillaume, what do we really know of her history? There is the question of Tom's state of mind. Was he even fully aware at the time of what he was doing? That woman has told us that, after they were "married" – I use the word until I can show that it is not the case – Tom fell ill; and on recovery rambled and was forgetful. Had he ever done that before? Was his mind wandering when he went through a marriage ceremony?'

I feared he might be grasping at straws, but at the same time the possibility existed. Thomas Tapley might have been muddled or coerced at the time he signed the register of marriage. Aloud I only said, 'I am sure the French police will check thoroughly. They have access to the necessary records.'

'I, also, shall be looking into it all thoroughly!' Tapley

made an irritable gesture as if swatting away a fly. 'At the moment, of course, she is playing the card of the loyal but deserted wife. She is standing upon her rights! His goods and chattels do not amount to more than his books and she would be welcome to those. But she is making preposterous claims on the estate. There are the two properties in Yorkshire and the income from them, and his investments. She seems well informed about them all.'

He leaned towards me. 'From where has she her knowledge, eh? I cannot imagine my cousin telling her every financial detail. We speak of a man who, throughout his time abroad, regularly sent home to his solicitors in Harrogate all his business correspondence. He did that because he meant it to be private! A man who made no new will providing for his new wife. A clear enough indication, I think, that he intended her to have nothing. This is not a man who would have taken her into his confidence concerning his personal wealth. So, then, how does she come to know so much about it, eh?'

He sat back again. 'We shall fight, Ross! We – *I* shall fight it vigorously, on Flora's behalf, taking it through any court necessary. Thank goodness there was no prenuptial contract made in France, before Tom embarked on this mad undertaking. My cousin was at least sensible enough to avoid that. He clearly did not intend her to have anything, and I shall make sure that she doesn't!'

'Mr Tapley,' I began cautiously, 'there are two points I should make. Firstly, neither Mrs Jameson, his landlady in this country, nor my wife, who spoke with your cousin on several occasions, got the impression his mind was wandering. Nor did young Fred Thorpe, in Harrogate, think him confused in mind. He thought him frightened, but that's something else; and we can't assume he was frightened of his wife. When Thorpe asked if he wanted to update his will, it was because Thorpe believed your cousin was of sound enough mind to do it.

'My second point is that I believe your cousin did not take the opportunity he had in Harrogate, to make a new will, because he didn't want anyone to know about his second marriage. *I stress we don't yet know why.* He must have realised his original will had been invalidated. Perhaps, as you say, he did not want to leave anything, or very much, to his second wife. Perhaps he simply did not want her to know where he was. He was not planning on dying just yet. Perhaps he had persuaded himself he had time to think of a way out of the predicament.'

Tapley rested his hands on the ivory skull pommel and raised his eyebrows. 'And your conclusion from that is?'

'My speculation, sir, not my conclusion, is that it does look as if your cousin was avoiding his wife. Was that simply because he had tired of the marriage, or was there another reason? We have to find out.'

Tapley gave a dry chuckle. 'I told you I thought you were in the wrong branch of the law, Ross!' He leaned forward, a gleam in his eyes, and added quietly, 'I believe – and you clearly suspect – Tom was in fear of his life when he fled to England from France.'

'As yet I cannot go so far, Mr Tapley. We should have to prove that. It will be difficult. It is a big step from saying that he'd fallen out of love, or decided the arrangement wasn't working out as he'd hoped, and so left the marital home, to saying he'd been threatened. We have no evidence of that. The lady may be quite innocent.'

'I don't harbour your generous thoughts towards her, Inspector. She has something to do with his death and I expect you to establish her guilt.' A wolfish gleam came into his eyes. 'Naturally, if she is guilty in any way, as an accessory to his murder or as the moving force, she cannot benefit from his demise. Her claim upon the estate falls away.' He rose to his feet. 'And now I must go. But we'll speak again, Inspector. Good day to you!'

'He wants Victorine Guillaume to be guilty,' I said to Dunn later, when I reported this conversation. 'Because then she no longer has any claim on the estate. We have to bear in mind that his anxiety to prove her guilt is greater than a desire for justice. This is a murder case, however, and if a list of suspects is to be drawn up, her name must be on it.

'So is his. I have not ruled him out, sir, or his wife. They were quite ferocious in their desire to protect the interests of Miss Flora, even before they learned of the existence of this Frenchwoman. Thomas Tapley had broken his agreement never to return to this country. He'd become a danger. From the moment they learned from Fred Thorpe that Thomas Tapley was back here, they will have been living in dread he'd turn up on the doorstep.'

'We must take care, he's a man of influence,' observed Dunn. 'What's your next move, Ross?'

'I shall call immediately on Victorine Tapley, née Guillaume, at her hotel, and question her again, sir. I don't believe, as she would have us believe, that his illness caused her husband to forget he was married! If he was the frightened man who came to see Fred Thorpe in Harrogate, it was because he had something to fear. I agree with Jonathan Tapley that the lady appears to know details of her husband's fortune, yet he deliberately avoided making a will including her. Something is wrong there, I feel it in my bones.'

'Good luck,' said Dunn.

'Thank you, sir.'

It was a little before noon when I arrived at the small hotel where Victorine Guillaume (to call her that for ease of reference) had established herself. The smell of boiling vegetables permeated the air. A maidservant was sent upstairs to fetch the lady.

I waited in the lobby at the foot of the staircase. Suddenly she appeared at the head of the flight, on the mezzanine. I confess I was so startled I took a step backwards. She was dressed in full mourning of black crêpe. The only item she wore that was not of sombre hue was a white 'widow's cap' with dangling ribbons around her ears. Her hair was as elaborately coiled as before, like a thick nest of shining jet-black serpents about her head. As her dramatic and handsome figure descended the staircase towards me, an idea occurred to me. It was quite equally startling; but it was also quite possible. Did the lady wear a wig? Was she, perhaps, a little older than she would have us believe?

I babbled an apology for coming just before a mealtime and hoped not to keep her long from the table.

She waved a hand in a graceful gesture that swept away either my apology or the smell of boiled greens.

'It is of no matter. I have little appetite. The hotel has a parlour through there.' She pointed with a hand encased in a black lace fingerless mitten. 'It's seldom occupied and perhaps we could use it.'

The parlour had that slightly musty unaired atmosphere that such places have in hotels. The furniture looked uncomfortable. The only painting on the wall was a gloomy Highland scene of cattle in a mist. Guests would not be encouraged to linger here and probably that, and the stale smell, was why the parlour was generally unused. It did, however, boast a copy of today's newspaper on the dusty table. The widow subsided on to a chair in a rustle of silk crêpe; and I identified an aroma of Parma Violets. Lizzie has a bottle of that scent.

'How are you otherwise today, madame?' I asked politely, as I took the opposite chair.

'Apart from the lack of appetite and my grief?' she returned sharply. 'Otherwise, as you put it, I am well. I slept but little.'

'That is understandable. May I ask, madame, where you learned to speak such excellent English?'

A slight smile touched her lips. 'To see me now, Inspector, you probably would not imagine that when I was young, I was a dancer. Oh, a respectable one! Although I now have a lodging house in Montmartre, I was not one of those so-called dancers who kick up their heels in the cabarets of that place and in Montparnasse, in an indecorous manner sometimes called *cancan*. Such women are no better than they should be. I was a *petit rat* of the Opéra, a ballet girl. The original company was founded by Louis the fourteenth, you know,' she added proudly. 'It has changed its official name so often and changed theatres almost as often, but it has always been known as the Opéra; and I am proud of having been a member, even a humble one, of its ballet company. Later, when I grew taller and heavier, I lost my place in the company. I came to England and was a member of the corps de ballet of several theatres here. That is where I learned my English. But a dancer's working life is short, monsieur. I had been prudent and saved my money. I returned to France and was able to set up my lodging house.'

'Mr Jenkins,' I said calmly, 'thought you had little command of the language.'

That checked her, but only for a moment. 'Mr Jenkins', she said drily, 'is not an intelligent man. The fact that I spoke good English probably never occurred to him. He insisted on addressing me in his appalling French. Where he learned *that*, I have no idea, although from the words he used I suspect it was in dockside bars.'

'You do not deny, then, madame, that you know of whom I'm speaking? That you engaged Mr Jenkins to look for your husband?'

'No, Inspector, I do not deny it.'

'You did not mention this yesterday.'

'*Yesterday* we did not go into great detail of my search here, Inspector. Had you asked me, I should have given the same reply. Why should I deny I engaged Mr Jenkins?'

'How did you come to know of his detective agency?'

She shrugged. 'There is a little board by the hotel reception desk, on which people leave messages. His card was pinned there. I thought it worth trying. But he turned out to be a rogue.'

'A rogue who found your husband, nevertheless . . .' I pointed out.

Her eyes flashed. 'No, Inspector, he did not! If he had done so, I should not have gone to Mr Jonathan Tapley in my desperation. As for Jenkins, *pah*!' She threw up her hands. 'I did not like the look of the man, or of his office, when I called there. However, having taken the trouble to seek him out, I explained I was looking for someone of the name of Thomas Tapley. I even gave him a photograph of my husband. A photograph he has failed to return, by the way. He asked for some money in advance, to pay for his expenses. I paid him a good amount. When I called back later to find out if he had made progress, he had the impudence, and the stupidity, to ask for more. I refused. I could see he was little more than a confidence trickster. I demanded my original money back. He said it was impossible. I demanded my photograph. He said he did not have it in his office. I told him his agency was no longer employed by me and he should send my photograph of Thomas to me at this hotel. He has not done so.'

'Mr Jenkins', I said, 'is dead.'

She was silent for a moment. 'How did he die?'

'He was murdered.'

'Ah . . .' Another silence. Then she said, 'Well, I am not surprised to hear it. Such a man would have enemies, other people he has tricked, no doubt!'

We sat looking at one another for a moment or two. She was a little flushed from indignation, or some other emotion. Questions chased one another pell-mell through my mind. She claimed to have been a dancer. Had she actually been an actress? Had her theatrical background inspired her to set the stage for her appearance when I waited in the hall? Was she possibly speaking the truth about Jenkins? I could easily imagine that Jenkins, from Lizzie's description of the man, had been something of a trickster. He might also have been a genuine private detective, but it would have been in his interest to string out his investigations for as long as possible, demanding continuing sums of money from his clients. The lady's description of Jenkins's attempts to speak French was amusing. It also had the ring of truth to it. Could he really have thought this capable woman spoke almost no English? But then, when she had called on him, she had had a companion with her. Had the unknown man done the talking? How I wished we could interview Jenkins again . . . or that someone had been able to interview him before his death. Lizzie had meant well, but she had delayed too long in reporting his existence.

'Madame,' I began again, 'I understand, from a witness, that when you first called on Mr Jenkins, you were accompanied by a gentleman.'

'What witness?' she demanded.

'A lady living upstairs in the building. Jenkins had an arrangement with her to bring down a tea tray when he saw new clients.'

'I do not remember such a woman. She claims she saw *me*?'

Well, no, Miss Poole did not claim that, only that she'd seen a back view of a lady and a hat with lavender rosebuds on it. There were probably other hats with such decoration. Miss Poole had not heard the lady speak.

I decided not to answer Victorine's question. It is the prerogative of the investigating officer that he asks, but does not answer, questions.

'You were not accompanied? You have told us, I know, that you are alone in London.'

'I *am* alone!' she snapped. 'But, as it happened, an old friend accompanied me on the journey across the Channel. I was nervous, you understand, at returning to this country after a number of years. Also I am a poor sailor. The gentleman, an old friend, agreed to come with me and see me settled here in London. He did also come with me to see Jenkins. But when Jenkins disappointed me, my friend could not remain here any longer. He had business in Paris to attend to. He returned to France. He suggested I return, too. But I explained to him I was now resolved to seek out Mr Jonathan Tapley, and would remain for as long as my finances allowed. He accepted that, but begged me not to waste more money on people such as Jenkins.'

'And the name of this gentleman?'

Again, the slightest hesitation. 'Hector Mas, I have known him many years. He knew Thomas, too. They were friends. Monsieur Mas was anxious to help me locate my husband.'

At that moment a gong sounded outside in the hall. She glanced in its direction.

'I think I shall try to eat some soup. The boiled meat puddings they serve here are disgusting beyond description.' Again the silk crêpe rustled and the scent of violets wafted by my nostrils.

Clearly, this conversation was at an end for now. I also stood up.

'Thank you for your time, madame. We shall speak again. You won't, I hope, leave this address? If you do, let Scotland Yard know. But, I beg of you, please don't return to France for the time being.'

'I must stay here,' she said. 'I now have some legal matters to attend to. My husband left no will. Also, I have learned I have a stepdaughter.'

'Your husband never mentioned his daughter?'

She shook her head. 'Never. I now understand he gave her away when she was an infant, to his cousin and his wife. They consider her their daughter. Thomas no longer had any responsibility for her and my belief is that he, too, considered her their daughter, rather than his.' She nodded. 'I shall make her acquaintance this afternoon, and that of Mrs Maria Tapley.'

'You will?' I exclaimed, unprepared for this development.

'Oh, yes. They are coming here to meet me.'

Oh, how I wished I could be a fly on the wall of this dingy parlour when that encounter took place later in the day!

On my way out, I paused by the reception desk. There was indeed a corkboard fixed to the wall with scraps of paper or card pinned to it. A glance at them showed them to be targeted at visitors to the capital, mostly cheaply printed bills advertising Turkish baths, cigar divans, theatres and the like. There was even . . . ah, yes, there it was, a small card advertising the services of Horatio Jenkins, private enquiry agent.

I took it down and showed it to the formidable, bombazine-clad female who guarded admission to the hotel. 'Did you see who placed this here, and when?'

She stared at it as if it might communicate some plague. 'I have no idea. The notices change continually. I could ask the page-boy. But I doubt he'd remember. Do you wish to speak to the boy?' She struck a bell on the counter.

A figure appeared in an ill-fitting page's uniform.

257

'This gentleman has a question for you,' said the woman, and left me with the page.

He was an unprepossessing youth, stunted in build, and with crooked teeth and a knowing look. 'Hullo,' he said. 'You're a rozzer, I'd bet my brass buttons on it.'

'Your brass buttons are perfectly safe. This card, advertising the detective agency, when was it pinned on that board?' I held it under his nose.

'What's it worth?' asked the youth.

'Let me explain something to you,' I replied. 'I am indeed an officer of the law. I am making some enquiries and if you withhold information, you will be in trouble.'

'I ain't got any information!' said the page in disgust. 'What information am I likely to have, stuck here? I'm run off my feet, I am. *She's* banging that ruddy bell every five minutes. There's someone wanting their luggage carried upstairs, or they want it carried down again. There's someone wanting me to run out and find a cab and another one wanting me to run half a mile with a message. If they give me a shilling I'm lucky. *She's* got me cleaning all their shoes, as well, because I'm boot boy, too, for my sins. I haven't got time to watch that cork-board. People come in and pin up their notices all the time. When it gets too full, *she* tells me to take 'em all down and chuck 'em on the fire. I don't read 'em. *She* might.'

'Then let me ask you another question,' I said. 'The French lady who is a guest here . . .'

'Oh, *her*,' said the page.

'Did she arrive alone?'

'Yus,' said the page confidently. 'I carried her bags, all of them, to the top floor and she only gave me sixpence. Oh, yes,

I remember *her* arriving. When she goes, she'll want me to carry them all down again, I don't doubt!'

'There was no gentleman, possibly a Frenchman, with her?'

He squinted at me. 'There was a fellow in the cab with her, the cab she arrived in, but he never got out, never gave a hand with the bags or nothing. She got out, the cabbie got down from his perch and whistled to me. I went out and the cabbie and me, we dragged out all the bags. I was given the lot to carry and the cab rattled off with the other fare still in it. I never heard the fellow inside speak, never got a proper look at him. There's not much light inside a four-wheeler and he had his hand up, sort of between his face and me. He might or might not have been a foreigner. He might have been the emperor of Russia. He might have had no legs. But it's no use asking *me* about him.'

So, I thought, Hector Mas, if the man in the cab had been Mas, who had travelled to England with Guillaume, had not lodged in the same hotel. Out of the same discretion that kept him veiled in the darkness of the cab when she arrived? Or for some other reason?'

I gave the page a shilling in case I needed to talk to him again. He might prove a useful spy.

'You want me to find out about that card?' asked the page, encouraged by my largesse. 'I could go round the other hotels hereabouts and see if they got one.'

'No matter,' I said. 'It is no use now. The agency it advertises is no longer in existence.'

'What do you think, then, Ross?' asked Dunn when I returned to the Yard.

'That she is either very plausible or telling the truth. Very likely, it is a mixture of the two. She tells me – us – nothing until she has to. Thus, she did not volunteer the information that she had used Jenkins's agency. She did not admit at first she had been accompanied by a man when she called there. She had forgotten the tea tray and would not, anyway, have seen Miss Poole, who was standing behind her in the doorway, and did not come into the room. She had to decide quickly whether to continue to deny a man had accompanied her, or admit he'd existed. Not knowing if Miss Poole got more of a look at her than we know she did – or if I could produce another witness – Guillaume decided to admit it.'

'And the reason for her reticence?' asked Dunn, drumming his fingers thoughtfully on the desktop.

I frowned and picked my words carefully. 'I would say, sir, that she has spent her life in a rather – shady – world. It is not in her nature to trust anyone or confide in strangers, even the police. Perhaps especially the police. Ballet girls, generally, are besieged by stage-door admirers, whose intentions are both dishonourable and quite apparent. As Guillaume said, the girls' dancing lives are short. When they stop being dancers, if they have not found a husband or a generous protector, they very often have little choice but to become courtesans. Victorine Guillaume was no innocent, but had a hard business head on her shoulders. She may well have saved her money – or earned it in a way she does not now care to acknowledge. At any rate, she had enough to buy and set up her lodging house. Her marriage to Tapley was probably to acquire the respectable status of married woman, nothing more. I don't think, with her theatrical background, she failed to recognise his sexual persuasion. Thomas Tapley had a reputation for sweet-talking older ladies into taking care of him . . . but no one would bamboozle Victorine Guillaume so easily. So, there was something else she hoped to get out of the marriage. By the way, I fancy she wears a wig, sir.'

'What?' asked Dunn, startled.

'Well, sir, her hair is very elaborately dressed and it looked today exactly the same as it did yesterday, although conceivably she may have called a hairdresser to the hotel. She could, if necessary, change her appearance quite easily, if she does wear a wig. Both Major Griffiths and Miss Poole described a woman with deep red hair. We have seen one with jet-black tresses. That is not to say they are not one and the same.'

'We shall have to keep an eye on her,' said Dunn grimly. 'In case she slips out of the country.'

'The French police should be able to find her, if she did. She wouldn't simply abandon her lodging house in Montmartre, unless she became desperate to disappear. I am more than a little interested in this fellow, Hector Mas. He wanted no one at the hotel to see him. Why was he so keen to stay out of sight? Guillaume tells us he has returned to France. I wonder, sir, if it is worth contacting the French police and asking if they know of him?'

'I'll get on to it,' Dunn promised.

'In the meantime, the lady is making claims on Thomas Tapley's estate. Until that is settled, she won't go away, sir.'

Later that evening Lizzie listened to all this in silence, paying close attention. After I'd finished speaking, she sat in thought for a moment or two before speaking.

'So Maria Tapley took Flora to meet this newly discovered stepmother this afternoon? I'm surprised she allowed Flora to go anywhere near her.'

'The Tapleys could hardly prevent her meeting the woman at some stage,' I pointed out. 'Better for it to be at once, so that Flora is prepared when the matter of the inheritance comes to court, if it does. She'd meet her then. She should know what she's up against. Perhaps it was Flora's own wish to meet the woman her father married in France?'

Lizzie thought that over and agreed. Her next question surprised me. 'You say Victorine was in deep mourning? Top to toe? Even a widow's cap?'

'To the last detail and all good quality – to my eye. Black silk crêpe, even little lace mittens.'

Lizzie leaned towards me, her face animated. 'Where did she get it all?'

'What?'

'The mourning ensemble, where and when did she acquire it?'

I confess I didn't at first see where this question was going and replied, 'I suppose, as a widow, it is quite proper she should dress that way.'

'Yes, yes!' said Lizzie impatiently. 'But one doesn't acquire such a complete set of widow's weeds overnight! Victorine did not know until quite late yesterday, when she met Jonathan and was taken to the undertaker's to see her husband's body, that she was a widow, or so she says. She had hoped to find Thomas alive, if mentally muddled. Did she rush straight out from the undertaker's to a dress shop, not pausing even to shed a tear?'

'No,' I replied. 'She came to Scotland Yard to surprise Dunn and me. She wore grey, a hussar jacket, and that hat you spoke of, with the lavender roses and ribbons.'

'Just so. She had no time to go shopping. She must have sailed from France to England with a travelling box or chest.'

'The hotel page told me she arrived with several bags.'

Lizzie nodded. 'So, did she pack this complete set of black clothes, just against the possibility that she might find out that he'd died here? If she thought he was alive, it seems unnecessary. It took up space and added to the weight of her luggage. It suggests to me she thought there would be a very good chance he would be dead, and she did not want the expense of equipping herself with black crêpe clothing here. But why should he have died? He had recovered physically from his bout of fever. At the very least, it seems very pessimistic of her to have filled her boxes with clothing she might not need.'

'Unless she was confident she *would* need it,' I said thoughtfully.

Lizzie beamed at me. 'Yesterday she wore grey. Grey is quite sombre enough a colour to wear for a week, until she had acquired some black clothes. If she'd done that, the puzzle of her sudden appearance in full mourning wouldn't have arisen. *But this afternoon Maria Tapley and Flora were to call on her for the first time.* Victorine wanted to make a good impression and set the stage. She could not resist taking out the black outfit she had brought with her and wearing it.'

Lizzie sat back and waited.

I had to confess my admiration. 'My dear Lizzie, distinctive headwear with lavender roses, black crêpe gowns: the clues in

263

this case seem all to lie with ladies' clothing. What is a mere male detective to do?'

'Exactly so,' said Lizzie with quiet triumph. 'It is as I told Superintendent Dunn. Scotland Yard needs some women employed there.'

Chapter Sixteen

Elizabeth Martin Ross

THE FOLLOWING morning I received a short note, posted early the evening before across town. It was from Flora Tapley.

> Dear Mrs Ross,
>
> I hope you will forgive my troubling you. I wonder if it is possible for you to meet me in the park in Bryanston Square, where we met before? I should very much like to speak to you.
>
> Again, I apologise for presuming on your kindness. But I should be most grateful.
>
> Yours sincerely,
> Flora Tapley

Ben had left for the Yard. Probably neither he nor Dunn would approve my taking further active interest, but Flora's request was a personal one. The poor child was clearly worried and not surprisingly!

We set out, Bessie and I. Bessie had assumed she would be coming along, too, and wouldn't be dissuaded.

'It's a very funny business, missus. You need someone to look out for you. At least I'll know where you are and what you're doing. If anything horrible happens, I'll be able to tell the inspector about it.'

'Nothing horrible is going to happen, Bessie!'

Bessie's small face contorted in a knowing sneer that added nothing to her already plain looks. 'I don't suppose as poor old Mr Tapley thought anything horrible was going to happen to him, not living with a respectable Quaker lady like Mrs Jameson. But he got his head bashed in, didn't he?'

'No one is going to bash – to knock me on the head in Bryanston Square!'

'Not while I'm there to watch out!' declared Bessie triumphantly, bringing her argument full circle.

So we went together. Flora was already there, waiting on a bench. Just as Bessie guarded me, so the suspicious Biddy lurked in the background to watch over Flora. Bessie promptly descended on the maid and engaged her in conversation.

'It is very kind of you to come, Mrs Ross,' said Flora, rising to greet me. 'I am taking up your time. The fact of the matter is, I have no one to talk to, no one except Aunt Maria; and I can't unburden my heart to her as I feel I can to you. I hope I am not presuming?' she concluded anxiously.

'Let us sit down,' I invited, 'and you can tell me everything on your mind. Don't worry about taking up my time. I can stay here as long as you like.'

'Well, I can't stay too long!' Flora managed a weak smile. 'Or Biddy will run to tell Aunt Maria. The inspector will have told you that a French lady came to see Uncle Jonathan and told him she is my poor father's widow?'

I nodded. 'Yes, she went to Scotland Yard and, I believe, showed her marriage certificate. I understand it's being checked but the police think there is little doubt it's genuine.'

'Both Aunt Maria and Uncle Jonathan are in a dreadful state about it,' Flora said wryly. 'It is because my father left no valid will, you see. He had made a will, but when he remarried in France, it was automatically revoked and he didn't make another.' She paused. 'We went, Aunt Maria and I, to a hotel yesterday afternoon to meet my stepmother.'

'What did you think of her?' I asked, rather tactlessly.

'Aunt Maria disapproved of her. She said afterwards that Victorine, that is my stepmother's name, is "vulgar". When Aunt Maria says that of someone, they have no chance of ever winning her approval. She also told Uncle Jonathan that Victorine was "brazen". Uncle Jonathan can hardly mention her name for rage.'

'But you?' I persisted. 'What did you think, Miss Tapley? How did you judge her?'

Flora's cheeks reddened. 'You see, dear Mrs Ross, this is why I asked you to come. I can speak so frankly and honestly to you and I couldn't speak so to the others. I didn't find her vulgar or brazen. She appeared rather more collected than I fancy Aunt Maria and I had expected, but I found her rather dignified. To tell the truth, I felt sorry for her, for Victorine.'

I must have shown my astonishment. Flora put out a hand and laid it on my arm.

'No one has any sympathy for her in her grief. Aunt Maria

said not a word of consolation and when I began to express sympathy, Aunt Maria interrupted me and signalled me to silence. I think Victorine must be so lonely in that nasty hotel. It is such a cramped place, not very clean, and smells dreadfully of kitchen odours. Not *good* kitchen odours, like freshly baked cakes, just unpleasant ones like cabbage water. I wouldn't wish to stay there. I think Victorine does not have very much money. That is one reason why I think Uncle Jonathan is unkind to oppose her claim for something from my father's estate. I think it must be very unpleasant and hurtful to know everyone dislikes you.'

'Perhaps that does not worry her so much, as it would worry you or me,' I said with some asperity, 'if it is true.'

'Oh, it is true. Uncle Jonathan and Aunt Maria don't like her. I think your husband and the other man, Superintendent Dunn, don't like her much. The people in the hotel don't like her. I could tell that from the way they looked at her. Think how awful it must be not to have a single friend in a strange city.'

'My dear Miss Tapley,' I said firmly. 'You are probably right. Being generally disliked must make some difficulty for Mrs Victorine Tapley socially. But it is her difficulty and not yours, do you understand? You have a very kind heart. Don't let it mislead you. You are not required to redress the balance all by yourself.'

'You see?' said Flora with a sad smile. 'Even you don't like her, and I do not believe you have met her.'

This was said with such a childlike spontaneity that the words contained no sarcasm.

'I stand corrected,' I said ruefully. 'I shouldn't judge the lady. I have never met her. But let me put it another way. If someone is disliked by everyone, perhaps it is because they are not a very nice person.'

'We don't know she is not a nice person,' objected Flora. 'She told us how she nursed my father when he was ill. He became very muddled after his illness, she said, and suspected everyone of plotting against him. Then he disappeared from their house on the outskirts of Paris and she has been seeking him ever since. Only think how worried she must have been. Now she's discovered he's dead. It is so sad, Mrs Ross. How can we not pity her?'

What could I say? In the event, I said nothing, and that is very unlike me, as Ben will tell you.

Flora grew brisker and continued, in a businesslike way, 'Arrangements are being made for my father's funeral. The service will take place at St Marylebone parish church, at the top of the High Street, so I trust you will not go to St Mary's Church in Wyndham Place in error, although that is nearer to our house. Uncle Jonathan and Aunt Maria were married at St Marylebone and we have always worshipped there. After the service we shall all go, with the coffin, to the Brookwood Necropolis railway station and travel by train out of London to Surrey as a funeral party. My father will be buried there, in the Necropolis burial ground. A plot is purchased and final arrangements are being made. I do hope that both you and Inspector Ross will come.'

'Of course,' I said.

'I will see you are sent proper notice.' Flora took my hand. 'Dear Mrs Ross, thank you again for coming and listening to me. I do so value your support. I must go back to the house now. I will see you at the funeral.'

★   ★   ★

'What do you make of all that?' I asked Ben that evening.

He had listened carefully to what I'd had to say and his expression had grown steadily more sombre. 'I don't like it; I don't like any of it.

'See here, Lizzie, if Flora's kind heart makes her generous towards her stepmother, Victorine will have sensed it instantly. From her point of view, she will already have won a valuable ally in the matter of the disputed estate. She will use any advantage ruthlessly. Jonathan Tapley is Flora's guardian, of course, and Victorine won't win him over. He is her implacable enemy.

'Moreover, she faces another problem. Jonathan Tapley will use all his legal skills to contest her claim and if necessary spin things out through the courts. Legal processes are notoriously slow. It could be many months before the estate is settled, perhaps a year or more. It's not unknown! If it's true that Victorine has limited funds, then she does indeed find herself in a very difficult situation. Even to stay in that cheap hotel will be eating away at her reserves. She may find herself forced to return to France, at least for a while. If she does that, and the estate is not yet settled, she will be at a great disadvantage, having abandoned the field. Napoleon did the same at Waterloo, and look what that cost him! Who would represent Victorine in any court proceedings? She probably can't afford a lawyer. Desperate situations sometimes lead to people taking desperate measures. Victorine is very clever and, frankly, as hard as nails. Of course I am worried on Flora's account.'

Ben gave a muted growl. 'I am worried on my own, also. All this means increased pressure on me to conclude the murder investigation. I can't let that drag on. Nor can I see any court deciding the matter of the estate while Tapley's murderer has not been named. I shall be pursued by a veritable pack of interested parties: the family, the widow, Dunn, the press, public opinion and the lawyers. In the meantime, I am concerned, as you are, that Flora is vulnerable. I don't doubt that. We must trust Jonathan and his wife to prevent Victorine playing on the girl's sympathy. But from your account of Flora dressing up to visit her father in disguise, it seems to me she can be a resourceful young lady, too.

'By the way, the French Embassy has informed us that the marriage certificate appears to be completely in order. We have not yet heard from the French police.'

'I have yet to meet Victorine,' I said. 'I'm looking forward to it, but it will have to be at the funeral.'

'As to the funeral, I should attend anyway, as investigating officer. Now we're invited to attend by the deceased's daughter, I shall be spared having to lurk in the background, trying not to offend by my presence.' Ben smiled grimly. 'As for Victorine Guillaume Tapley, well, I have not yet played all my cards.'

Inspector Benjamin Ross

The following day, with the help of Sergeant Morris and Constable Biddle, I scoured London seeking a hotel where anyone named Hector Mas had been a recent guest. We drew a blank at each enquiry. We were told of several French visitors who had registered at all manner of establishments, expensive and cheap. We managed to speak to one or two who were still there, and establish none was our man. Of the others, none sounded likely to have been the fellow we sought. They were too old, too young, had been accompanied by their wives, or were known to the hotel staff from previous visits. We described Victorine Guillaume to the staff, but no one remembered seeing her. Morris remarked to me that he thought Victorine the sort who'd be remembered.

'And this chap, Mas,' Morris went on, 'he could either have stayed in a private house or, most likely, some sort of bed and breakfast establishment, a rooming house, or a public house with a bed or two to rent. There are hundreds of them, sir, in London. We'd need a dozen men to go round them all and take probably over a week about it. Even then, if Mas paid the owners a couple of guineas to deny he'd ever been there, they'd be happy to oblige.'

'So, what sort of a man was he, Morris?' I asked.

'One who was up to no good,' opined Morris. 'That's my view of it, sir. But, there again, he might be what they call eccentric, or just very thrifty. But my best bet would be, he don't want to be noticed.'

The following afternoon I was able to set in motion, with Dunn, a little plan I had hatched. I was confident of its success but knew I'd look a fool if it failed, and the best-laid plans, as the poet wrote, can go so very wrong. I know he wrote something Scottish, but I cannot quite recall what it was. I should ask Lizzie. She would know the reference. At any rate, he was right.

Victorine Guillaume had been requested to come to the Yard at two that afternoon. I waited with Dunn in his office.

The door of my office, a little way down the corridor, was left open. Anyone coming to see Dunn would have to pass by it.

Accordingly, a few minutes before two, I was waiting nervously with the superintendent. A thump of boots announced Constable Biddle who appeared, red faced, to tell us, 'The lady's on her way up, Mr Ross, sir – and Mr Dunn, sir!'

Perhaps reflecting he had got the names in the wrong order of seniority, Biddle's face grew even redder.

'Yes, yes! Get yourself out of sight, boy!' snapped Dunn.

Biddle vanished. He had barely disappeared when a lighter footstep heralded our lady visitor. We could see her, through the open door of Dunn's office, coming along the corridor towards us, clad in her mourning attire. She had just passed by the open door of my office when a voice from within that room boomed, 'Bless my soul! If it isn't Miss Guillaume. A great pleasure to see you again, mademoiselle, and a great surprise!'

Victorine gasped and spun round as a gentleman in a tweed suit emerged from my office, hat in hand, and bowed to her in a military manner.

'Major Griffiths, ma'am, if you remember me?' he identified himself. 'You called at my home, The Old Hall near Harrogate, together with your brother, some time towards the end of last year.'

She may have been taken by surprise, but she was aware that Dunn and I listened from his office and she was not so foolish as to deny it. I had to admire the quickness with which she rallied.

'Indeed I do, Major! May I ask what brings you here?'

'Well, it's all rather unexpected for me, too,' returned the major cheerfully, 'I admit I seldom come to London these days. The fact of the matter is, I have travelled down this morning to attend the funeral of my landlord, Mr Thomas Tapley, later in the week. I mean also to spend a few days looking out my old haunts. I never knew Tapley personally but I have lived in his house for a number of years. All my household staff know of the family. It seems right to show my face, pay my respects. Poor Tapley was murdered, you know. That is why I am here at the Yard, asking how the investigation progresses.' Griffiths leaned towards her and added in a confidential tone, 'And I don't mind telling you, my dear Miss Guillaume, that I was also dashed interested to see the famous Scotland Yard, what?'

Well done, Major! I thought as I walked down the corridor to join them.

'Ah, madame!' I greeted her. 'So you know Major Griffiths? This lady, Major, is the widow of your landlord.'

'Is she, b'gad?' replied the major, frowning. 'You didn't make yourself known as such, ma'am, when you called on me with your brother. I feel I was remiss in not offering you more hospitality at the time. I should have done, had I known.'

'You were quite hospitable enough, thank you, Major Griffiths,' said Victorine icily. 'Inspector Ross, I understand I have an appointment with Superintendent Dunn. Please excuse me, Major Griffiths.'

'Delighted to see you again, ma'am, delighted,' he said.

Clearly Victorine was not delighted, but she swept past him and into Dunn's office.

I lingered long enough to murmur, 'Thank you, Major

Griffiths. I was a little afraid you might not recognise her.'

'Well, she wasn't all in black when I saw her last,' admitted Griffiths. 'And her hair was a different colour, I fancy, reddish. But she isn't the sort of woman one forgets. I knew her the moment I saw her pass the doorway of your office there.'

'Again, my thanks for waiting and identifying her. Perhaps you would give us a little more of your time, and sign a statement to the effect that she called on you in Harrogate and in what circumstances? Sergeant Morris will look after you. If you are to attend Tapley's funeral, I'll be meeting you again, sir.'

'Thought I should attend the funeral,' Griffiths repeated. 'Proper thing to do. I confess I'm also interested to see if I can find out what's likely to happen about my tenancy. Glad to have been of service, Inspector.'

I joined Dunn and Victorine Guillaume in Dunn's office. Victorine was seated on the chair where I'd first seen her. Her dark eyes sparkled with anger as she watched me enter. Dunn looked relieved to see me. However, I was not prepared, this time, to carry the burden of the interview. I stationed myself by the closed door, and waited in silence.

'Ah, yes, Ross . . .' mumbled Dunn. He then straightened up and, turning to Guillaume, began briskly, 'Well, madame, I am sorry for the little subterfuge, but it seems you have not been entirely frank . . .'

He got no further. She turned that blazing gaze from me to him and Dunn visibly blanched.

'I am also very sorry, because I believe that neither you, Superintendent, nor you, Inspector Ross, has behaved as a

275

gentleman should.' The dark eyes flashed at me again, 'Particularly in your case, Inspector!'

'I am afraid, madame, I am only a simple police officer,' I said. 'I have never made any claim to be a gentleman.'

'It is as well!' she said icily.

'Now, look here, madame . . .' Dunn wrested back control of the conversation. 'You have not been frank with us, you know. You cannot blame us for our little trick. This is a murder inquiry. You should not keep information of any sort from us. You should have told us you travelled to Harrogate in search of your husband. You did not go unaccompanied. You presented yourself under false colours, madame, at The Old Hall. We should like to know why.'

'Pah!' She threw up her hands. 'I do not keep secrets! I simply did not know you wished to be told all this. You have misunderstood. Why should my visit to Harrogate be of interest to you? My poor husband was not there and he had been living, I now know, here in London. He was murdered here. There is no connection with Harrogate, only a wasted and expensive journey made by myself. Of what interest or use is all that to you? I am not accustomed to being interrogated by the police.'

Oh yes, you are, I thought but did not say aloud. You'd be a lot more nervous if you'd never been through any official interrogation before. Innocence acts guilty, and the guilty present themselves as white as driven snow, that's my experience. I wonder how you earned the money that bought you the lodging house in Montmartre?

'You gave a false name . . .' Dunn began. He must have been flustered to make such an elementary mistake.

She leaped on it. 'I gave no such thing! I gave my maiden name, Guillaume.'

'The gentleman with you also gave that name,' Dunn persevered. His manner was growing terrier-like. She was doing her best to shake free of his line of questioning, but he'd got a grip.

'If you would allow me to explain, Superintendent!' We waited. Victorine's manner grew calmer. She folded her hands in her lap and began composedly. 'I told Inspector Ross...' (A malicious glance at me.) 'That I had travelled to this country with an old friend, a friend of both my husband and myself, Hector Mas. He has returned to France. But for a few weeks after we arrived, he stayed here to support me in my enquiries. When we landed in England, we travelled to Yorkshire. My husband had spoken of his boyhood there and I thought it possible that, if he had come back to England in a confused state of mind, he might have gone to his boyhood home. As a married lady, it would not appear proper to travel with an unrelated gentleman of a different name. So Monsieur Mas agreed it best that he present himself under the name of Guillaume and, as such, we travelled as brother and sister. Now, of course, it appears suspicious to you. But at the time, to us, it only appeared practical.'

She waited for our comment but since neither of us made any, she gave a cross sigh and continued.

'On our arrival in Harrogate, we found it is a spa town with many visitors coming and going, often from the Continent, and our arrival did not occasion any surprise. We asked about a family called Tapley. We were told the name was very well known but no Tapley had lived in Harrogate or nearby for many years. No one had seen Mr Thomas Tapley recently. However, the family still owned some property, The Old Hall, as it was called, now occupied by a tenant, and some farmland and farmhouse. So Hector, Monsieur Mas, suggested he walk over the moor towards The Old Hall, in the hope of encountering an employee of the estate or a servant at the Hall, whom he could ask about my husband, and whether he'd been seen in the area. Thomas might not have gone into the town, we thought, but he might have stayed at an inn, for example, near his old family home.'

I decided this was all going too smoothly and decided to toss a pebble into the water. 'I believe, madame, that Monsieur Mas adopted the disguise of an artist, carried a painter's satchel, perhaps?'

That did catch her off guard. Dunn looked surprised as well. I admit I'd only just made the connection myself.

'Monsieur Mas,' Victorine said firmly, 'is an accomplished amateur artist. That is why he took his satchel of drawing paper and materials. The scenery around there interested him. However, he didn't get any chance to draw nor any chance to speak to anyone. The only person he encountered was a ruffian declaring himself a gamekeeper, and carrying a gun. He was aggressive and abusive and drove poor Hector away. Hector was alarmed and didn't stay to argue.

'We decided to present ourselves at The Hall as tourists, respectable people who could not be driven off with threats of violence. We hired a barouche, which was an expense I could ill afford, but we needed it. We called at The Hall, met Major Griffiths, were invited into the house by him and shown some of the rooms. We tried to talk to him about the family, but he became almost as surly as his gamekeeper and we found ourselves dismissed with little ceremony.'

'And yet, madame,' said Dunn, 'had you presented yourself as Mrs Tapley, you would have received a far kinder reception.'

'Yes, I realise that now,' Victorine said irritably. 'It is possible to be very wise after the event, as you say. In France, we call that *l'esprit de l'escalier* . . .'

We both stared at her uncomprehendingly.

'The wit of the staircase,' she translated obligingly. 'It is the thing you should have said, but did not think of, and only occurred to as you were leaving. As we were returning to Harrogate in the barouche, Hector and I, we agreed it would have been better to present ourselves as Mrs Tapley and Monsieur Mas, and let the gossips make of that whatever they liked. But we had not. So, having found no trace of Thomas, or anyone who could help us, we decided to go to London. I knew that Thomas had a cousin, Jonathan, living there. Thomas had given me to understand he and his cousin were not on good terms. They had quarrelled. But I thought I might contact him, even so. However, when we arrived here I found, at my hotel, a card advertising a detective agency. I hesitated for some time but eventually decided to enquire first if they could help. I have explained all this to you, Inspector Ross.'

'Indeed you have, madame,' I agreed. 'Tell me, while in Harrogate, you did not think to consult Newman and Thorpe, the firm of solicitors there who handle all your husband's business?'

'I did not know of Newman and – who?'

'Thorpe, madame.'

'I did not know of them.' She frowned. 'That is a great nuisance. If I had known, I should certainly have gone to them.'

'If you had presented yourself in the town as Mrs Tapley, you might have been directed to them by someone,' I said mildly.

'Again, Inspector,' was the chilly response, 'you are wise after the event. Obviously, as I realise now, I was wrong not to give my married name in Harrogate. However, the fact remains I did not.'

She stood up. 'Is there anything else you wish to know?'

'Is there anything else you wish to tell us, madame?' asked Dunn politely.

'No!' was the curt response. 'I remind you I am recently widowed. I am very upset by all of this. I should like to return to my hotel and rest. I have the ordeal of my dear husband's funeral ahead of me. What's more, that man Griffiths will be there, he tells me.'

'Before you leave, madame,' I said. 'Perhaps you'd be so kind as to repeat all you have told us in the form of a statement and sign it? I'll call my sergeant.'

'You are impertinent!' she snapped. 'To ask me to make a statement, to sign things, at this time and in these circumstances, is unkind, unnecessary and ungentlemanly. But we have discussed your lack of gentlemanly qualities already, Inspector.'

'I fear I have lost your good opinion, madame, and I am sorry for it. But there, it is the way of police work. It cannot be helped,' I told her ruefully.

An extraordinary thing happened then. I swear, she almost

laughed. She didn't, but cast me a quizzical look as she swept past. I found myself smiling foolishly.

'Take that sentimental grin off your face, Ross!' ordered Dunn, when she had left with Morris. 'You are not conducting a flirtation with the lady.'

'No, sir, sorry. But she, well, she has a way of catching one off guard.'

'Hum!' growled Dunn. 'Is she a liar?'

'Ah, sir,' I said. 'There's the thing. She doesn't exactly lie. That is to say, she doesn't, as far as we can prove anything. What she does is give out the truth in dribs and drabs; and then in such a way that it appears quite differently, as related by her, to the way it has been seen, previously, by us. She holds up a prism to the facts. They divide and become confusing. One can't be sure what one's looking at.'

'So, are we wrong? Or just thick-headed policemen?'

'She makes me feel like a thick-headed policeman,' I confessed. 'I do sometimes think she is playing some sort of game with me.'

'Ross! I remind you that you are a married man, an officer of the law, and investigating officer in this case!'

'I am not flirting, Superintendent! I wouldn't dare. Lizzie would kill me.'

'So, did Victorine Tapley kill her husband?' Dunn asked grimly.

'Beat him over the head with a blunt instrument, sir? No, I can't see it. It would be too crude. I can imagine her poisoning his soup, perhaps? But that's not how the poor fellow died.'

'Because he ran away from her before she could do it?' asked Dunn.

'We don't know, sir.'

Dunn looked thoughtful. 'I said she was a clever woman,' he said at last.

I'd thought I was the one who'd said that.

Dunn ran his fingers through his cropped hair, making it stand up on end like a hearth brush. 'I, too, shall attend this funeral, Ross,' he announced.

'I am glad to hear it, sir. There are things about this funeral I should like to discuss with you. We shall have all parties gathered together in one place. I think it may prove a day of reckoning.'

Chapter Seventeen

Elizabeth Martin Ross

THE DAY of the funeral dawned dank and chill, as if recently departed winter had decided to make a surprise return visit, just when we all thought we'd seen the last of it for a while. Overnight a fog had rolled up from the river and swirled about, trailing its fingers through the streets as if a fire smouldered nearby. It was not so bad as to be categorised as a 'London Particular', that thick brown soup which fouls the air, causes pedestrians to cough and choke, and cabs and carts to collide with one another. But still, it was bad enough. Air in our street and around was made worse by smoke from the engines at the railway terminus nearby, trapped at low level. By the time the day is over, and we have reached home again, I thought, we shall all of us smell like kippers.

'It will be better in the Marylebone area,' said Ben optimistically.

Mrs Jameson accompanied us. She had expressed a wish to see her late lodger decently laid to rest. The three of us squeezed into Wally Slater's four-wheeler, hired for the purpose, and proceeded at a painfully slow pace north of the river. Wally, in honour of the occasion, had tied a black scarf round his hat, and Nelson had black rosettes pinned to his bridle. Ben had found a black armband, and I had donned the mourning I had last worn for my poor father. The clothes had been packed away in a box since then and suffered for it. So, in a way, I was glad of the poor light because then my skirt and fitted jacket would not display its creases and darns so obviously. Mrs Jameson was dressed in her habitual sober manner, but not in black. It was not the Quaker custom, she informed us, to wear 'outward trappings' or make a ceremony of the occasion.

'Sorrow is in the heart, Mrs Ross. Indeed, I am very sorry for what happened to poor Mr Tapley. I still find it difficult to imagine that some ruffian forced his way into my house and struck the poor man down dead in the upstairs parlour. We pray he is now at peace; and that his assailant may yet repent of his crime.'

Despite Ben's optimism, the air wasn't so very much better by the time we reached St Marylebone church. We waited outside, with damp dripping from the trees and seeping through our clothing, for the arrival of the hearse with the coffin. I took the opportunity to look around to see who might be attending. I didn't expect there would be much of a crowd. Superintendent Dunn was already there ahead of us. The family had not yet arrived and apart from Ben and myself, and Mrs Jameson, there was only an elderly female. She told us, between much sniffing into a handkerchief, she had been governess to 'dear little Flora' from her arrival at the age of three in the household until she grew old enough to be sent away to school.

'The family has always been so good to me,' she confided. 'Mr Tapley – Mr Jonathan Tapley – settled a small annuity on me in recognition of my services. But now to think that the other Mr Tapley, dear Flora's papa, is to be buried today. The poor child.' She took refuge in the handkerchief.

'Did you know Mr Thomas Tapley?' I enquired.

She shook her head. 'I never met the gentleman. He did call a few times to see his child in the early years, before he went away to France. But I did not meet him, only glimpsed him, on the few times he came, when Flora was called down to the parlour by her aunt. I would take Flora down and leave her at the door. He never stayed long, her papa, I mean.'

Another party arrived, swelling our numbers. It consisted of four gentlemen, three of them, as it turned out, known to Ben. All four had come down from Harrogate for the occasion. They were two solicitors by the name of Thorpe, father and son, I gathered; and Major Griffiths. The fourth gentleman was a real John Bull of a figure, of stout build, red in face, and wearing a low-crowned hat, a broadcloth coat and old-fashioned breeches and gaiters. He informed us he had been a boyhood friend of Thomas.

'Though I've heard nothing of him for years,' he explained. 'Not since he went off to live abroad. I little thought I'd be coming down to London to see him buried.' He shook his head. 'Poor fellow, he were a sorry horseman and a poor shot, but come to book-reading, well, he could quote you Shakespeare by the yard.'

At this point the rumble of wheels and clatter of hooves announced that the hearse had arrived in sombre splendour, drawn by a pair of jet horses, black plumes nodding above their ears. The Tapley carriage followed close behind. Now I saw for myself the matched carriage pair of 'golden horses', so vividly described by Joey. I confess they appeared inappropriately showy for the sad occasion, even though they, too, sported black plumes and rosettes. Down from the carriage stepped Jonathan, a black silk scarf tied round his top hat, and holding up his hand to help down first his wife and then Victorine. I had been wondering if they would allow her to come with them, as a family member. Whatever their feelings towards her, and Jonathan's suspicions, I supposed they could hardly *not* have brought the widow with them. It would have occasioned gossip, and the Tapleys had a horror of that.

I studied Victorine Tapley as closely as I could without staring at her too openly. She was undeniably a handsome woman, even if not in the first flush of youth. She carried herself like a queen. But then, she had been a trained dancer. An expensive-looking hat, trimmed with ostrich feathers dyed black, was securely pinned to her intricately coiled hair. Surely such a fashionable hat came from Paris, I thought, awkwardly aware of my own old-fashioned mourning bonnet. More than ever I was convinced Victorine must have brought her entire mourning wardrobe with her from France, despite it taking up at least two boxes besides the hatbox for the millinery. She expected poor Thomas would soon be dead, I decided, if he wasn't already. But was I looking at a murderess?

Flora stepped down last, appearing almost to have been forgotten. She wore a small mourning bonnet with a leafy patterned veil. She followed her uncle, aunt and stepmother with bowed head. Maria Tapley glanced back at her once, but otherwise, I got the impression both Jonathan and his wife were keeping their eyes firmly fixed on the widow.

The coffin was carried into the church, the family following behind and the rest of us following them. Our small gathering seemed even more modest in the spacious, elegant, white and gold interior. The service was brief. We left again. Ben and I, with Mrs Jameson, climbed back into Wally's growler, joined there by Superintendent Dunn. We set off behind the hearse, the family carriage and the vehicle that had been hired to carry the Thorpes, Major Griffiths and the John Bull incarnation, together with the little former governess whom they had kindly taken up with them. Our destination was the modest railway station, situated near to its bigger brother at Waterloo, which was the starting point of the private line running to the huge burial area, known as the Brookwood Necropolis, some twenty-five miles out of London.

By the time the coffin and the pallbearers had been loaded aboard, and we mourners had entered a separate carriage, our party had gained two more members. There was a couple, apparently husband and wife, of middle age and stolid appearance. They did not introduce themselves, spoke to no one en route and I did not remember seeing them in the church. I did wonder if they had somehow attached themselves to the wrong funeral. Ours had not been the only party at the station waiting to be taken to Brookwood and there would be at least two other funerals that afternoon. I didn't know if they suspected that they had got mixed up, if indeed they had. But if so, they were sitting it out with true British determination.

Mrs Jameson seemed fascinated both by Victorine and by Jonathan Tapley. After a baffled look or two at the

Frenchwoman, Mrs Jameson fixed her gaze on him throughout the journey to Brookwood, although, if she thought he had noticed or anyone else had observed, she looked quickly away or down. On one occasion she caught my eye, watching her as she watched him, and she blushed quite pink. It's not surprising, I thought, that she should find it hard to connect such a prosperous figure of a successful man with the spindly form of her shabby lodger. She must wonder anew how it could be that Thomas Tapley had ended his life in her first-floor parlour.

Flora remained behind her veil. The pattern of leaves that sprinkled it meant that her features could only be glimpsed dimly in small areas. As the veil quivered in the rocking of the carriage, these areas flickered like a magic lantern show. I saw an eye and then one side of her mouth, then her cheek, all frozen in a misty gloom. Sometimes I had the eerie feeling that, if the veil were suddenly removed, there would be no Flora behind it, only a doll's porcelain face. From time to time, her Aunt Maria glanced at her again, but did not offer any words of comfort, nor even touch her arm. Flora was 'bearing up'; and that was all that mattered.

The Necropolis had two platforms at which mourners could descend: one for the area used for Church of England funerals, and another for Nonconformist ones. It would have given the unknown couple the opportunity to slip away and await the right funeral, but they stuck with us. Perhaps, after all, they had come to see Tom Tapley buried.

The twenty-five miles travelled from London had not proved far enough to shake off all traces of the fog. A perceptible mist filtered across the cemetery grounds, a huge area of parkland. It had been designed to be a resting place for the dead of London, for whom little or no burial space remained in the city and whose families could afford to buy a plot here. The mist snaked between the trees and around the headstones and monuments, hovering above the areas of green sward and restricting our view. The day appeared darker than it should have been at this hour. The sun's rays had not penetrated the cloud cover at all that day.

We walked in a sedate procession, our feet crunching on the gravel paths, passing by stone urns, decked with carved draperies; and angels who cast down their sightless eyes at us, spreading wings that would never flap free of the earth. It had grown much colder. The mist grew thicker by the minute. It was a fairly long walk at our slow pace and by the time we reached the appointed site, the light was failing fast. The clergyman who had come with us from the church, conveyed in the Tapley carriage, spoke the necessary words and poor Tom Tapley was lowered into the ground, amid the smell of freshly turned soil. We all set off back to the platform for the train.

Now that the task was over, a sense of relief could be felt. Our disciplined procession had broken up and become more of a scattered group. The undertaker's men walked in a little group, to one side. The stolid husband and wife had at long last approached Jonathan and Maria and were expressing some condolences. The Tapleys were accepting these with equanimity, although I had a strong suspicion they had no idea who these people were. Tom's widow had dropped back and walked by herself. Ben was talking to Major Griffiths; Superintendent Dunn chatted with the stout gentleman in breeches. The little governess was whispering to the pair of solicitors, and Flora . . .

I looked round, sensing a spurt of alarm. Where was Flora? Quickly I looked in all directions. I saw only trees, headstones and stone figures on plinths.

I shouted out her name as loudly as I could, heedless of the impropriety in the surroundings. 'Flora!'

Immediately our party was in disarray and panic set in. Jonathan shouted, 'Where the devil is she?' His wife gave a shriek and fell back to be supported, unhappily, by the clergyman. The four gentlemen from Harrogate split up and ran in different directions. The stout gentleman in breeches was crying, 'Halloo!' as though he were on the hunting field and we saw he was pointing in the distance. Indistinctly, amid the trees and difficult to discern in the gloom and mist, something moved, some strange shape, constantly changing. Suddenly as it broke free of the sheltering trees it could be seen to be made up of a man and a woman, struggling. All the men, including the pallbearers but with the exception of the clergyman who was still encumbered with Maria Tapley, began to race in that direction, shouting. Ben was yelling, 'Police! Stop!' The male struggling figure broke away and the female one sank to the ground. Dunn began roaring, 'Mas! Devil take it, it must be Mas! Catch the scoundrel!'

Then the hunt was on, as the fleeing male figure darted and dodged among the monuments and headstones. The pursuers had spread out and were attempting to cut off his escape. Maria Tapley had recovered her senses, and she and the governess were both running towards the form of Flora collapsed on the ground. The clergyman, his surplice flapping, hastened behind them, clutching his prayer book and trying to keep some dignity. I looked for Victorine and saw that she was running, too, but not with the rest. She was heading in the opposite direction.

I picked up my skirts and set off after her. I didn't know where she was going, or her purpose, and I had no one to help me by heading her off. I made every effort, jumping over graves and sprinting across the grass. She knew I was behind her. She glanced back once and then dashed on. But I was younger and fitter and I began to gain on her. At that point, she stooped and picked up a small marble flower vase and hurled it at me with the force and accuracy of a bowler in a cricket match. I ducked and it whizzed over my head. Our chase was on again. But she had wasted time in stooping to take up her missile and hurl it. I had reached within a few feet of her. I hurled myself forward, arms outstretched, and grasped a handful of the material of her skirt.

She turned on me, hissing in rage, and tried to shake me free but I was not to be cheated of my prey, now that I had her in my grasp. At that moment, she stumbled over the granite kerbstone of a grave and fell to her knees. I threw myself on her and wrapped my arms round her waist. She was abusing me ferociously in French. It awoke memories of those long-ago French lessons of my girlhood and I replied vigorously in the same language.

I fancy it was that, hearing me speak to her in French, which surprised her so much. She ceased struggling. We were both on the ground now, the pair of us exhausted and breathless. My bonnet had fallen off my head and was caught round my neck by its ribbons. Victorine was collapsed with her back to a gravestone, drawing breath in ragged gasps. Her fine Parisian milliner's creation with its ostrich feathers had also fallen off . . . but with it so had her gleaming black hair. The elaborate wig lay on the ground. Victorine's own hair was short and almost white. It was an old woman who sat, panting and still spitting defiance, opposite me.

Ben pounded up to us, out of breath. He, too, was hatless. 'Are you all right, Lizzie?' he demanded anxiously.

'Yes, I'm fine,' I assured him. 'But how is Flora? Is she harmed? Did you catch that man who was running away?'

'Miss Tapley has had a fright, but is recovering. She had lagged a little behind and suddenly, she says, an unknown man stepped out from behind a monument, put his hand over her mouth and began to drag her away from our party. Enterprisingly, she bit his palm. He relaxed his grip and the tussle began which we saw. We didn't catch him, I'm sorry to say. The light is poor and we found ourselves running into another funeral party. In the confusion, he got clean away.'

Ben turned his attention to Victorine, still sitting on the floor. 'But I think I know who he is. It was Hector Mas, wasn't it, madame? What was he trying to do? Strengthen your claim on the estate by removing the other main claimant?'

Victorine had regained her composure. She stretched out a hand to pick up her wig, and set it carefully on her head. Turning to me, she asked, 'Is it straight?'

'Yes, quite straight,' I heard myself say.

'You speak very good French,' she told me.

I heard Ben give an exclamation of impatience. 'It will not do, madame. You cannot play the innocent as if nothing had happened! You are under arrest for plotting the kidnap, with

Hector Mas, of Flora Tapley with intent to do her some grievous harm. You will also be charged conspiracy in the murders of Thomas Tapley and Horatio Jenkins.'

'Monsieur Mas', she said coldly, 'has returned to France. I don't know who that man was you were chasing. Probably some tramp, intent on robbery. To say that I plotted to murder my poor husband is disgraceful! Of course I did not. As for Jenkins,' she shrugged, 'anyone might have killed him.'

'We'll discuss it further at the Yard, madame.'

Proceedings now took an ironical twist, for there was nothing for it but for the funeral party to return on the special train to London, all sitting together, as before, in one carriage. The only difference was that this time, Victorine Tapley sat between Ben and Superintendent Dunn, and no one looked in her direction except for John Bull. From time to time, he remarked, 'By Jove!' He seemed pleased he would have a tale to tell when he got home.

The governess had learned the identity of the stout couple. She whispered to me that the woman's mother had, when young, been in service with the first Mrs Tapley. At the terminus, we all parted, Ben, Dunn and Victorine in one cab, the Tapley family in their carriage and others by cab. Mrs Jameson and I walked back to our street. Before her front door, we paused to say our goodbyes.

'It is an extraordinary business, Mrs Ross,' said Mrs Jameson, in the first comment on the events at the Necropolis made in my hearing by anyone. (I did not count the 'By Jove!' remarks of the gentleman in breeches.)

'Yes, it is,' I said. 'And we haven't heard all of it yet.'

'No, indeed.' She was silent a moment. 'Can it really be

293

that the Frenchwoman, wearing that extraordinary hat with the feathers, is the widow of poor Mr Tapley?' she asked next.

'It would seem so,' I said.

'And that fine-looking gentleman in the beautifully tailored coat, that is his cousin?'

'Yes, Mrs Jameson, he is.'

'Well,' said Mrs Jameson. 'It's very puzzling and I shall have to think it over. Goodnight, Mrs Ross, I am glad to have had your company today.'

With that, she went indoors and I continued to my own home, where Bessie was waiting agog to hear about the day. I had rather more to tell her than she'd expected.

Chapter Eighteen

Inspector Benjamin Ross

AN ATTEMPT to interview Victorine Guillaume that evening, on our return to Scotland Yard from Brookwood, proved unproductive. At first, the lady simply refused to speak. She had unpinned her hat with the feathers and placed it on the table between us where it reminded me irresistibly of a dead game bird laid out like a trophy. She sat with her eyes fixed on it and her hands folded in her lap.

'You do yourself a disservice, madame,' I told her. 'By saying nothing at all, when your behaviour has been so strange, it suggests you have some guilty motive for your silence.'

At that, she did ask, in her normal composed manner, 'What behaviour?'

'At the cemetery. When all were either hastening to help Miss Flora, or running in pursuit of her attacker, you ran in the opposite direction and resisted my wife's attempt to prevent you.'

That earned a flicker of an eyebrow. 'I did not know what was happening. I am in a foreign country. My husband has been murdered here. We were gathered in that cemetery to bury him. My mind was occupied with that and nothing else. Then, for some reason I had not understood, all began to shout and run. So, I ran. In the poor light I did not realise it was Mrs Ross behind me. I thought a gang of ruffians had set upon us in that lonely place. Why did Mrs Ross run?'

'Because you ran, madame.'

'Then I suggest it is your wife who behaved illogically, not I.'

And with that well-placed dart she'd found her target and would say no more.

'We'll leave her in a cell overnight,' I told Dunn. 'She may well have changed her mind about talking in the morning. Or we may have heard from the French police. I certainly hope so, because at the moment we can't charge her with anything . . . except running away when everyone else was panicking and running. We'll have to let her go tomorrow if we learn nothing new. We risk making fools of ourselves. If we can find the man who attacked Flora Tapley, and if he is Hector Mas, then that changes the picture. He may talk. In any case, she will find it hard to deny complicity.'

I knew I sounded frustrated and bitter. Dunn shared my mood.

'If that fellow in the cemetery was Mas,' he fumed. 'Where the devil is he now? Find him! He should stick out like a sore thumb, wherever he is!'

I went home to my wife, there being for the moment nothing else I could do that day. It was now late but Lizzie was waiting up for me.

'There has been no time to cook today,' she announced. 'I thought I'd be home from the cemetery in time to make something, and you would be here, too, so I didn't tell Bessie to get anything ready.'

'I've eaten Bessie's dry meat pies and scorched rice puddings,' I replied. 'I'm glad you didn't ask her. After being made to look and sound an idiot by Victorine Guillaume, and having lost Mas at the cemetery, Bessie's cuisine would be the last straw.'

'She is improving as a cook,' Lizzie defended our maid. 'But as it happens, there is the rest of the steak and kidney pie we had two days ago in the larder. It's still quite fresh. It's cold in the larder even in warm weather and at this time of year, there's no fear of anything going off in a few days.'

So we ate three-day-old steak and kidney. I must say, it tasted fine.

The following morning when I reached the Yard I found that, at long last, something had gone right for us. The French police had sent a long communication answering our queries.

The marriage between Thomas Tapley and Victorine Guillaume had been conducted according to French law and properly registered. The groom had declared himself a widower. The bride had described herself as a spinster. The lady was not altogether unknown to the police. Before establishing herself as owner of a respectable lodging house, she had been a dancer, the mistress of an exporter of wines and spirits and, at the same time, a procuress of young women to train up as the better sort of courtesan. This had eventually led to the close interest of the police and the subsequent loss of her protector. Before matters got too hot for her, she had vanished from Paris and been absent some years. It was believed she had moved to England. When she had finally returned it was to buy the property in Montmartre. Though she had never been imprisoned, she was a known acquaintance of a range of petty criminals. These included one Hector Mas, about whom we had also enquired; although much younger he was widely believed to be her lover.

Mas was originally from Marseilles. He had lived for a number of years in Paris where he made his living chiefly as a small-time confidence trickster and cardsharp, who preyed on newcomers to Paris from the provinces. He had served two prison terms, one in his native Marseilles and one in the capital. Mas had not been seen in Paris in recent months. Neither had Victorine Guillaume. The lodging house still existed, run, in the absence of the owner, by a manager. As a business, it appeared to be perfectly in order. A suspicion, a few years earlier, that it operated as an unregistered brothel had not been supported by enquiries.

'Well,' I said to Dunn. 'So Mas is the usual sort of smooth-talking petty crook. London is also full of rogues like him, plying the same trade fleecing the gullible.'

'And despite what that woman insists, he is not at present in France. We know that now!' snorted Dunn. 'He is lurking somewhere around London. He knew the details of the funeral, where and when, and only Guillaume could have told him that. He waited in the cemetery for a chance to abduct Flora Tapley. It was a bold step but our conspirators have grown desperate.' Dunn shook a thick forefinger at me. 'The discovery of Flora's existence was a development with which they had not reckoned when they followed the wretched Tapley to England. It must have come as a real shock to them.'

'I think, sir,' I said, 'that with the new information to help, I am now ready to interview the lady again.'

'Well, now, madame,' I said when I found myself seated opposite that lady a little later. 'I hope you did not spend too uncomfortable a night.'

She did not deign to reply to that but cast me a look of scorn and spite that spoke volumes.

She was still neat, still in her widow's weeds, and the black wig was firmly in place. Her composure must be assumed, but it was convincing enough at the moment. I hoped to shake it very soon.

'You should know, madame, that we have now heard from the French police.'

Her eyelids drooped briefly over her dark eyes but then she was staring at me again in her usual direct manner. 'Then they will have informed you my marriage was legal,' she said.

'Yes, madame, they have told us that . . . and a good deal more. You have led an eventful life, madame.'

'You are not a fool, Inspector,' she said coldly. 'You know that the world is not kind to women who find themselves alone. I was born the illegitimate child of a singer in the cabarets of Montparnasse. She placed me in the ballet school at a young age in the hope I would have an occupation that would keep me from the streets; and, eventually, help me find a protector rich enough to take care of both of us. My mother died only a few years later of consumption. I have always had to rely on my own resources, and survived because I have always done what it was necessary for me to do. But I have never been charged with any crime, Inspector.'

'There is always a first time, for everything, madame, or so they say. The French police also inform us that you were once accused of procuring young girls . . .'

Her eyes snapped with anger! 'One girl! One girl only and let me tell you about her, Inspector, before you lecture me! She was being forced by her parents to marry an old man, an old man she detested and feared. So she ran away from her home. I found her begging on the streets. I took her home with me and I tried to help her by finding her someone who would take care of her. I did find her a protector, a decent man who would have treated her well. But then, of course, the parents reappear. They must have their daughter back! I have seduced their innocent child into a despicable and immoral life. They complain to the police. The police come to me. The wretched child is forced back to her parents' home. Because they want to be reconciled to her? No, because they fear the gossip and scandal. The old suitor comes forward again and this time, having no hope of escaping him, the girl swallows rat poison, arsenic. It is a terrible death, Inspector. The police suddenly have no further interest in pursuing me. No charges were ever brought against me in court. No one, of course, pursues the parents or the filthy old lecher who was the cause of it all.'

'Yet the matter remains upon your police file, madame. If what you tell me is true, that is indeed unfortunate.'

'Policemen, in the whole of Europe and probably even further afield, like to keep files,' Victorine Guillaume said. 'It encourages the taxpayer in France and here, I suppose, to believe their money is well spent.'

I decided to abandon this line of enquiry. But I was getting very tired of being out-argued by her.

'Let us talk of your associate, Hector Mas. Now, he's a different kettle of fish. His police file is fat and none of the reports in it has been doubted. He has spent at least two spells in gaol. He has not been seen in Paris or elsewhere in France for some time. He is here in London, isn't he? We believe it was Mas who attempted to abduct Flora Tapley from the cemetery. The only explanation for his knowing where to position himself for the attempt is that you told him: the hour, the place and the day. I assure you, madame, you will be charged with conspiracy to kidnap.'

This was a chance throw of the dice by me. It might be possible to make such a charge stick, but without Mas in our hands, it would be difficult.

'I do not know who was the man in the cemetery—' she began.

I interrupted her. 'Please, madame,' I said gently. 'You were kind enough just now to say I was not a fool, so, I beg you, don't start now to treat me like one. Equally, I believe you to be an intelligent woman. You must know you can't rely on Mas. We shall catch him, without question. He is fleeing like a hunted fox at the moment. But we shall run him to earth. The French police are now on the lookout for him also. If he returns there, they will arrest him. He will seek to save himself. I know the type. His own skin is all that matters to him. He knows no loyalties.'

She said nothing but watched me warily. A tiny flicker of hope sprang up in me that she could be persuaded to bargain. She would do what she said she had always done, anything necessary, and that would include abandoning Mas, but only if I proceeded cautiously.

'Madame,' I began again, 'let us begin again differently. Let me tell you the history of what has happened, as it seems to me. You will then tell me if I am right. Is that in order?'

'I cannot prevent you,' she said coldly.

'Thomas Tapley is an Englishman who has lived many years in France, kept by personal reasons from returning to his own country. He is growing older and beginning to regret his lack of a permanent base. You are the owner of a lodging house on the outskirts of Paris. One day, into the lodging house walks Tapley.

'He appears down at heel, but he *is* a gentleman, you identify him as that. He begins to lodge with you. It soon becomes apparent to you, because you have a sharp eye, that this "poor" Englishman in his shabby coat is not so penniless after all. He pays his rent regularly with no delay. Money is coming from somewhere. He doesn't, perhaps, realise how well you speak and read English. One day, while he is out, you go into his room and manage to gain access to his personal papers. He is in correspondence with a bank in England, with a firm of solicitors. There is mention of property . . .'

She had made no attempt to interrupt me and was watching me keenly. I am on the right track! I thought.

'You tell your good friend, Hector Mas, about him. Mas can smell a mark. He is very interested. I don't know whose idea it was that you should persuade Tapley to marry you, in order to gain himself a comfortable home in his old age. Perhaps it was yours, because in the past, at least once, you have lived in the care of a protector. You are no longer young enough, forgive my bluntness, to seek out a protector of that sort. But perhaps the situation is now reversed. You can

302

present yourself as a kind of protector to Tapley, a wife who will care for him and is in the position to offer him a comfortable home. At any rate, the marriage takes place.

'At first all is well, but then Tapley falls ill. You take care of him devotedly. But when he recovers, instead of being grateful, he is suspicious. Perhaps Mas has been hanging around and Tapley has recognised Mas for what he is. Perhaps Mas is asking you why you tried so hard to help your husband recover, when, had you let him die, you could have written to England with the news and claimed any estate. You are both of you quite sure, by now, that there is money. During his illness, you have probably either read some mail directed to him, or again rummaged through his papers.

'But Tapley has realised it. He begins to fear a plot against him, that his very life is at risk. Should he "fall ill" again, no doctor would think it odd, after the serious illness he's already had. Perhaps Mas has said as much to you, madame. One day, when you are out of the house, and Mas out of the way, Tapley packs his box and flees. So desperate is he, that he feels nowhere in France safe, and returns to England. When he arrived in Harrogate and spoke to his solicitor there, he deposited some personal papers, stressing the need for them to be kept secure, and spoke of "an incident". He appeared a frightened man. Am I more or less right so far, madame?'

'You are taking facts I have told you, and interpreting them in a different way, Inspector,' Victorine replied. 'You have said nothing new, except to speculate about what Hector Mas may have said. As to that, you would have to ask Hector himself.'

'You failed to find your husband in France and decided he

must have come to England, you also told me that,' I continued. 'You knew if you did find him he would not return with you to France. I believe you and Mas planned to locate him and murder him.'

Victorine jumped to her feet, eyes blazing with rage. 'This is an insult and stupid, as well! Why should I plan to kill my dear husband for some money which might not exist?'

'Sit down, madame. You are both of you sure now that money *does* exist. You have been to Harrogate and seen The Old Hall. You have been to Bryanston Square where Mr Jonathan Tapley lives, and seen his fine house. You have made enquiry about Mr Jonathan, and learned he is a wealthy man. This is a family of well-to-do, well-regarded people. You have also learned something alarming. Mr Jonathan Tapley is a lawyer. You will have to tread carefully. You cannot simply knock at his front door and ask if he knows the whereabouts of your husband.

'So you decide to use a detective, Horatio Jenkins. You give Jenkins a photograph of your husband and Jenkins locates him. You pay Jenkins off but he declines, using some excuse, to return the photograph. In so doing, he has signed his death warrant. Mas goes to where Thomas Tapley is lodging. In the absence of the maidservant he enters the house by the kitchen door, goes up the back stairs, finds your husband reading and strikes him down. He looks round the room quickly but there are no signs of any correspondence with the solicitor in Harrogate, or anything else that Tapley might have written down to indicate he was living in fear of his life, should his wife find him. No diary, for example, and no "letter to be opened in the event of my death". He goes into the next room, Tapley's bedroom. He does not want to linger, with a recently slain corpse stretched upon the carpet next door, but a solution presents itself. Lying on a bedside cabinet is a door key. Mas pockets it, intending to return later to search again. He leaves.'

'*You are wrong!*' Victorine screamed at me, losing her composure at last. 'Hector did not go there! He did not kill my husband!' She made an effort to pull herself together. 'The wretched Jenkins did not give us my husband's address. He only asked for more money!'

'Who else would want your husband dead? Who else would enter a private house belonging to a respectable Quaker widow, creep upstairs and kill her harmless, apparently penniless, lodger?'

'Hector did not kill him,' she repeated obstinately. 'Nor, in case you are thinking it, did I!'

'What of Jenkins, the detective you employed? Someone killed that unfortunate fellow. Someone searched his room thoroughly. Was that Mas? Was he looking for the photograph? It was not there. But we have discovered its whereabouts and we have it in our possession!'

That surprised her so much, she blurted, 'Where was it?'

'Jenkins had given it to someone to keep for him. Come, madame, the circumstantial case against you and Mas is very strong. You are certainly going to be charged regarding the attempted kidnap of Flora Tapley. The time has come to help yourself, because, without Mas, you will face the charges of conspiracy to murder and conspiracy to kidnap alone. You told me, madame, that you have always done what was necessary to survive. Do it now.'

She drew a deep breath. 'Very well, I will tell you what happened. If you do not believe me . . .' She shrugged. 'I cannot help it. Hector did not go to that house and did not kill my husband. He did go to Jenkins and demand the return to the photograph. Jenkins refused. Hector threatened him with a knife, foolishly. Jenkins tried to seize it, there was a struggle and Jenkins was stabbed. The man's death was an accident. It was not Hector's intention to kill him. Hector did search the room, but could not find my photograph. Now you say you have it. I repeat, I did not conspire with Hector Mas to kidnap Miss Tapley. I do not know the identity of the man in the cemetery and neither, Inspector, do you! There is nothing, Mr Ross, no evidence that allows you to charge me with any crime!'

'But I shall have evidence,' I told her confidently, 'when I have Mas, because he will talk. He will confess everything to save his skin. He will blame you. He'll say it was all your idea, your plan to come to England, that you persuaded him, paid him, tricked him, anything. You have just confessed to me that you've concealed knowledge of a crime, the stabbing of Jenkins. You say Hector Mas was responsible. If you know where Mas is to be found, and refuse to tell us, then you are guilty of concealing the whereabouts of a wanted man, as well as knowledge of the crime. Before you refuse to tell us, please consider, madame, whether Mas will show the loyalty to you that you are showing him? He is a miserable petty crook and trickster. For him there is no honour, even among thieves.'

She heaved a deep sigh, rolled up her eyes, and shrugged. My heart rose. She was going to talk! Not reveal everything, perhaps, but at least tell us about Mas.

'Very well, he is in Wapping.' She spoke more quietly and looked away from me, as if ashamed to betray a man she must know to be a worthless wretch. 'He has been lodging at an inn called the Silver Anchor. He is using another name, Pierre Laurent. I don't know if he's still there. He may be trying to get passage overseas, working as a deckhand, on one of the ships docked there. When he was young, he sailed on trading vessels all around the Mediterranean. Perhaps he's already left this country for ever. If he has, I cannot help you any further. I have said all I have to say.' She pressed her lips together.

'You have been wise, madame,' I told her, trying to keep my tone sober and not betray my elation.

She stared at me with hatred. 'You will never prove that Hector and I conspired to kill my husband,' she said. 'Because we did not; and you will never get the evidence to show otherwise.'

Chapter Nineteen

THERE ARE still people who remember when pirates were hanged at Wapping. Whether their twitching limbs and swollen faces, or their tarred remains left hanging in iron cages as a warning, did anything other than provide the residents with a good spectacle is doubtful. Occasionally, even now, a yellowed bony hand pokes out of the stinking mud when the tide goes out.

Crime is still breathed in at Wapping with its fetid air. Seamen still throng its narrow streets and rat-infested wharves and warehouses, and lurch drunkenly from its alehouses. Between the walls of its crammed, tottering buildings run dark alleys into which it would be rash to venture. Chandlers' shops spill their wares upon the cobbles. Smuggled goods change hands in smoky back rooms. Grog-shops, taverns, opium dens and bawdy houses jostle one another. If you want a bed for the night, no questions asked, it can be had for a shilling or two, if you don't mind the squalid condition. It might be cheaper if you are prepared to share it.

Here Hector Mas had gone to earth, another face, another foreign accent, and another bearer of a false name among a crowd of such. He had begun life in the slums of Marseilles and he blended in here perfectly.

It had grown dark by the time we reached the Silver Anchor tavern, a low, board-fronted building with a shingled roof, which looked as if it might originally have been a storehouse. We had enquired among the ships' captains and shipping agents about anyone signing on as crew in the name of Laurent, or Mas, or speaking with a French accent. Most said they didn't know of anyone of that description. Only one agent remembered an enquirer who possibly might have been our man. He had asked about ships wanting crew, but the agent had sent him away, not liking the look of him.

'We are not fussy about a man, provided he's fit and healthy and can do the job,' said the agent. 'But that one had a look in his eyes I have seen before. It was a look you see in the eyes of men with blood on their hands.'

Now we gathered before the Silver Anchor, reasonably sure our quarry was within. Our numbers were swelled by officers of the River Police. The tavern was doing good business. The noise of raucous laughter, female shrieks and quarrelling male voices, snatches of music, all streamed with the light from the tavern's mullioned windows. We had checked the area carefully and I'd made sure men were stationed round the building at all points from which an exit could be made. I opened the door and, followed by Sergeant Morris, went in.

Before they saw us, they sensed the presence of the law. Silence fell at once over the company. Card-players froze with the next card to be laid down between their fingers, now held suspended in the air. The accordion player broke off in mid-note with a tuneless squawk. Someone spat audibly on the floor. We walked through the crowd to where a stout, bearded man in a stained apron leaned on a rickety bar.

'You have a guest lodging here, a Frenchman, name of Pierre Laurent,' I said to him. 'I am Inspector Ross, of Scotland Yard, and I am anxious to speak to him. Where is he?'

The innkeeper began to wipe down his bar with a rag so dirty, it would only make the surface grimier. 'Well, sirs, I don't know that he is here.' Somewhere above, faintly, my ear caught the ting of a very small bell: the sort operated by a cord to summon a servant. Behind me, I heard Morris growl.

'Where is he?' I snapped. 'Don't play for time. The building is surrounded. If he's here, he can't escape.'

The man straightened up and glanced at the staircase running up beside the bar. 'Second door left.'

Careful though we had been, there had been time enough for someone to communicate with the fugitive upstairs. The bell was probably a time-honoured signal given whenever the police entered the place. It needed only a jerk on a cord operated by someone below in the crowded taproom. The host might have done it with his foot while the movement of the grimy rag had distracted our attention. As Morris and I reached the first floor, we saw the bell, still quivering on its metal spring. The second door on the left gaped open, and the room beyond was empty.

We threw open other doors as we ran along the corridor. In the first we discovered only a seaman, so far gone with drink that he sprawled semi-conscious on a grimy pallet and stared up at us blearily, probably unable to focus on our faces. In the

311

next we disturbed an indignant bawd and her customer. He was not our quarry and demanded to know what we meant by bursting in. I ignored his protests, threw open a casement and shouted to my men below.

'Has anyone left?'

'No, sir! We're watching all the doors and windows!' yelled back the officer in the street.

I hurried back to the main corridor, followed by one of the bawd's shoes as an encouragement.

Morris was standing by a narrow ladder and looking up at an open hatch. As I appeared, he pointed. 'He's not gone down, sir, he's gone up! There must be an attic up there at least.'

The ladder debouched into a long, low loft running the length of the building. Rows of straw mattresses indicated this was where you could buy your bed the most cheaply. Two old men sat staring at us with rheumy eyes, mildly surprised to see us pop up through the hatch like a pair of jack-in-the-boxes. There was no sign of Mas, or anywhere he could be hidden.

'He's on the roof, sir!' shouted Morris, pointing upward at an open skylight. As he spoke we heard above our heads the scrape of a foot sliding on the tiles.

We clattered back downstairs. The crowd in the taproom raised a derisive cheer as we raced through them and out into the street. Our quarry's whereabouts was signalled by upturned faces and pointing fingers of our River Police colleagues outside. High above, outlined starkly against the blue-black of the night sky, a darker silhouette picked its way across the roof as delicately as a tightrope walker.

'Mas!' I yelled up to him. 'You cannot escape! Come down!'

His response was to jump, to make a graceful, athletic leap across the narrow space between this roof and that of the next building and land there. A couple of tiles were dislodged, fell to the ground and shattered. The silhouetted figure teetered wildly and appeared on the verge of falling backwards. He flung out his arms to either side, to gain balance, and wavered like an aspen before the wind. A sizeable crowd was gathering fast below now, and from it came a united intake of breath.

'He's going to fall! He'll break his neck!' cried someone. A woman shrieked.

But Mas didn't fall. He regained his balance and, bent double, scrabbled rapidly on all fours, like the rat he was, across that roof, over the ridge tiles and disappeared. The crowd cheered.

I reflected that Mas had been a seaman in his youth and learned to swarm up the rigging in blustery weather. He did not fear heights.

We ran after him and the crowd ran after us. There then followed a weird and frantic chase. Mas scuttled across roof after roof, leaping from one to the other with the same balletic grace. We crashed and stumbled our way along below, trying to keep him in sight, waiting for the moment, which must come, when there wasn't another roof to which he could jump. The sightseers, among them the patrons of the Silver Anchor, their ranks swelled by the customers of every taproom we passed, ran along with us, despite our orders to keep clear. They hindered our progress – their intention – and shouted their encouragements to the fleeing man.

So we came to the end of the row of buildings where it abutted a narrow wharf beyond which lay the river, gurgling and slapping against the stonework.

'He'll have to climb down now,' said Morris. 'Fetch a ladder, someone! Hey, you up there!' he added, bellowing to the fugitive. 'Stay where you are and we'll get you down.'

But Mas had no intention of accepting our offer. He was in his own waterside element. We saw his slim figure stand erect at the very point of the gable. He raised his arms and we all fell silent in awe and apprehension as the silhouetted form, starkly outlined again the moon, took flight, arching into the air, and then flying outward and downward in a swallow dive. By some miracle he cleared the wharf, and plunged into the murky waters of the Thames.

He caused a waterspout that sent a great fountain high into the air and across the wharf to drench those nearby. We all ran to the edge. Lanterns were held out. The surface of the river was black, choppy, and slicked with oil. Debris of all sorts bobbed about. Moored craft creaked and rocked with the wave. But nothing resembled the head of a man treading water, or showed us the progress of a swimmer.

'He can stay underwater for so long,' I muttered. 'But not for ever.'

'He'll have knocked himself out and drowned,' murmured Morris, as the seconds ticked by.

'No, sir, look!' shouted one of the River officers, pointing.

There in the distance, caught in the light of lanterns hung from the bow of a moored vessel, we could see the water breaking, and a stream of foam, as a swimmer struck out strongly.

Perhaps his intention was to lose himself among the moored craft, and come ashore at a different spot. He might have been successful. But crewmen aboard a barge anchored further out had spotted the man in the water. Not knowing what was happening, they were reacting instinctively.

We heard their cry of 'Man overboard!' They were already lowering a boat. Figures, one armed with a boathook, were waiting to scramble into it to the rescue.

'Mr Ross!' shouted the sergeant of the River Police who had come with us. 'We have a police launch ready, sir. This way!'

We ran after him, and found ourselves crammed into the police launch, heading towards the spot. As we neared it we saw a remarkable sight, as if we had not already seen so many that evening.

The would-be rescuers had reached the man in the water, but he was declining to be rescued. Hands stretched out to him. A rope was thrown. Voices implored him to 'Grab hold, matey!' He ignored all offers and struck out in another direction.

The River Police sergeant put a loud-hailer to his mouth. 'Detain him! Detain that man!'

The crewmen heard him. The one with the boathook stretched it out and hooked it into the swimmer's clothing. The swimmer threshed about, trying to free himself without drowning in the effort. But he was caught as surely as a fish on a line, and soon we had him landed.

'Hector Mas?' I gasped at the sodden figure sprawled on the deck of the launch at our feet. 'Otherwise known as Pierre Laurent? You are under arrest.'

The half-drowned creature rolled on to his side and spewed out half a gallon of filthy river water. Then he looked up and disgorged another stream, this time of French, directed at me.

I don't understand French and, if Lizzie had been with us, I doubt her knowledge included the words Mas was using. But, no matter, I got his meaning quite clearly.

It was late when I arrived home that evening, damp and exhausted. I was eager to tell the tale of our triumph. But I was forestalled. To my surprise, not only had Lizzie waited up for me, but she also had Mrs Jameson with her.

'I am surprised to see you, ma'am,' I said to her, 'at this late hour. I hope nothing more has gone amiss.'

Not waiting for her answer, I couldn't help but add eagerly, 'You should know, ma'am, that we have him! We have the man who killed your lodger. He is a Frenchman and is now sitting, still awash with river water, in the cells.'

It struck me that this intelligence was not being received with the cries of amazement and delight I had anticipated. I saw the two women glance at one another. My heart sank.

'What is it?' I asked.

'Ben,' began Lizzie. 'We're delighted you've caught Mas, of course. You must all be so pleased and Superintendent Dunn in particular. But Mrs Jameson has waited to see you, even though it's so late, because she has something very important she wants to tell you.'

I sat down, feeling the heat from the hearth begin to dry my damp clothes. I suspected I was starting to steam like a racehorse and probably smelled abominably of the river.

'The fact is this, Mr Ross,' Mrs Jameson began. 'I should offer an apology. I should have told you of this before, but it was not until the funeral of poor Mr Tapley that it occurred to me you might like to know about it. Indeed, I had almost forgot it until today.'

'Yes?' I encouraged her. She looked very nervous.

'I was very surprised, when we attended the funeral, to meet Mr Tapley's cousin, Mr Jonathan Tapley, and see what a fine, prosperous gentleman he was – is. Such a beautifully tailored coat . . . The coat particularly, and the cane.'

'Yes . . .' I repeated dully, apprehension growing in me.

'I do realise you asked me, and Jenny, too, on the day of the murder, whether we'd seen any strangers loitering about the house. I said I had not because, you see, my mind was running on suspicious-looking strangers, ruffians, murderers . . . I had forgotten the gentleman with the cane.'

I closed my eyes briefly. 'Go on, ma'am.'

'It was earlier that afternoon – on the day of the murder. It would have been some time after three o'clock. I am not usually in my front parlour at that time of the afternoon, unless I have visitors. But I had gone in to fetch some item I'd left there the evening before. Something attracted me, a movement in the street outside that just caught the corner of my eye, and caused me to look out of the parlour window. I saw a gentleman walk past my house and glance up at it. He was very well dressed and carried a cane, A few moments later, he walked past again. I did not know him, and thought perhaps he was looking for an address. When he did not come back a third time, I assumed he'd found it. He was a most respectable-looking man, a *professional-looking* man, very

317

dignified. It was not until the funeral, and to tell the truth, not until we were on the Necropolis railway train, travelling out to Brookwood, that I was able to study Mr Jonathan Tapley close at hand. I became convinced that it was the same man. And yet, I thought I *must* be mistaken. But the more I looked at him, the more I became sure.'

'Forgive me, ma'am,' I said. 'But do you sometimes wear spectacles? I ask because this is what a barrister may one day ask.'

'I do not wear spectacles, Inspector, not even when reading by artificial light. I have always been blessed with excellent eyesight!' Mrs Jameson sounded nettled. She resumed her usual placid tone to continue, 'I hesitated to speak to you at once. You told us, the doctor's opinion was poor Mr Thomas Tapley had died no earlier than five that afternoon. But I saw the other gentleman – I am now sure it was Mr Jonathan Tapley – so much earlier in the afternoon. I cannot give you a time o'clock, but it was certainly not so very long after three when he first passed by my house and about two minutes after that when he passed by the second time. You can see my predicament and why I have waited until tonight to tell you? But then I decided, you should know of it, even if it makes no difference. You say you have the culprit? Well, then, I suppose it does make no difference and I have troubled you with this to no purpose.'

'Thank you, Mrs Jameson,' I told her hollowly. 'I – we, the police, are much obliged to you. You did quite the right thing in telling me.'

'Thank you,' she said with relief, rising to her feet. 'And now I must go home.'

'I'll walk with you,' I said. 'It's late.'

When I returned to my own fireside, my wife wasted no time. 'But he couldn't have done it, surely? Why should he? Mrs Jameson must be wrong. You have Mas in the cells, and Victorine as well. What will you do?'

'I shall tell Dunn', I said, 'first thing tomorrow morning. What he will say, I dread to imagine.'

Chapter Twenty

'THE WRONG man?' roared Dunn. His eyes bulged. 'What on earth are you talking about, Ross?'

'I mean, it would be dangerous to congratulate ourselves too soon, sir. We may not have solved this case yet.'

'Of course we've solved it! Do you seriously mean to suggest that, with Mas downstairs in the cells, we have arrested an innocent man!' Dunn gurgled into silence, gulping for air in the manner of a stranded fish.

'No, no, Hector Mas is not an innocent man, sir,' I hurried on. 'Except, possibly, of the murder of Thomas Tapley. On other counts I'm quite sure he's guilty and we have the right villain locked up in the cells. He killed Jenkins and tried to abduct Flora Tapley. It may have been his original intention – and that of his accomplice Guillaume – on coming to England, that they seek out Thomas Tapley and that Mas murder him. But we cannot place him at the scene of that murder. Let us suppose that it's just possible someone else was there. Someone found Thomas Tapley before Mas did.'

'Let us suppose, for the sake of a mental exercise, that the moon is made of blue cheese,' offered Dunn sarcastically.

'All I am saying, sir, is that I don't think we have yet

established beyond doubt that it was Mas who killed Thomas Tapley.'

'Of course he did!' bawled Dunn. 'Who else had a motive and opportunity?'

'For that we must widen the scope of our enquiries, sir. But we have a starting point. We have agreed that there is a clever woman involved in this case, Victorine Guillaume. But I'm thinking there has also been a clever man.'

'Aha!' Dunn looked up at me under bushy eyebrows. 'Hector Mas is your clever man.'

'He has the quickness and ruthlessness of a wild beast, sir. But he is all instinct. The brains belong to Victorine Guillaume. No, I am thinking of Jonathan Tapley.'

'Tapley and Guillaume in league? Nonsense!'

'Yes, sir, that would be nonsense and I don't suggest it for a moment. I mean they have acted separately and in ignorance of one another. Victorine and her henchman, Mas, have been playing one deadly game. Jonathan Tapley has been playing another. Normally we have one set of villains. This time, I fancy we have two.'

Dunn shook his head. 'No, no, it won't do, Ross.'

I persisted. 'Mrs Jameson saw a man in the street, as I have been telling you, sir, walking up and down outside her house on the afternoon of the murder. When she saw Jonathan Tapley at the funeral, she recognised him as that man. She is quite certain. So, we have no witness to put Hector Mas in front of the house, but we do have a reliable one to put Jonathan Tapley there.'

'Reliable? We have an elderly lady, whose sight, for all we know, may be failing. She saw a man through her window, some distance away, and now she is ready to swear that it was Jonathan Tapley? Come, come, Ross, no jury would accept that.'

'We have to consider it. Of course, Mrs Jameson saw the man at around three in the afternoon or shortly thereafter—'

Dunn interrupted. 'In that case, how on earth is Jonathan Tapley supposed to have done it? In the medical man's opinion, the murder took place some time between five and the discovery of the corpse at a little after seven. *Jonathan Tapley could not have done it.* His actions at the time of the murder are accounted for. He was in court all day! By four thirty he was at his chambers, eating cold chicken. At five he held a case conference there. All these things during the period when we know, from our medical man, that the murder was committed! He has given us a list of those people who saw and spoke to him at his chambers. Anyway, why, for pity's sake, should he kill his cousin?'

'Mr Dunn,' I began. 'Let me explain my thinking.'

'Please do so,' said Dunn sarcastically, with a broad gesture of his hand and arm. 'I confess myself fascinated, Ross. Proceed!'

I did so, carefully laying out my reasons.

'Guillaume repeatedly tells us that she was told by her husband, or that he gave her clearly to understand, that the cousins had quarrelled. There was a bitter rift, she suggests, between them. Well, now, that might be so. Because Guillaume is thrifty with her evidence, it does not mean everything she says is to be disbelieved. She twists the facts to suit her purpose, but in a curious sort of way, she sticks to them. So, was there animosity between the two men?

323

'Only consider, sir, Jonathan had forced his cousin to leave the country, had taken away his cousin's only child, his daughter Flora. We have good reason to believe Thomas was devoted to his child. Lizzie discovered how he had sought out Flora secretly here in London and how worried he was that she was about to make a disastrous marriage. We have this from Flora's own lips.

'But Jonathan's account of the arrangement made with his cousin is that it was entirely amicable; that Thomas was grateful to Jonathan and his wife for taking in little Flora and raising her as their own. Thomas found visiting the child "difficult", says Jonathan, and that is the reason his visits were so few and brief. But is that true? According to Jonathan, Thomas agreed it was best he leave the country for France and never return. Did he put up no argument against the plan? We don't know, because if he did, then Jonathan has been careful not to tell us so. To my mind, there is a discrepancy between what Jonathan has told us, and what we know from Flora herself of her father's actions when he was back in London.

'Because Jonathan is a respected barrister at law, our instinct is to believe his version of events. Because Victorine appears to have led a rackety life when young, has been difficult to deal with and obviously mistrusts the law, we are tempted to be suspicious of everything she says. That includes her report of some old quarrel she says took place between the two men. It could be that Victorine is simply her own worst enemy. Consider, sir, that Thomas never tried to contact Jonathan when he returned to England over a year ago. He lived in London, south of the river, near to Lizzie and me. He crossed the river, using Waterloo Bridge, regularly on his way to spend his day in town. Lizzie met him in the area. Jenkins, waiting about in his clown's costume, ran him to earth there. Yet Thomas did not walk as far as his cousin's house; or even his cousin's chambers in the Gray's Inn Road. Thomas sought out his daughter in a public library, and swore her to secrecy about their meeting. He agreed to her dressing up and visiting him in disguise. This, to me, is a man who did not trust his cousin Jonathan and was anxious, above all, that Jonathan never learn Thomas was back in London.

'Was this just because Thomas knew he had broken his word about never returning? Because he feared Jonathan's anger? Did he fear resurrection of old scandal? Or something else altogether? You know, when I first met Jonathan, he said something odd. It struck me at the time as merely tasteless, but now I wonder. I had noticed his cane, with the skull pommel. He saw it had taken my interest. He held it up, saying that he had not used it to beat in his cousin's brains. I would not have thought him a man to make such a crude joke at so inappropriate a time. So, then, why did he say it? Was he meeting my suspicion head-on in order to deflect it?'

'Supposition . . .' growled Dunn.

'At least give me a chance, sir, to go through Tapley's alibi again. If I can crack it . . . find a loophole somewhere . . .'

'You'll but offend him and make us look ridiculous!' Dunn grumbled. 'How are you going to crack his alibi for the time of the murder, when we have medical evidence that the victim died after five that afternoon?'

'Well, sir,' I said, 'as to that, I have an idea I'd like to try out.'

Dunn threw up his hands and brought them palm down on his desk with a thump. 'An idea? It seems to me you're full of ideas, Ross, each one crazier than the last. Where, if I may ask, did you get this latest idea?'

I allowed myself a smile, which seemed to alarm the superintendent. 'I got it from a steak and kidney pie, sir.'

At that, Dunn looked even more alarmed, until I explained. 'Hum,' he muttered. 'Forty-eight hours, Ross, I give you forty-eight hours. If you haven't got a case against Jonathan Tapley in that time, I shall personally charge Hector Mas with the murder of Thomas Tapley.'

Elizabeth Martin Ross

'I heard your old man has arrested a Frenchie for the murder of the gent living in your street.'

The voice appeared out of nowhere and made me jump. I looked around and a movement in the shadow of a doorway materialised into the familiar ragged form of Coalhouse Joey.

'Oh, Joey!' I exclaimed in relief. 'Where have you been recently? I've been looking out for you.'

'Was you?' Joey's features twisted into a scowl. 'I thought as you might be, so I cleared off, didn't I?'

'Why did you do that?'

'Because,' said Joey patiently, as if speaking to someone slow on the uptake, 'you would have told your old man what I told you, about the young swell what I spotted signalling to old Tapley from the street. Then your old man, being a rozzer, would have come questioning me. I don't like talking to rozzers. So I cleared off. But now I heard he's gone and nabbed the villain, he won't be interested in me no more, and I can come back.' Joey paused. 'So I have, and here I am!' he concluded.

'My husband would have liked to talk to you,' I admitted. 'But not now, because the mystery of the young man you saw has been cleared up.'

'Oh? Has it?' Joey looked disappointed. 'Nuffin' to do with the murder, then?'

'No, not exactly. But you were right to tell me what you saw. If you ever see anything else unusual like that, you can always tell me. Witnesses are always very important.'

Joey obviously liked the idea of being important, but tempered his enthusiasm with the knowledge it meant talking to rozzers.

'A Frenchie, eh?' He stared at me thoughtfully. 'I heard they went chasing him all round Wapping, River Police, too. The Frenchie climbed up a building and stood on the top of a chimney, shaking his fists and defying all the p'licemen. Then ran across all the roofs in Wapping before he leaped into the river. He swam across the Thames to escape 'em; but they went after him in a boat and hauled him out of the water, swearing and cussing and fighting for his life. It took six of 'em to hold him down.'

'Well, more or less,' I agreed. I could see why the chase after Mas, witnessed by so many bystanders, would become folklore immediately. At each retelling, Mas's exploits would grow and become more fantastic until he turned into the Springheeled Jack of legend.

'But I am still very pleased to see you, because I want to talk to you, Joey. You like horses, don't you?'

'Yus . . .' agreed Joey cautiously.

'I know a cabman by the name of Wally Slater. He's a very nice man, Joey. He used to be a prizefighter so he looks rather frightening, but really, he's very kind. He needs someone to help him look after his horse, and clean his cab – it's a growler – when he gets home at the end of the day. So, I told him about you and he's agreed to give you a trial. I don't suppose he'll pay very much, but it would be a regular wage and far better than just living on the streets.'

Joey's expression had gone through surprise to incredulity to alarm to something like panic. 'Yes, an' very likely knock the living daylights out of me if I don't do it properly, if his horse don't kick my head in first!'

'Mr Slater would not do that, Joey. He'd know I would find out about it and he wouldn't want to upset me.' I was reasonably sure of this. I wasn't certain Wally Slater was worried about upsetting me so much, as he'd be worried I'd lecture him. 'You can't stay on the streets, doing nothing for the rest of your life, Joey.'

'I don't go thinking about the rest of me life,' objected Joey. 'That's a waste of time, that is. I might not have one.'

'What? A life?'

'No one knows it,' said Joey, in a surprising recourse to philosophy. 'I might get the cholera. I might get murdered meself, like that old feller, Tapley. I might . . .' he added, squinting up at me ferociously, '*get run down by a cab!*'

'Yes, you might,' I agreed. 'And if you go on living on the streets as you do, it's more than likely. Why don't you let me take you along to meet Wally Slater? It's worth a try.'

'All right . . .' agreed Joey unwillingly. 'But if he starts hitting me or his 'orse starts biting me, I'll be off!'

'Good! Agreed, then. Nelson is a very placid horse and I'm sure he doesn't bite. Now then, we'd better clean you up a bit.'

'*Clean me up* . . .' Now there was no disguising Joey's horror. 'Whatcha mean?'

'Well, I can't take you to Wally without a wash and some proper clothes . . .'

'*WASH!*'

If I hadn't grabbed him, he'd have been off down the street and this time, I doubt he would have come back. He wriggled but I clung on. He could have got free if he could have given rein to his normal tactics of biting and kicking, but he didn't feel free to kick me or bite me, so in the end he gave up and stood glowering at me resentfully.

'I'd never have agreed to it, if I'd known it meant all this . . .' he grumbled as I hauled him along to our house. 'It's just like being arrested, it is!'

I must say Bessie looked just as horrified when she saw him. 'Wash him?' she yelled.

'I'll give you a hand. Get the tin tub down, out in the yard, and put on some kettles for hot water.'

'I'll drown . . .' said Joey despondently.

'Not in a tin tub, Joey, with Bessie and me standing by.'

'I ain't taking all me clothes off in front of no women.'

'All right, I'll give you the soap and a towel; and Bessie and I will wait in the kitchen.'

He looked pathetic. 'I'll get a chill on me chest. I'll cough me lungs up. Lungs carry you off in no time, lungs do.'

'Not if you're quick about it. Come on, now. And don't forget to wash your hair.'

We filled the tub, handed Joey a bar of soap and the towel, made him promise not to run off, and told him to get on with it. He sniffed at the soap and said he'd smell like a ladybird.

We retired to the kitchen. Bessie, peeping from the window, reported that Joey had climbed into the tub, and was amusing himself by flicking water at a neighbour's cat.

'At least some dirt will come off,' I told her. 'Here's some money. Run along to the old man who keeps the barrow of second-hand clothing, down by the bridge. Get some trousers and a shirt, a jacket if you can. I don't know about boots, what size.'

'I'll get them plenty big enough. We can stuff them with paper if we need to,' said Bessie.

When she returned, Joey, wrapped in his towel, was sitting damply before the kitchen range with a mug of tea in hand. The range was smoking rather badly because I had stuffed his old clothes into it to burn, but smoke didn't worry Joey. I had trimmed his hair and, although I'm no barber, it was at least tidy. Joey had allowed me to do it without much protest. I think he had resigned himself to the inevitable. Dressed in his new (old) clothes, he looked transformed from his former self. He wasn't sure about the boots, never having worn any. He walked up and down the kitchen in a comical fashion, raising each foot too high and placing it carefully on the stone floor.

'You'll get used to them,' we promised him.

Now that we were all ready, I thought it well to be on our way at once to Kentish Town where I knew the Slaters lived. Joey's willingness was already fading. I think the boots in particular had something to do with that.

'It don't seem normal,' he muttered, as we set out. 'That's what feet are for, walking on.'

'In boots,' I pointed out, 'you are safe from sharp stones or bruises from having someone stand on your foot. Your feet are dry in wet weather and warm in cold weather.'

'They slows you up!' argued Joey. 'You can't run in these things. If I had to run, I'd have to take 'em off first, and while I was doing that, I'd be caught!'

'Stop making a fuss!' Bessie ordered him. 'You'd make a fuss to be hung, you would!'

We took an omnibus for the third time in our recent adventures and set off for Kentish Town. I think Joey liked the omnibus ride, but did not wish us to think he had no experience of this vehicle.

'It ain't the first time I took the ommybus, you know,' he informed us. 'Only the first time I've been sitting inside one.'

'You've travelled on the open top before?' I asked.

'No, I hung on the back and rode for free.'

I knew Kentish Town to be a place with some history behind it. It had not begun to grow from its original village until comparatively recent years. Now there were new buildings of all sorts, and a railway line running through it, but plenty of older houses remained. We were directed to one of these in a side street. Wally was well known, as I'd guessed he would be, and our first enquiry told us the way.

Wally's home was still a cottage with an entrance beside it, wide enough to admit his cab, and leading into a yard. At the back of the yard was a wooden building, Nelson's stable. Family washing flapped on a line.

The door was opened to us by a small, plump woman who

331

barely stood as high as my shoulder; she had a great deal of fluffy fair hair pinned up on top of her head in a bun, so that she resembled a cottage loaf.

'Hullo,' she said, by way of greeting, looking the three of us up and down. 'What's all this, then?'

'Mrs Slater?' I asked. 'I am—'

I got no further before I was interrupted. 'Oh, I know who you are, I do!' said Mrs Slater merrily. 'You're that Miss Martin as my husband is always talking of!'

'Yes, well, I am Mrs Ross now.'

'He told me that, and all. Married to a policeman, he said. He reckoned that would suit you. Come on in, then.'

We trooped into her spotless parlour where I introduced Bessie and finally, Joey. I then explained our purpose. 'I did speak to your husband about Joey, perhaps he mentioned him? I do hope so.'

'He told me all about it, never you fear. But tea first, business after,' said Mrs Slater firmly. 'You sit there, Mrs Ross, that's the best chair. You, Miss Bessie, you sit over there on that one. It rocks a bit but it won't tip you on the floor. I keep on to Wally to fix the legs. And you, young feller-me-lad, you come into the kitchen with me. You can carry things.'

Bessie, delighted at being treated as a proper visitor, was beaming as she took her seat on the wobbly chair. I sat in a vast wing chair that was obviously normally reserved for Wally. A table and cupboard were the only other articles of furniture in the room, and a well-worn scrap of carpet on the stone flags, but everything was spotlessly clean. Mrs Slater, I was sure she was responsible, had compensated for lack of furnishing by adorning the walls with all manner of pictures.

Most, I suspected, had been bought from a street barrow for a few pence. There was one, in pride of place, of Her Majesty Queen Victoria in her coronation robes. Another, beside it, featured the Prince Consort, looking very much the dandy in his younger years. Sadly, this picture was crowned with a black ribbon bow, in recognition of his death a few years earlier. There were images of the royal children, two or three paintings of flowers, a representation of the Parting of the Red Sea, and several images of prizefighters. The largest of these was displayed above the hearth and showed a fearsome figure, bare chested and in breeches, whose feet appeared remarkably small for the rest of him to balance on. He crouched, holding out his clenched fists and fixing us with a menacing scowl.

'That's my Wally,' said Mrs Slater with cheerful pride, returning from the kitchen to find me studying this one. 'In his prime, as you might say. That's when I first knew him. But I told him straight away, once I saw he was sweet on me, I'm not being married to no prizefighter. They've always got a black eye, or a thick ear and coming home covered in blood. So make your choice, I told him, and he did.' This last was said with deep satisfaction. 'His family was in the licensed hackney carriage trade,' she went on. 'Father and grandfather before him, so Wally turned to that.

'Now then,' continued Mrs Slater, turning to a miserable-looking Joey who stood behind her, shuffling in his new boots, and carrying the tray of tea things. 'You can put that on the table, over there.'

Joey obeyed, but not without remarking loudly, 'I come here to look after a horse. I never come to be no footman!'

'No backchat!' ordered Mrs Slater sternly. 'Now then, Mrs

Ross, I've had a look at this young feller and a bit of talk to him in my kitchen. We will give him a try, a shilling a week to begin with. He can sleep in the stable loft and I'll feed him, is that all right?'

'That would be excellent,' I spoke up for Joey. 'Thank Mrs Slater, Joey.'

'Much obliged, I'm sure,' mumbled Joey.

'No taking of strong drink, no using of foul language, no blaspheming and no hanging out in bad company,' ordered Mrs Slater. 'No going in the pubs. No gambling. You keep the horse groomed, the cab fit for a gentleman or lady to ride in, and you keep yourself clean. You can wash out in the yard under the pump.'

Joey rolled his eyes at me in despair.

'Certainly,' I agreed. 'You understand all that, Joey?'

'Yus, I understand all right,' said Joey.

'Mutton stew for dinner tonight,' said Mrs Slater in a careless sort of way, with the suspicion of a twinkle in her eye. 'That all right, too?'

'Oh, yus! That's all right!' exclaimed Joey, brightening.

'It will work out splendidly,' I would tell Ben much later.

'If he doesn't run off,' warned Ben.

'He won't run away from a hot dinner every night and shelter in bad weather,' I said firmly. 'Besides, if he did, I fancy the Slaters would have every cabbie in London looking out for him.'

But I had to wait a little before I could recount my success, because Ben had other, more important, matters on his hands.

Chapter Twenty-One

Inspector Benjamin Ross

I HAD found Sergeant Morris drinking a mug of tea in a shadowy nook between a cupboard and a wall. This hideaway was sacred to Morris and known throughout the Yard, at least among the constables, as 'the sergeant's earth'. The query, 'Where is Morris?' might, if you were lucky, be answered, 'He's gone to earth, sir.' Then, if you knew the code, you knew exactly where to find him.

Morris made to put down the mug and stand up as I approached. I waved him to take his seat again and sat down beside him. If anyone deserved a mug of tea on the quiet, it was Morris. Besides, he wasn't going to get much chance of a few minutes' relaxation for the next two days.

'Well, Sergeant,' I said to him. 'We have forty-eight hours to save my reputation or ruin it.'

'How's that, then, sir?' he asked, eyeing me over the rim of his mug.

I explained. Morris drained his tea and sat with the mug nestled in the palms of his hands, staring thoughtfully ahead of him. 'It'll take a bit of doing, Mr Ross.'

'Then we'll have to get started. What I want you to do is find out which case Jonathan Tapley was appearing in on the day of the murder. Find out what time court rose, and if his actions can be accounted for thereafter.'

'Beg pardon, sir,' said Morris, 'but he'd be a bit of an idiot to say he was in court, if he wasn't appearing that day.'

'I don't suggest he didn't appear at any time that day in court. I am particularly anxious to know the *latest* time he was seen there. If I am right – that is to say if Mrs Jameson is right – and Tapley was walking up and down outside her house shortly after three in the afternoon . . . We must allow the lady's estimate of "shortly after" to be any time up to half past. But if he was there, then it follows he wasn't in court. To turn the argument around, if he wasn't in court, he could have been walking outside the house.'

'Very well, sir. Where will I find you? Should I need to, that is.'

'I am going to seek out Dr Harper. Then I'll meet you back here.'

We went about our separate ways.

By one of those quirks of detection – which generally take you in directions you don't anticipate – I found myself going back to Wapping. Enquiry at the hospital where he was normally to be found told me Dr Harper had been called to the River Police morgue there, on account of a drowning.

Accordingly, I found myself in the somewhat ramshackle structure that dignified itself by the name of morgue and was used for the reception of bodies pulled from the Thames. Its latest arrival, a young woman, lay on the table awaiting the attention of Harper, who was standing by, scalpel in hand, with an assistant at his elbow.

'Ah, Dr Harper!' I hailed him. 'I am sorry to disturb you, but glad to see you haven't started yet.' That was true. 'Could I have a word?'

'If it doesn't take long,' replied Harper. He indicated the woman on the table. 'This will turn out a suicide, of course. Well nourished. Clothes good quality and nothing darned or mended.' He indicated the pile of sodden clothing on a nearby bench. 'Hands . . .' He lifted one of the drowned girl's hands and turned it palm upward for my inspection. 'Never done a day's work in her life.' He stared thoughtfully at the subject. 'It will be the old, old story, I dare say, seduced and abandoned. She is with child, of course.' He replaced the girl's hand on the table surprisingly gently.

We moved away from the table and the assistant tactfully went out of the room.

'Dr Harper,' I began. 'You will recall the night I fetched you away from your dinner to a murder in a house not far from Waterloo Station, in the same street in which I live myself, as it happens.'

'I do,' said Harper, eyeing me suspiciously. 'You'll not be wanting me to carry out a second post-mortem examination? I have a very busy day ahead of me. I have to go straight from this one to another case elsewhere, in which the victim supposedly shot himself. But it wouldn't be the first time a dead man has shot himself, eh?'

'No, Doctor. The body I called you to that night . . .'

'Oh that,' said Harper. 'Cause of death was clear.'

'We buried the victim yesterday, or rather his family did. I don't anticipate applying for an exhumation order. We are agreed on cause of death.'

'Good,' said Harper. 'Once they've been in the ground a while, it all gets more difficult.' He frowned. 'Something else bothers you?'

'Yes. I wonder if you would cast your mind back to that evening. Do you remember anything about the room in which the body was found?' I waited apprehensively for his reply.

'Small sitting room of some sort, or gentleman's study, perhaps?' Harper offered. Seeing this vague memory was not enough, he asked, 'What is it you have in mind?'

'Nothing else about the room, Doctor? Anything . . .' I urged. I must not lead him, but if his recollection was no more than that, I was done for.

Harper was scowling in effort. 'Well, it was simply furnished . . . couple of chairs, a bookcase . . . no fire in the grate.' He caught the expression on my face. 'Oh, so that's what you're getting at? The room was very cold. I did notice that.'

'It was very cold. Apparently he could have had a fire lit, had he wanted it. But since midwinter he'd done without. He said it didn't trouble him. I have this from the landlady and the maidservant. Dr Harper, I have read, or been told, that if a newly slain body is kept very cold, the onset of rigor may be delayed?'

'So it is time of death that troubles you, not cause?' Harper indicated the door. 'Let us go outside, Ross. I fancy a pipe of tobacco.'

We went outside the building and stood in the sharp breeze blowing across the water. Gulls wheeled above and uttered their discordant cries. Out on the river, a vessel sounded a warning whistle blast. Harper took his time filling and tamping down his pipe. Then he had to get the thing going and only then, when it was drawing satisfactorily, did he take it from his mouth and, holding it by the bowl, point the stem at me.

'If a body is cooled rapidly, or kept at a very low temperature, it is true rigor may take longer to set it. But, mind you, once the surrounding temperature returns to normal, rigor not only proceeds but may even speed up. These things are notoriously hard to judge, Ross. Sometimes I've found it easier to state cause of death than estimate time it occurred.'

'By the time you got the body to the hospital, what state was it in then?'

'Stiffening nicely,' he said. 'But you want me to reconsider my estimate of time of death, I assume?'

'I do, Doctor. Please don't take offence, but on the night in question it was very late in the day, I'd called you from your dinner table . . .'

'And I might, therefore, have been in a hurry to get back to it, eh? Made a quick judgement as to time of death when I should have looked around me and thought a bit more?'

'Believe me, Doctor . . .'

He waved the pipe stem at me again. 'And so I might have done. However, does that mean that now, in retrospect, I am ready to change my opinion?'

'Are you?' I was on tenterhooks.

Annoyingly – and I am sure on purpose – he puffed a few clouds of tobacco at me. 'It's important to you, eh?'

'Doctor, it is very important.'

'Well, then, Inspector, let me put it this way. I repeat that it is not always easy, and seldom possible, to be exact about time of death – especially if, as in this case, you have no other evidence than the body itself. I believe I gave the time of death as no earlier than five o'clock that afternoon?'

'You did, sir.'

'I could, you know, if I wanted to be awkward, stick to my guns and what I said then.' Another wave of the pipe stem.

'You could, Doctor, and I couldn't blame you.'

'Oh, couldn't you? Personally, I hope I shall always be open to revising my judgement if necessary, and not become one of those touchy fellows who cling to a point, even when they've been proved too quick in reaching it! Now then, I don't say that I was wrong . . . but I may not have been right. Do you understand me?'

'I think so, Dr Harper.'

'Mm . . . Given that the room was so very chilly and the deceased appeared to have been sitting in it reading for some time even before he was struck down, it is just possible that rigor was slightly delayed. If so, then it is also just possible that he died before five.'

'How much earlier than five?' I asked eagerly.

'Now that's a tricky one to answer,' he said aggravatingly. 'Four o'clock?'

'How about three o'clock?' I asked.

He frowned and my heart sank. 'Three would be very early.' He shook his head. 'I would hesitate to put my money on three o'clock. Not even to oblige you, Ross. Half past three might be a possibility.'

Mrs Jameson had seen Tapley walking up and down the

340

street shortly after three. He was looking up at the house fronts. He might have glimpsed his cousin at the window upstairs and made a note of the room. He might then have gone away and returned twenty minutes later. That might give us a time of half past three.

I was reasoning frantically. Why did he go away? Because just as Mrs Jameson noticed him, he, too, was aware that someone was looking out of a downstairs window? So he leaves, and returns at half past three, enters the house from the kitchen, unseen, goes upstairs and strikes down his cousin, then he leaves as he's come . . . Oh, yes, oh yes! He could still have got back to his chambers in the Gray's Inn Road by half past four. Only just, perhaps, but he could have done it. Then, clever fellow that he is, he sends out the office boy for half a roast chicken, making some remark about having just time to eat it before the people attending the case conference arrive. Thus the boy remembers with certainty what time he was sent out on the errand. If Morris can establish Jonathan Tapley wasn't in court all afternoon, then I do believe we have him! Or at the very least, we have enough to bring him in and question him. And to think that, had Lizzie not served up a three-day-old meat pie with a remark about how well it had kept in a cold larder . . .

'Dr Harper,' I said, 'I am exceedingly obliged to you. You may have to go into the witness box over this. Will you stand by it?'

'I will say in the witness box what I have just said to you,' said Harper. 'Whether that proves good enough for judge and jury isn't up to me.'

No, I thought ruefully, it is up to me.

Morris arrived back at the Yard nearly an hour after I returned there. I was on tenterhooks by then.

'Well?' I asked him eagerly.

Morris permitted himself a smile and my heart began to rise. 'Seems, sir, that proceedings were interrupted in the case in which Mr Tapley was appearing. Court had just reconvened after lunch when one of the main witnesses was suddenly taken ill, in mid-testimony. There was no likelihood the witness would be able to continue that day, so the case was adjourned. Court rose at a little after half past two. Tapley was conferring with fellow counsel for a further ten minutes or quarter of an hour. After that, the gentlemen of the bar concerned all dispersed for the day. As far as I could find out, no one else there saw or spoke to him. The other cases being heard were proceeding, and those involved were in attendance on those. I asked ushers and doorkeepers and such, and while none of them can swear to the exact time he left, they are sure it wasn't late.'

'Let's say he left at about ten minutes to three,' I conjectured. 'He could have jumped in a cab...there's always plenty waiting around there. Yes, he went directly by cab south of the river. He had the cabbie set him down a couple of streets away from his destination. By twenty minutes past three he was outside Mrs Jameson's house. She is not exact as to time, but says it was "some time after three". I take that to mean before half past. If he then went away and came back when he was satisfied she was no longer at her window, he could still have returned by a quarter to four. He slips into the house, up the back stairs, comes upon his cousin, strikes him down, and leaves. He probably goes to the railway station and picks up another cab there. At half past four he is entering his chambers in the Gray's Inn Road.'

'It's a tight timetable, sir,' warned Morris.

'But not an impossible one. Let me speak with the superintendent.'

'Yessir,' said Morris, looking relieved. 'Best have Mr Dunn on our side, if you don't mind me saying so.'

'Very well,' said Dunn, when he'd heard me out. 'I must consult the deputy commissioner about this, given who Tapley is. But I suggest you proceed immediately, without waiting for me to return, and let me deal with objections from on high. I will take responsibility. Go on, man. Strike while the iron is hot!'

I hastened back to Morris. 'All goes well, Sergeant. I think we may invite Mr Jonathan Tapley to call upon us here at the Yard!'

Chapter Twenty-Two

'WELL, INSPECTOR, I am here at your request...'
Jonathan Tapley seated himself in my office and placed his
folded hands over the skull pommel of his cane. 'I take it you
have something of interest to tell me? Since you have the
culprits safely under arrest, I cannot imagine what it is that
necessitated my coming here with such urgency.'

Morris had stationed himself discreetly behind our visitor
and, even more discreetly, young Biddle had slipped into the
room and sat in a corner with notebook and pencil in hand. I
was sure that Jonathan Tapley had not yet noticed him. He'd
have remarked on it, if he had done.

'I do indeed have something of interest to tell you, sir,' I
began politely. 'New information has reached us.'

'How? From the French police?'

'No, Mr Tapley, fresh evidence from a witness.'

He stiffened slightly. 'A witness? To what?'

'This witness has come forward, admittedly a little late, to
tell us you were seen on the afternoon of the murder, at some
time shortly after three, walking up and down outside the
house where the murder took place. You were seen to glance
up at the front of the house, as if seeking something.'

Coldly, Tapley said: 'My movements on the day, and particularly for the period during which my cousin's death could have occurred, have been accounted for. I have given you a list of witnesses.'

'You have give us a list of witnesses from four thirty onward.'

He looked annoyed. 'Well, then! That is sufficient. The medical man gave his opinion my cousin died after five of the afternoon.' He tapped the cane on the floor. 'What is all this about?'

'The medical man has reconsidered the time of death. He is now of the opinion it could have occurred as early as four or even before that, possibly half past three.' I waited to see how he'd take that.

Any other man with a heavy conscience might have betrayed shock or panic. But Tapley was used to courtroom tactics, including a witness making an unexpected and unwelcome statement.

'Indeed?' he said drily. 'And what has caused this medical fellow to revise his opinion, originally made at the time with my cousin's body on the floor in front of him?'

'I don't recall telling you the body was on the floor,' I said. 'I told you, I think I am correct, that the assassin came upon your cousin as he sat reading in a chair.'

'Pah!' Tapley dismissed this as a quibble. 'Chair . . . floor . . . If he was sitting in a chair when he was struck, then he presumably fell on to the floor? Do you agree?'

'Oh, yes, he did that,' I had to admit.

'It seems obvious to me. I repeat, what has caused the doctor to change his mind? It seems extraordinary that he can reduce the time of death from five in the afternoon to, what, a full hour and a half earlier?'

'The doctor has been reconsidering,' I said carefully, 'because he is now taking into account the very low temperature of the room. That can slow the onset of rigor. It was the absence of rigor in the body that had prompted him to make his first assessment of five o'clock.'

By now he knew what this was leading up to, and he was ready for me.

'I do not practise in the criminal law courts,' Tapley said with a touch of disdain. 'But I have heard cases discussed between those who do. I understand, from such conversations, that a corpse left in a cold place may remain remarkably flexible, as you say. Equally, however, the body might not. There is no hard and fast rule about it. If your doctor were to be questioned in the witness box, he would admit that. He is unwise to revise his estimated time of death on that alone.'

A rustle in the corner as Biddle turned a page of his notebook caused our visitor to look over his shoulder.

'Why is that young fellow writing all this down?' he asked sharply.

'It is the procedure, Mr Tapley.'

Tapley permitted himself a faint smile. He leaned back in the chair. 'Well, well,' he said. 'I might be tempted to imagine you mean to charge me with the murder of my cousin, Inspector.'

'You might be right, sir.'

'You would be foolish. Even if my cousin died earlier than five, something that is not established fact despite the vacillations of your doctor, I was—'

'You were not seen in court after about ten to three,' I interrupted. 'A witness in the case with which you were concerned that day was taken ill. Court rose at half past two. You chatted with fellow counsel for a few minutes and then you left.'

'You have been thorough, Inspector,' Tapley said after a pause. 'You have a witness who saw me leave the building?'

This I did not have. He had unerringly picked a weak spot. This was not going to be easy. 'No, sir, but no one in the building saw you or spoke to you after that time, a little before three.'

'No witness, in other words. Tut, tut, Inspector. Another supposition on your part. Another statement you cannot back up. I dare say that you're about to claim, in another flight of fancy, that I leaped into a cab and was carried immediately to where my cousin lived?'

'Yes, sir, I think that is what happened. I suspect you asked the cabbie to take you to Waterloo railway station, because that would have allowed you to ask him to make all possible speed. You had a train to catch, you told him. If you'd asked him to set you down in the street where your cousin lived, he might have remembered you and the address – should we find the cabbie. We are looking for him, by the way. But you would have calculated that no cabbie troubles to remember a particular fare among many delivered to a railway station. The destination is too commonplace.

'You could not have planned it, because you could not have known court would rise early. But you were intending at some point soon to face your cousin. You had earlier learned that your cousin was back in London. I think you had also learned that your niece, Miss Flora, had been in contact with her father. I fancy your coachman told you of the escapade when he drove the young lady, in disguise as a young boy, accompanied by a friend, to the vicinity of the house. The coachman had told your wife. She was anxious you did not learn of the adventure and asked the coachman not to tell you. But you are his employer. It is upon your recommendation he depends. I think he did tell you. You quizzed your wife. She admitted it.

'Unlike your wife, you did not imagine Flora had made a romantic tryst with some unsuitable young man. You immediately and rightly guessed it was her father she'd gone to see. You were furious and alarmed. Thomas had broken his word to you about returning to England. You already knew that because Fred Thorpe had told you. You had been hoping your cousin had returned to France. Now you had discovered he was living in London and, even worse from your point of view, he had contacted his daughter. This had led to a potentially scandalous escapade involving Miss Flora dressed as a boy. You and your wife had set your highest hopes on Flora marrying her highly connected young suitor. Now the possibility of dangerous gossip loomed. I don't think the noble family into which you plan Flora to marry would take kindly to news of her travelling round London in male attire. As for Thomas appearing, like Banquo's ghost, at the marriage festivities . . . You had to take some action.

'As soon as you learned what Flora had done, you had your coachman take you to the same spot where he had set down Flora. It did not take long, asking around, to locate your cousin and where he lived. You did nothing there and then;

because the less Joliffe saw or heard, the better. You had him drive you home again to Bryanston Square. While you were still debating what to do, a few days later, court rose unexpectedly early in the afternoon. You seized the opportunity to go to the house, face your cousin and have it out with him. You meant, perhaps, only to insist he write out a formal consent to the marriage, then return to France immediately, after which there must be absolutely no more contact between him and Miss Flora. You would not allow, could not allow, Thomas to ruin everything.'

I concluded my exposition of the situation leading up to the murder as I saw it, and fell silent.

'Even if I did all that, Inspector, and I am not admitting any such thing, it is a far cry from "having it out with him" to killing him in cold blood,' Tapley pointed out. He had been listening carefully to my case as I laid it out, just as he would have listened to an opponent in a courtroom.

I was not finished yet. But I had to go slowly and carefully, because I was now dealing not with what Jonathan Tapley must have felt, but with what he did.

'You entered the house secretly. You did not announce yourself at the front door because you did not want to be seen and remembered. There must be no link with Bryanston Square! You slipped in through the kitchen in the absence of the single maidservant, went up the back stairs, located the room, opened the door quietly ... Your cousin sat there reading peaceably. The sight fuelled your anger. There he sat, the man who had broken his word and caused so much trouble, apparently without a care in the world. Your rage overcame you. You raised your cane – that cane . . .' I pointed at it. 'You struck the back of his head and he toppled from his chair to the floor. You struck him again when he lay on the carpet, to make sure he was dead. Having struck him once, you could not risk that he might be conscious enough to identify his assailant, or survive to tell of the attack.'

Tapley rested the cane against his knee and placed his fingertips together. 'You are ingenious, Inspector, I'll grant you that! You make me curious. How did I know – again I ask without admitting anything – which room my cousin was in?'

'You had a bit of luck. You were looking up at the front of the house – the witness saw you do that – and glimpsed him through an upstairs window.'

'Did I indeed? I must ask you again, Inspector, to identify your witness. Otherwise, how do I know such a witness really exists?'

'The owner of the house saw you, through her parlour window.'

'The owner of the house?' He looked stupefied. 'Do you mean that elderly Quaker lady who attended the funeral?'

'Yes, sir.'

'She did not know me. When she saw a stranger in the street how on earth could she tell it was I?' Anger broke into his voice.

'She recognised and identified you, having had a good opportunity to observe you closely, during the short train journey from the church to the Necropolis on the day of the funeral.'

'That was quite some time later than the day my cousin died,' he objected. 'She could not be sure I was someone she had, she claims, seen briefly, for the first time in her life, at a distance, through a window, and many days earlier! Good heavens, Inspector, you have been an investigating officer long enough to know that even several witnesses of one event can give wildly differing accounts. Asked to describe someone, one witness will say he was tall, another that he was short. One swears he saw a walking stick –' Tapley indicated his cane – 'but to another this same object appeared to be an umbrella! They cannot all be right, obviously. So, how can you, Inspector, who have a single witness, be so sure she is not mistaken? The lady is of advanced years, I recollect. She is a religious female and no doubt spends much time reading her Bible. I doubt her eyesight is first rate. She probably wears spectacles to read.'

'No, sir, she does not. I asked her.' I smiled at him.

Of course he was right: Mrs Jameson's confident assertion, that she had seen Jonathan Tapley before the house, would easily be demolished by a competent defence barrister. But I knew both she and I were right too. Jonathan had been there; and now he knew he'd been seen. Frustration struck me as a physical ache in my stomach. I had to have something more. But what?

Tapley gripped his cane again and rose magisterially to his feet. 'Inspector Ross, I have sat here with remarkable patience and listened to this farrago. Your two main witnesses, the doctor and the house owner, wouldn't last five minutes under cross-examination. Nor would a cabbie's testimony, even if you found a cabman who said he took me on the day, at the time, to the destination, hold up in court. As you yourself said, I would have been one fare among many. Let us say – again this is purely hypothetical – that I remember I left court early. Let us say I admit I went to the street and walked up and down before the house, debating whether to go in and face my cousin. But suppose I also say I changed my mind as I walked there, and left without doing so. What then, Ross? You cannot put me in that house, in that room, with my cousin. If you have nothing more to say, then I shall leave, unless you care to arrest me? Or you can lose your senses altogether and charge me. Otherwise, I shall go.'

He stood there before me, that same dapper figure who had entered my office not so very long ago, and told me he thought he could identify the victim. I remembered him standing in the morgue looking down at his cousin's body and showing not a scrap of emotion. Here was that same man, in that elegant coat and holding that same distinctive cane, looking down at me with something very like triumph. And he was a murderer! I could not let him win. I would not let him win. We were like a pair of duellists, facing one another in a misty dawn, pistols drawn and having one shot each. But he had fired his pistol shot. Now it was my turn. Now it was a test of whether his nerve would hold out the better . . . or my resolve.

'Your appearance is impressive, Mr Tapley,' I said. 'Because it is part of your stock in trade to look the part, is it not? It impressed me when we first met. It is even possible a cabman might recall such a distinguished gentleman. Your distinctive appearance is why Mrs Jameson took a good look at you from her window; and was so sure when she saw you again on the train, that it was you she'd seen in the street. She particularly mentioned to me your well-tailored frock coat and . . .'

I saw it then. It lasted but a split second but I saw the alarm in his eyes. I caught the involuntary twitch of his shoulder as if he would have moved his arm but stilled it. The coat! I thought. *That well-tailored coat, it is something to do with his coat . . .*

Now I dared not let him walk out of here. If he had forgotten something that might incriminate him, he would immediately put it right the moment he left the Yard. It could not be a bloodstain, because anything like that he'd have looked for and cleaned off at once. So, what else could a coat have? *It has pockets,* I thought. Can it be . . . ?

He had already told me he thought me a fool in my attempt to build a case against him. I might as well be hanged for a sheep as for a lamb.

'Mr Tapley,' I said, 'would you be so kind as to turn out your coat pockets and put the contents on my desk?'

'What?' he shouted, suddenly losing his temper. 'Am I to be treated like a delinquent schoolboy? Like a common pickpocket?'

'If you would oblige me?' I persisted in a polite tone. His loss of composure confirmed to me I was on the right track.

'Damned if I will! You shall hear more of this, Ross! I shall complain to your superiors! I am a professional man of some standing in the community. I practise the law myself and have represented many eminent men and their cases before the courts. When they hear of this, this nonsense of accusing me, they will laugh the Yard to scorn and your superiors will not thank you for it!'

'I discussed matters with my immediate superior, Superintendent Dunn, before I sent a request to you to come to the Yard, Mr Tapley. Mr Dunn is even now, I believe, in a meeting with the deputy commissioner about the case. It is not unusual, Mr Tapley, that when an investigation strikes near to home, a gentleman such as yourself threatens the officer with a complaint to his superiors.'

Tapley scowled. But he had run out of delaying tactics. Slowly, and with very bad grace, he set down his cane, put his hand into his right-hand pocket and withdrew a handkerchief and some loose coins. He put these on my desk. From his left-hand pocket he produced a stub of pencil, at which he looked mildly surprised. He put that down also.

'Do you want my wallet also? It is in my inside pocket.' He opened his coat and took out a fine pigskin wallet to add to the collection on the desk.

None of these items was what I was looking for. 'The procedure, sir,' I said to Tapley, 'is to turn the pockets inside out, to make sure nothing is missed. If you would oblige us?'

'Oblige you? Why the devil should I do any such thing?' he exploded again, his face reddening. 'I object in the strongest terms. This is confounded impertinence and nothing more, Ross! I refuse.'

'Why so? If you have not omitted anything, there is nothing to worry about. Come now, Mr Tapley, let us get it over with.'

For a moment Tapley stood there rigid with rage and I really began to think he would be obstinate in his refusal. I was now sure that there was something in one pocket he did not want us to see, because if there really was nothing more, surely he wouldn't pass up the opportunity to make me look a fool.

Yet, what would I do if he did continue to refuse? I did not

want to ask Morris to investigate the fellow's pockets. That
would lay the sergeant open to an accusation, should anything
be found, that he had placed it there. I held Tapley's gaze and
waited. He must do it, I told myself. He must . . . not because
I ask him as a police officer, but because he is a guilty man
and we both know it. Because he must deal with *all* the
evidence against him as he has dealt with my argument so far.
He will now have to brazen it out, come what may, to the
bitter end that is the scaffold.

At long last, with infinite slowness, Tapley turned out the
lining of the right pocket of the frock coat, which produced
nothing. Even Biddle in the corner was holding his breath
now, pencil suspended in his hand. Morris was sweating. I did
not like to think what the expression on my face showed.
Tapley's hand moved to the left pocket . . .

Some small object clattered to the floor.

'Something's fallen out, sir,' said Morris hoarsely.

He looked down at the floor. Tapley, too, looked down. I
came round my desk to join them and Biddle got up from his
chair and edged nearer to have a view.

We were all staring down at a metal object. It was a key.
Had Tapley, in desperation, tried to palm it, slip it into his
sleeve, and lacked the dexterity? I thought I caught a brief
expression of disappointment on his face. But it was quickly
gone and he was impassive.

'Perhaps,' I suggested, 'you would be so kind as to pick it
up and put it on the desk?'

Morris, realising Biddle had joined us, signalled him crossly
to go back to his corner.

I thought Tapley might explode in protest again, but he

simply bent down and retrieved the key, tossing it on to my desk with a contemptuous gesture. It landed noisily, slid a little way, and came to rest in the middle.

'Well now,' I said. 'Where does this come from, Mr Tapley?'

'I have no idea,' he said tightly. 'I must have picked it up in error somewhere.'

'No, you picked it up from the bedside table in your cousin's bedchamber. It is, I think we'll find, the street-door key to Mrs Jameson's house. We know your cousin had one, but we have so far failed to find it, despite a diligent search. Having killed your cousin, you were anxious lest there were anything in his rooms you would not wish anyone to see. Perhaps he'd begun to write a letter to his daughter? Perhaps, even worse, she had written to him during his stay in London, once she knew where he lived. It was important, in your view, that any direct connection between father and daughter be destroyed. Flora had to be presented as totally unaware of her father's presence in London, if – in your view – her reputation was to be saved. You could not linger long, with a dead body on the floor. Someone might come at any moment. You were expected back at your chambers for a case conference later. You must not be late for that! That would require an explanation, complicate your story. You looked quickly round the sitting room, went into the bedroom next door and made a superficial search of that. You found nothing but were dissatisfied. You needed more time. There was a key looking like a street-door key in a tray on the bedside table. Ideal! You picked it up and slipped it into your pocket, intending to return. Then you left the house as you'd entered it.

'But events moved rather too quickly for you, as you realised when you saw a report of the murder in the evening papers. You had to abandon your plan to return to the house . . . at least for a while. But the key remained in your pocket. Perhaps you thought it the best place for it. No one would see it there.'

'If', Tapley said in measured tones, 'you believe that to be the key to Mrs Jameson's house, then I suggest you take it there and open the front door with it.' His gaze challenged me.

I was equal to it and for the second time I allowed myself a smile. 'You suggest I do that, because you know it will not now open it. The lock has been changed. It was changed the very next morning on my recommendation. But you have just revealed that you're well aware of that. So you did return, after all, didn't you? And you couldn't get in. You did not risk entry through the kitchen again. Or perhaps you tried the kitchen door and found the maid had shut that fast, too. Given that a murderer had entered that way the last time she'd left it open, when she was out of the kitchen, she was now being extra careful.'

'If the front-door lock has been changed,' said Tapley, 'then how will you prove that was formerly the key?'

'You know,' I told him, 'I have met some interesting people in the course of this investigation. One of them was a taxidermist.'

Tapley looked astounded. 'What the devil has that to do with it?'

'Only that he had a large number of keys on a ring, far more than he needed. I remarked on it to him. He told me he never threw away a key because you never knew when it might come in useful. There are many people like that, Mr Tapley, who hoard old keys. They usually have a box they keep them in, or a drawer in the kitchen or in a desk, or they put them on a ring like my taxidermist. If the key to something is lost, trying an old key or two may sometimes open a recalcitrant lock. I think I myself have a couple lying about at home somewhere. Perhaps that's what inspired me to take possession of the old door lock to Mrs Jameson's house, when the locksmith changed it, together with Mrs Jameson's own key to it. That same unwillingness to part with a key, you could say, that might be useful. Particularly useful in this case, because there was a house key missing, the one we knew Thomas Tapley had in his possession. We hoped to find it. Should it turn up, well, then, it would be important to be able to establish beyond doubt that it was your cousin's key. Constable, go and fetch the bag with the lock in it, the one I removed from the murder house.'

Biddle put down his notebook and pencil and scurried away. We all waited in uneasy silence. I think I must have been as nervous as Tapley must surely be. He didn't show it, other than by a tapping of one hand upon the other. I had to admire his refusal to admit defeat, and I hoped I looked as confident.

Biddle returned, nursing the bag in his arms like a baby. He carried it to the desk where he set it down reverently.

'Well, open it, then, boy!' growled Morris.

'Yessir!' Biddle flushed and pulled open the drawstring securing the neck of the bag. He tipped it up and the old lock slid out on to the desk. It was a fine bit of lockmaker's art. It wouldn't have surprised me if it had been set into the door of the Jameson house more than seventy years ago. No villain, intent on house-breaking, could have picked his way through that one, just as the locksmith had told us. Without a key, the intruder would have to depend on forcing a window – or on a careless maid, leaving the back door ajar.

'Here it is,' I said, 'and there's Mrs Jameson's key in the bag with it.' I took it out and set it down beside the key from Tapley's pocket. 'Yes, they look to me to be a pair. But we can make quite sure. We'll try the key from your pocket in the lock. Will you do the honours, Mr Tapley, or shall I?'

Tapley was now as still as a statue, and as silent. I smiled and, picking up the key that came from his pocket, put it into the keyhole of the old lock. It turned easily with a distinct click and the bolt leaped out smoothly. I turned it back and the bolt obligingly slid out of sight. I took out the key and set it down again. Tapley said nothing. But his eyes were filled with fury as he stared down at the little object that would send him to the gallows.

'You invited me to arrest you earlier,' I said. 'I think I will now accept your offer and do so. Jonathan Tapley, you are under arrest, charged with the murder of Thomas Tapley.'

It is quite something to have Lizzie listen in silence, but she spoke not a word as I told her of all this later. She hardly moved a muscle.

'Jonathan must be gnashing his teeth in rage,' I concluded, 'as he sits in a cell and reflects on how unnecessary it all was! He should have tossed the key into the river when he found it was no more use to him. I wonder if he gave way to that instinct so many of us have, to keep odd keys? In any case, his speciality has not been criminal law, and he has never learned to think like a criminal and make careful disposal of evidence. After all, he never dreamed he'd be a suspect. Even more galling for him than his failure to get rid of the key is the knowledge that, had he not gone to his cousin's lodgings, Hector Mas would probably have gone there not many days later, Jenkins having located their target, and carried out the foul crime. Jonathan need have done nothing! Mas would have done it for him.'

Lizzie heaved a deep sigh. 'Poor Flora,' she said. 'First she loses her father, horribly murdered. Now it seems the man she has grown up regarding as a substitute father may well end on the gallows. Just to know that he killed her father . . . and perhaps, even worse, her own action, in persuading the family coachman to drive her to a spot nearby to where her father was living, led to the fatal confrontation.'

'When the truth comes out in these matters, all suffer,' I told her, 'the innocent as well as the guilty. What of Maria Tapley? Not a likeable woman, perhaps, but she'll suffer, too. The reputation of the family, which means so much to her, is utterly destroyed.'

'What of Victorine and that wretched man, Hector Mas?' demanded Lizzie.

'Oh, they'll be charged concerning the death of Horatio Jenkins and the attempted abduction of Flora. Victorine will do her best to wriggle free of any foreknowledge of either. But she covered up for Mas afterwards, at the very least.'

Lizzie looked thoughtful. 'Victorine had nothing to do with the murder of her husband. She may, dreadful though the thought is, have been planning such an unspeakable crime with Mas, but they didn't carry it out. So, do you think she will continue to press her claim to a share of Thomas Tapley's estate?'

'My dealings with Victorine Guillaume, or the widow Tapley as we should call her,' I told Lizzie, 'have taught me that the lady never gives up, no matter how tricky a situation she finds herself in!

'But I understand,' I went on, 'that the matter of Thomas Tapley's estate, in the absence of a valid will, will have to be decided by a court. When such things go to court, Lizzie, they are likely to linger there a long time. It may be a few years before it's finally settled. Let us at least hope that the whole value of the estate does not finish by being swallowed up in legal fees! Flora may well need to make a good marriage now, if she can. She is tainted by events, alas.'

'That young man who wanted to marry her before this', said Lizzie firmly, 'was not suitable, no matter how highly Jonathan and Maria thought of him. Flora has written to tell me the marriage will now not take place. It is not surprising. The noble family feared the stories in the press. I hope that one day she'll meet someone who will love her for the intelligent, loyal and courageous person she is, and not worry about old scandal. Then she'll be truly happy . . .' Lizzie reached out and took my hand . . . 'like you and me.'